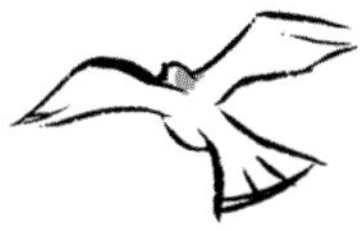

ICHIRO

ICHIRO

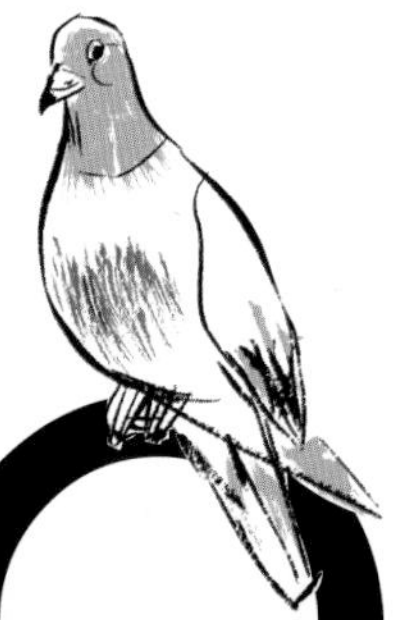

Written & Illustrated by Ryan Inzana

Houghton Mifflin
Houghton Mifflin Harcourt
Boston New York 2012

Lyrics to "New York Is Gonna Burn" by The Don't Stop
recorded 2002 at Funhouse Studios, Brooklyn, New York,
reprinted with permission.

Verse from "Flower of Summer" ("Natsu no Hana") by Tamiki Hara
reprinted with permission.

For information about permission to reproduce
selections from this book, write to Permissions,
Houghton Mifflin Harcourt Publishing Company,
215 Park Avenue South, New York, New York 10003.

www.hmhbooks.com

The text of this book is set in TimSale.
The illustrations are mixed media.

The Library of Congress Cataloging-in-Publication Data
is on file.

ISBN: 978-0-547-25269-8

Manufactured in China
LEO 10 9 8 7 6 5 4 3 2 1
4500337969

For Yuko

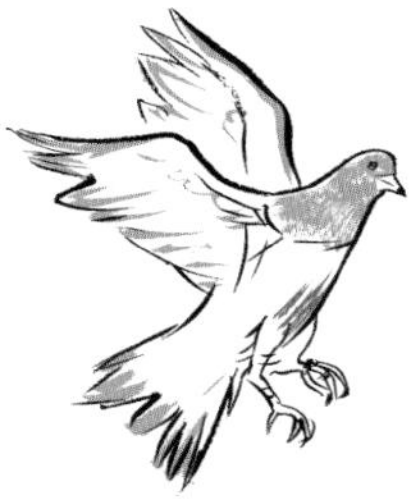

ICHIRO

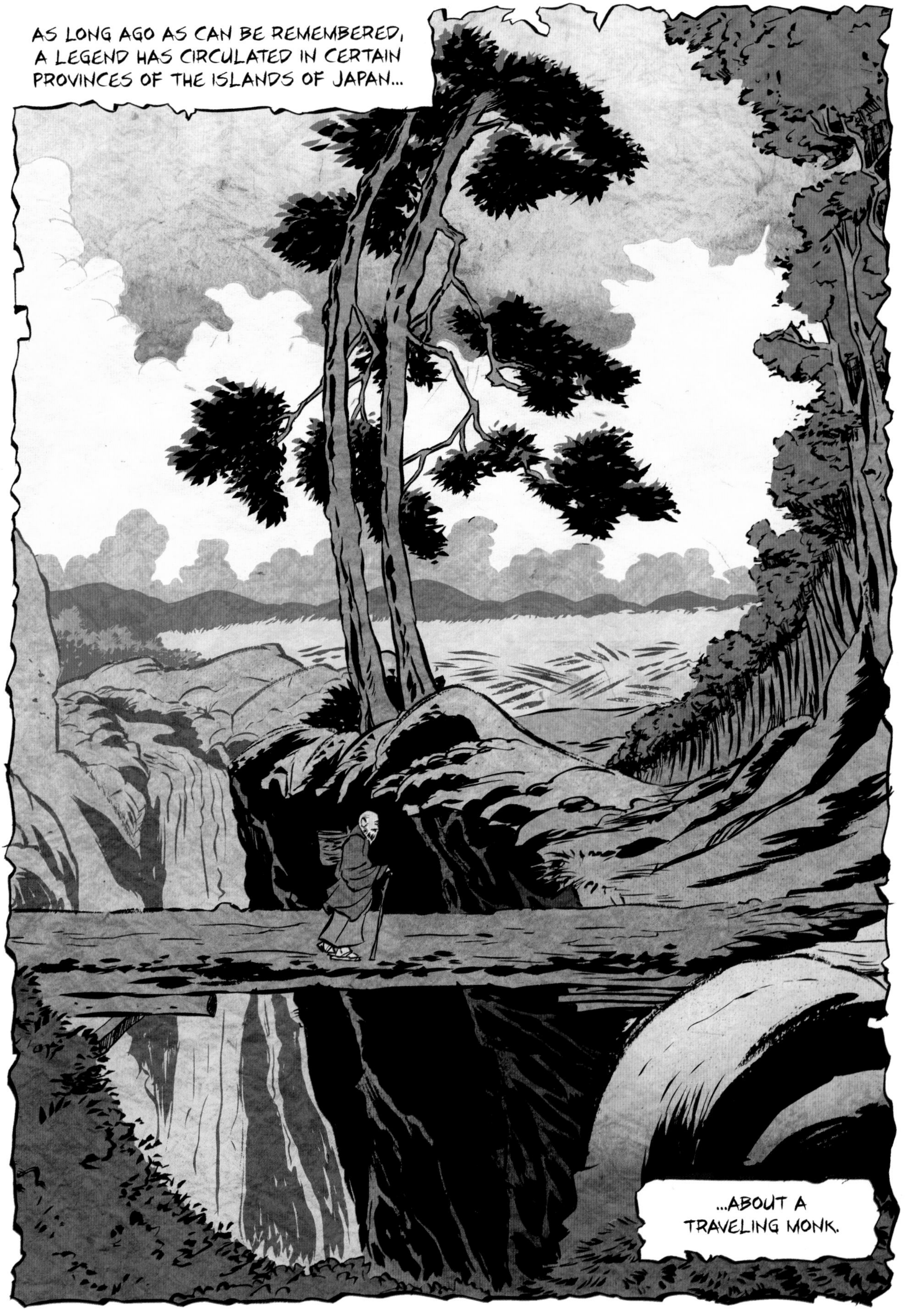
AS LONG AGO AS CAN BE REMEMBERED, A LEGEND HAS CIRCULATED IN CERTAIN PROVINCES OF THE ISLANDS OF JAPAN...
...ABOUT A TRAVELING MONK.

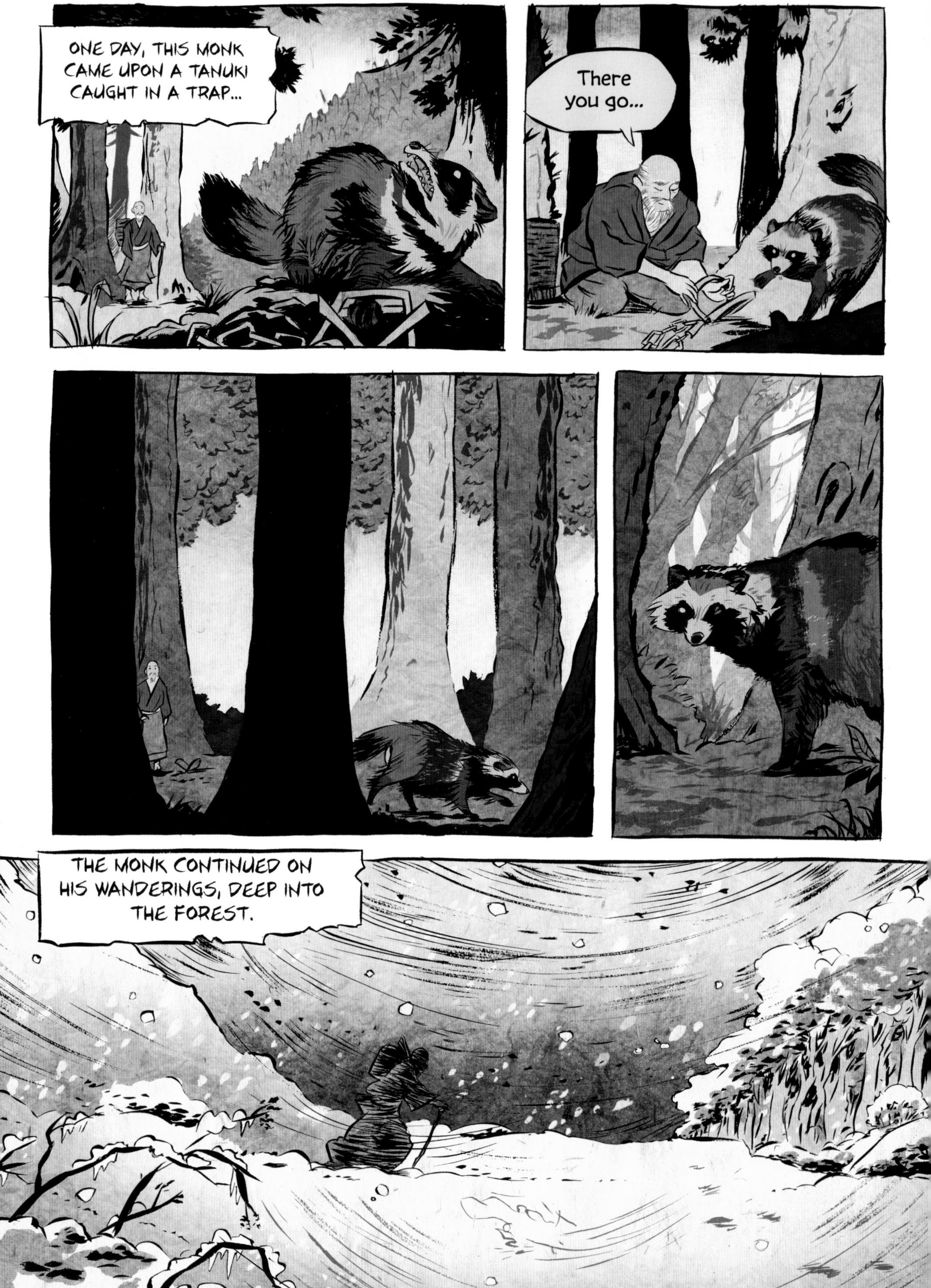
ONE DAY, THIS MONK CAME UPON A TANUKI CAUGHT IN A TRAP...
There you go...
THE MONK CONTINUED ON HIS WANDERINGS, DEEP INTO THE FOREST.

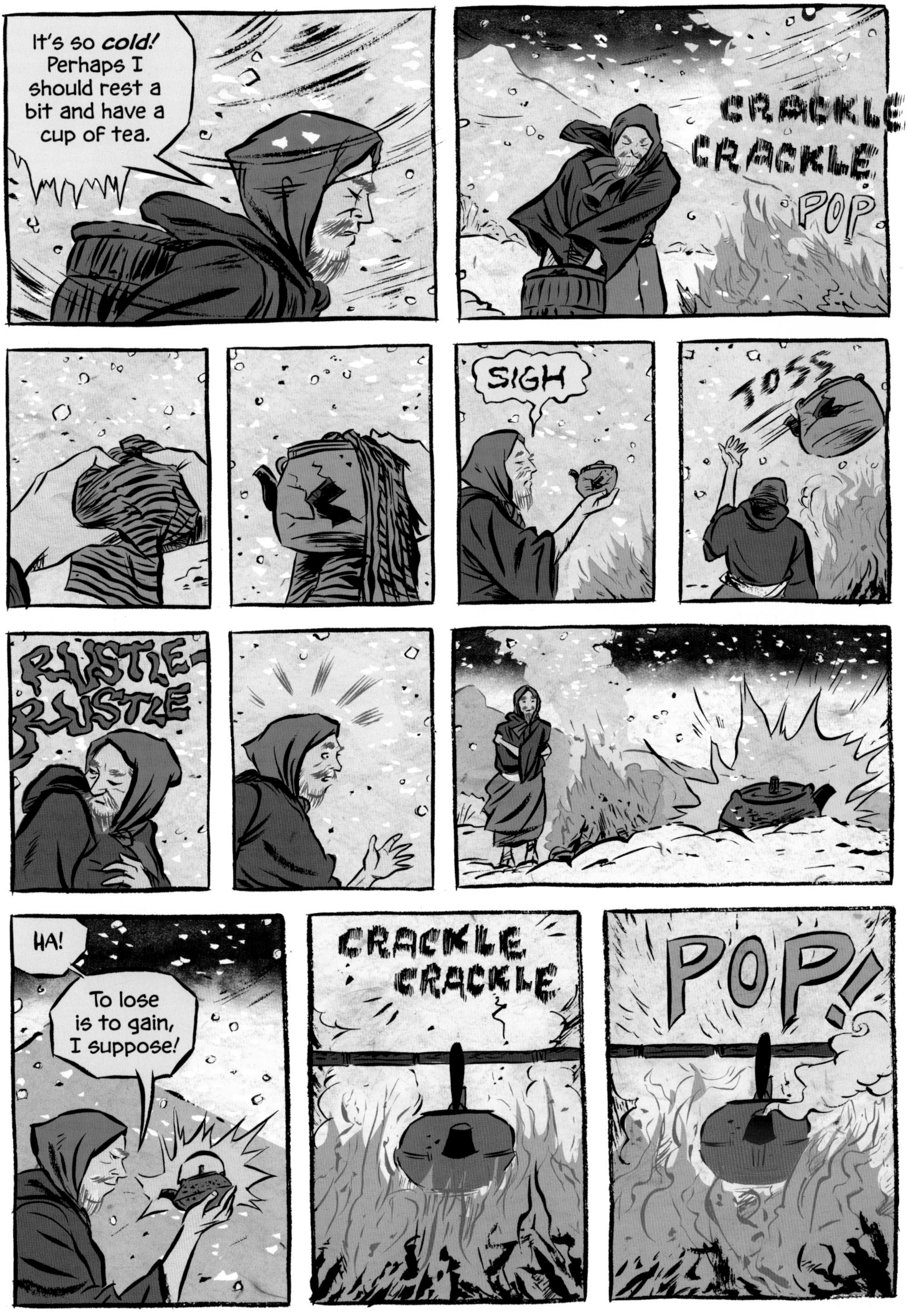
It's so *cold!* Perhaps I should rest a bit and have a cup of tea.
CRACKLE
CRACKLE
POP
SIGH
TOSS
RUSTLE-
RUSTLE
HA!
To lose is to gain, I suppose!
CRACKLE
CRACKLE
POP!

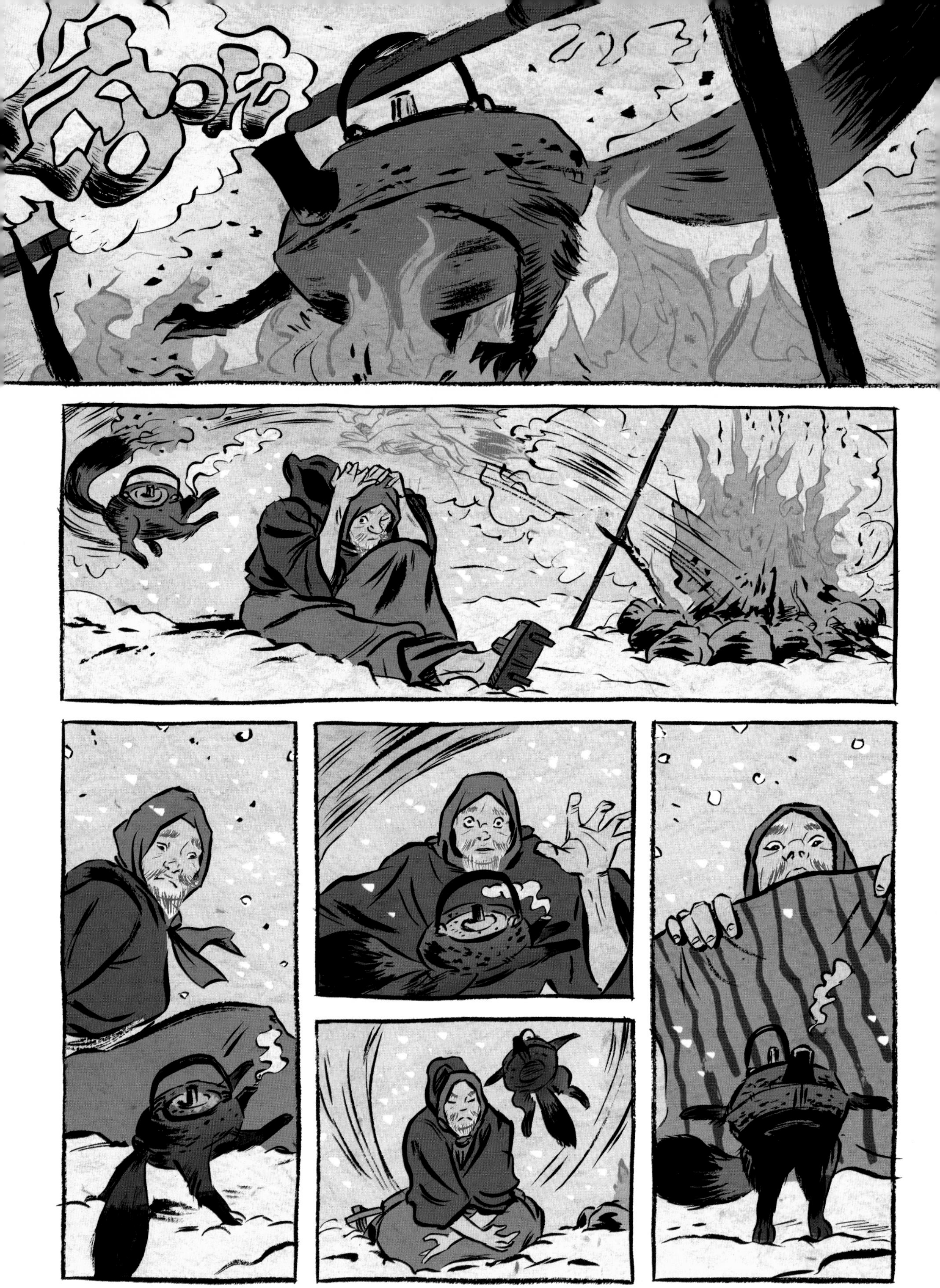

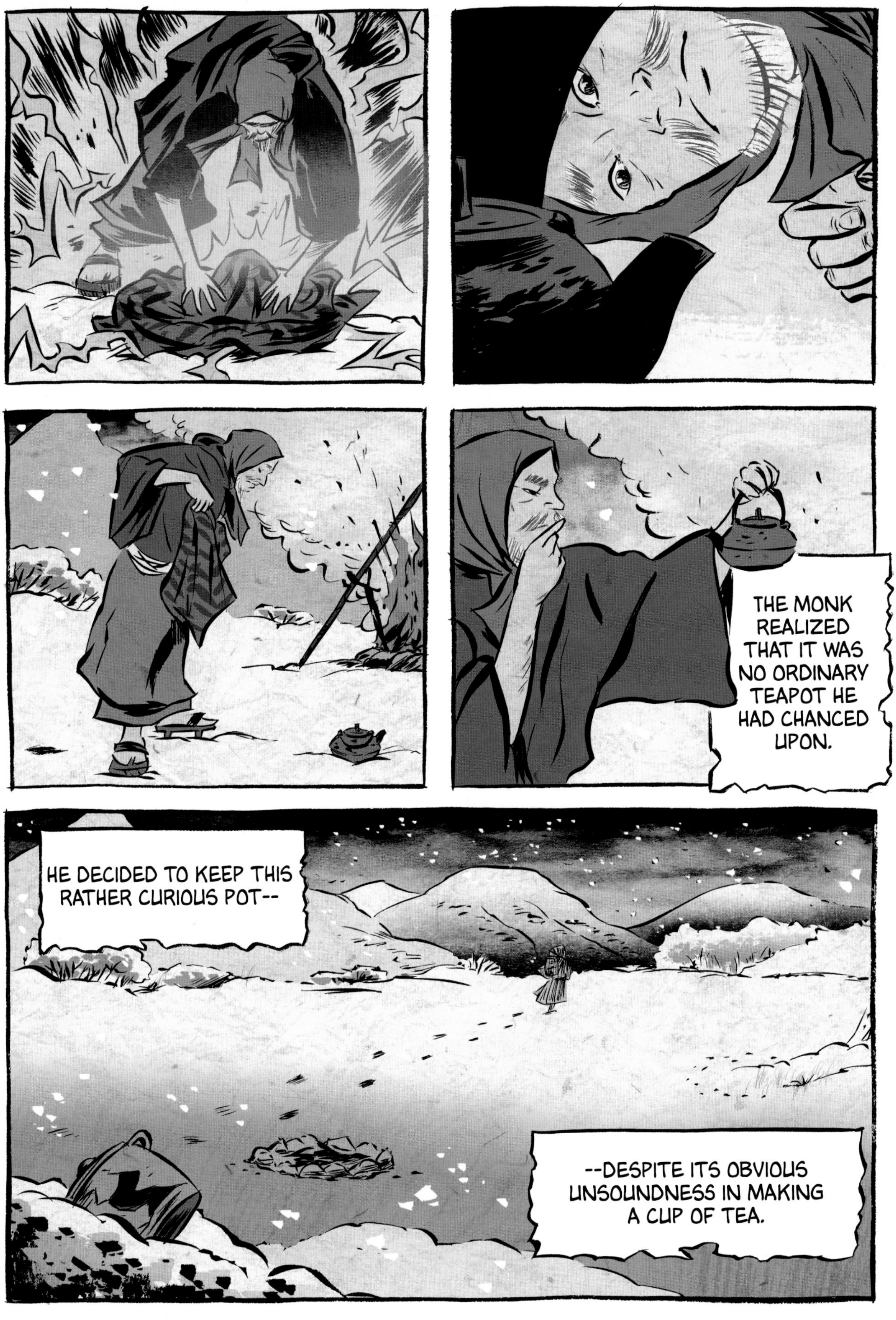
THE MONK REALIZED THAT IT WAS NO ORDINARY TEAPOT HE HAD CHANCED UPON.
HE DECIDED TO KEEP THIS RATHER CURIOUS POT--
--DESPITE ITS OBVIOUS UNSOUNDNESS IN MAKING A CUP OF TEA.

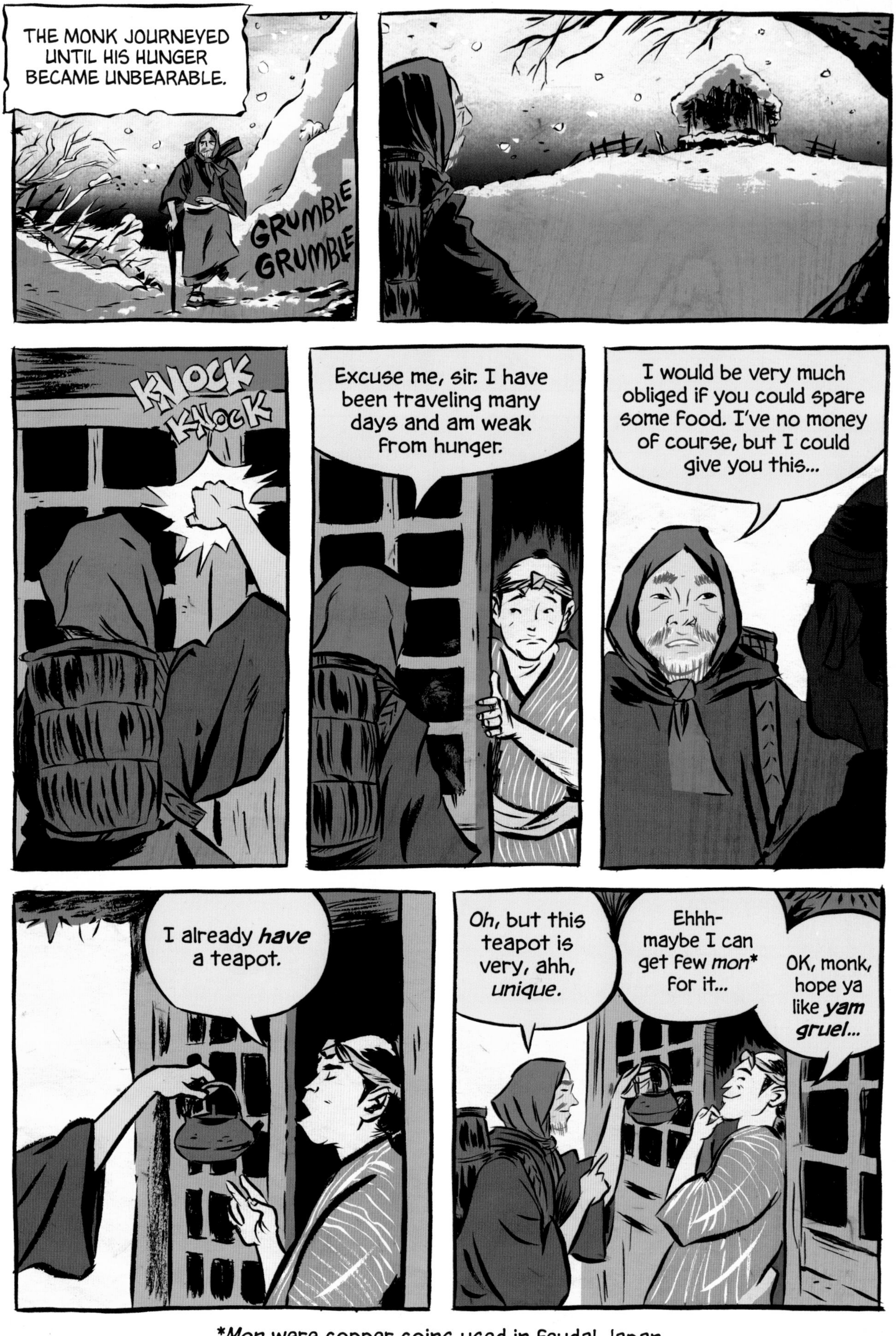
THE MONK JOURNEYED UNTIL HIS HUNGER BECAME UNBEARABLE.
GRUMBLE GRUMBLE
KNOCK KNOCK
Excuse me, sir. I have been traveling many days and am weak from hunger.
I would be very much obliged if you could spare some food. I've no money of course, but I could give you this...
I already *have* a teapot.
Oh, but this teapot is very, ahh, *unique*.
Ehhh- maybe I can get few *mon** for it...
OK, monk, hope ya like ***yam gruel***...

**Mon* were copper coins used in feudal Japan.

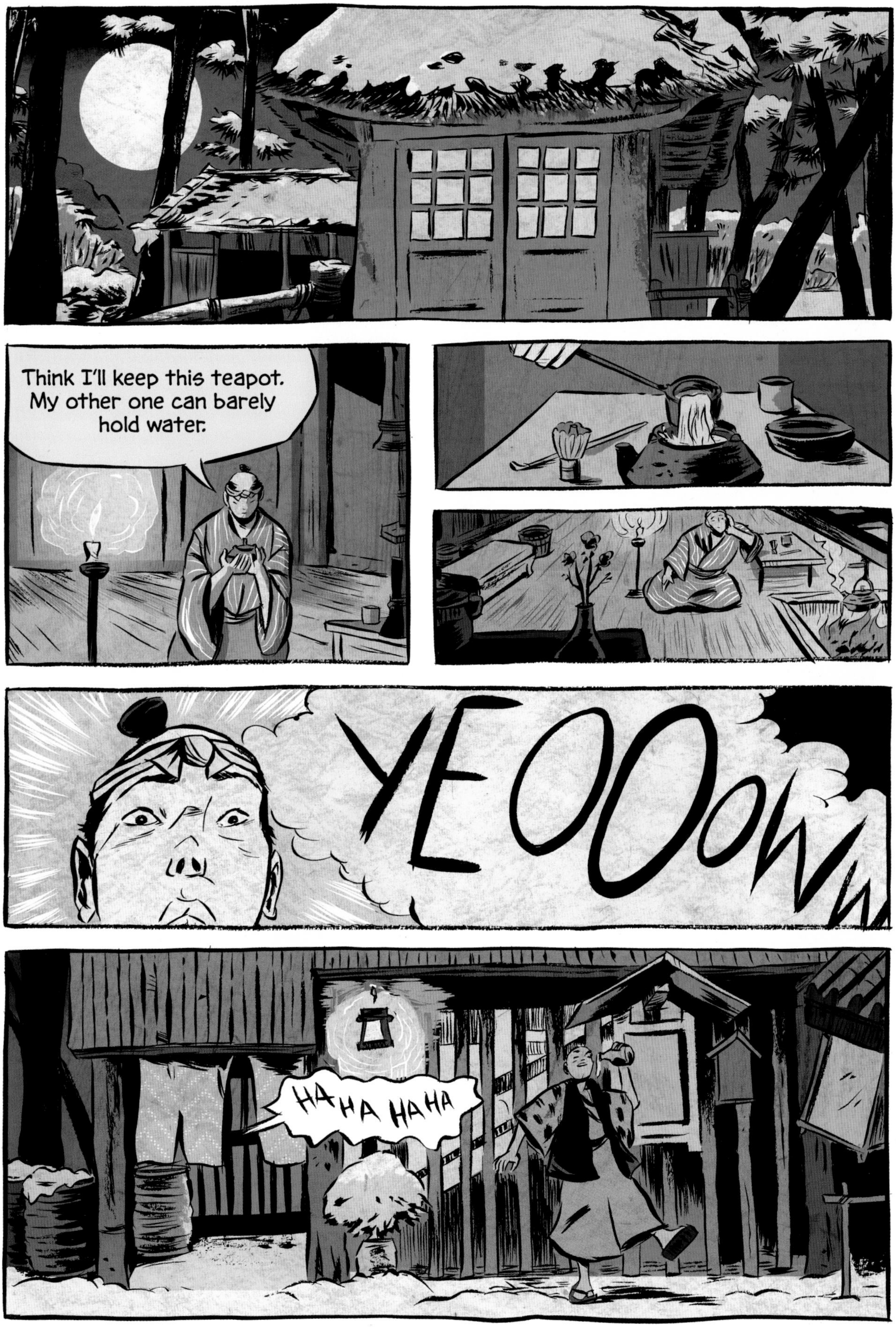
Think I'll keep this teapot. My other one can barely hold water.
YEOOOWW
HAHA HAHA

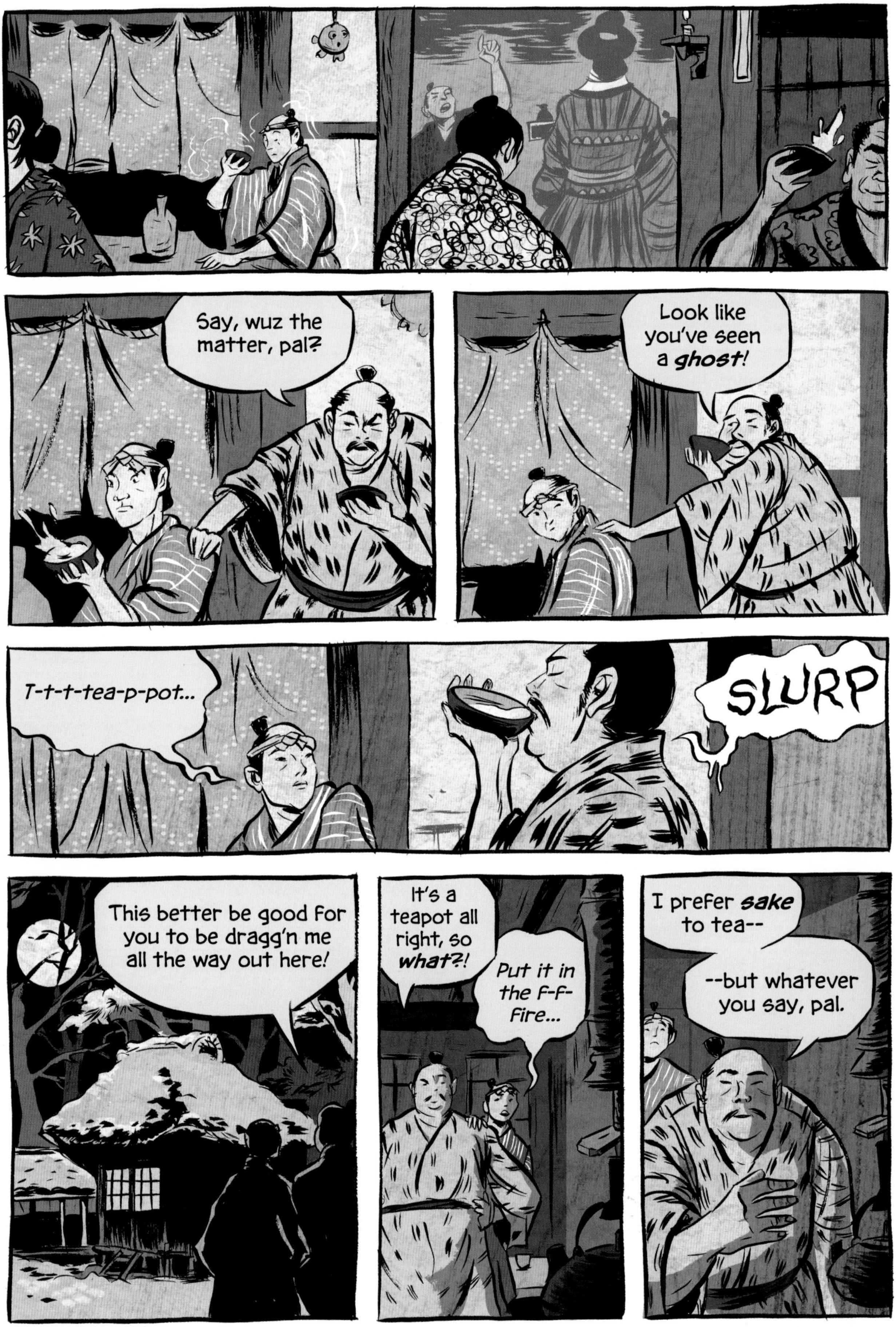
Say, wuz the matter, pal?
Look like you've seen a *ghost*!
T-t-t-tea-p-pot...
SLURP
This better be good for you to be dragg'n me all the way out here!
It's a teapot all right, so *what?!*
Put it in the f-f-fire...
I prefer *sake* to tea--
--but whatever you say, pal.

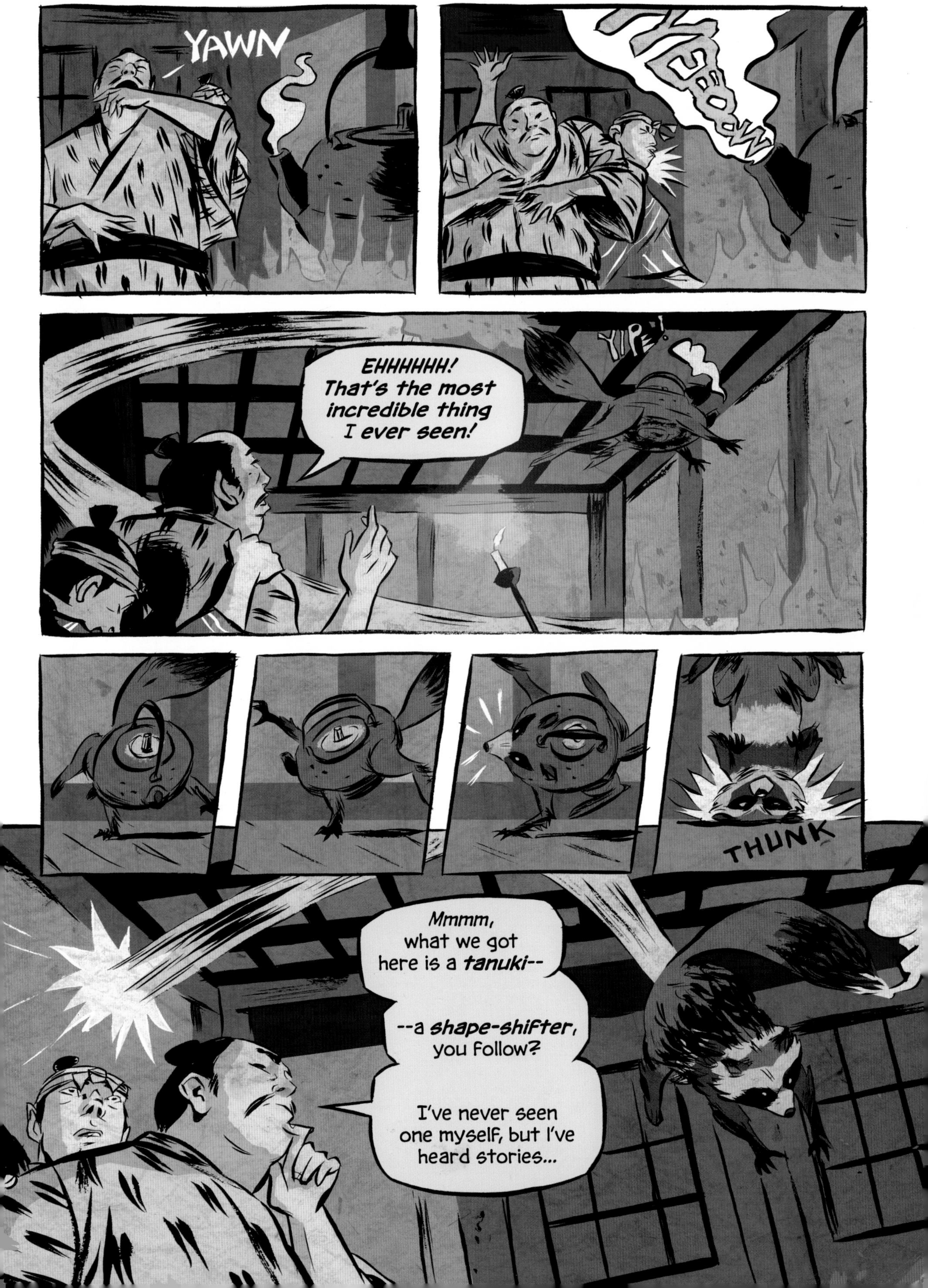
YAWN
YEEOW
YIP
EHHHHHH! That's the most incredible thing I ever seen!
THUNK
Mmmm, what we got here is a *tanuki*--
--a *shape-shifter*, you follow?
I've never seen one myself, but I've heard stories...

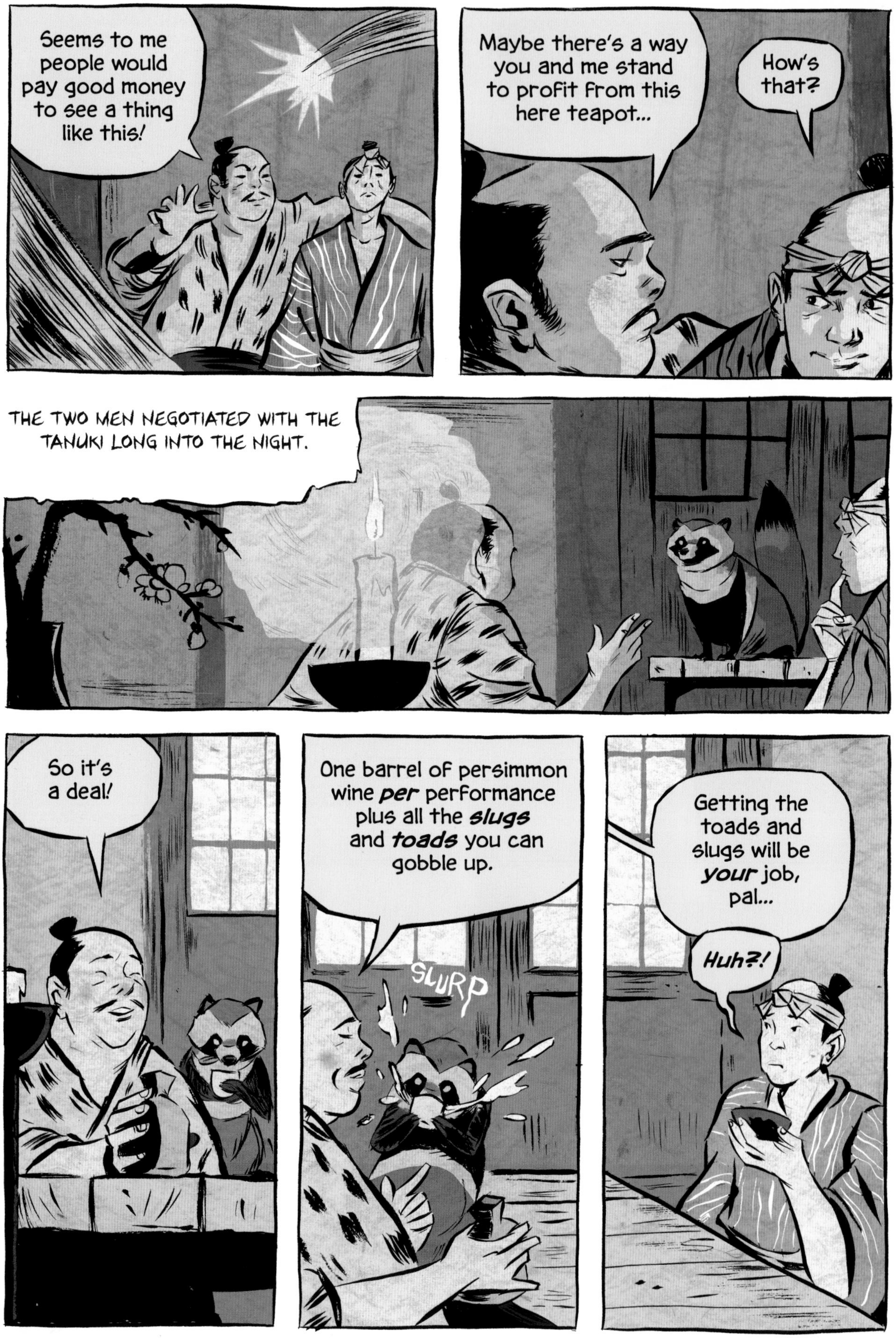
Seems to me people would pay good money to see a thing like this!
Maybe there's a way you and me stand to profit from this here teapot...
How's that?
THE TWO MEN NEGOTIATED WITH THE TANUKI LONG INTO THE NIGHT.
So it's a deal!
One barrel of persimmon wine *per* performance plus all the *slugs* and *toads* you can gobble up.
SLURP
Getting the toads and slugs will be *your* job, pal...
Huh?!

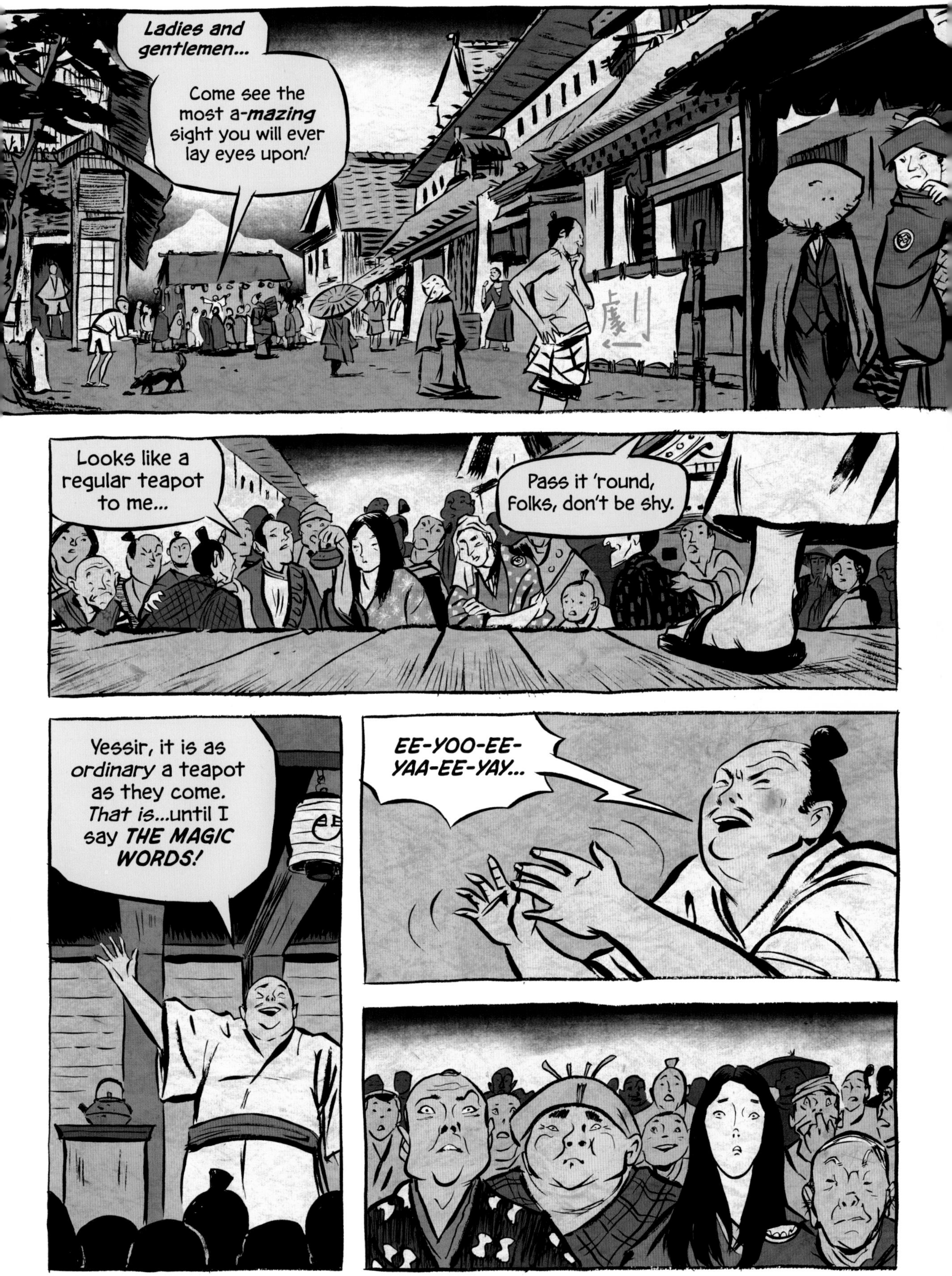
Ladies and gentlemen...
Come see the most a-mazing sight you will ever lay eyes upon!
Looks like a regular teapot to me...
Pass it 'round, folks, don't be shy.
Yessir, it is as ordinary a teapot as they come. That is...until I say THE MAGIC WORDS!
EE-YOO-EE-YAA-EE-YAY...

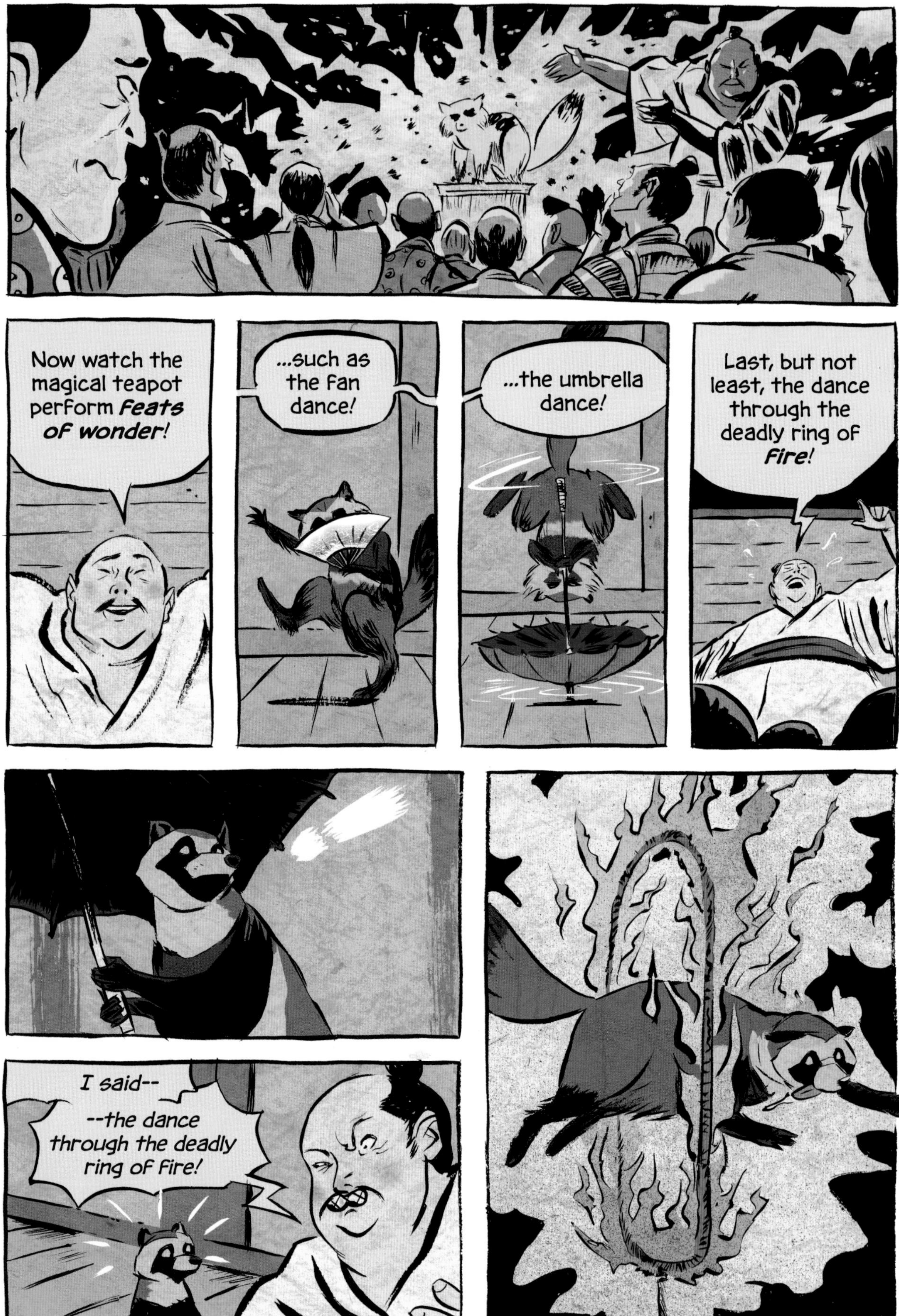
Now watch the magical teapot perform *feats of wonder*!
...such as the fan dance!
...the umbrella dance!
Last, but not least, the dance through the deadly ring of *fire*!
I said--
--the dance through the deadly ring of fire!

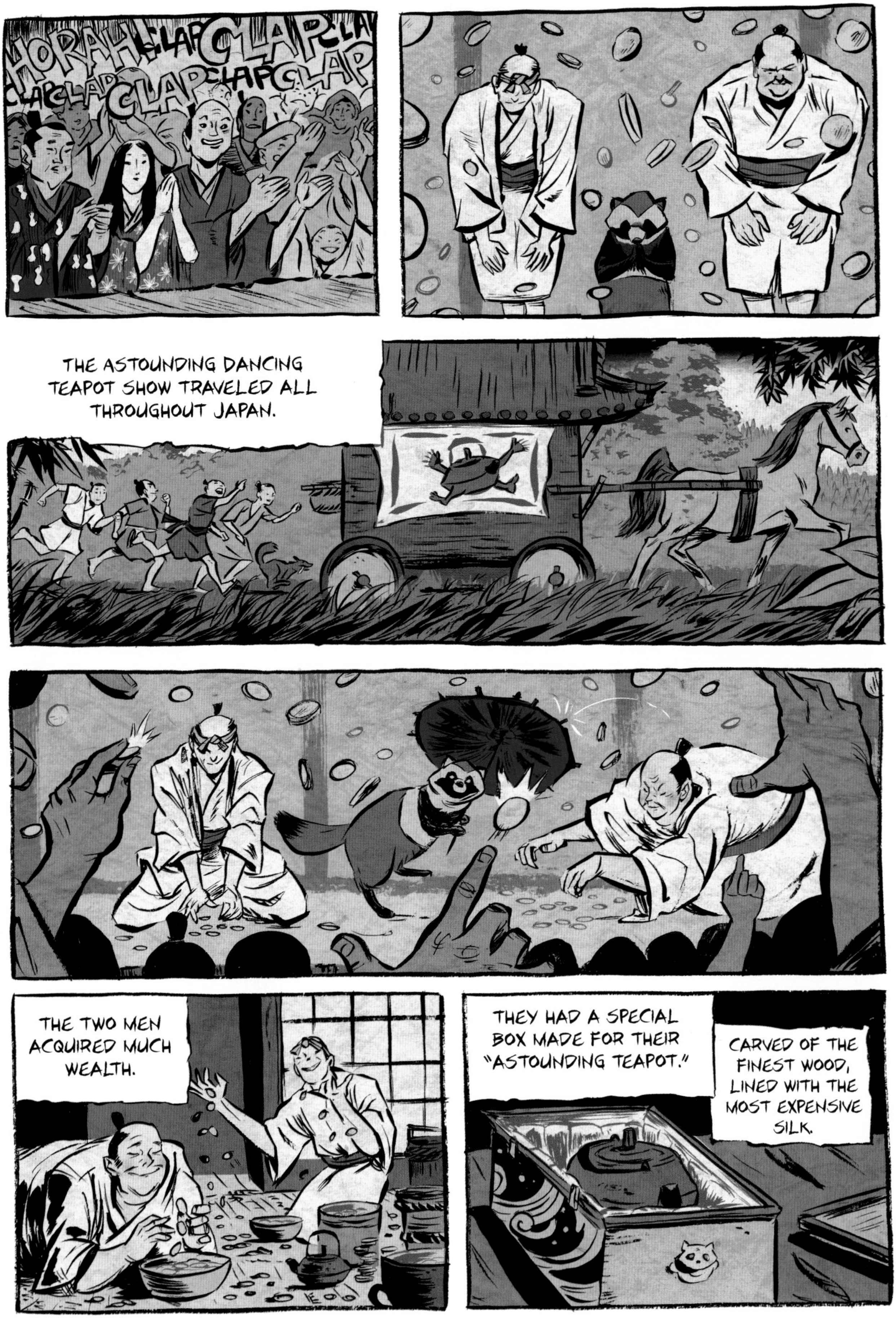
HORAH CLAP CLAP CLAP
CLAP CLAP CLAP CLAP CLAP
THE ASTOUNDING DANCING TEAPOT SHOW TRAVELED ALL THROUGHOUT JAPAN.
THE TWO MEN ACQUIRED MUCH WEALTH.
THEY HAD A SPECIAL BOX MADE FOR THEIR "ASTOUNDING TEAPOT."
CARVED OF THE FINEST WOOD, LINED WITH THE MOST EXPENSIVE SILK.

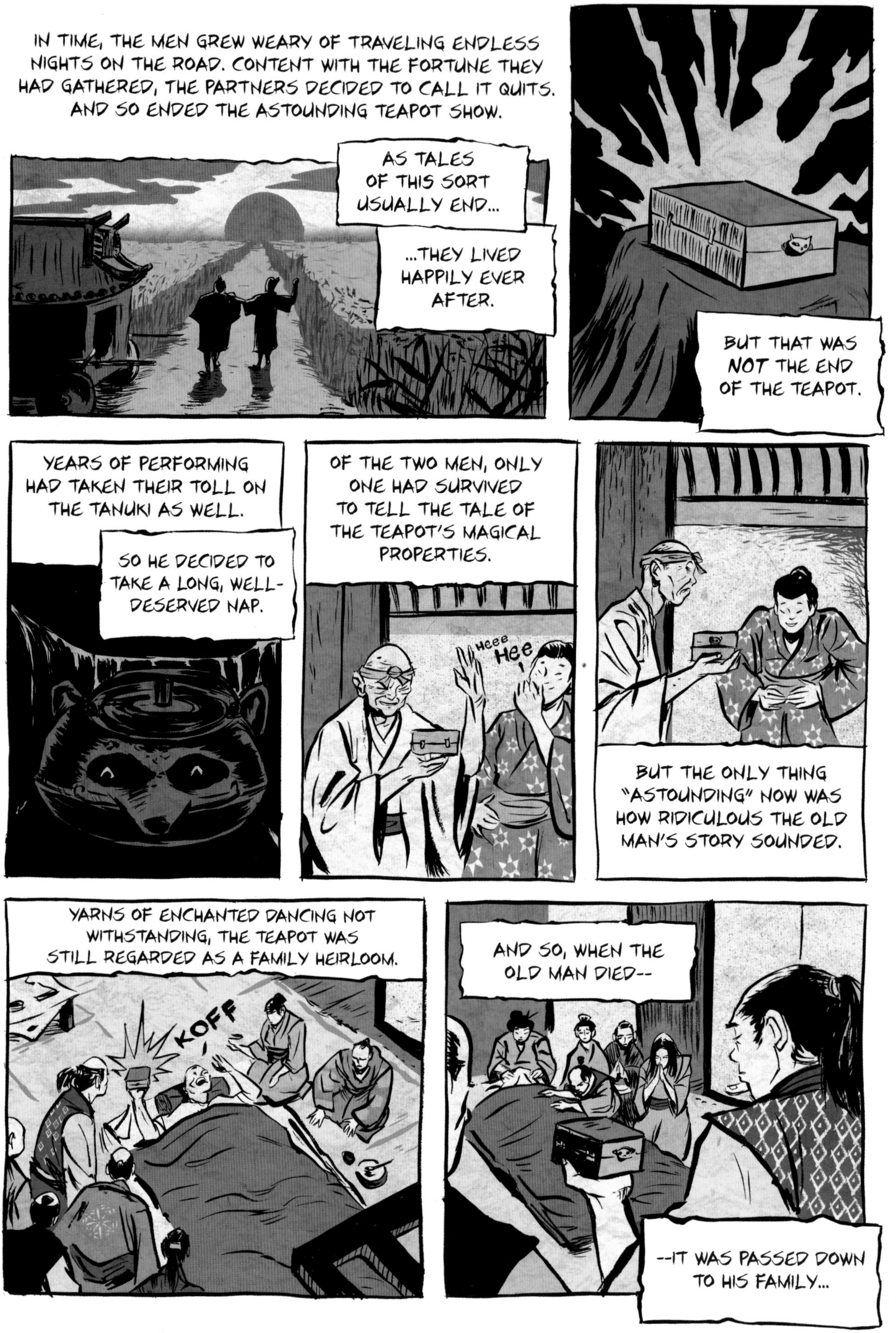
IN TIME, THE MEN GREW WEARY OF TRAVELING ENDLESS NIGHTS ON THE ROAD. CONTENT WITH THE FORTUNE THEY HAD GATHERED, THE PARTNERS DECIDED TO CALL IT QUITS. AND SO ENDED THE ASTOUNDING TEAPOT SHOW.
AS TALES OF THIS SORT USUALLY END...
...THEY LIVED HAPPILY EVER AFTER.
BUT THAT WAS NOT THE END OF THE TEAPOT.
YEARS OF PERFORMING HAD TAKEN THEIR TOLL ON THE TANUKI AS WELL.
SO HE DECIDED TO TAKE A LONG, WELL-DESERVED NAP.
OF THE TWO MEN, ONLY ONE HAD SURVIVED TO TELL THE TALE OF THE TEAPOT'S MAGICAL PROPERTIES.
Heee Hee
BUT THE ONLY THING "ASTOUNDING" NOW WAS HOW RIDICULOUS THE OLD MAN'S STORY SOUNDED.
YARNS OF ENCHANTED DANCING NOT WITHSTANDING, THE TEAPOT WAS STILL REGARDED AS A FAMILY HEIRLOOM.
KOFF
AND SO, WHEN THE OLD MAN DIED--
--IT WAS PASSED DOWN TO HIS FAMILY...

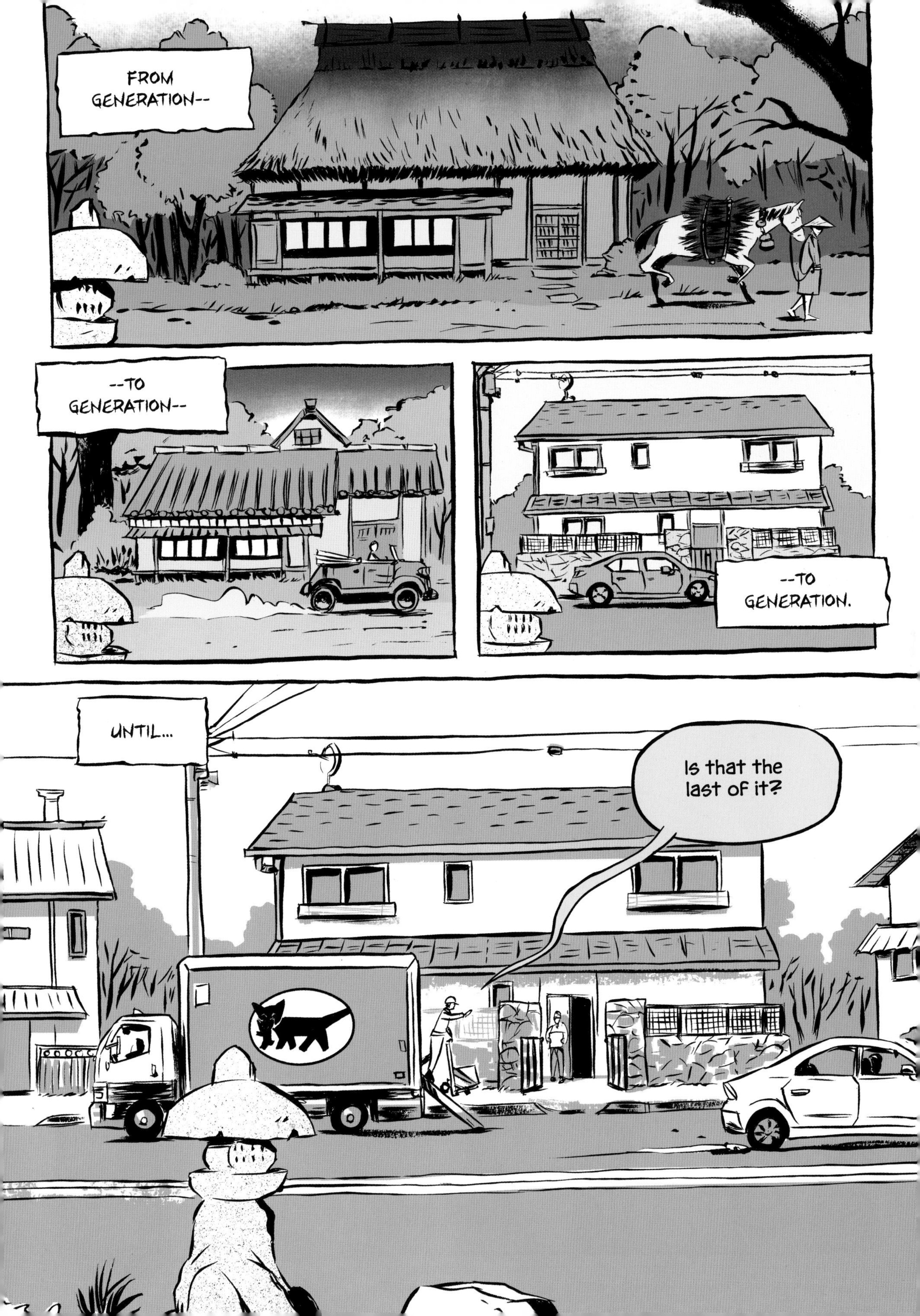
FROM GENERATION--
--TO GENERATION--
--TO GENERATION.
UNTIL...
Is that the last of it?

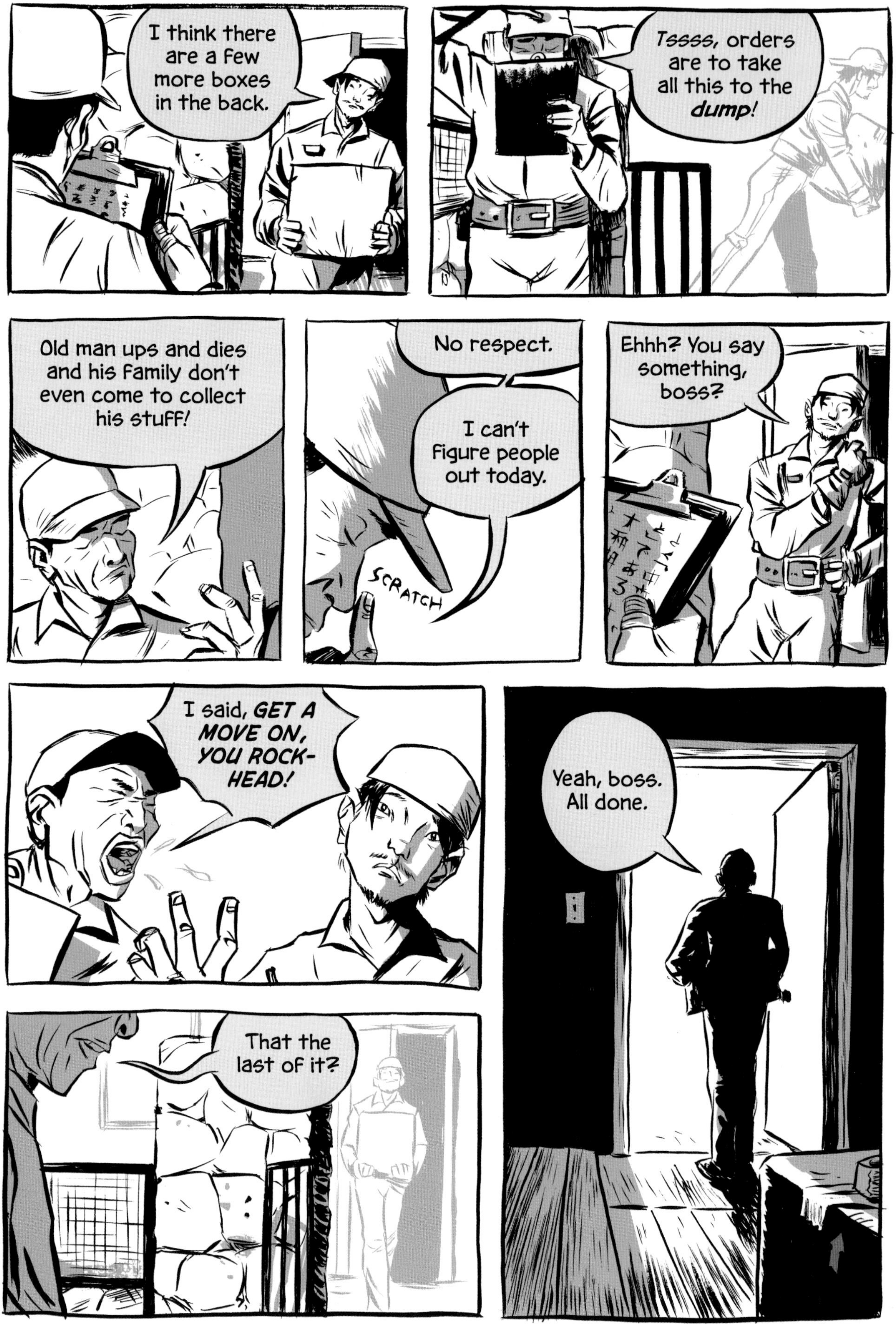
I think there are a few more boxes in the back.
Tssss, orders are to take all this to the dump!
Old man ups and dies and his family don't even come to collect his stuff!
No respect.
I can't figure people out today.
SCRATCH
Ehhh? You say something, boss?
I said, GET A MOVE ON, YOU ROCK-HEAD!
That the last of it?
Yeah, boss. All done.

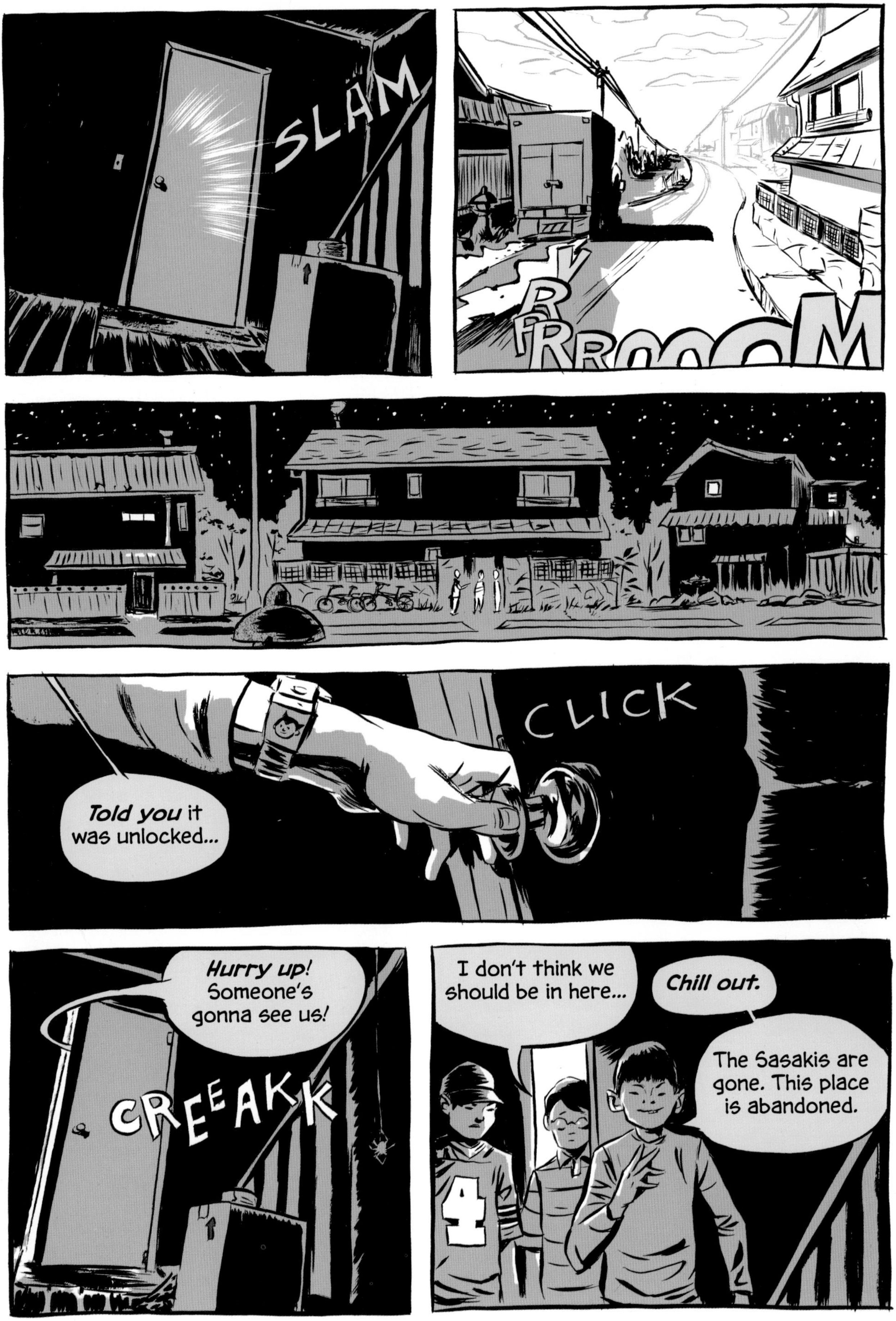
SLAM
VRRROOOOM
CLICK
Told you it was unlocked...
Hurry up! Someone's gonna see us!
CREEAKK
I don't think we should be in here...
Chill out.
The Sasakis are gone. This place is abandoned.

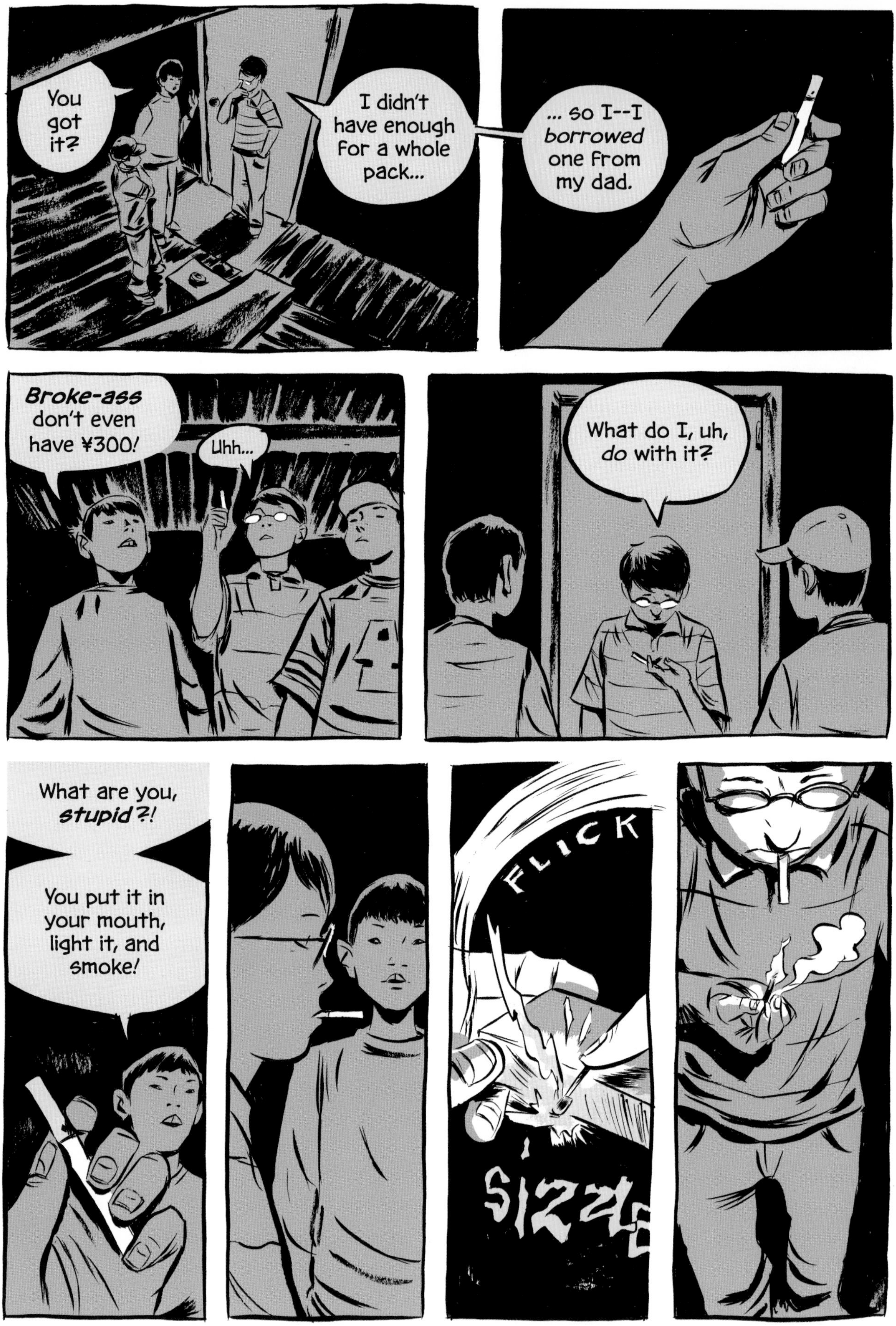

You got it?
I didn't have enough for a whole pack...
... so I--I *borrowed* one from my dad.
Broke-ass don't even have ¥300!
Uhh...
What do I, uh, *do* with it?
What are you, ***stupid***?!
You put it in your mouth, light it, and smoke!
FLICK
SIZZLE

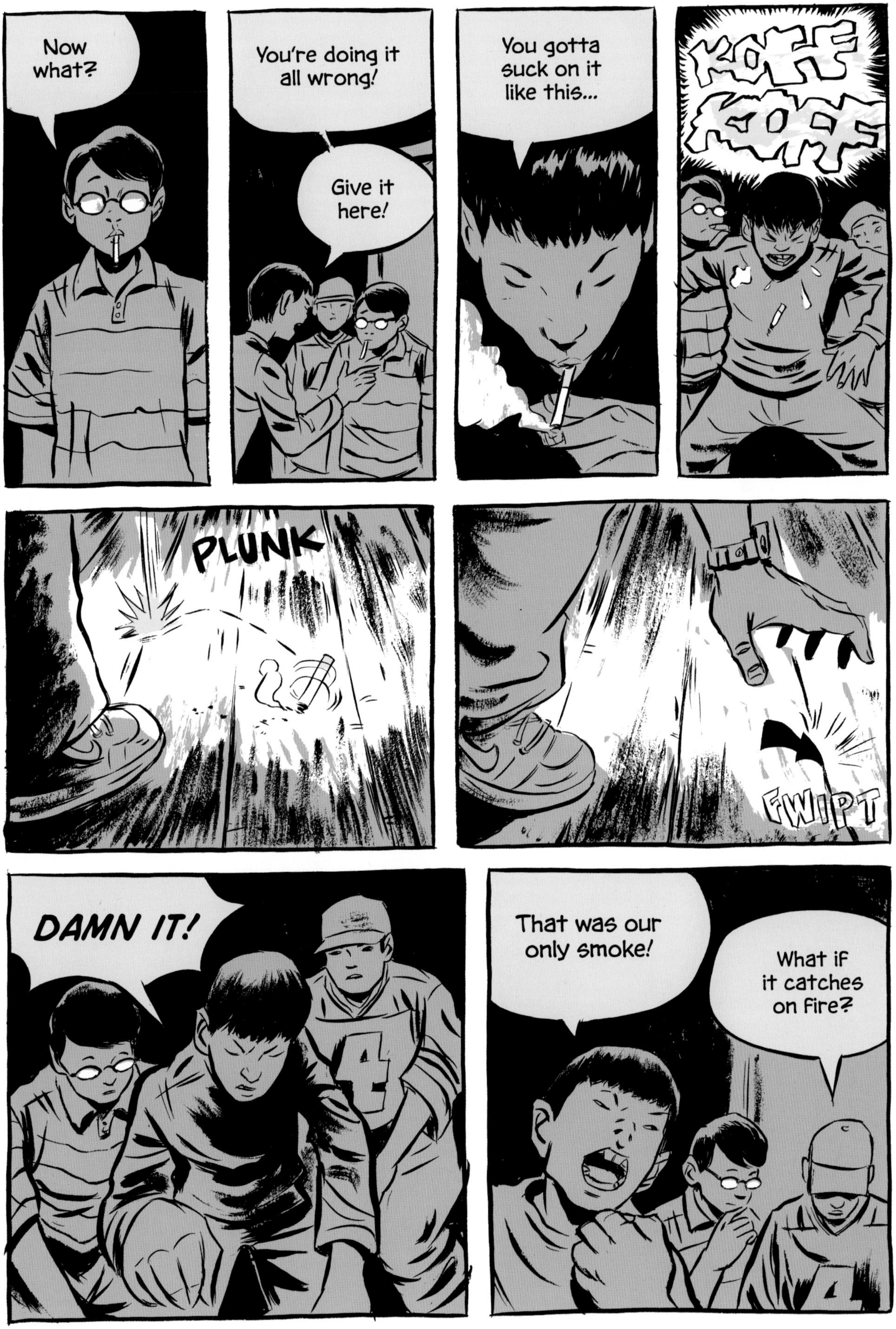
Now what?
You're doing it all wrong!
Give it here!
You gotta suck on it like this...
KOFF KOFF
PLUNK
FWIPT
DAMN IT!
That was our only smoke!
What if it catches on fire?

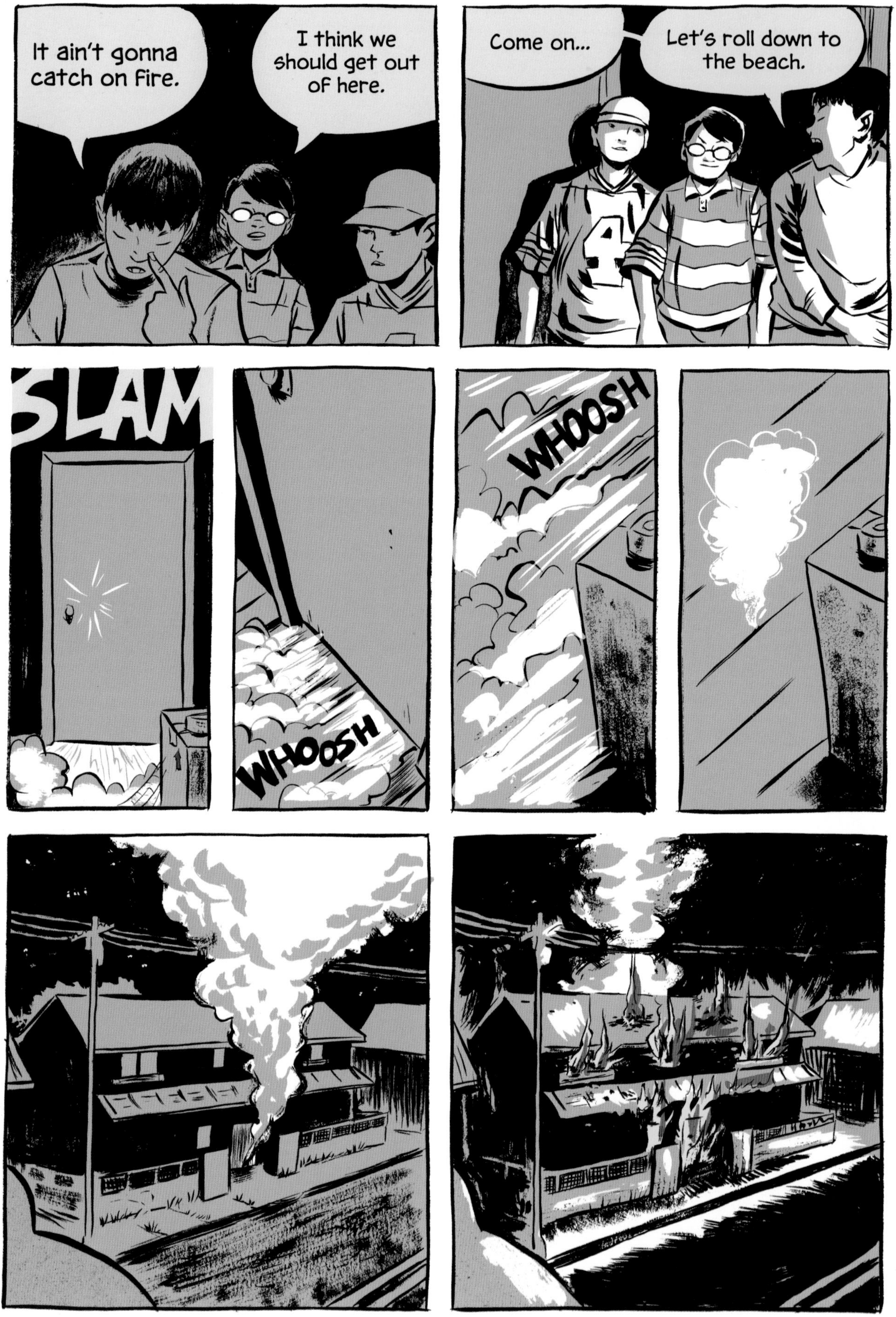
It ain't gonna catch on fire.
I think we should get out of here.
Come on...
Let's roll down to the beach.
SLAM
WHOOSH
WHOOSH

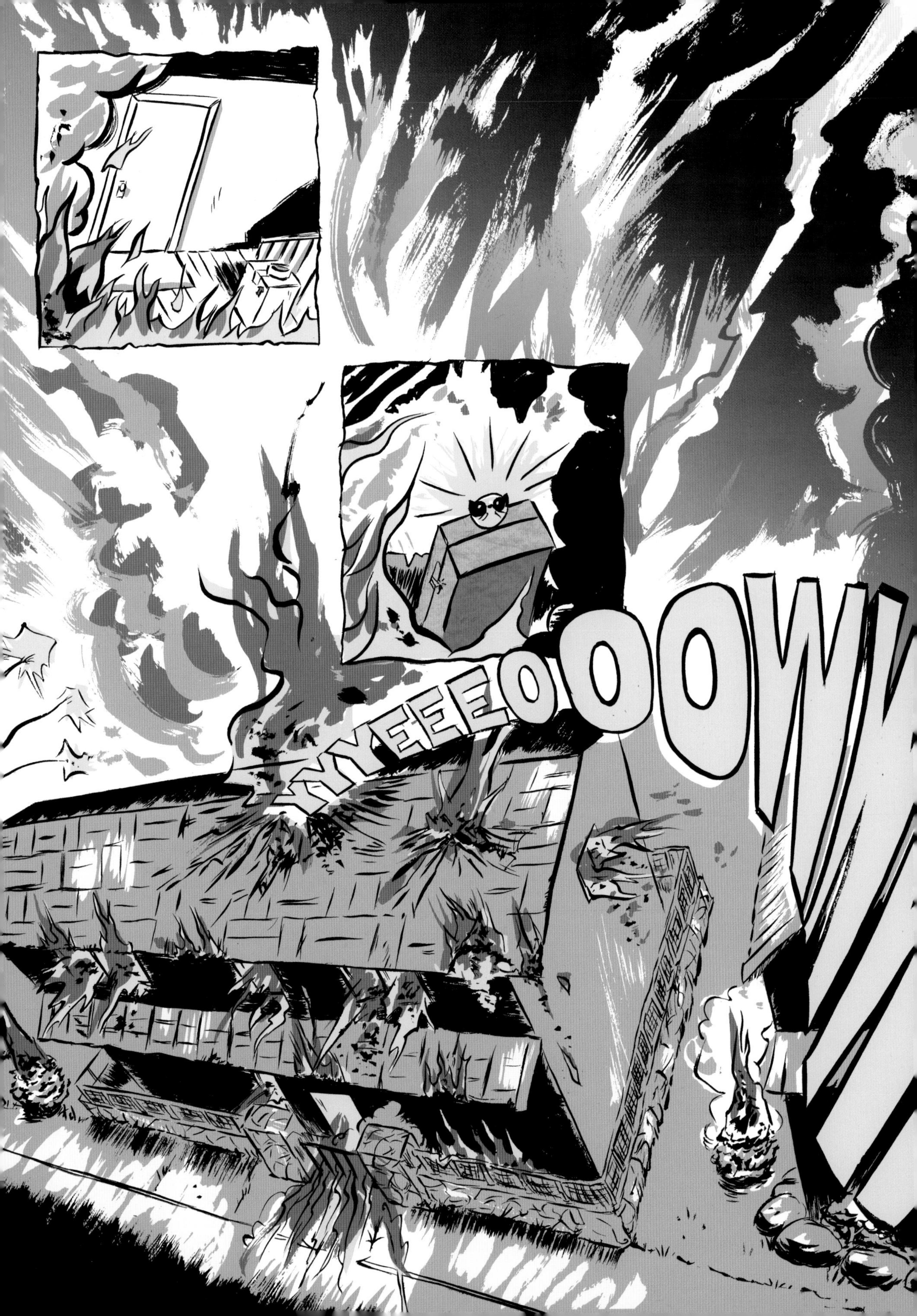
NYEEEOOOW

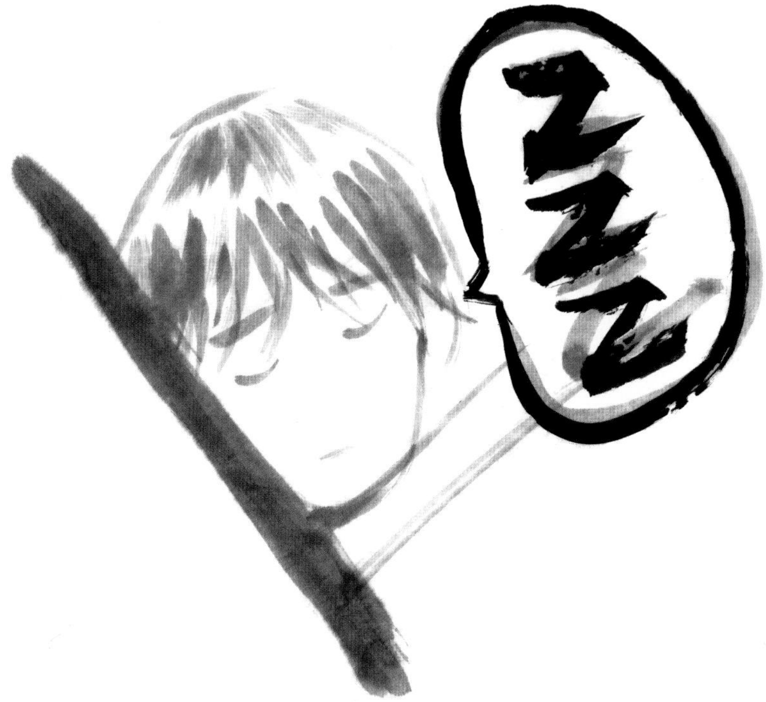
ZZZ

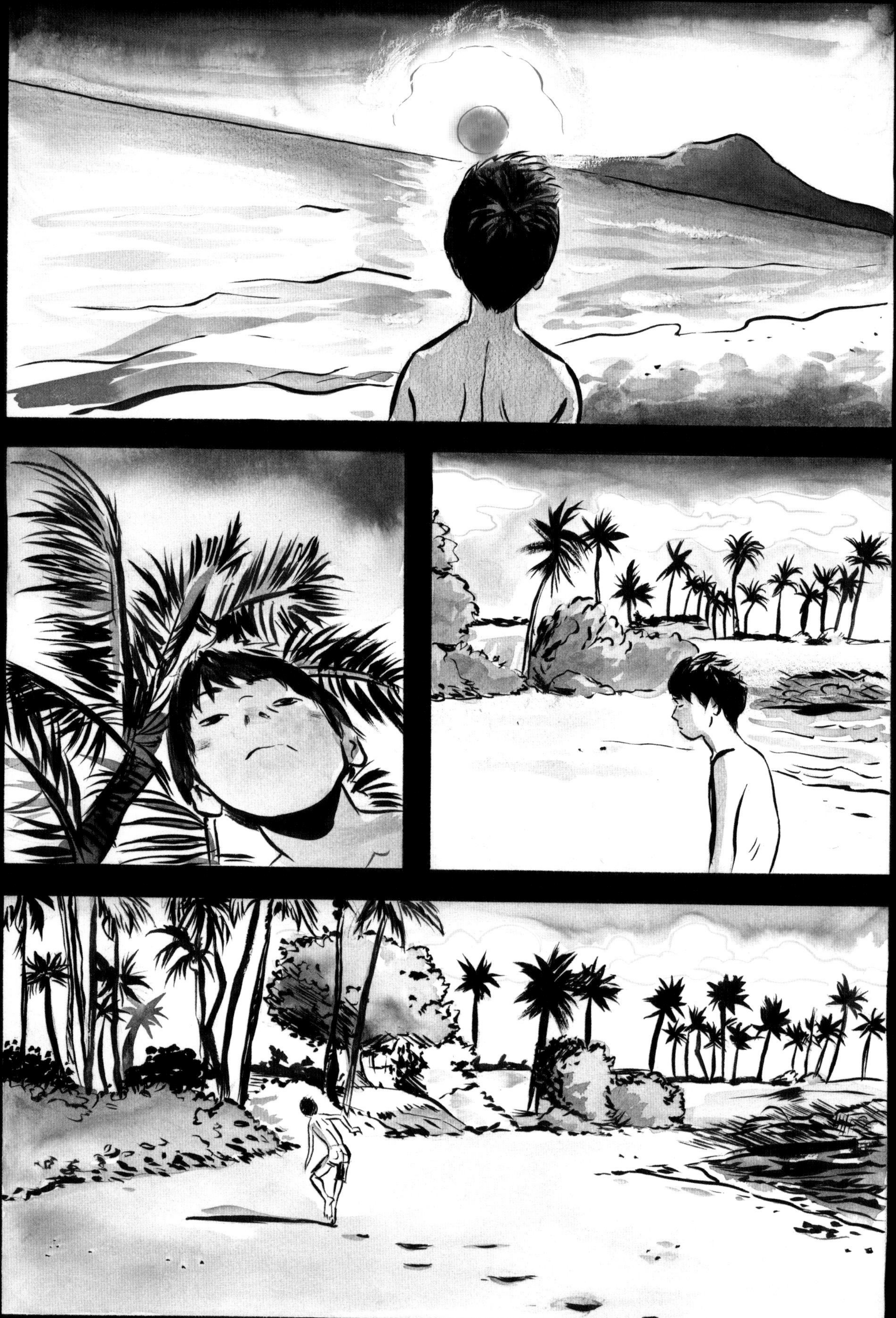

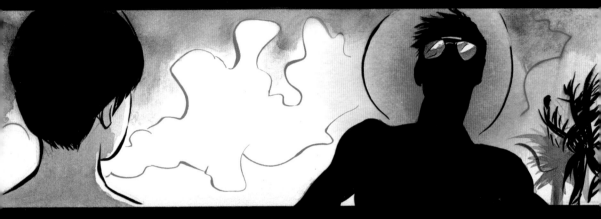

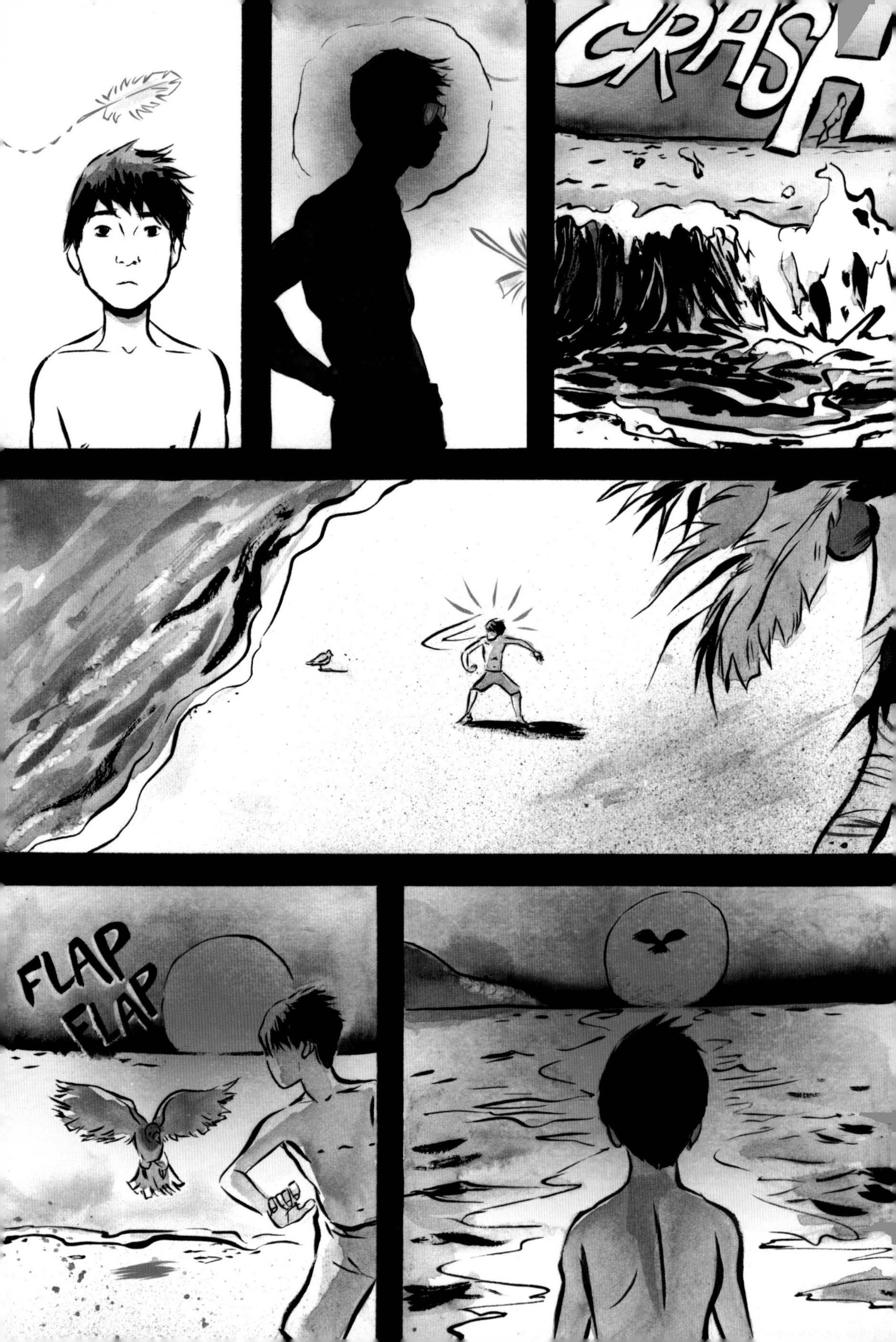
CRASH
FLAP
FLAP

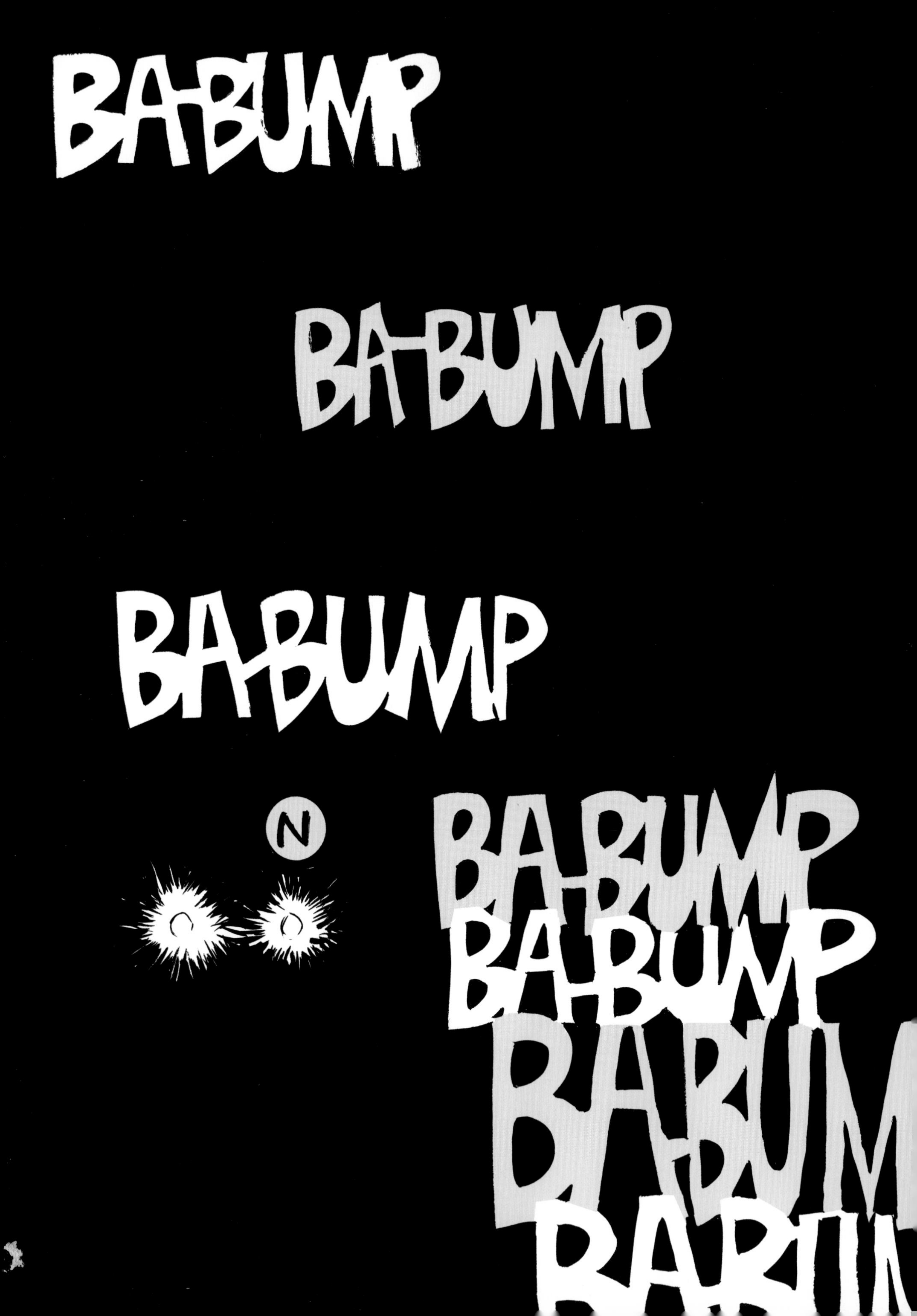
BA-BUMP
BA-BUMP
BA-BUMP
N
BA-BUMP
BA-BUMP

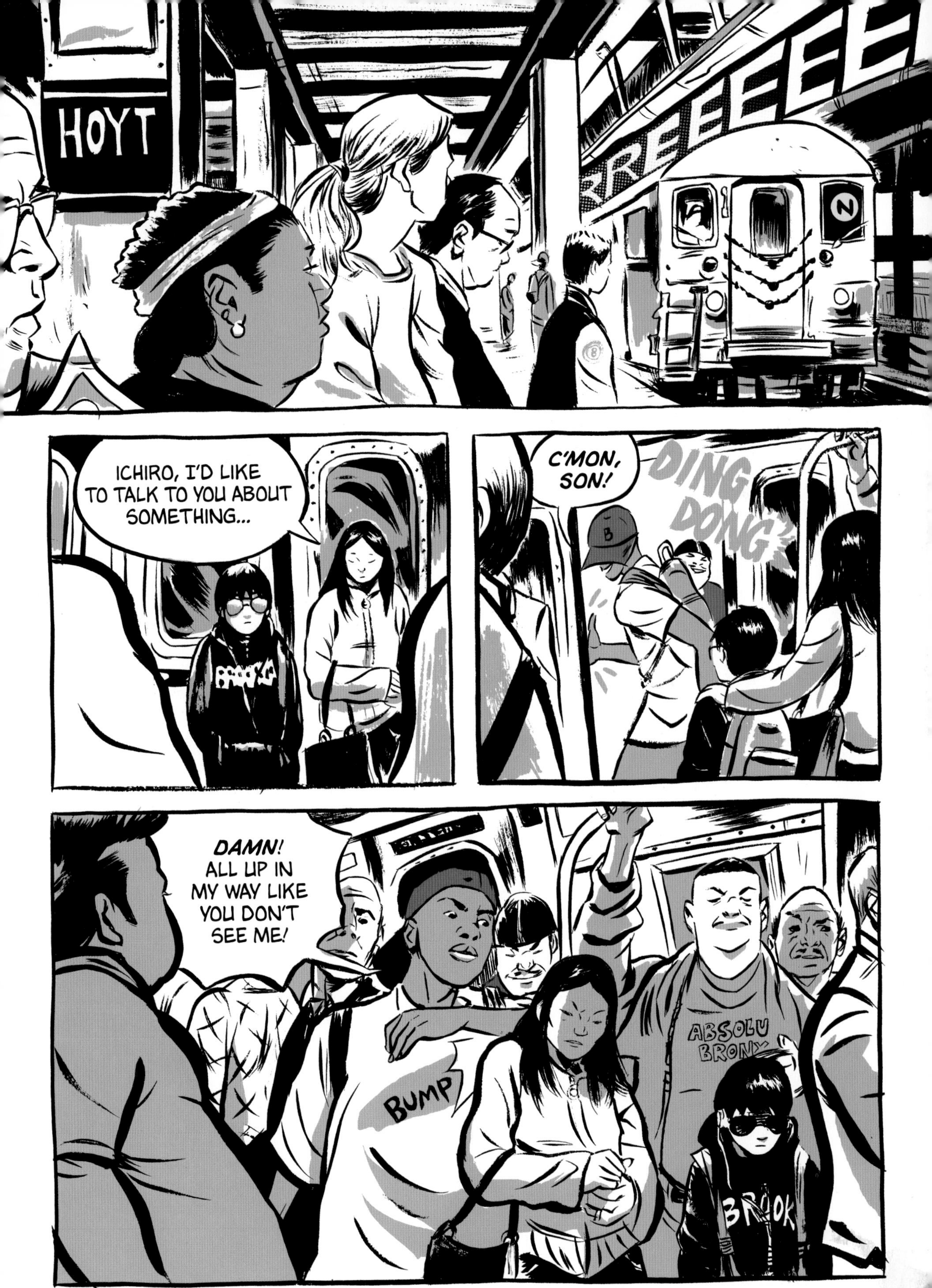
HOYT
RREEEEEEE
ICHIRO, I'D LIKE TO TALK TO YOU ABOUT SOMETHING...
C'MON, SON!
DING DONG
DAMN! ALL UP IN MY WAY LIKE YOU DON'T SEE ME!
BUMP
ABSOLU BRONX
BROOK

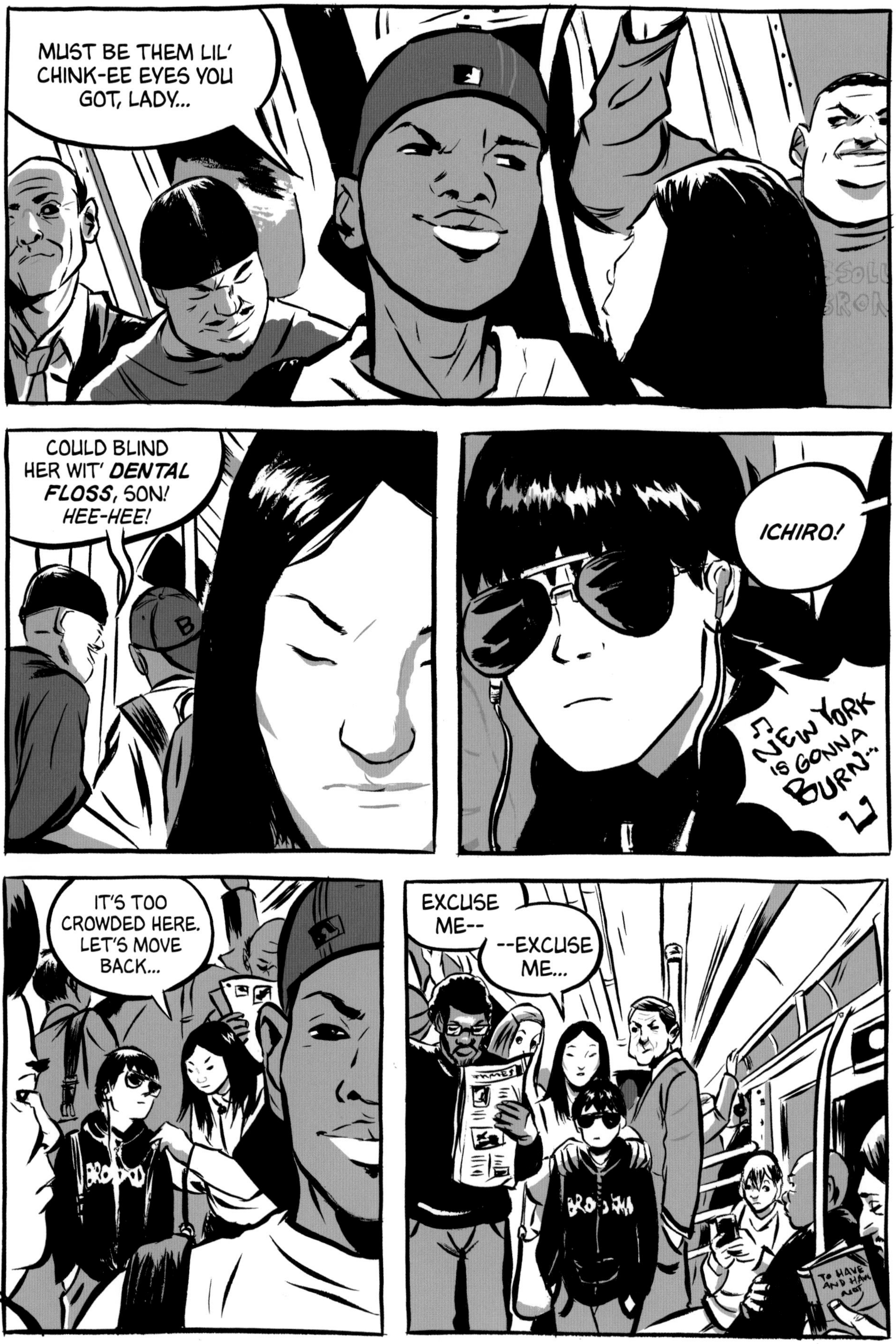
MUST BE THEM LIL' CHINK-EE EYES YOU GOT, LADY...
COULD BLIND HER WIT' *DENTAL FLOSS*, SON! HEE-HEE!
ICHIRO!
♫ NEW YORK IS GONNA BURN... ♫
IT'S TOO CROWDED HERE. LET'S MOVE BACK...
EXCUSE ME--
--EXCUSE ME...

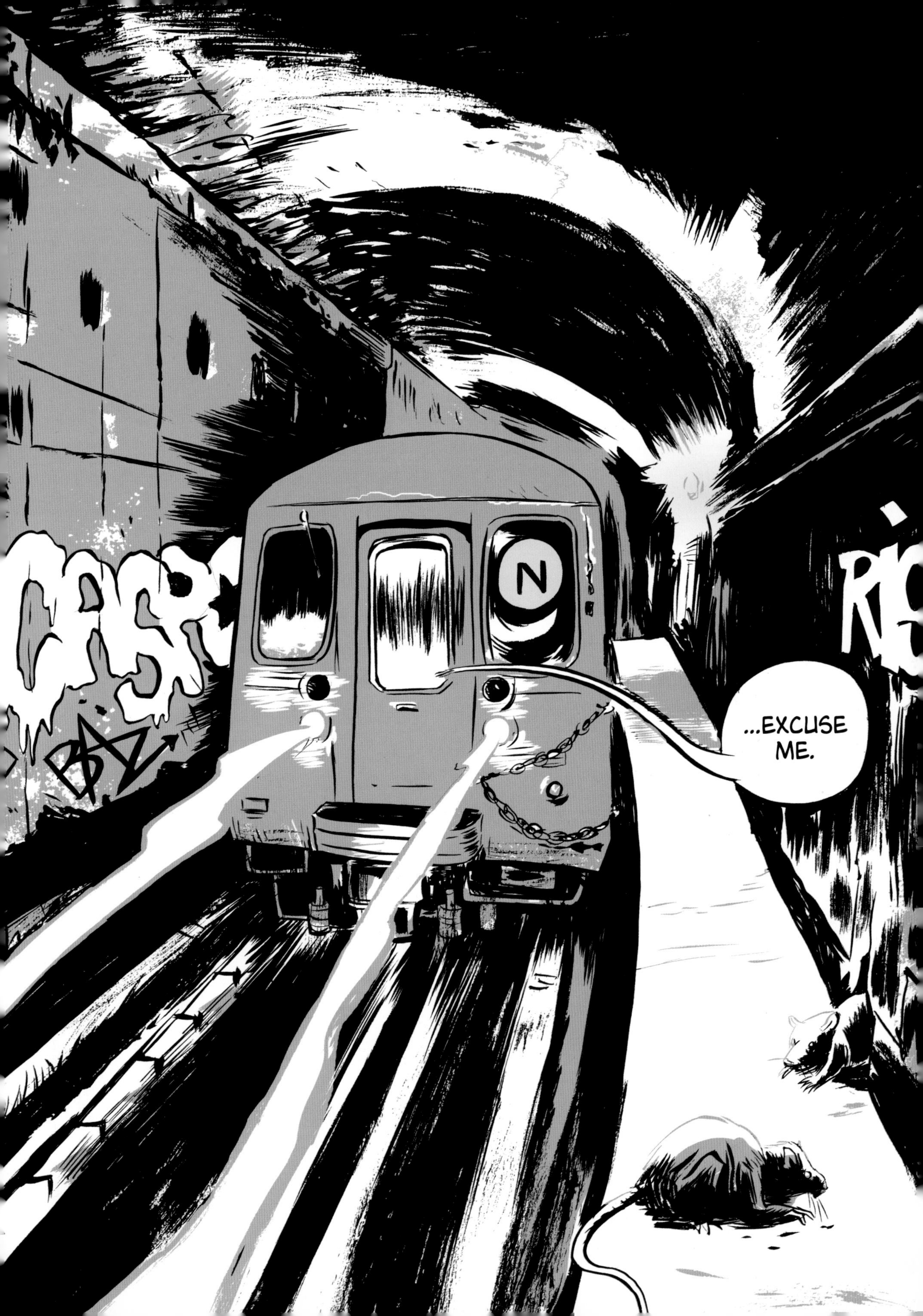
N
...EXCUSE ME.

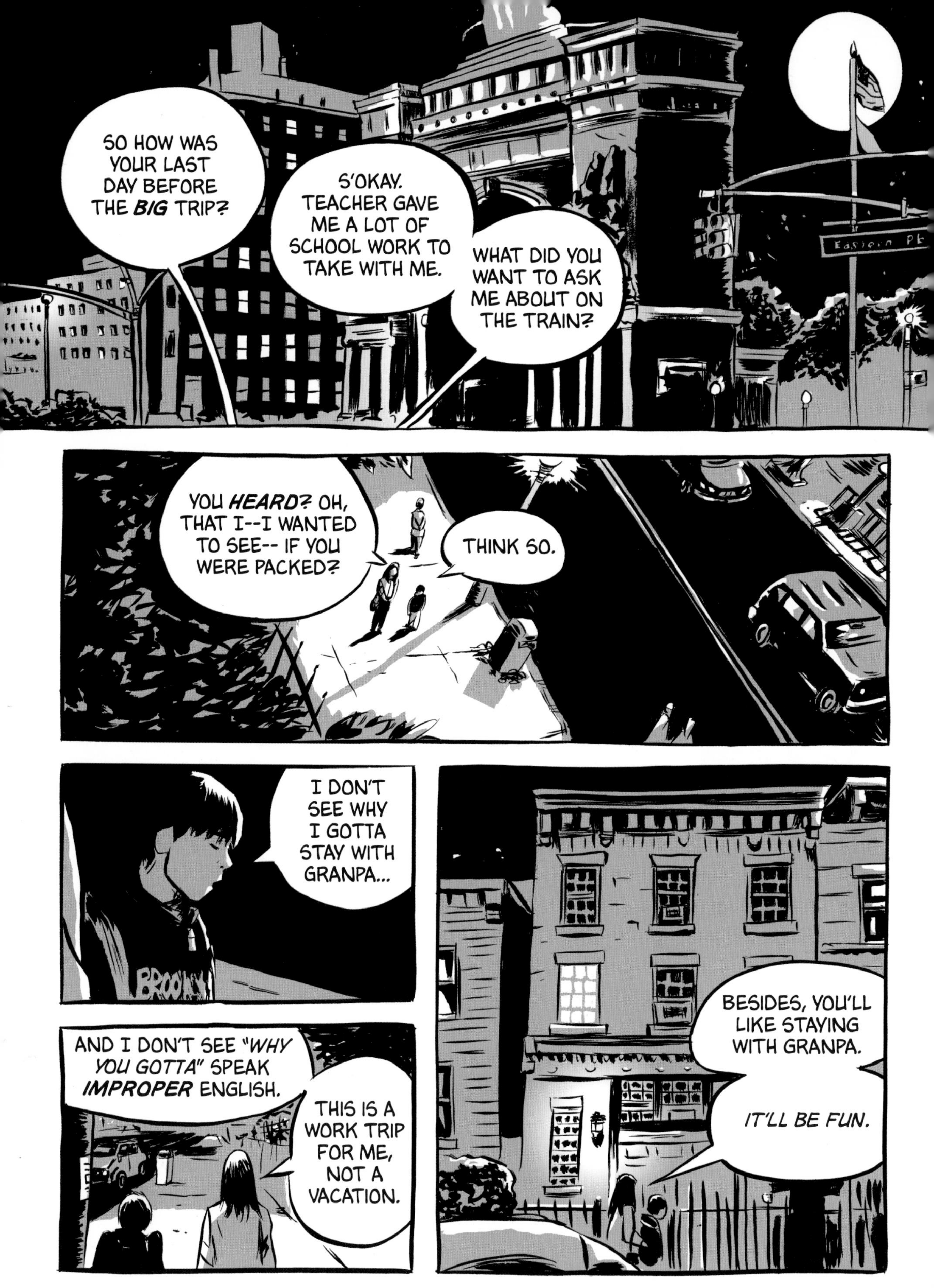
SO HOW WAS YOUR LAST DAY BEFORE THE *BIG* TRIP?
S'OKAY. TEACHER GAVE ME A LOT OF SCHOOL WORK TO TAKE WITH ME.
WHAT DID YOU WANT TO ASK ME ABOUT ON THE TRAIN?
YOU *HEARD*? OH, THAT I--I WANTED TO SEE-- IF YOU WERE PACKED?
THINK SO.
I DON'T SEE WHY I GOTTA STAY WITH GRANPA...
AND I DON'T SEE "*WHY YOU GOTTA*" SPEAK *IMPROPER* ENGLISH.
THIS IS A WORK TRIP FOR ME, NOT A VACATION.
BESIDES, YOU'LL LIKE STAYING WITH GRANPA.
IT'LL BE FUN.

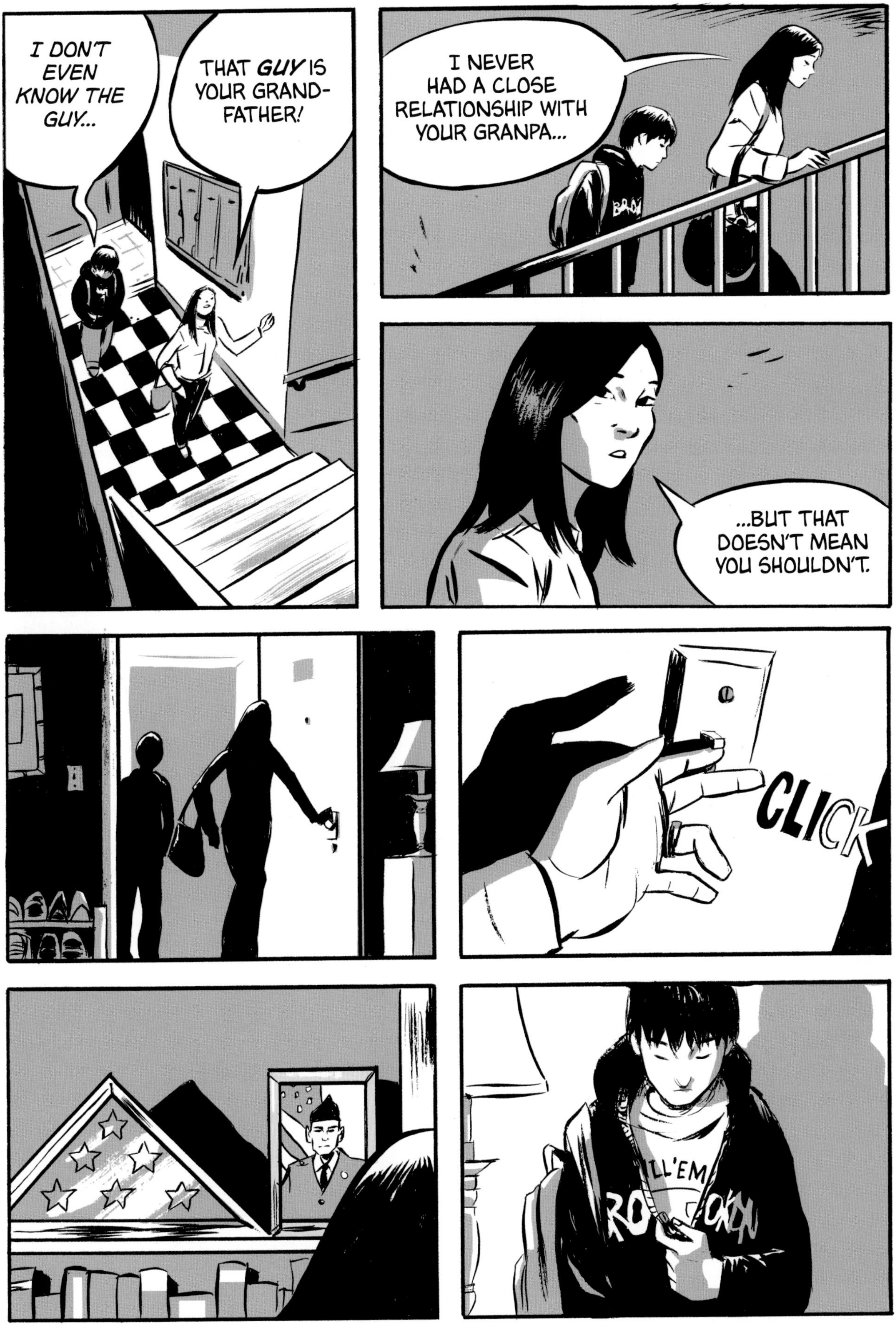
I DON'T EVEN KNOW THE GUY...
THAT *GUY* IS YOUR GRANDFATHER!
I NEVER HAD A CLOSE RELATIONSHIP WITH YOUR GRANPA...
...BUT THAT DOESN'T MEAN YOU SHOULDN'T.
CLICK

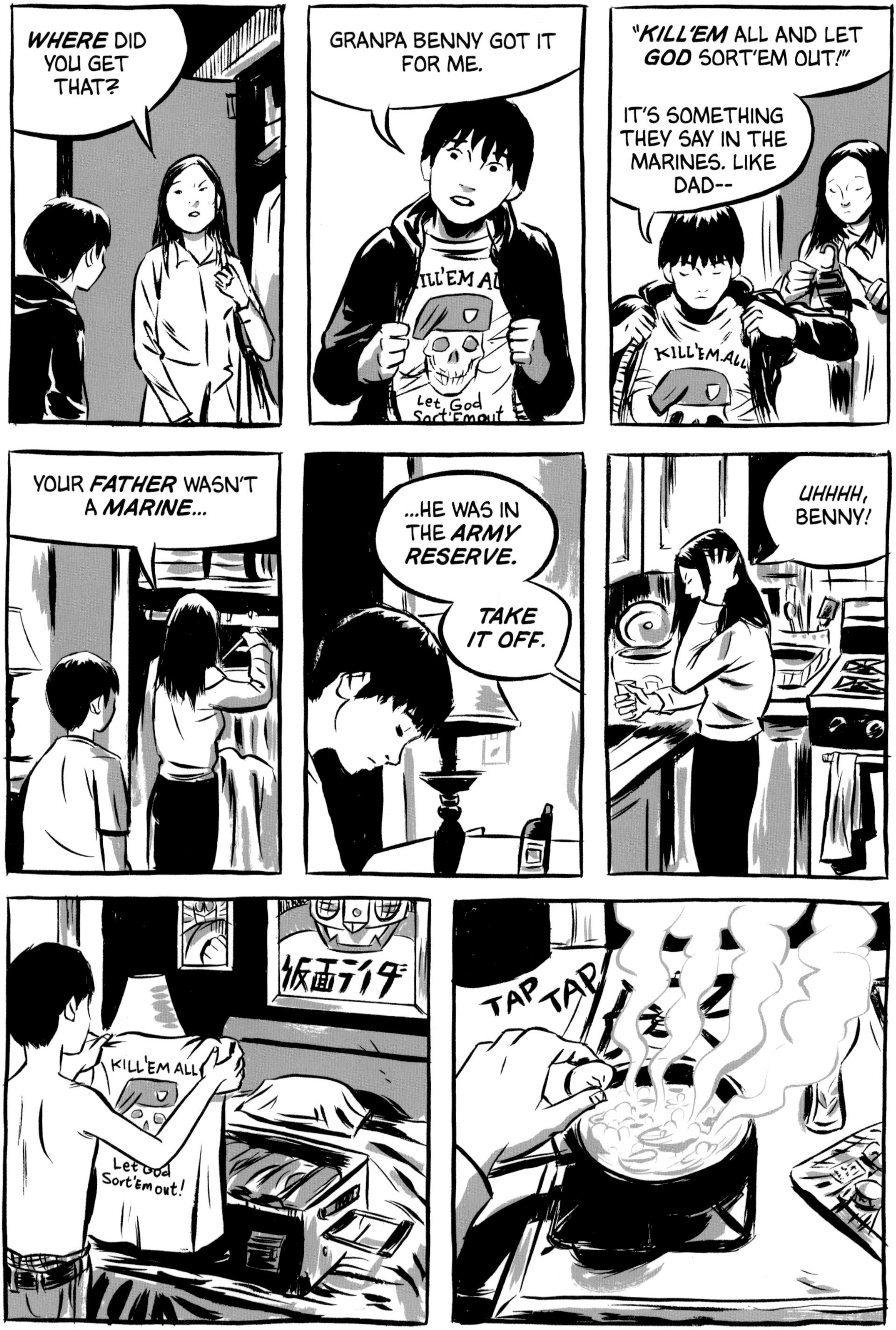
WHERE DID YOU GET THAT?
GRANPA BENNY GOT IT FOR ME.
KILL'EM ALL
Let God Sort'Em out
"KILL'EM ALL AND LET GOD SORT'EM OUT!"
IT'S SOMETHING THEY SAY IN THE MARINES. LIKE DAD--
KILL'EM ALL
YOUR FATHER WASN'T A MARINE...
...HE WAS IN THE ARMY RESERVE.
TAKE IT OFF.
UHHHH, BENNY!
仮面ライダ
KILL'EM ALL
Let God Sort'Em out!
TAP
TAP

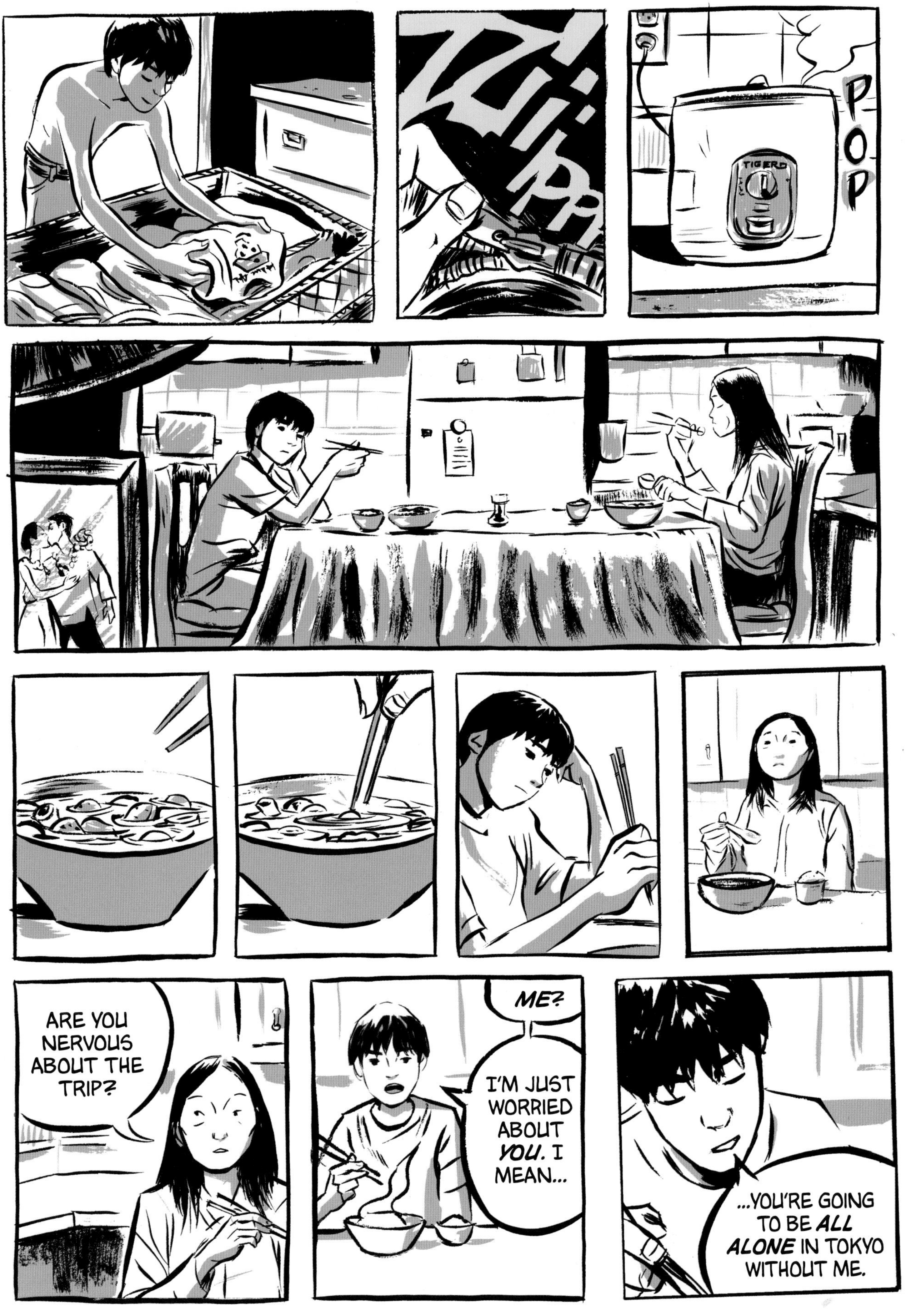
ZIIIPP
POP
TIGER
ARE YOU NERVOUS ABOUT THE TRIP?
ME?
I'M JUST WORRIED ABOUT YOU. I MEAN...
...YOU'RE GOING TO BE ALL ALONE IN TOKYO WITHOUT ME.

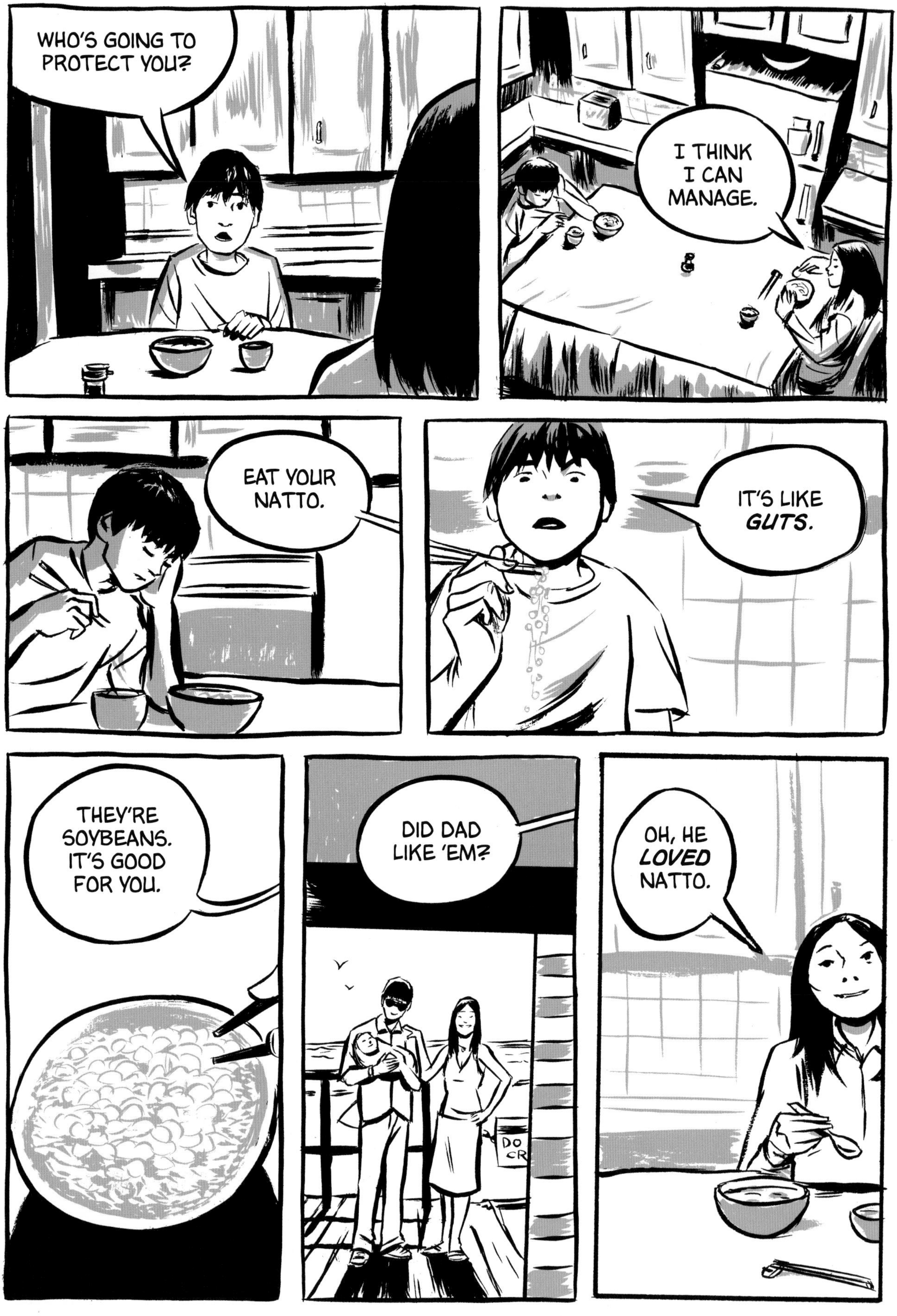
WHO'S GOING TO PROTECT YOU?
I THINK I CAN MANAGE.
EAT YOUR NATTO.
IT'S LIKE *GUTS*.
THEY'RE SOYBEANS. IT'S GOOD FOR YOU.
DID DAD LIKE 'EM?
OH, HE *LOVED* NATTO.

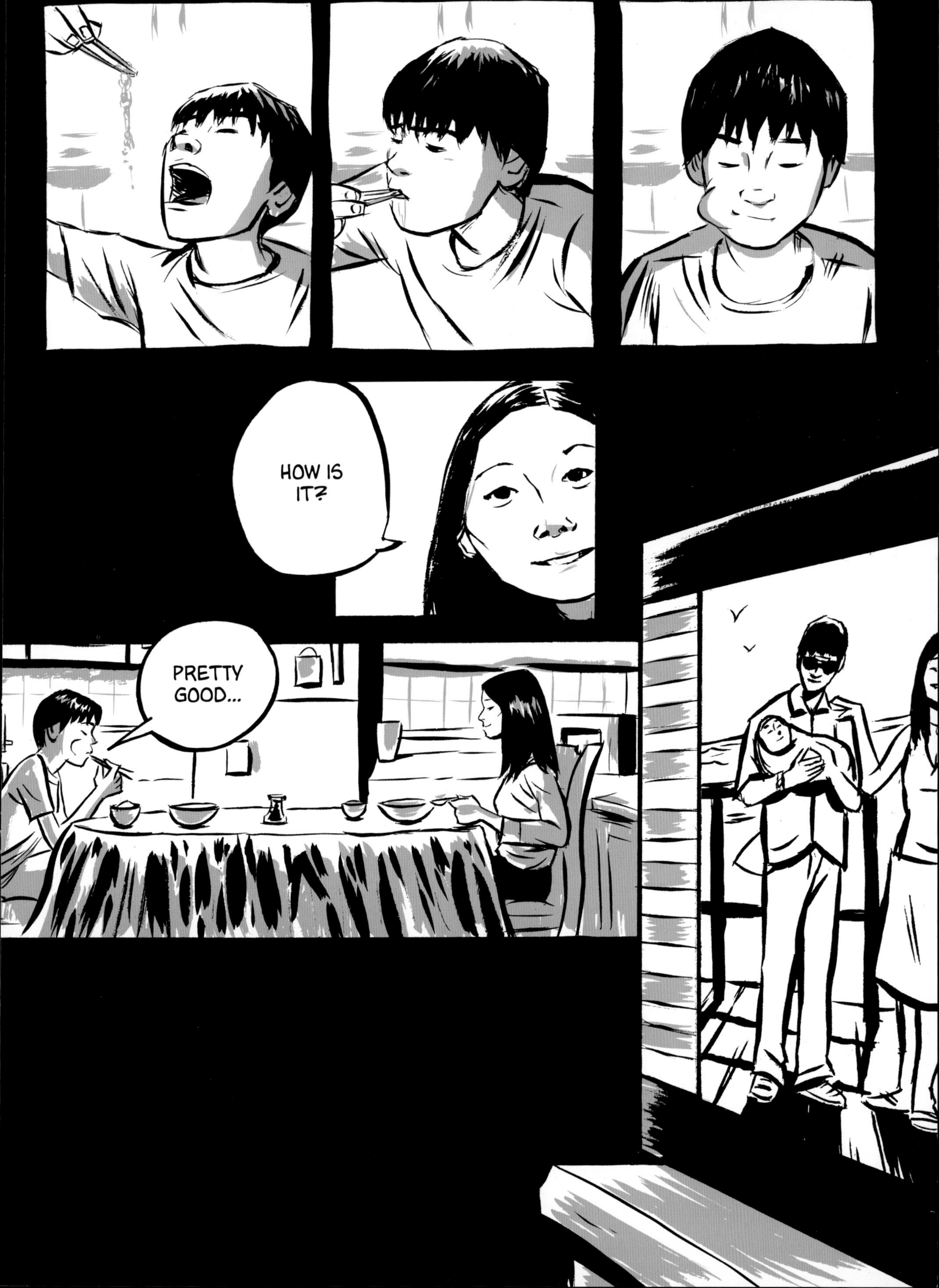
HOW IS IT?
PRETTY GOOD...

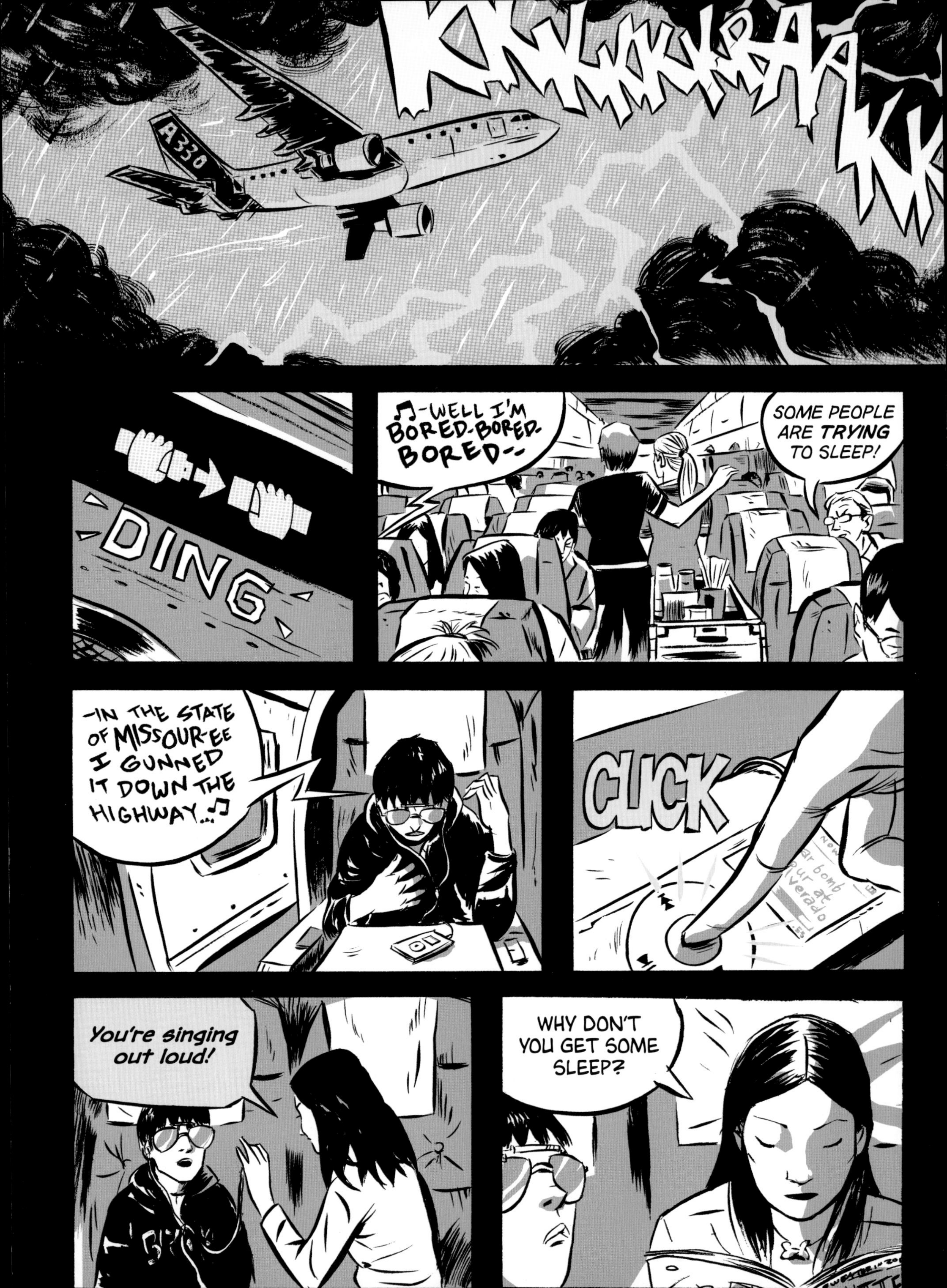

A330
DING
♫-WELL I'M BORED-BORED-BORED--
SOME PEOPLE ARE *TRYING* TO SLEEP!
-IN THE STATE OF MISSOUR-EE I GUNNED IT DOWN THE HIGHWAY...♫
CLICK
You're singing out loud!
WHY DON'T YOU GET SOME SLEEP?

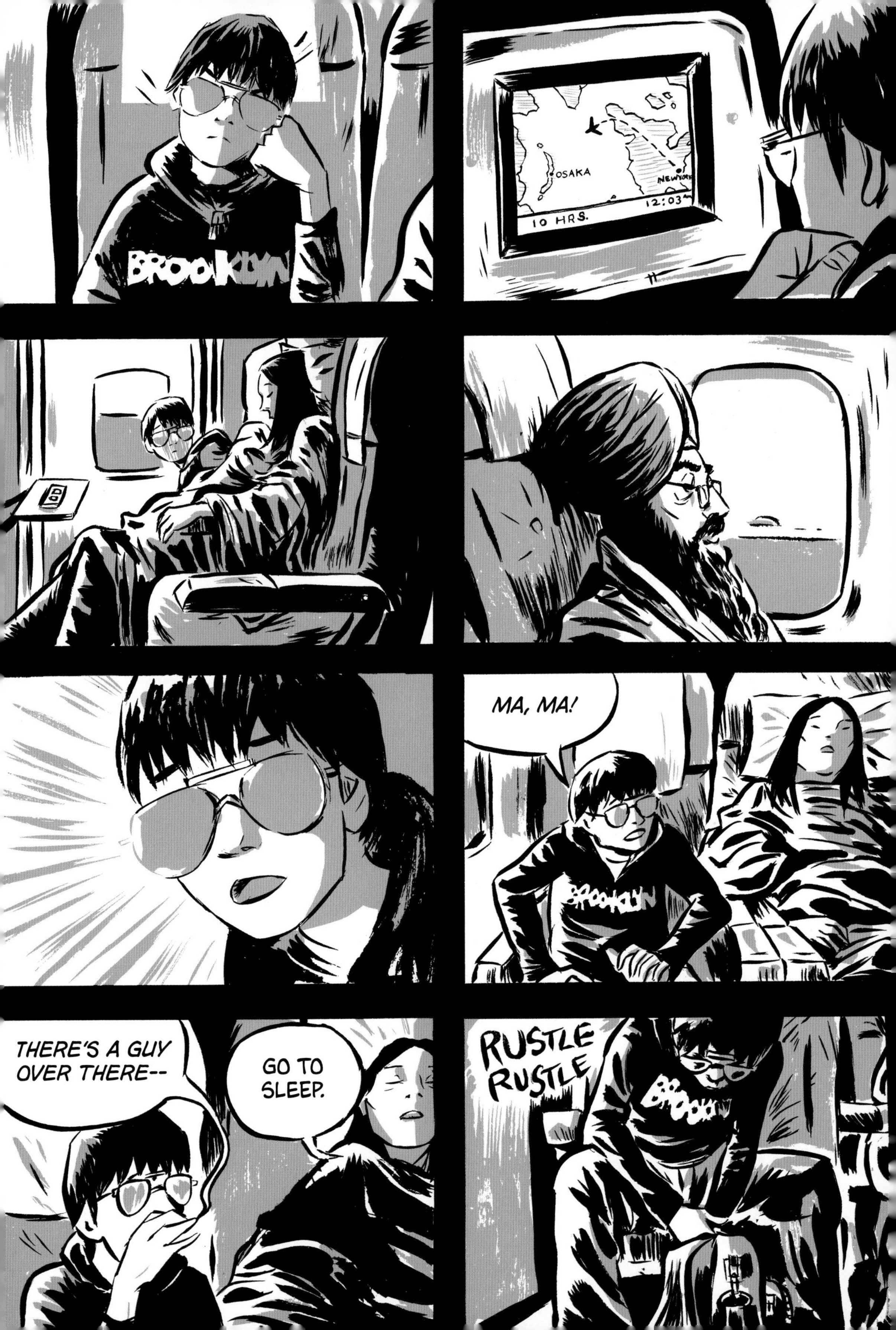
BROOKLYN
OSAKA
NEW YORK
10 HRS.
12:03
MA, MA!
BROOKLYN
THERE'S A GUY OVER THERE--
GO TO SLEEP.
RUSTLE RUSTLE

SOLDIER'S HANDBOOK
HEADQUARTERS DEPT. OF THE ARMY
YAWN
Where did you get this?
IT WAS IN A BOX OF DAD'S OLD STUFF IN THE CLOSET.
IT TEACHES YOU ALL SORTSA WAYS TO TAKE A GUY OUT.
VITAL TARGETS
TOP OF HEAD
TEMPLE
EYE
NOSE
SIDE OF NECK
THROAT
CAROTID ARTERY
WHY DO YOU NEED TO KNOW HOW TO "TAKE A GUY OUT"?

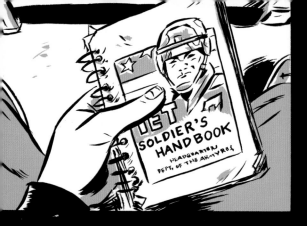

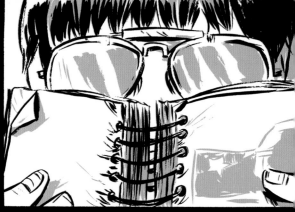

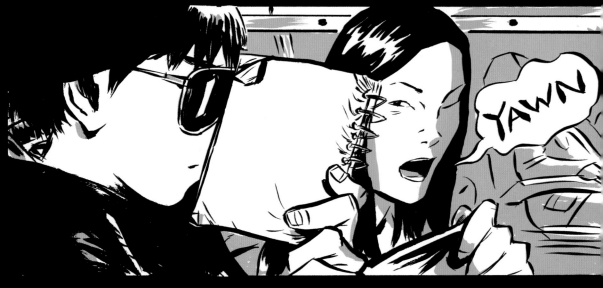

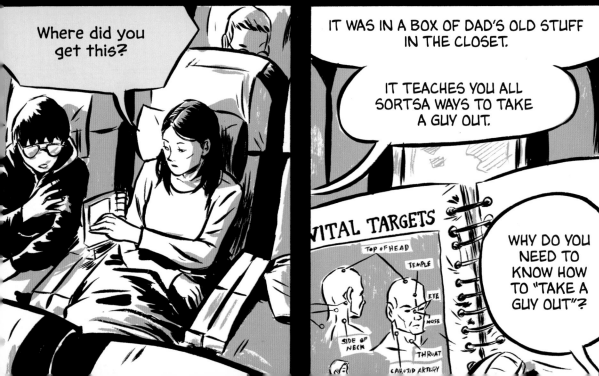

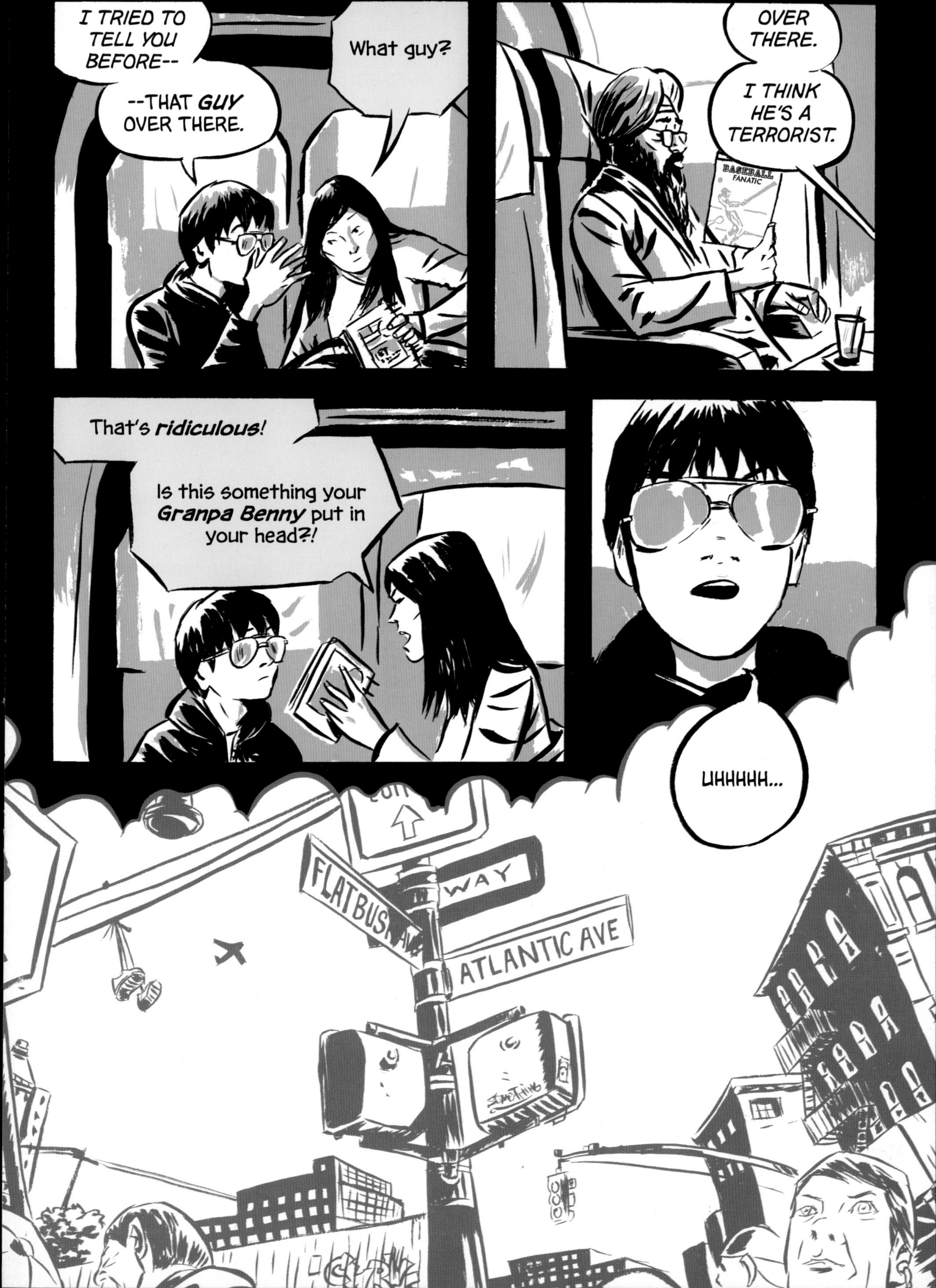
I TRIED TO TELL YOU BEFORE--
--THAT GUY OVER THERE.
What guy?
OVER THERE.
I THINK HE'S A TERRORIST.
BASEBALL FANATIC
That's ridiculous!
Is this something your Granpa Benny put in your head?!
UHHHHH...
WAY
ATLANTIC AVE

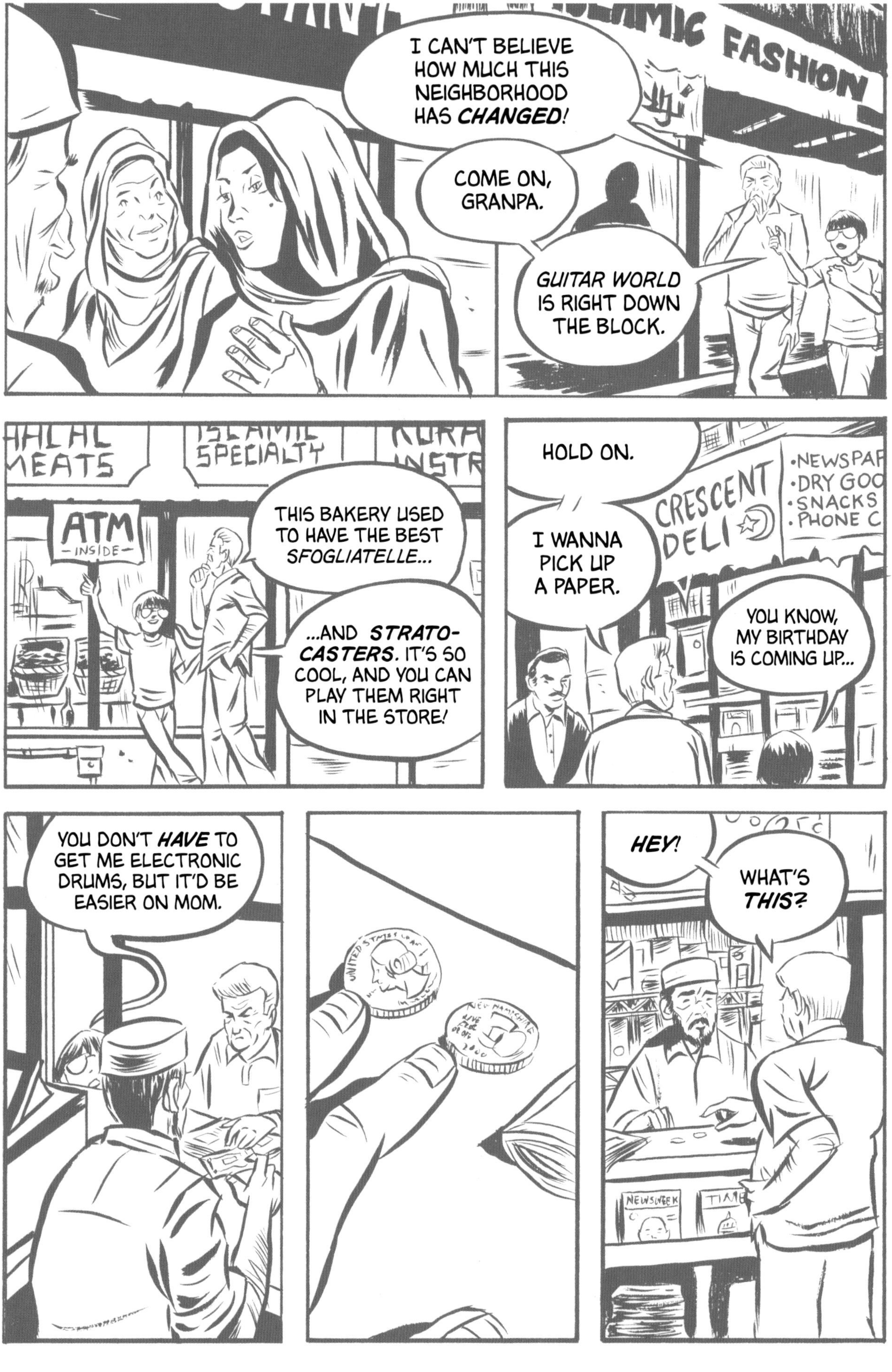
FASHION
I CAN'T BELIEVE HOW MUCH THIS NEIGHBORHOOD HAS *CHANGED*!
COME ON, GRANPA.
GUITAR WORLD IS RIGHT DOWN THE BLOCK.
SPECIALTY
ATM
INSIDE
THIS BAKERY USED TO HAVE THE BEST *SFOGLIATELLE*...
...AND ***STRATO-CASTERS***. IT'S SO COOL, AND YOU CAN PLAY THEM RIGHT IN THE STORE!
HOLD ON.
I WANNA PICK UP A PAPER.
CRESCENT DELI
YOU KNOW, MY BIRTHDAY IS COMING UP...
YOU DON'T ***HAVE*** TO GET ME ELECTRONIC DRUMS, BUT IT'D BE EASIER ON MOM.
HEY!
WHAT'S ***THIS***?

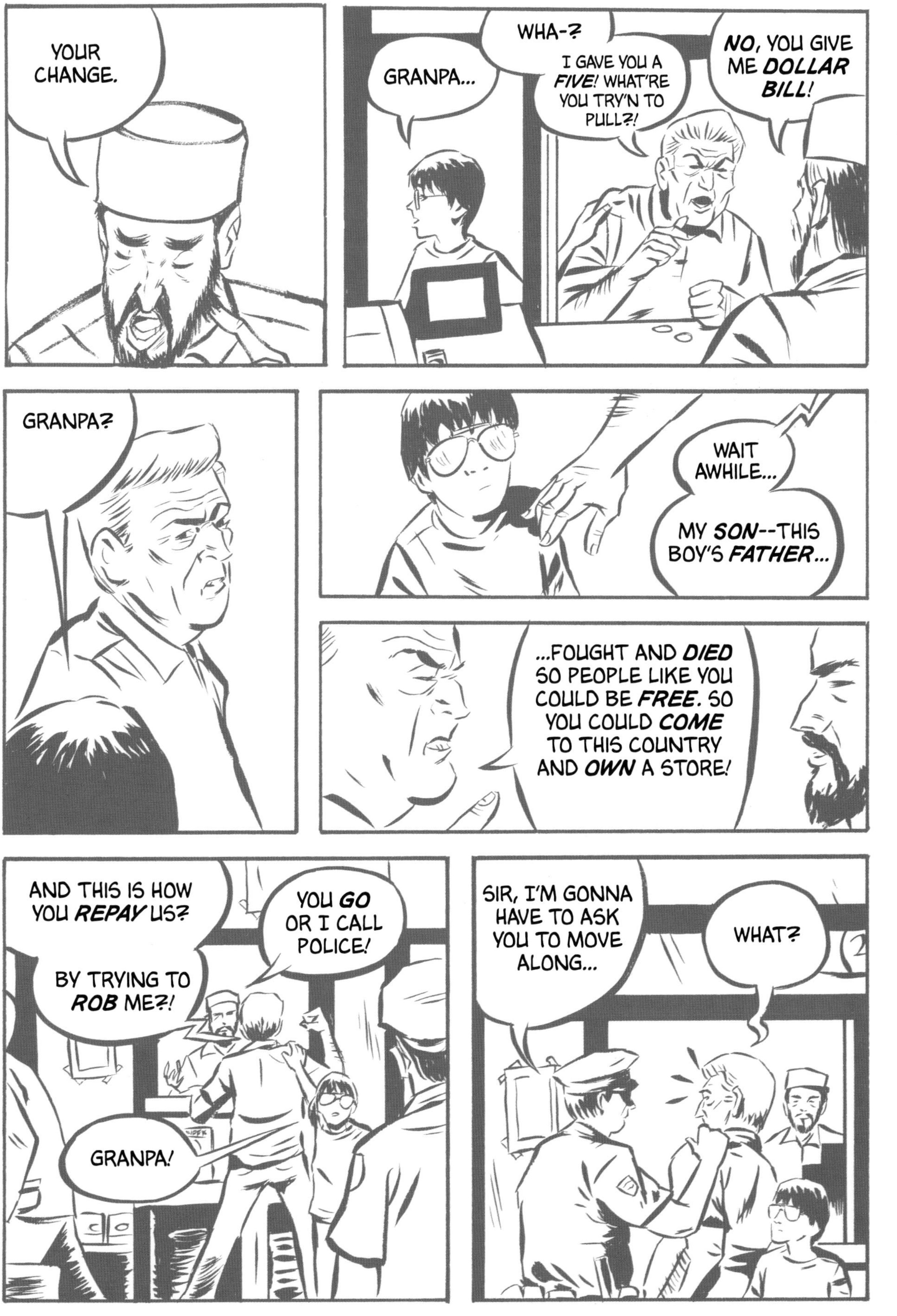
YOUR CHANGE.
GRANPA...
WHA-?
I GAVE YOU A FIVE! WHAT'RE YOU TRY'N TO PULL?!
NO, YOU GIVE ME DOLLAR BILL!
GRANPA?
WAIT AWHILE...
MY SON--THIS BOY'S FATHER...
...FOUGHT AND DIED SO PEOPLE LIKE YOU COULD BE FREE. SO YOU COULD COME TO THIS COUNTRY AND OWN A STORE!
AND THIS IS HOW YOU REPAY US?
BY TRYING TO ROB ME?!
YOU GO OR I CALL POLICE!
GRANPA!
SIR, I'M GONNA HAVE TO ASK YOU TO MOVE ALONG...
WHAT?

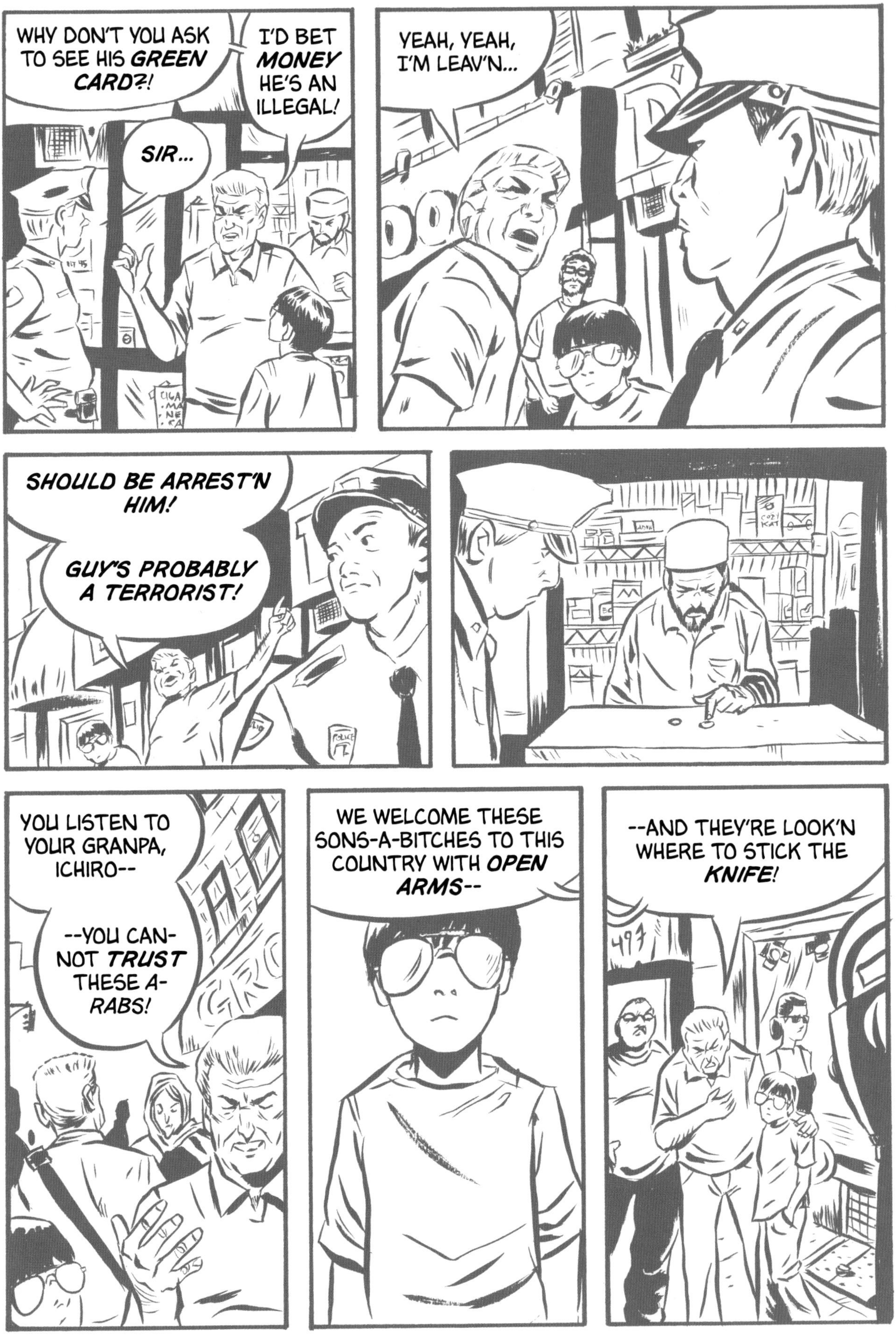
WHY DON'T YOU ASK TO SEE HIS *GREEN CARD?!*
I'D BET *MONEY* HE'S AN ILLEGAL!
SIR...
YEAH, YEAH, I'M LEAV'N...
SHOULD BE ARREST'N HIM!
GUY'S PROBABLY A TERRORIST!
YOU LISTEN TO YOUR GRANPA, ICHIRO--
--YOU CAN-NOT *TRUST* THESE A-RABS!
WE WELCOME THESE SONS-A-BITCHES TO THIS COUNTRY WITH *OPEN ARMS--*
--AND THEY'RE LOOK'N WHERE TO STICK THE *KNIFE!*

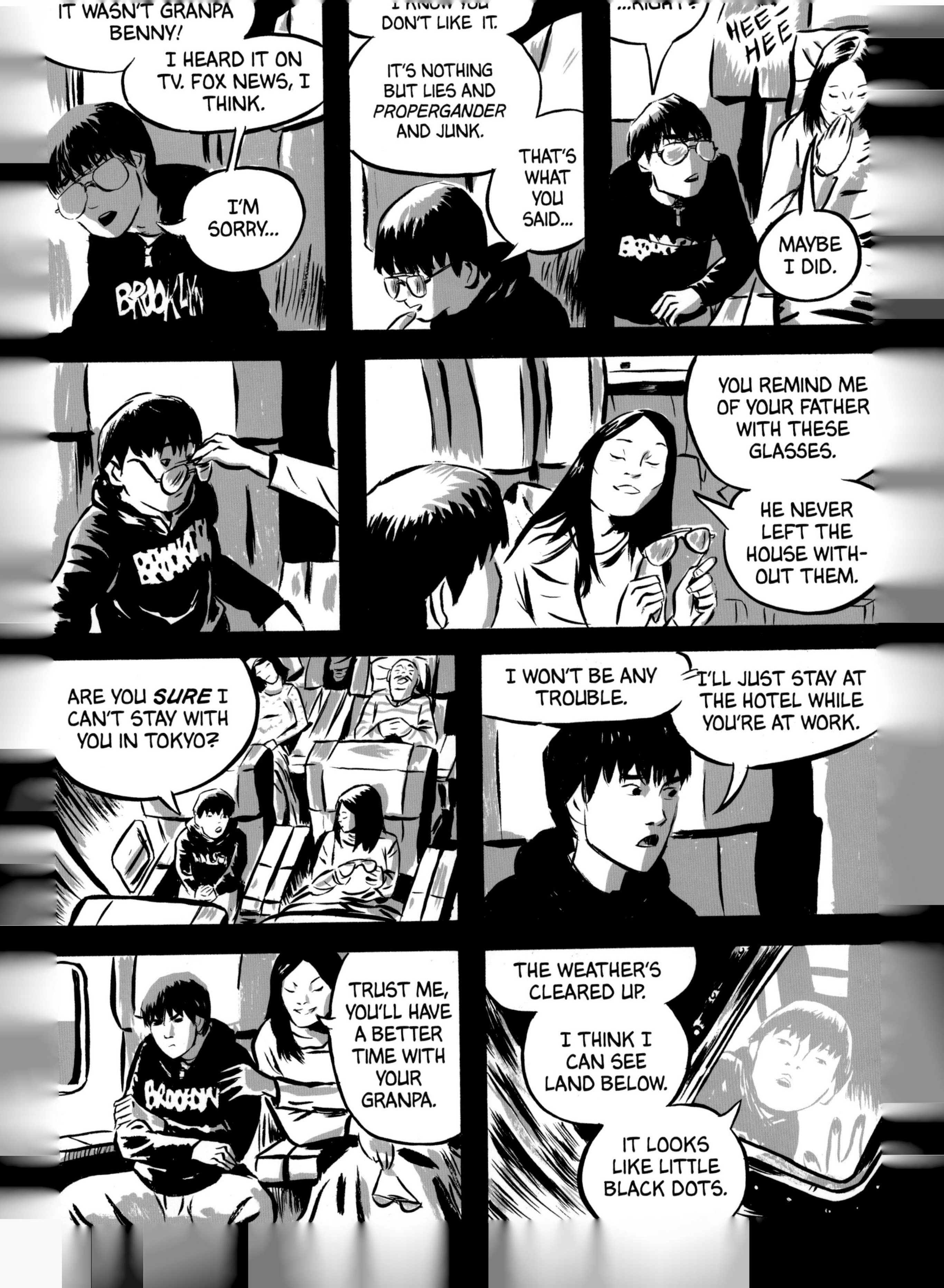
IT WASN'T GRANPA BENNY!
I HEARD IT ON TV. FOX NEWS, I THINK.
I'M SORRY...
DON'T LIKE IT.
IT'S NOTHING BUT LIES AND *PROPERGANDER* AND JUNK.
THAT'S WHAT YOU SAID...
HEE HEE
MAYBE I DID.
YOU REMIND ME OF YOUR FATHER WITH THESE GLASSES.
HE NEVER LEFT THE HOUSE WITH-OUT THEM.
ARE YOU ***SURE*** I CAN'T STAY WITH YOU IN TOKYO?
I WON'T BE ANY TROUBLE.
I'LL JUST STAY AT THE HOTEL WHILE YOU'RE AT WORK.
TRUST ME, YOU'LL HAVE A BETTER TIME WITH YOUR GRANPA.
THE WEATHER'S CLEARED UP.
I THINK I CAN SEE LAND BELOW.
IT LOOKS LIKE LITTLE BLACK DOTS.

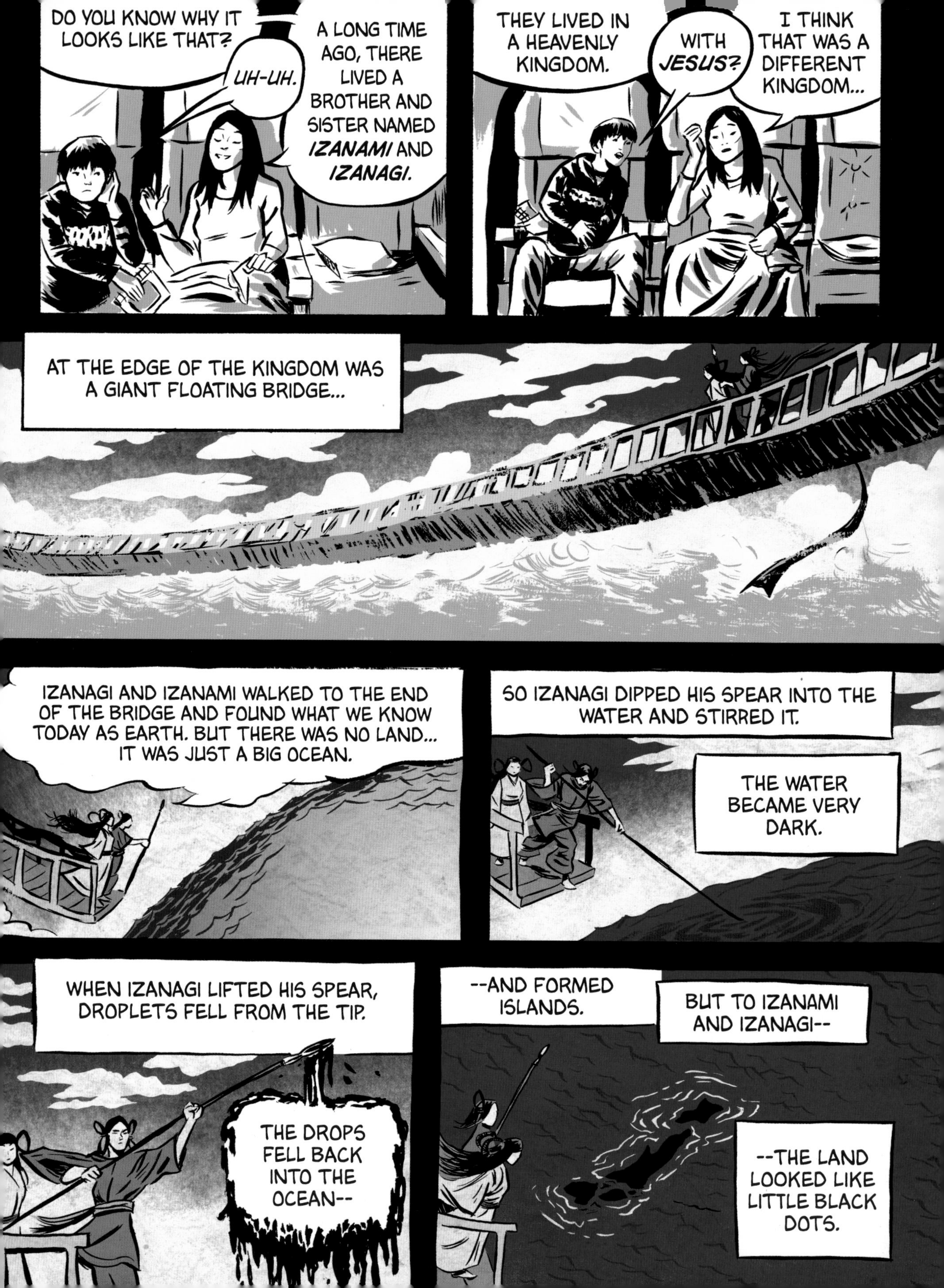

DO YOU KNOW WHY IT LOOKS LIKE THAT?
UH-UH.
A LONG TIME AGO, THERE LIVED A BROTHER AND SISTER NAMED *IZANAMI* AND *IZANAGI*.
THEY LIVED IN A HEAVENLY KINGDOM.
WITH *JESUS*?
I THINK THAT WAS A DIFFERENT KINGDOM...
AT THE EDGE OF THE KINGDOM WAS A GIANT FLOATING BRIDGE...
IZANAGI AND IZANAMI WALKED TO THE END OF THE BRIDGE AND FOUND WHAT WE KNOW TODAY AS EARTH. BUT THERE WAS NO LAND... IT WAS JUST A BIG OCEAN.
SO IZANAGI DIPPED HIS SPEAR INTO THE WATER AND STIRRED IT.
THE WATER BECAME VERY DARK.
WHEN IZANAGI LIFTED HIS SPEAR, DROPLETS FELL FROM THE TIP.
THE DROPS FELL BACK INTO THE OCEAN--
--AND FORMED ISLANDS.
BUT TO IZANAMI AND IZANAGI--
--THE LAND LOOKED LIKE LITTLE BLACK DOTS.

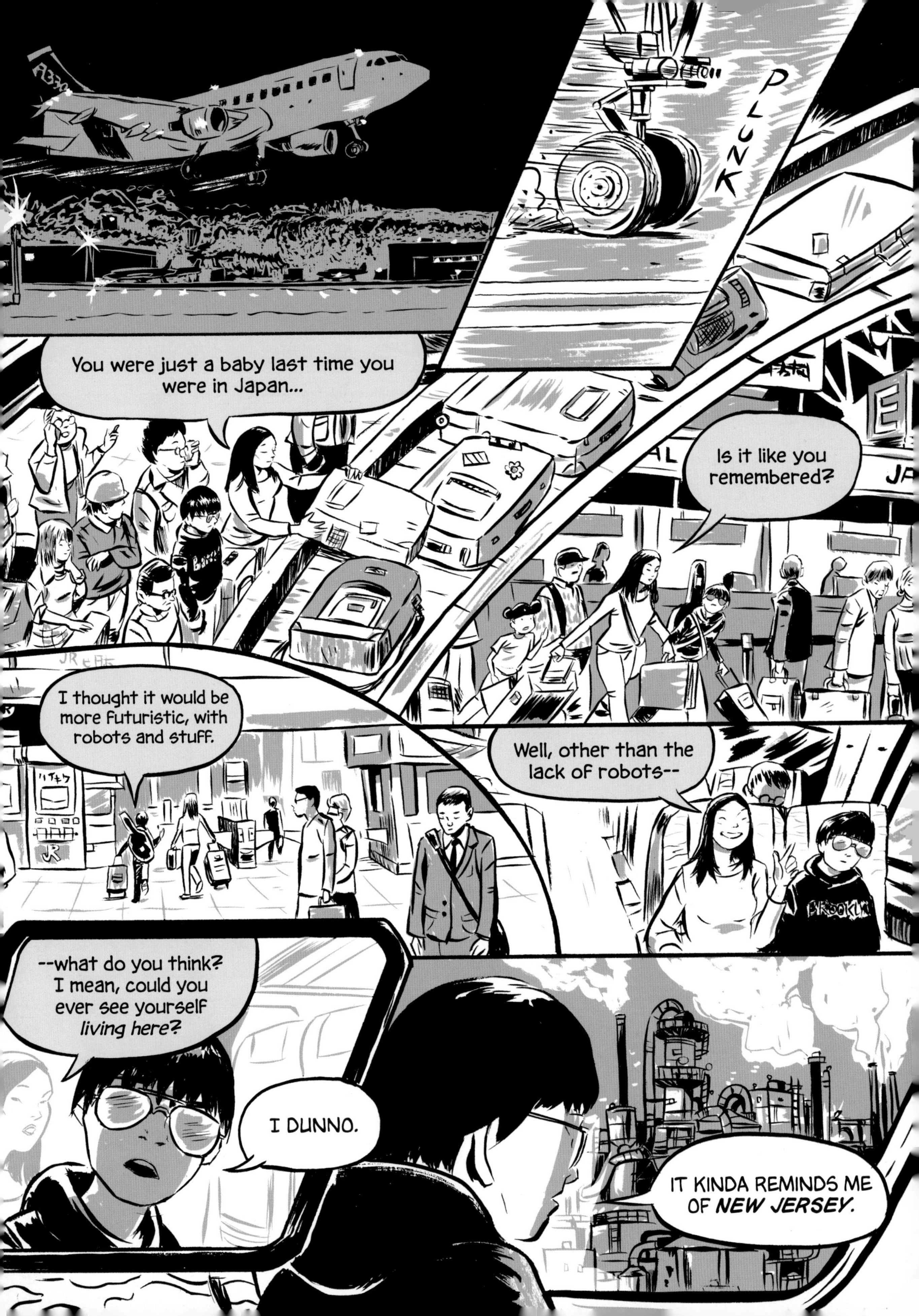
PLUNK
You were just a baby last time you were in Japan...
Is it like you remembered?
I thought it would be more futuristic, with robots and stuff.
Well, other than the lack of robots--
--what do you think? I mean, could you ever see yourself *living here*?
I DUNNO.
IT KINDA REMINDS ME OF ***NEW JERSEY.***

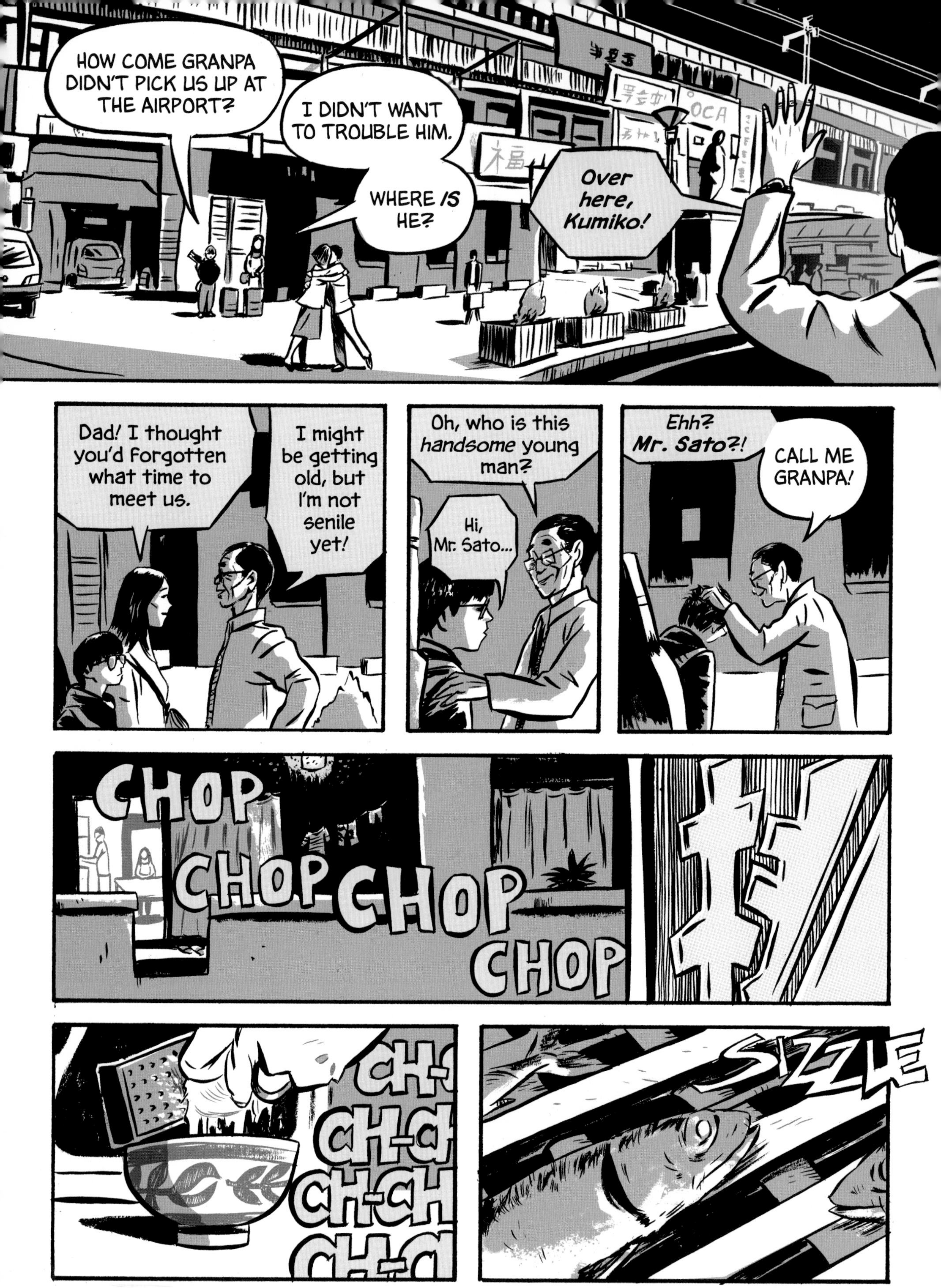
HOW COME GRANPA DIDN'T PICK US UP AT THE AIRPORT?
I DIDN'T WANT TO TROUBLE HIM.
WHERE *IS* HE?
Over here, Kumiko!
Dad! I thought you'd forgotten what time to meet us.
I might be getting old, but I'm not senile yet!
Oh, who is this *handsome* young man?
Hi, Mr. Sato...
Ehh? Mr. Sato?!
CALL ME GRANPA!
CHOP
CHOP CHOP
CHOP
CH-C
CH-C
CH-CH
CH-C
SIZZLE

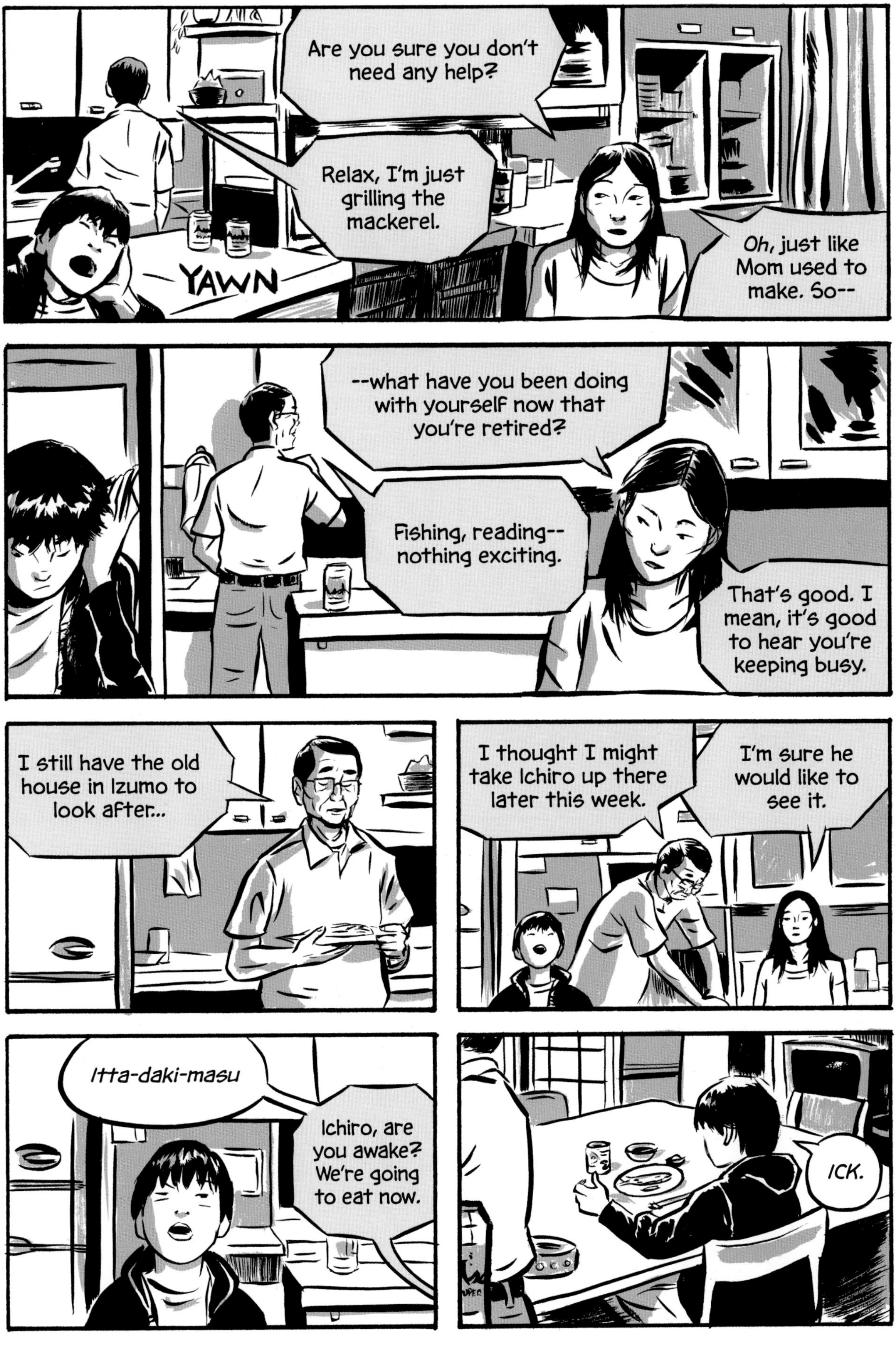
Are you sure you don't need any help?
Relax, I'm just grilling the mackerel.
YAWN
Oh, just like Mom used to make. So--
--what have you been doing with yourself now that you're retired?
Fishing, reading-- nothing exciting.
That's good. I mean, it's good to hear you're keeping busy.
I still have the old house in Izumo to look after...
I thought I might take Ichiro up there later this week.
I'm sure he would like to see it.
Itta-daki-masu
Ichiro, are you awake? We're going to eat now.
ICK.

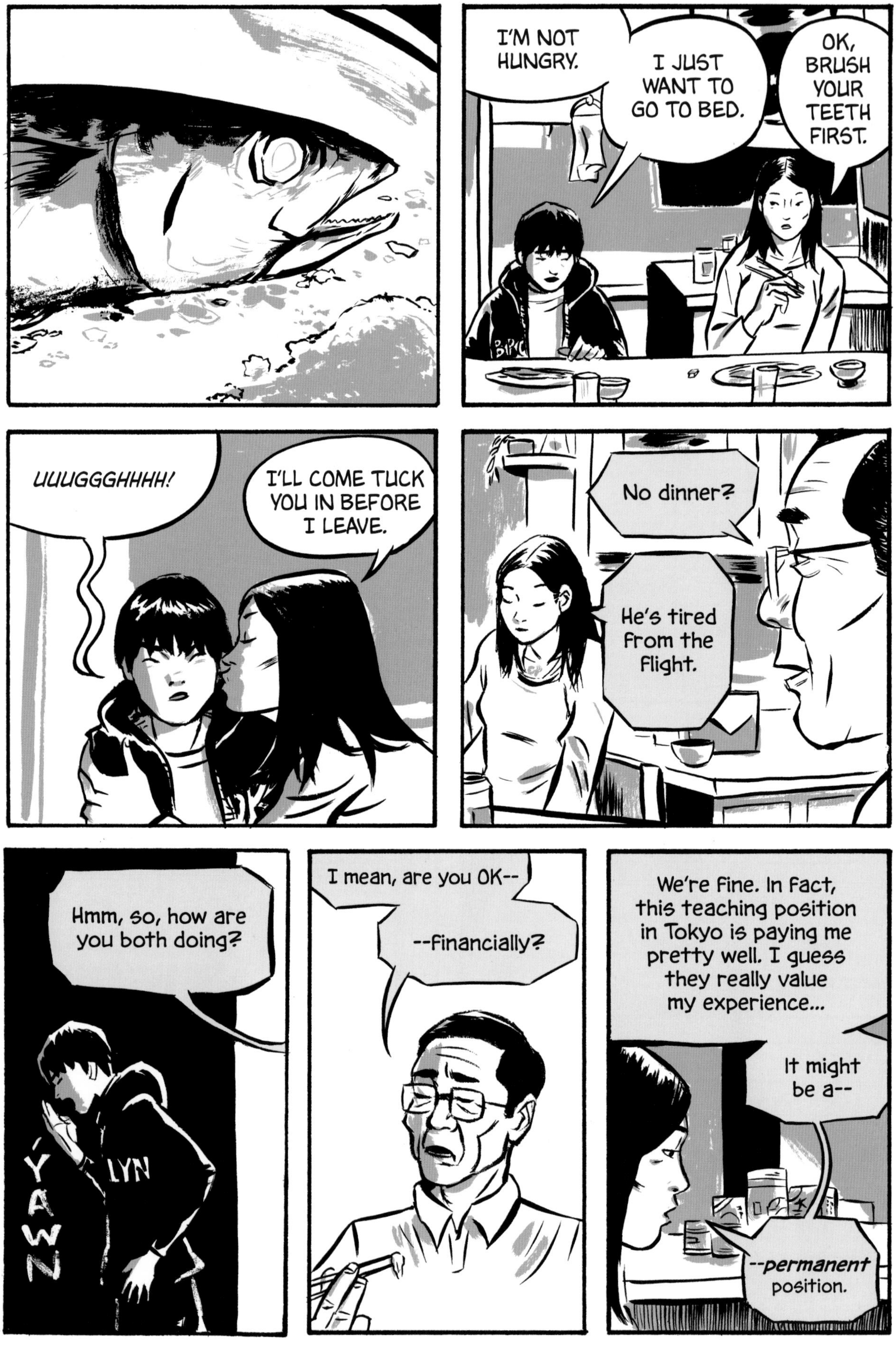
I'M NOT HUNGRY.
I JUST WANT TO GO TO BED.
OK, BRUSH YOUR TEETH FIRST.
UUUGGGHHHH!
I'LL COME TUCK YOU IN BEFORE I LEAVE.
No dinner?
He's tired from the flight.
Hmm, so, how are you both doing?
YAWN
LYN
I mean, are you OK--
--financially?
We're fine. In fact, this teaching position in Tokyo is paying me pretty well. I guess they really value my experience...
It might be a--
--*permanent* position.

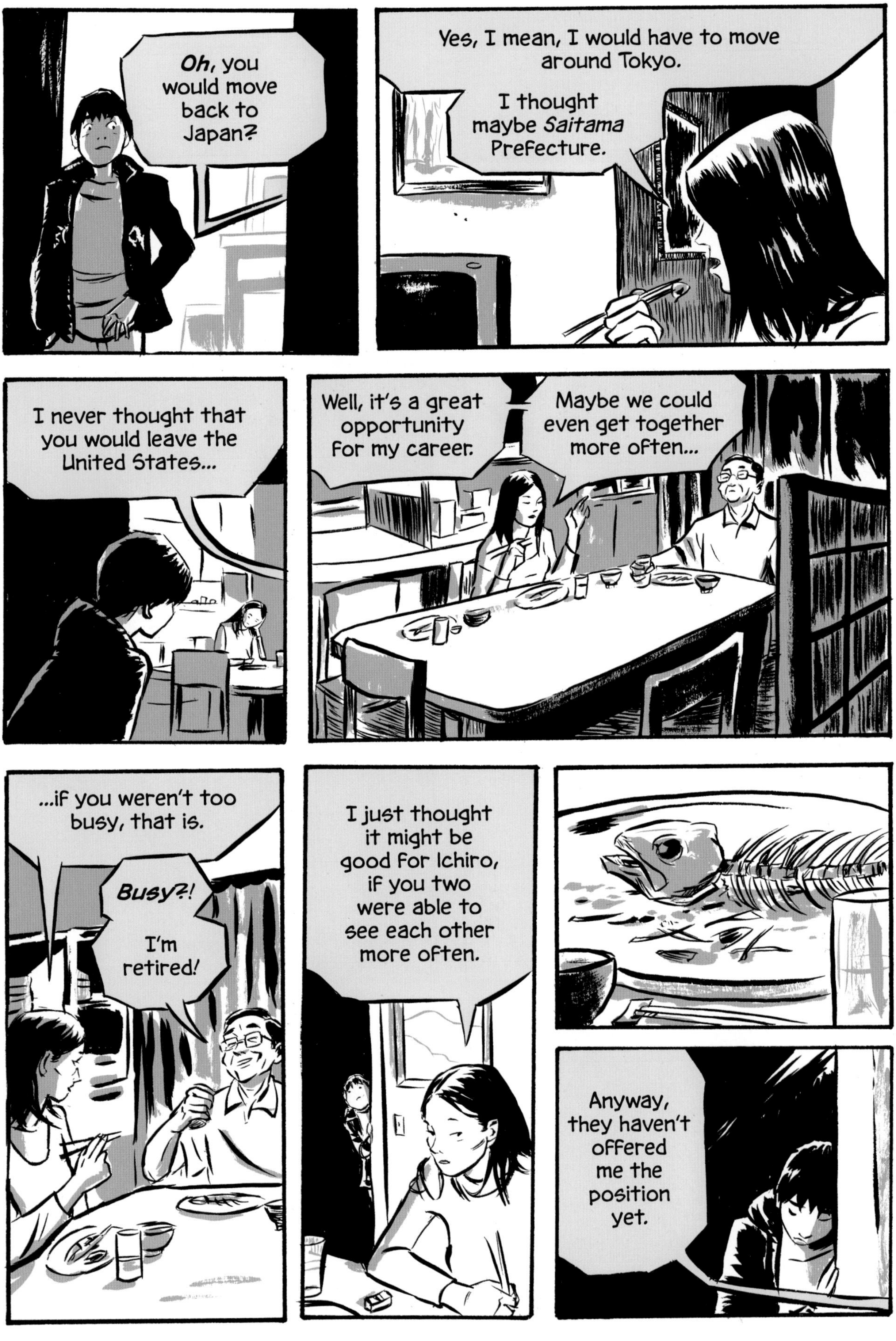

Oh, you would move back to Japan?
Yes, I mean, I would have to move around Tokyo.
I thought maybe Saitama Prefecture.
I never thought that you would leave the United States...
Well, it's a great opportunity for my career.
Maybe we could even get together more often...
...if you weren't too busy, that is.
Busy?!
I'm retired!
I just thought it might be good for Ichiro, if you two were able to see each other more often.
Anyway, they haven't offered me the position yet.

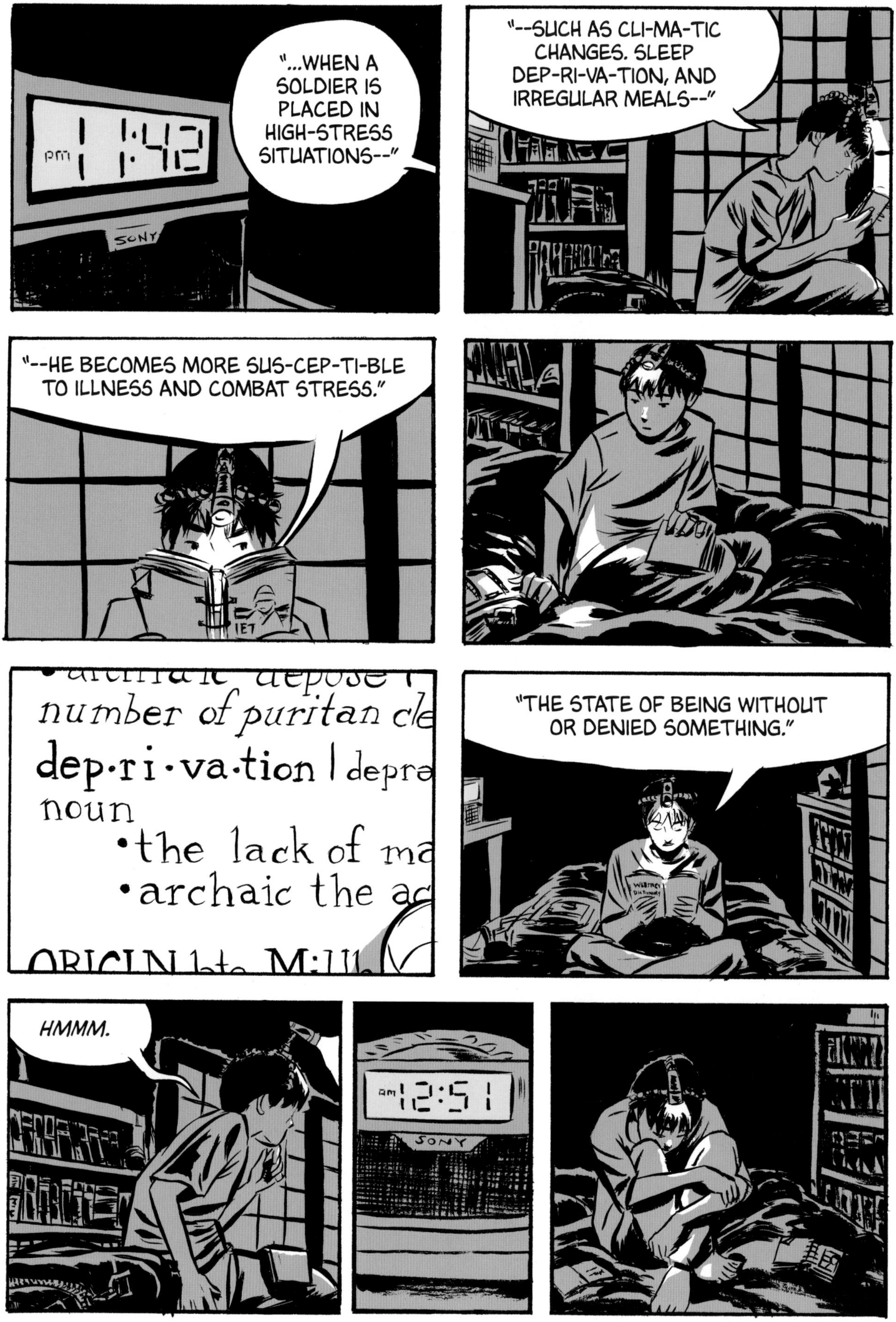
pm 11:42
"...WHEN A SOLDIER IS PLACED IN HIGH-STRESS SITUATIONS--"
SONY
"--SUCH AS CLI-MA-TIC CHANGES. SLEEP DEP-RI-VA-TION, AND IRREGULAR MEALS--"
"--HE BECOMES MORE SUS-CEP-TI-BLE TO ILLNESS AND COMBAT STRESS."
number of puritan cle
dep·ri·va·tion | depre
noun
•the lack of ma
•archaic the ac
"THE STATE OF BEING WITHOUT OR DENIED SOMETHING."
HMMM.
am 12:51
SONY

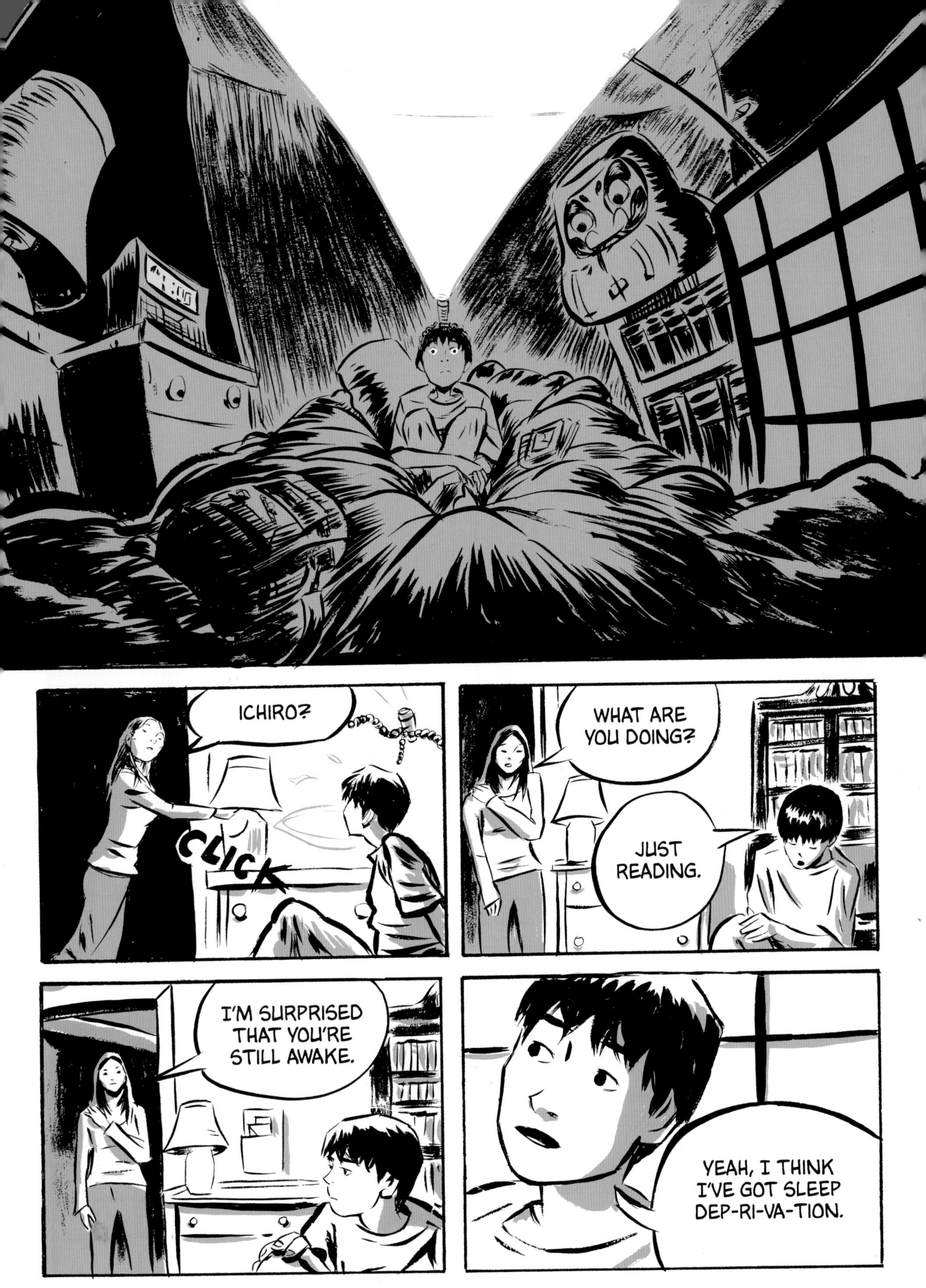
ICHIRO?
CLICK
WHAT ARE YOU DOING?
JUST READING.
I'M SURPRISED THAT YOU'RE STILL AWAKE.
YEAH, I THINK I'VE GOT SLEEP DEP-RI-VA-TION.

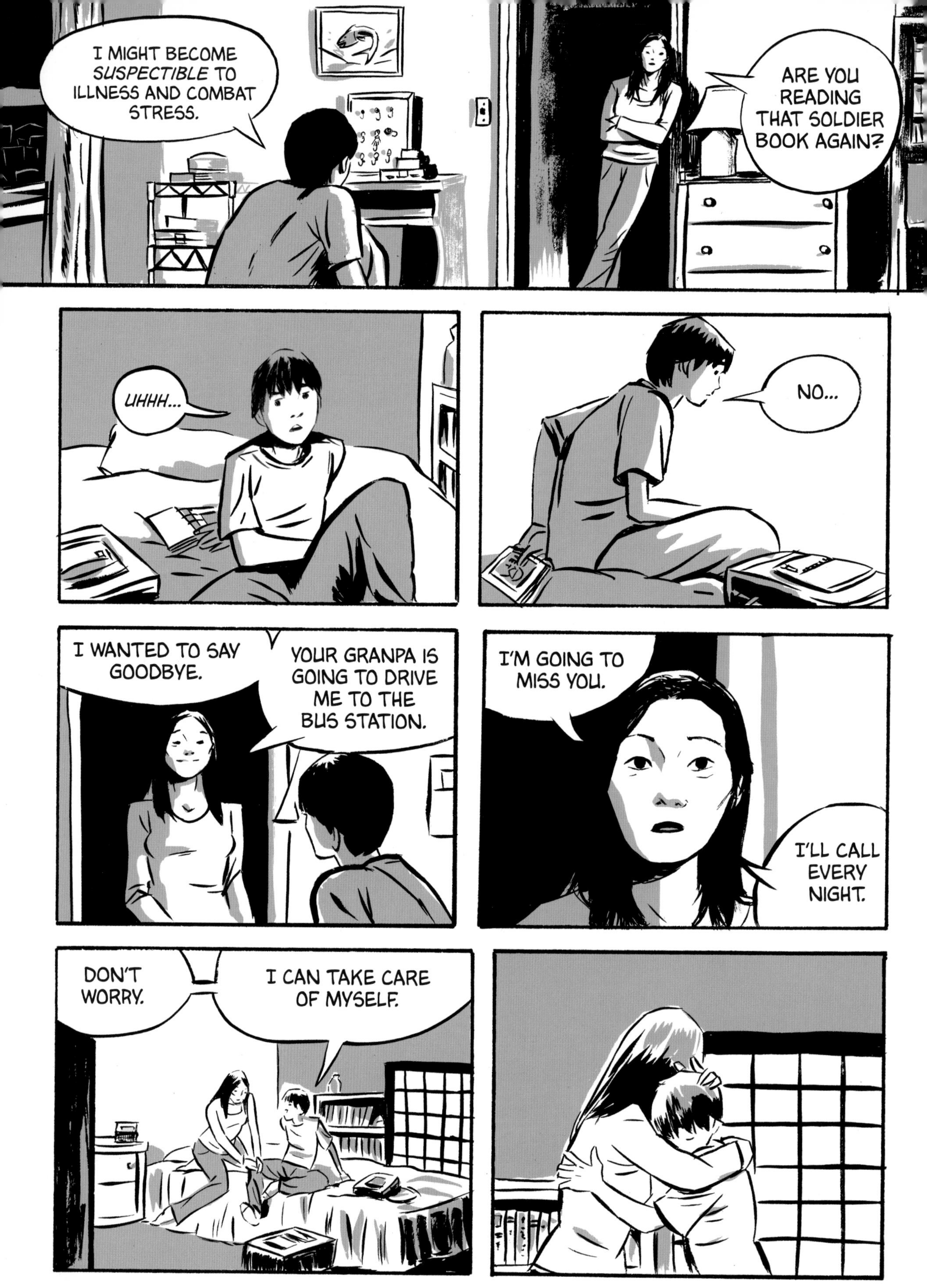
I MIGHT BECOME *SUSPECTIBLE* TO ILLNESS AND COMBAT STRESS.
ARE YOU READING THAT SOLDIER BOOK AGAIN?
UHHH...
NO...
I WANTED TO SAY GOODBYE.
YOUR GRANPA IS GOING TO DRIVE ME TO THE BUS STATION.
I'M GOING TO MISS YOU.
I'LL CALL EVERY NIGHT.
DON'T WORRY.
I CAN TAKE CARE OF MYSELF.

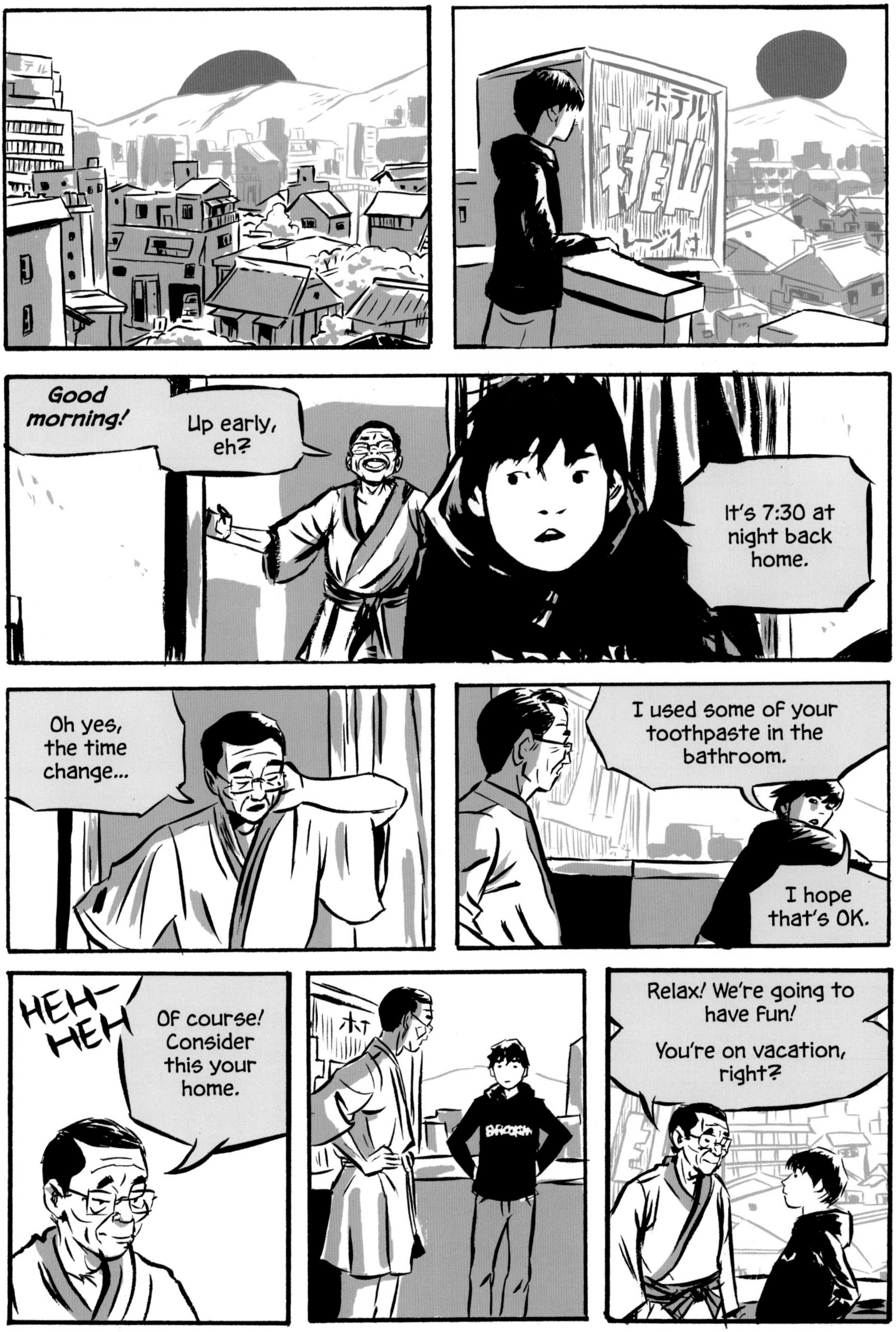

ホテル
Good morning!
Up early, eh?
It's 7:30 at night back home.
Oh yes, the time change...
I used some of your toothpaste in the bathroom.
I hope that's OK.
HEH-HEH
Of course! Consider this your home.
Relax! We're going to have fun!
You're on vacation, right?

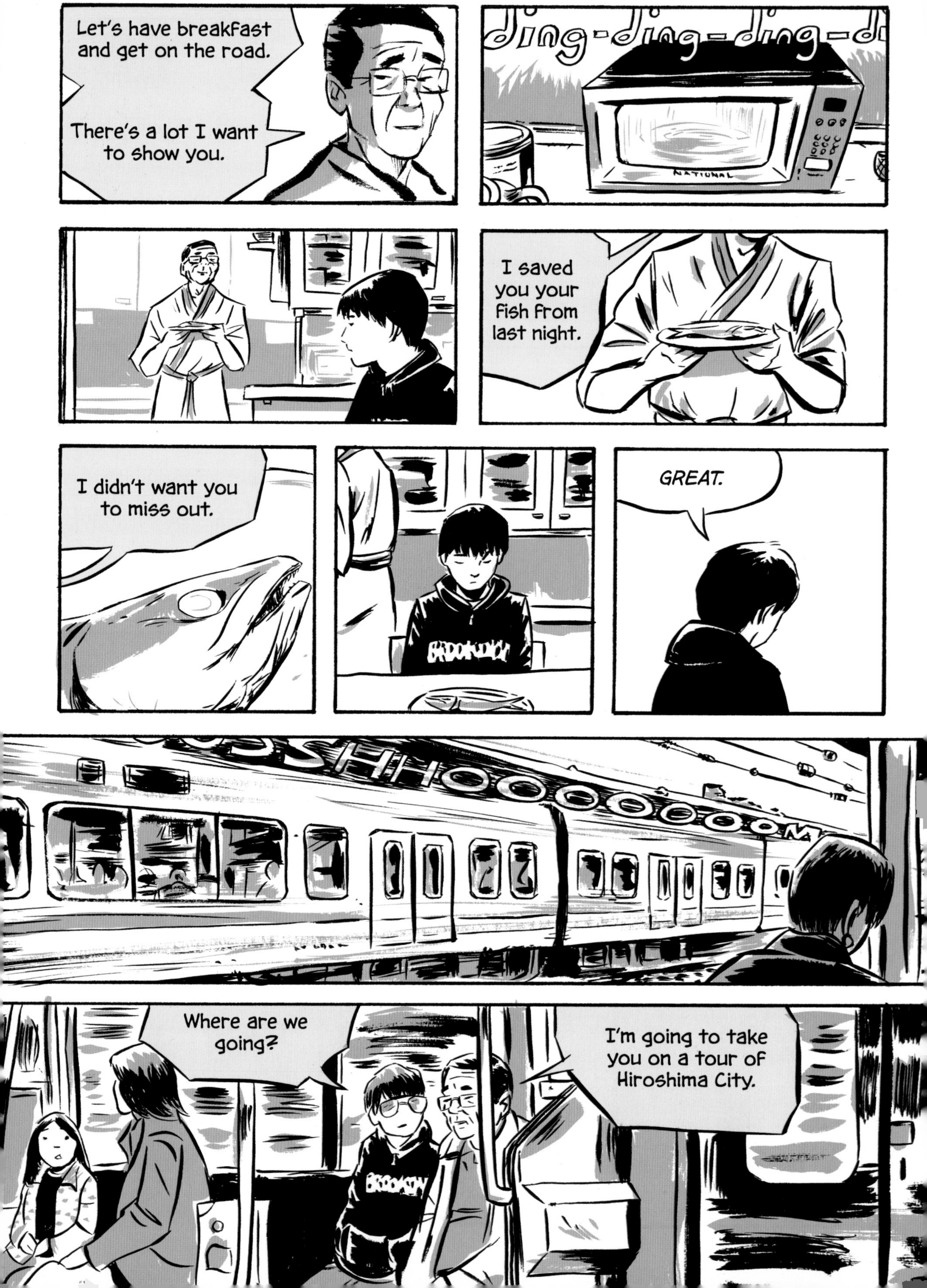
Let's have breakfast and get on the road.
There's a lot I want to show you.
ding-ding-ding-di
NATIONAL
I saved you your fish from last night.
I didn't want you to miss out.
GREAT.
SHHOOOOOOOOOM
Where are we going?
I'm going to take you on a tour of Hiroshima City.

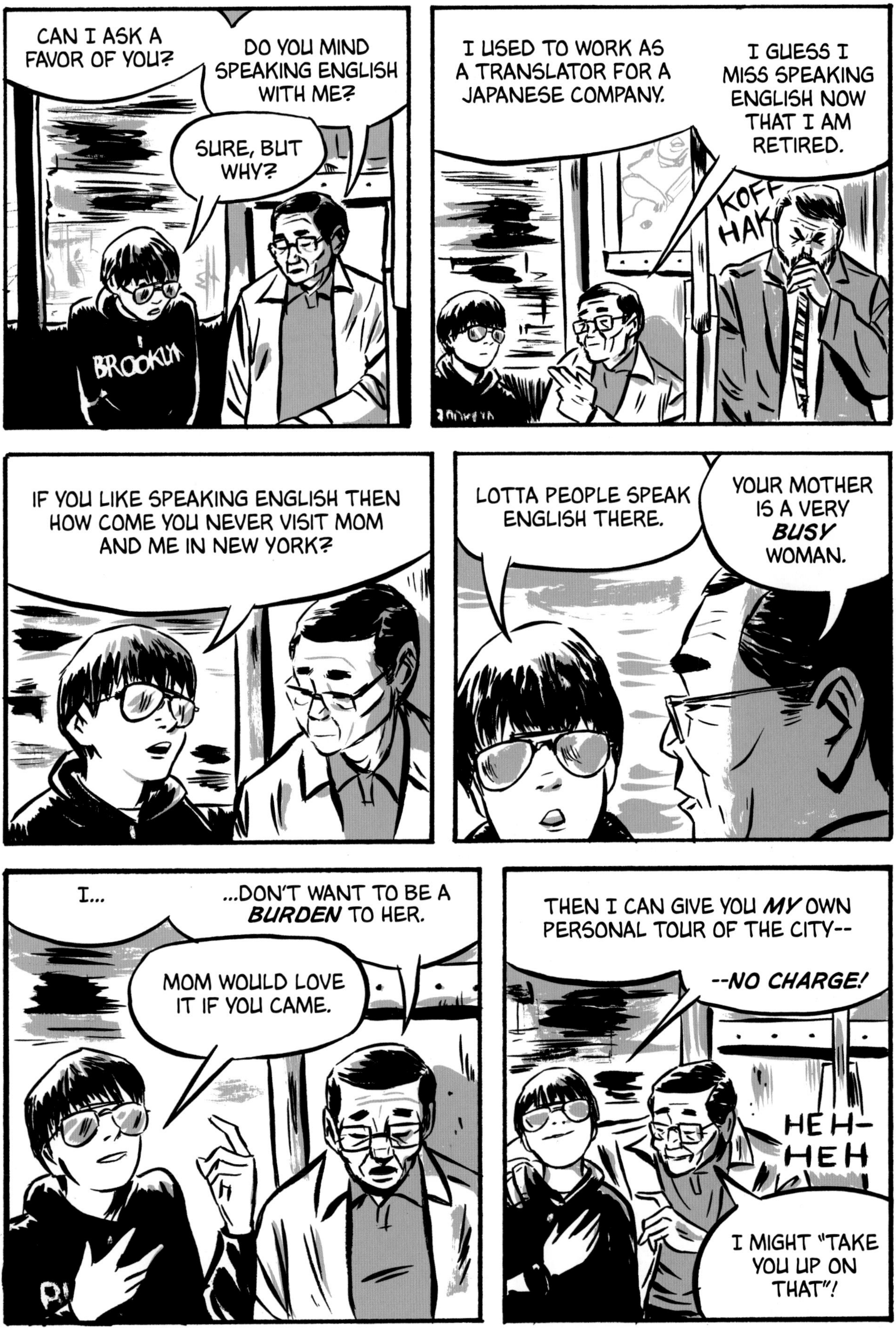
CAN I ASK A FAVOR OF YOU?
DO YOU MIND SPEAKING ENGLISH WITH ME?
SURE, BUT WHY?
BROOKLYN
I USED TO WORK AS A TRANSLATOR FOR A JAPANESE COMPANY.
I GUESS I MISS SPEAKING ENGLISH NOW THAT I AM RETIRED.
KOFF HAK
IF YOU LIKE SPEAKING ENGLISH THEN HOW COME YOU NEVER VISIT MOM AND ME IN NEW YORK?
LOTTA PEOPLE SPEAK ENGLISH THERE.
YOUR MOTHER IS A VERY *BUSY* WOMAN.
I...
...DON'T WANT TO BE A *BURDEN* TO HER.
MOM WOULD LOVE IT IF YOU CAME.
THEN I CAN GIVE YOU *MY* OWN PERSONAL TOUR OF THE CITY--
--*NO CHARGE!*
HEH-HEH
I MIGHT "TAKE YOU UP ON THAT"!

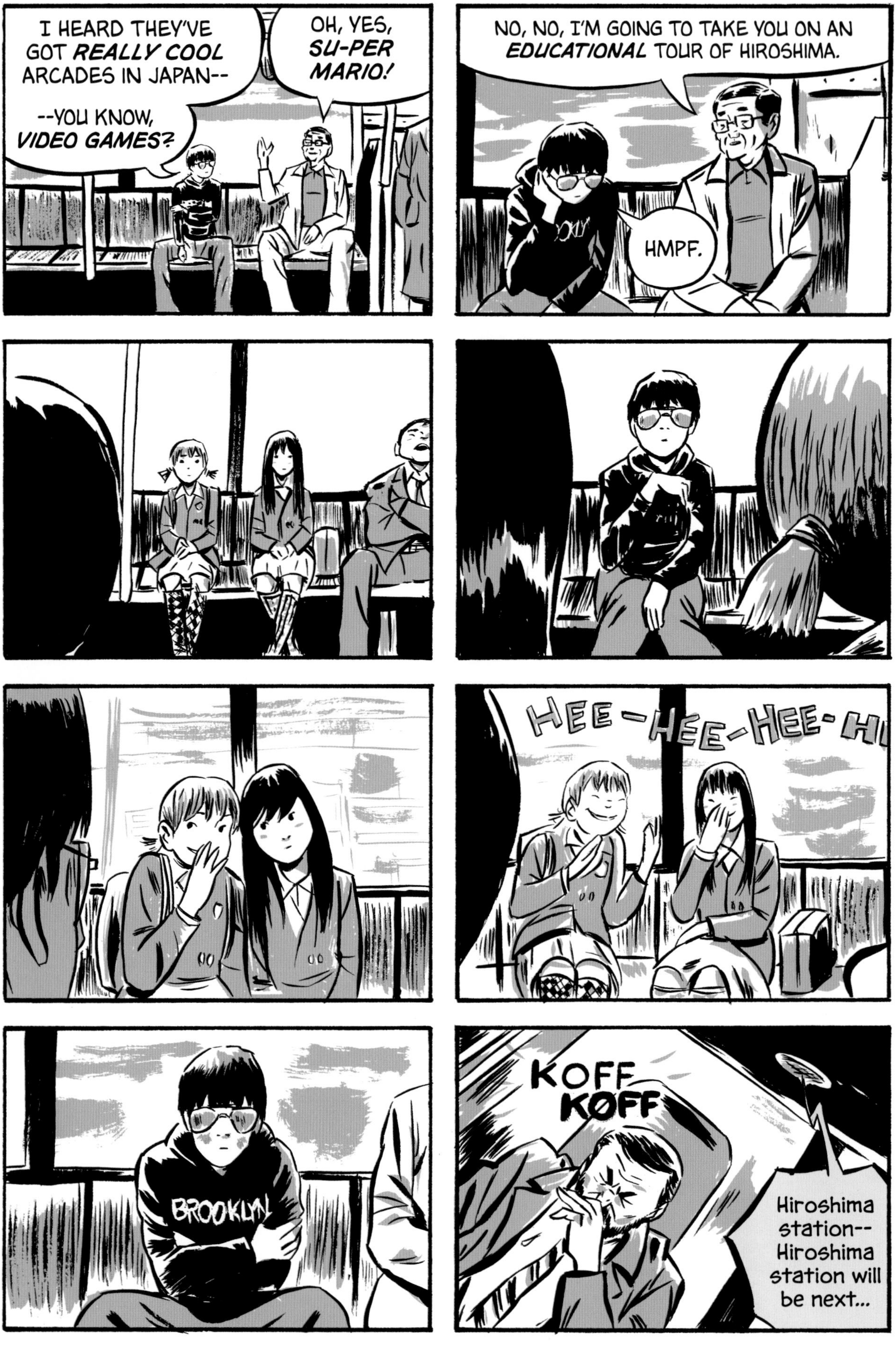
I HEARD THEY'VE GOT *REALLY COOL* ARCADES IN JAPAN--
--YOU KNOW, *VIDEO GAMES?*
OH, YES, *SU-PER MARIO!*
NO, NO, I'M GOING TO TAKE YOU ON AN *EDUCATIONAL* TOUR OF HIROSHIMA.
HMPF.
HEE-HEE-HEE-HI
BROOKLYN
KOFF KØFF
Hiroshima station-- Hiroshima station will be next...

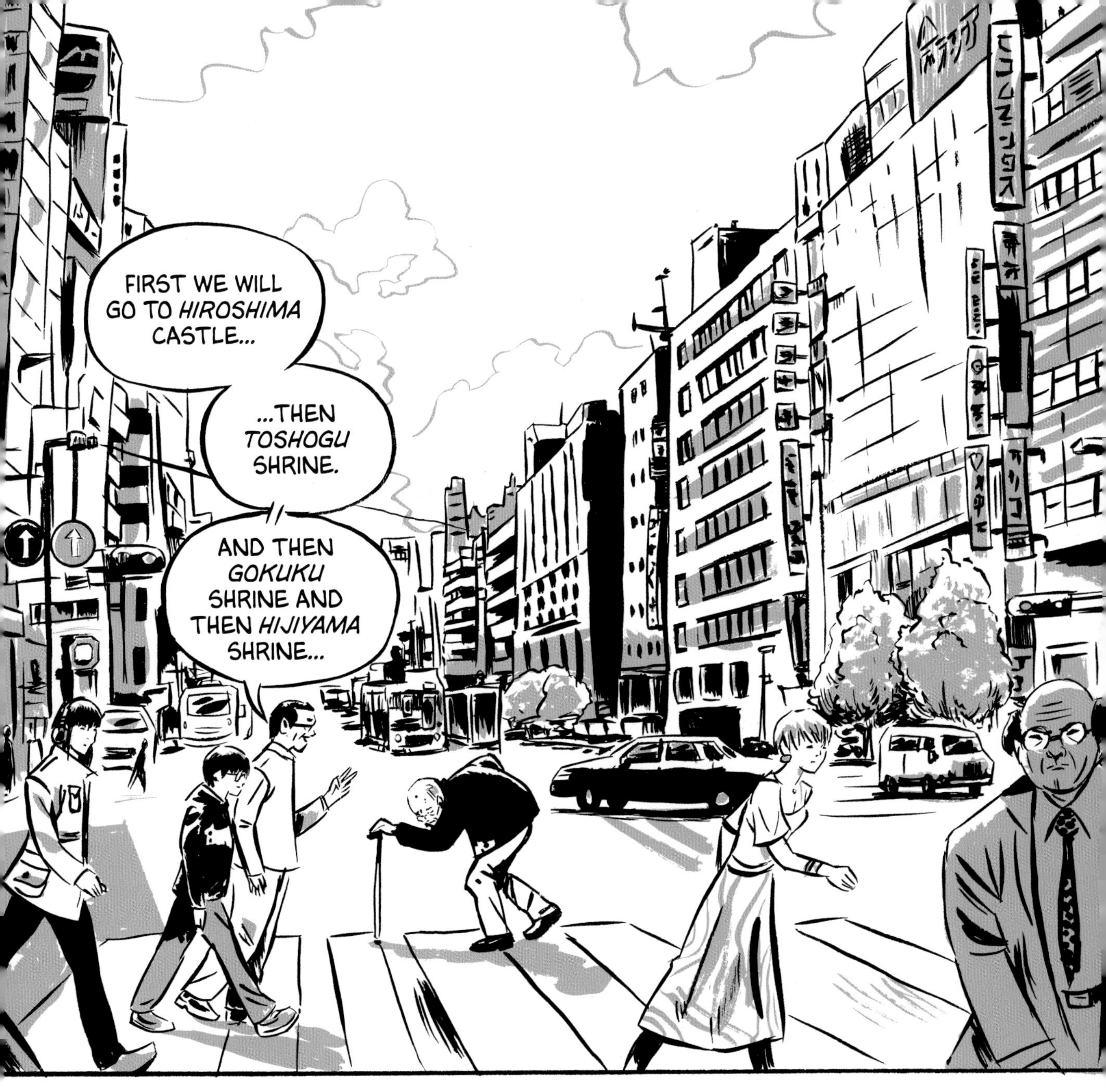
FIRST WE WILL GO TO *HIROSHIMA* CASTLE...
...THEN *TOSHOGU* SHRINE.
AND THEN *GOKUKU* SHRINE AND THEN *HIJIYAMA* SHRINE...

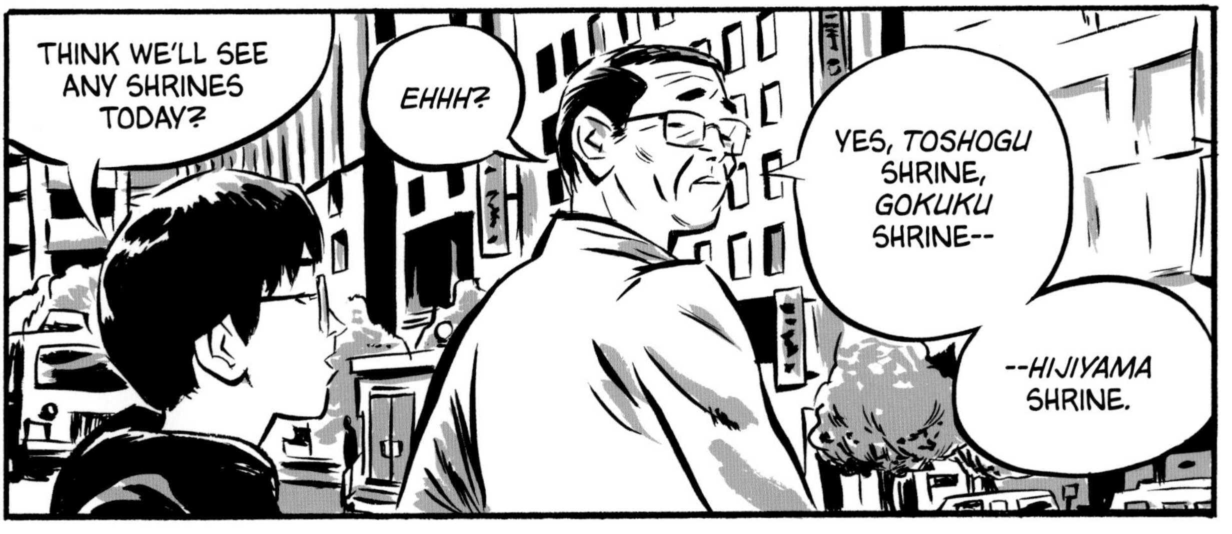
THINK WE'LL SEE ANY SHRINES TODAY?
EHHH?
YES, *TOSHOGU* SHRINE, *GOKUKU* SHRINE--
--*HIJIYAMA* SHRINE.

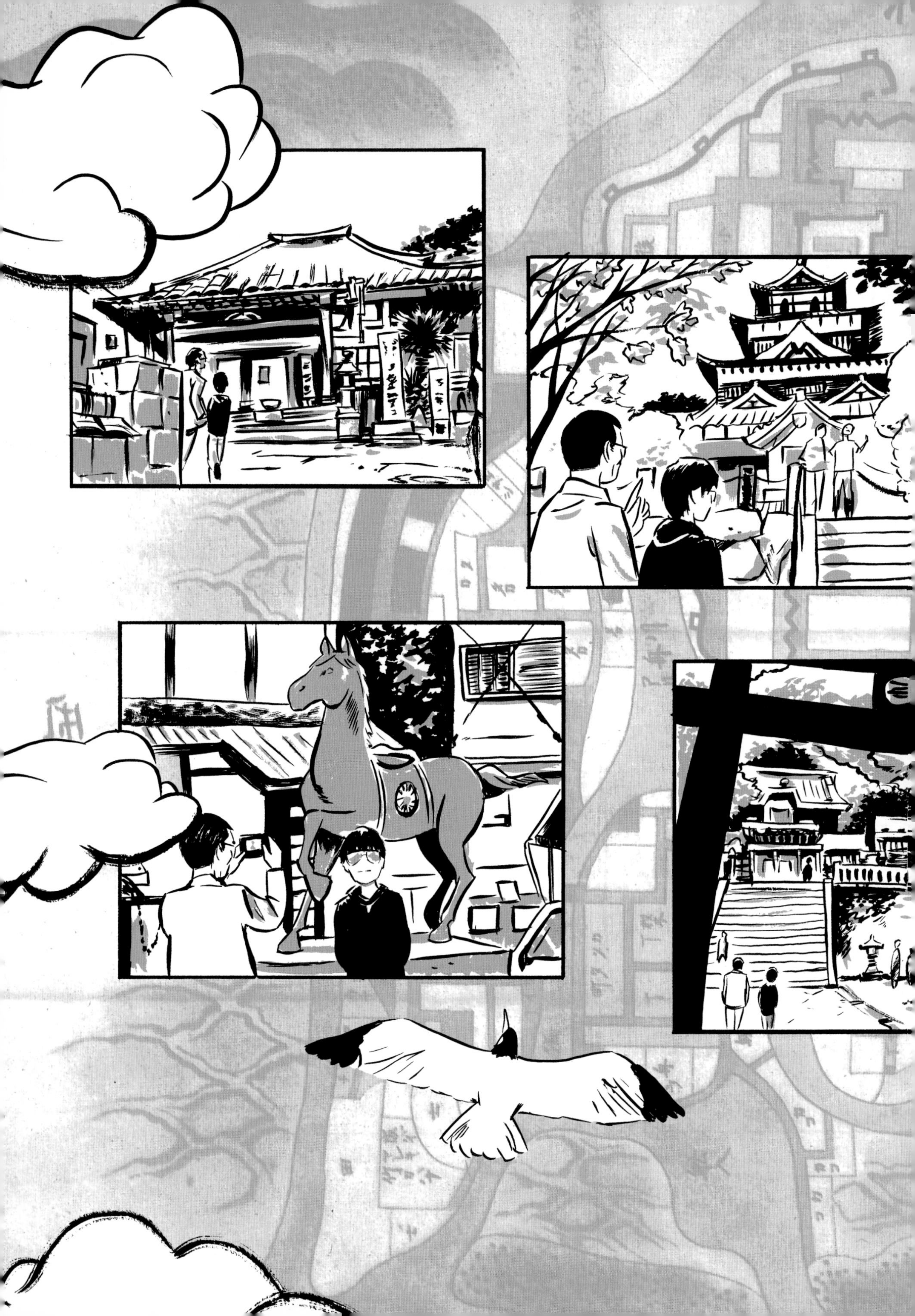

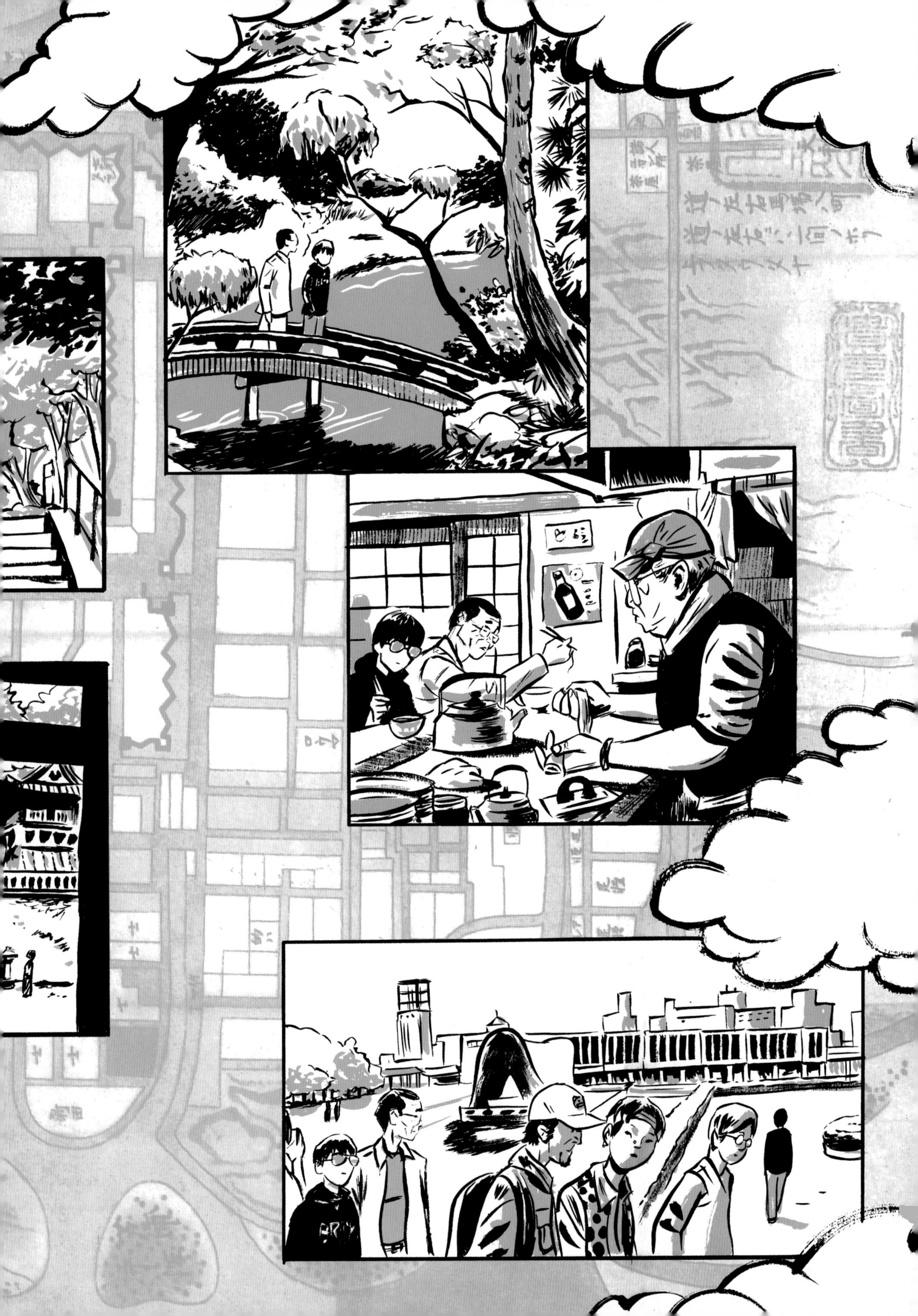

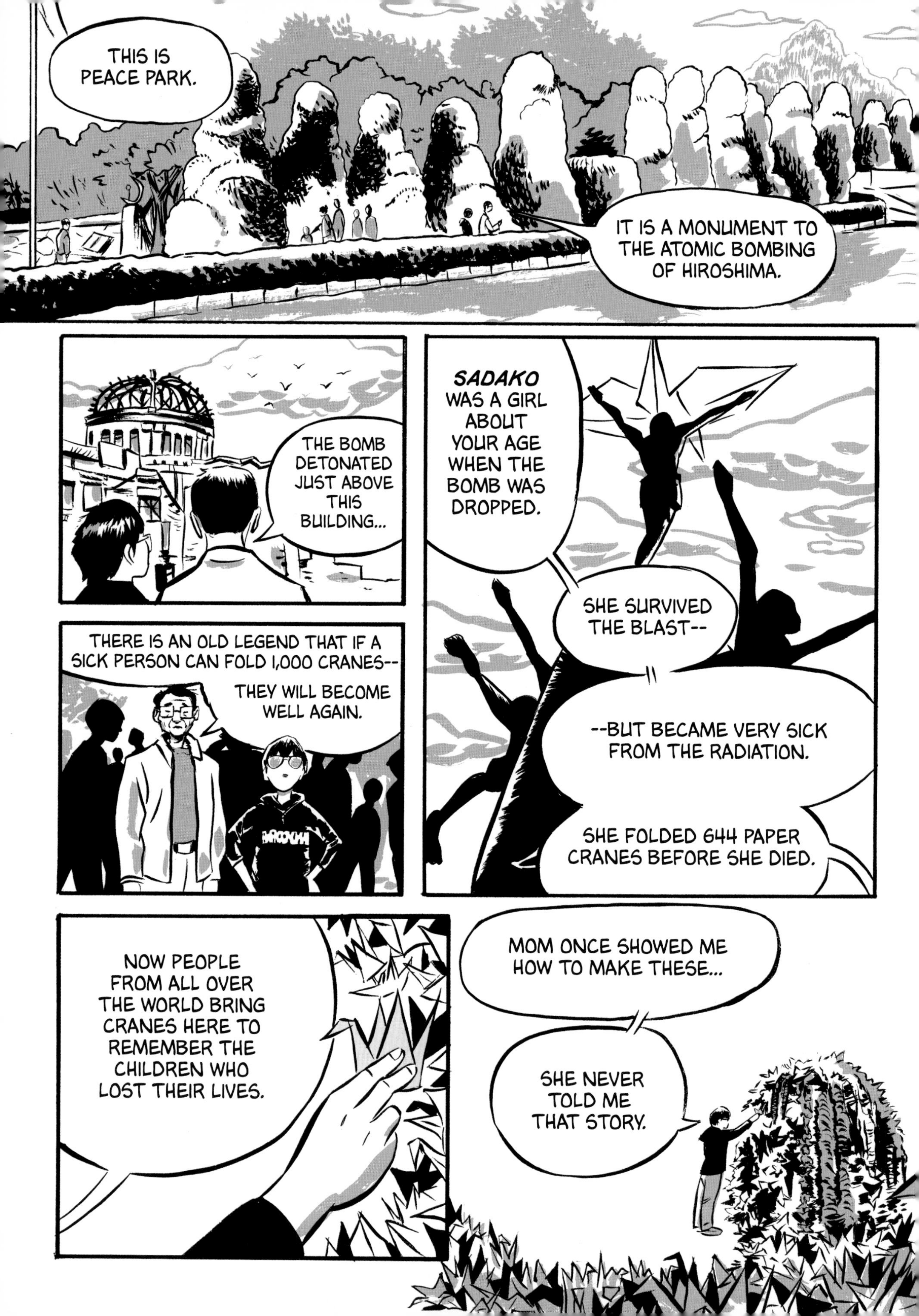
THIS IS PEACE PARK.
IT IS A MONUMENT TO THE ATOMIC BOMBING OF HIROSHIMA.
THE BOMB DETONATED JUST ABOVE THIS BUILDING...
SADAKO WAS A GIRL ABOUT YOUR AGE WHEN THE BOMB WAS DROPPED.
SHE SURVIVED THE BLAST--
--BUT BECAME VERY SICK FROM THE RADIATION.
SHE FOLDED 644 PAPER CRANES BEFORE SHE DIED.
THERE IS AN OLD LEGEND THAT IF A SICK PERSON CAN FOLD 1,000 CRANES--
THEY WILL BECOME WELL AGAIN.
NOW PEOPLE FROM ALL OVER THE WORLD BRING CRANES HERE TO REMEMBER THE CHILDREN WHO LOST THEIR LIVES.
MOM ONCE SHOWED ME HOW TO MAKE THESE...
SHE NEVER TOLD ME THAT STORY.

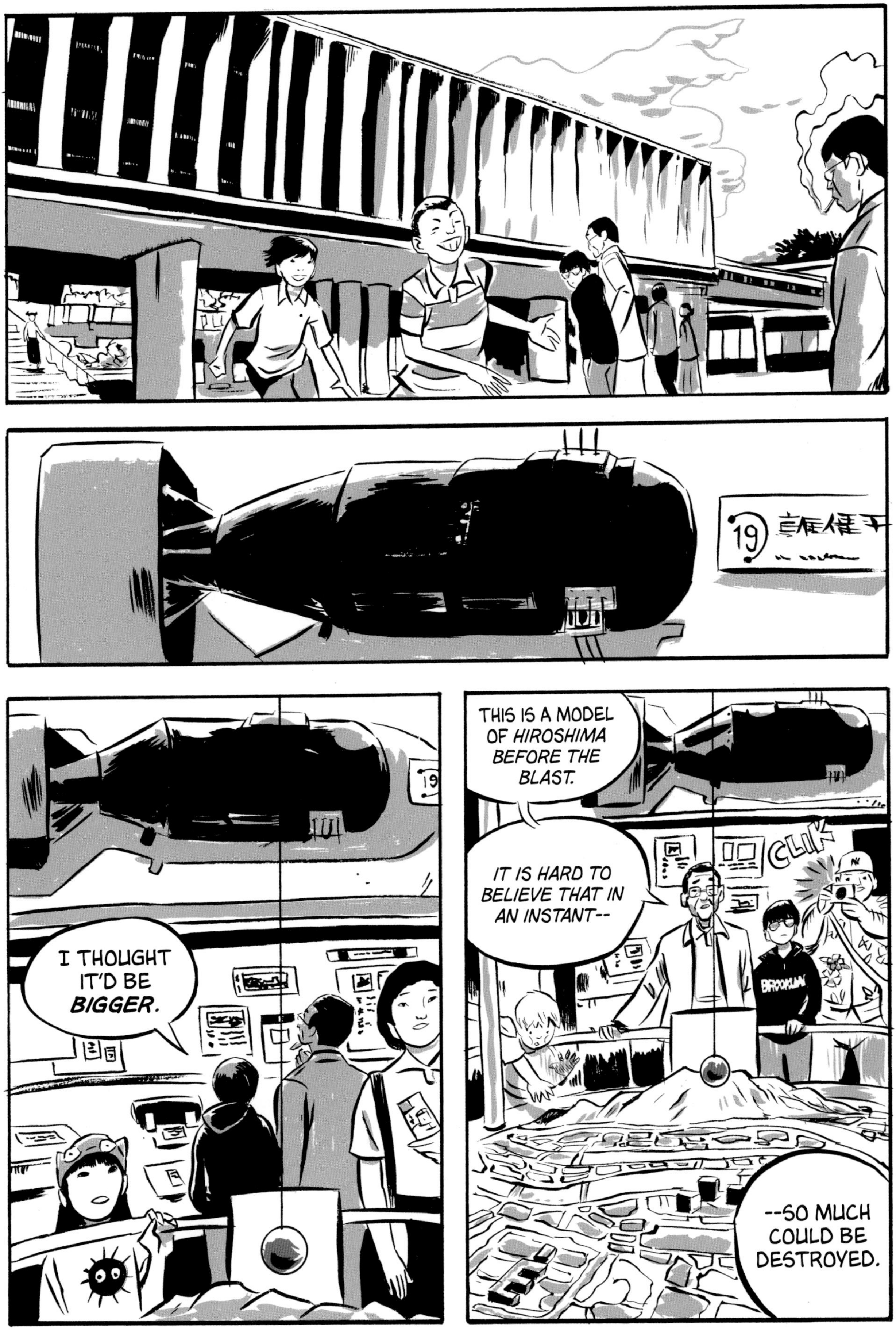
I THOUGHT IT'D BE *BIGGER*.
THIS IS A MODEL OF *HIROSHIMA* BEFORE THE BLAST.
IT IS HARD TO BELIEVE THAT IN AN INSTANT--
CLIK
--SO MUCH COULD BE DESTROYED.

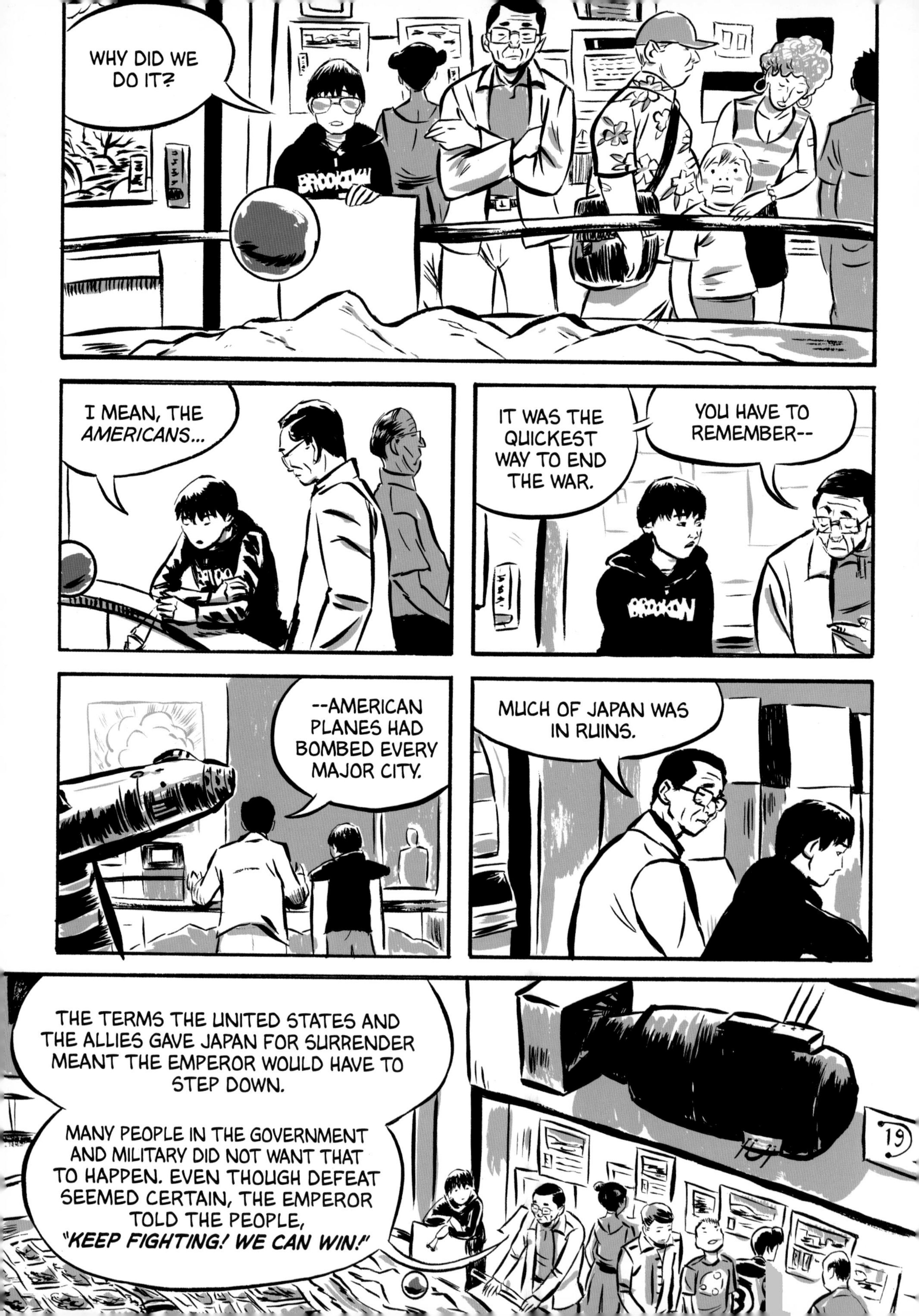
WHY DID WE DO IT?
I MEAN, THE *AMERICANS*...
IT WAS THE QUICKEST WAY TO END THE WAR.
YOU HAVE TO REMEMBER--
--AMERICAN PLANES HAD BOMBED EVERY MAJOR CITY.
MUCH OF JAPAN WAS IN RUINS.
THE TERMS THE UNITED STATES AND THE ALLIES GAVE JAPAN FOR SURRENDER MEANT THE EMPEROR WOULD HAVE TO STEP DOWN.
MANY PEOPLE IN THE GOVERNMENT AND MILITARY DID NOT WANT THAT TO HAPPEN. EVEN THOUGH DEFEAT SEEMED CERTAIN, THE EMPEROR TOLD THE PEOPLE, ***"KEEP FIGHTING! WE CAN WIN!"***
19

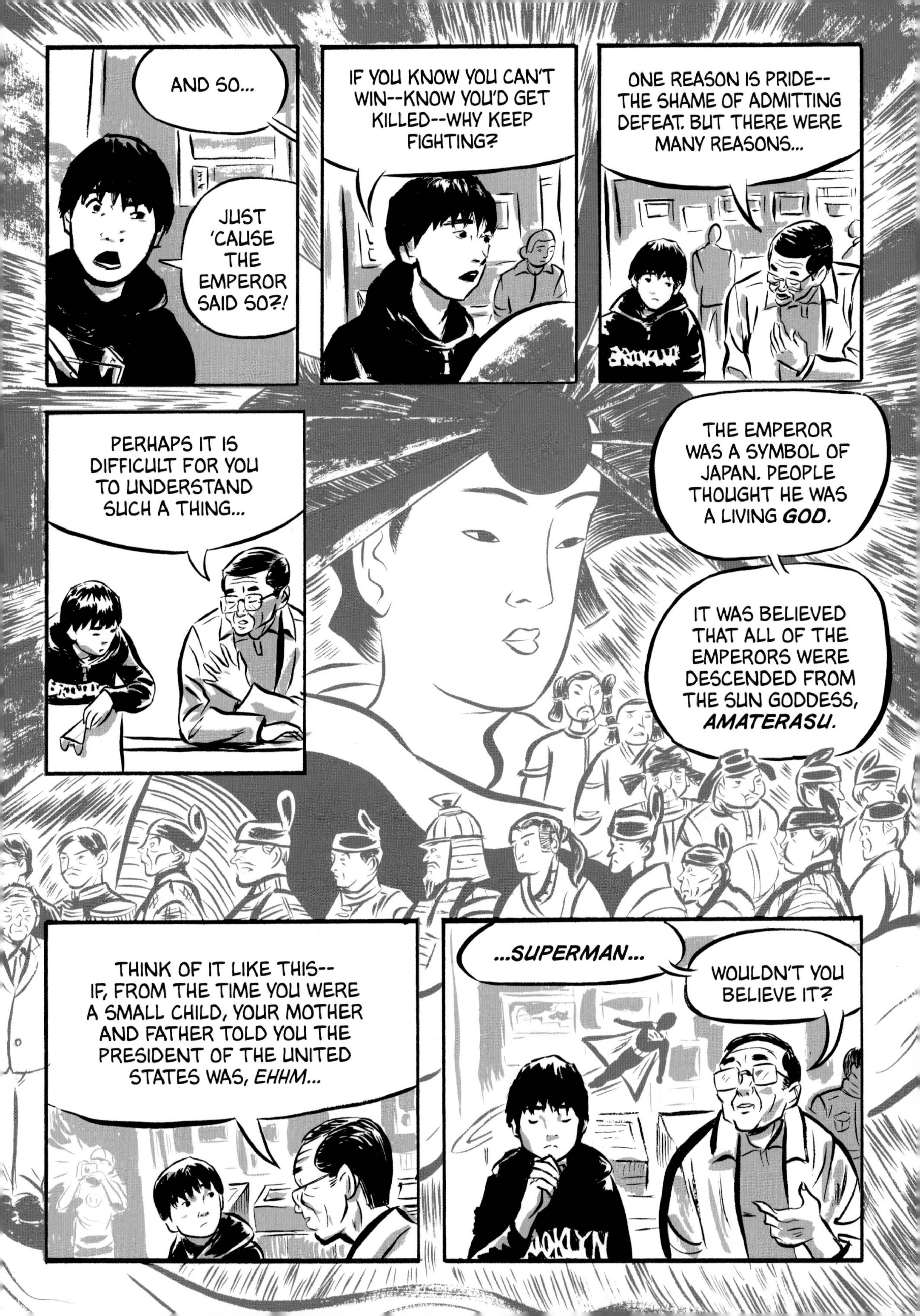
AND SO...
JUST 'CAUSE THE EMPEROR SAID SO?!
IF YOU KNOW YOU CAN'T WIN--KNOW YOU'D GET KILLED--WHY KEEP FIGHTING?
ONE REASON IS PRIDE-- THE SHAME OF ADMITTING DEFEAT. BUT THERE WERE MANY REASONS...
PERHAPS IT IS DIFFICULT FOR YOU TO UNDERSTAND SUCH A THING...
THE EMPEROR WAS A SYMBOL OF JAPAN. PEOPLE THOUGHT HE WAS A LIVING *GOD.*
IT WAS BELIEVED THAT ALL OF THE EMPERORS WERE DESCENDED FROM THE SUN GODDESS, *AMATERASU.*
THINK OF IT LIKE THIS-- IF, FROM THE TIME YOU WERE A SMALL CHILD, YOUR MOTHER AND FATHER TOLD YOU THE PRESIDENT OF THE UNITED STATES WAS, *EHHM...*
...SUPERMAN...
WOULDN'T YOU BELIEVE IT?

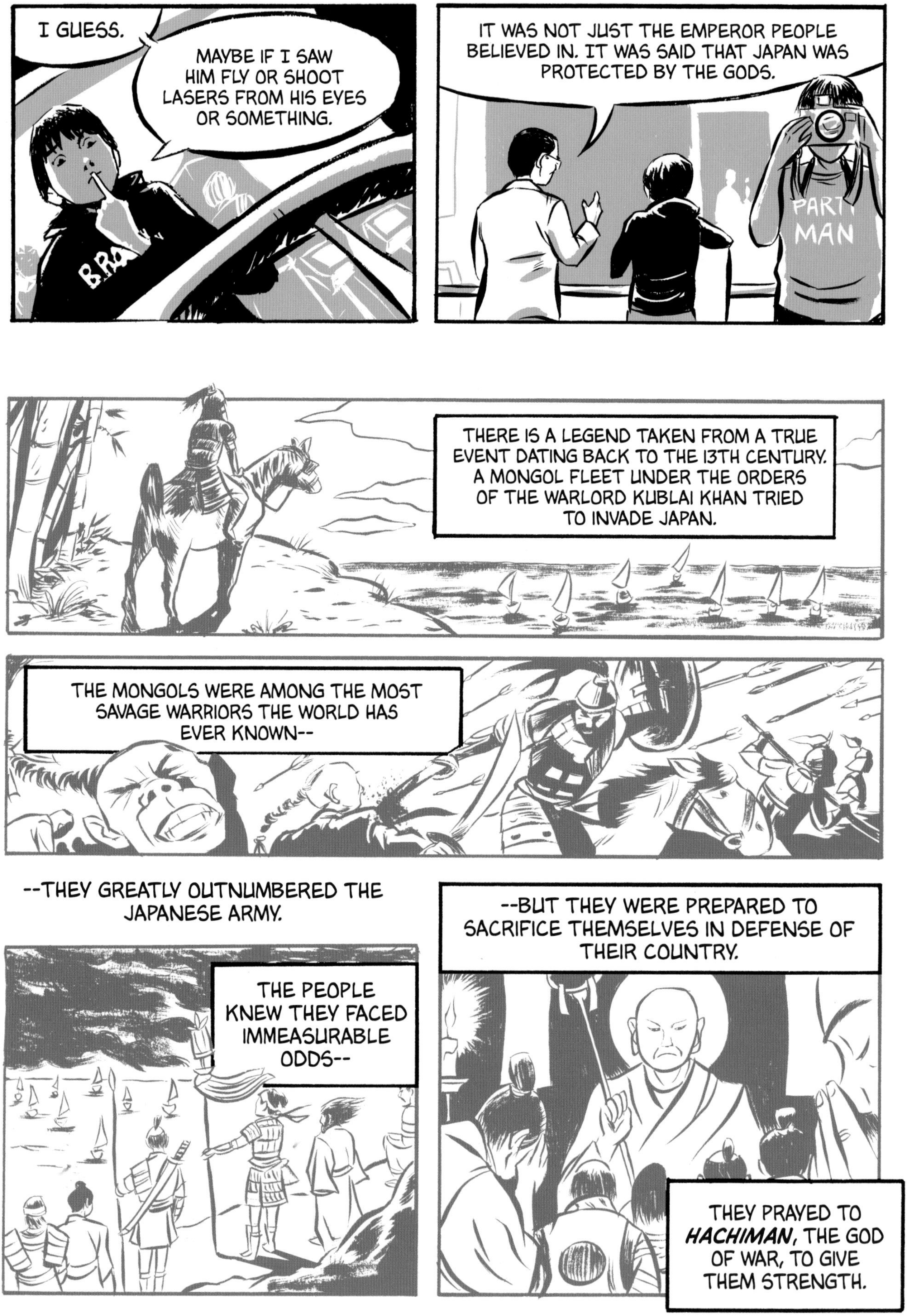
I GUESS.
MAYBE IF I SAW HIM FLY OR SHOOT LASERS FROM HIS EYES OR SOMETHING.
IT WAS NOT JUST THE EMPEROR PEOPLE BELIEVED IN. IT WAS SAID THAT JAPAN WAS PROTECTED BY THE GODS.
THERE IS A LEGEND TAKEN FROM A TRUE EVENT DATING BACK TO THE 13TH CENTURY. A MONGOL FLEET UNDER THE ORDERS OF THE WARLORD KUBLAI KHAN TRIED TO INVADE JAPAN.
THE MONGOLS WERE AMONG THE MOST SAVAGE WARRIORS THE WORLD HAS EVER KNOWN--
--THEY GREATLY OUTNUMBERED THE JAPANESE ARMY.
THE PEOPLE KNEW THEY FACED IMMEASURABLE ODDS--
--BUT THEY WERE PREPARED TO SACRIFICE THEMSELVES IN DEFENSE OF THEIR COUNTRY.
THEY PRAYED TO ***HACHIMAN***, THE GOD OF WAR, TO GIVE THEM STRENGTH.

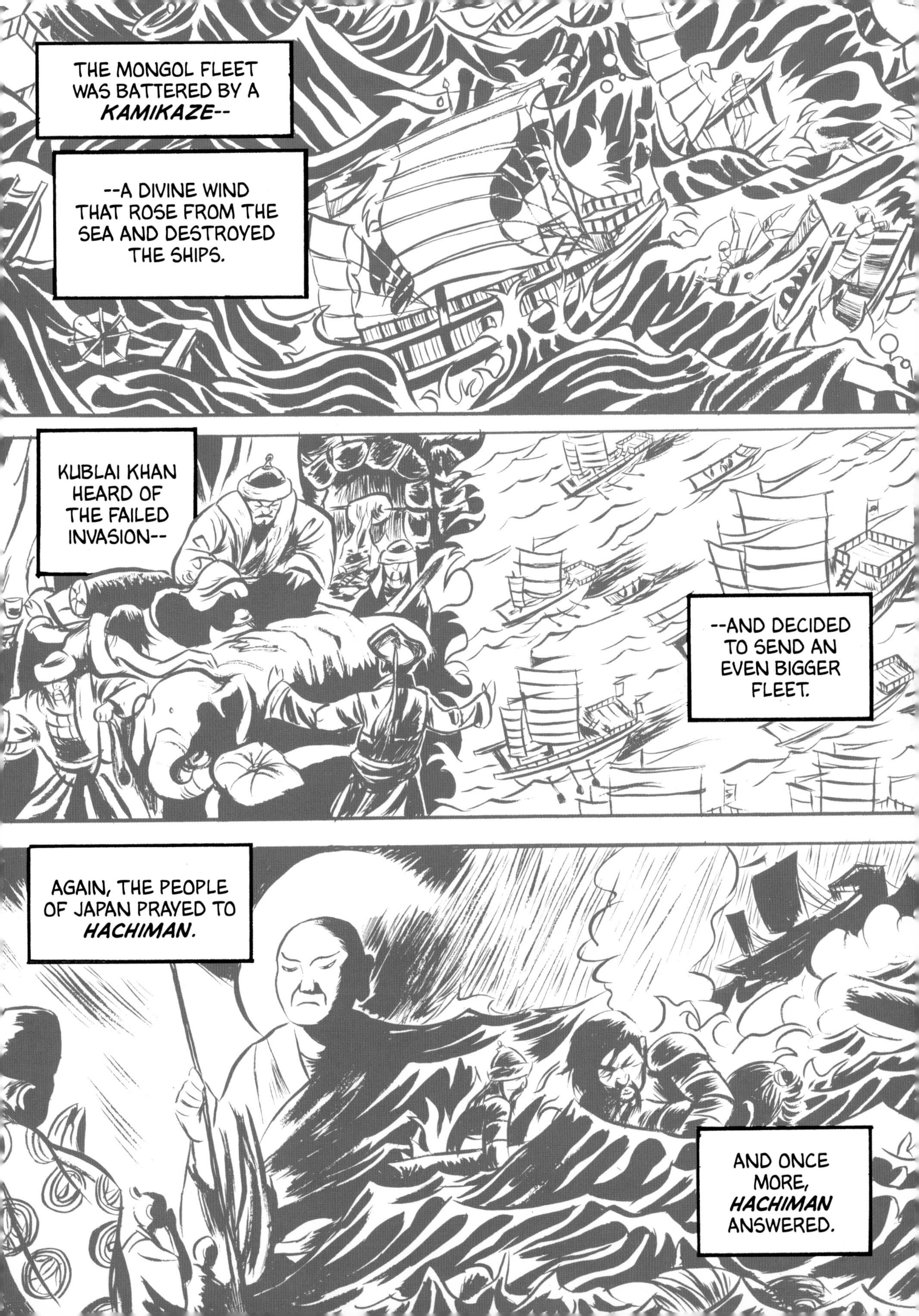
THE MONGOL FLEET WAS BATTERED BY A *KAMIKAZE*--
--A DIVINE WIND THAT ROSE FROM THE SEA AND DESTROYED THE SHIPS.
KUBLAI KHAN HEARD OF THE FAILED INVASION--
--AND DECIDED TO SEND AN EVEN BIGGER FLEET.
AGAIN, THE PEOPLE OF JAPAN PRAYED TO *HACHIMAN*.
AND ONCE MORE, *HACHIMAN* ANSWERED.

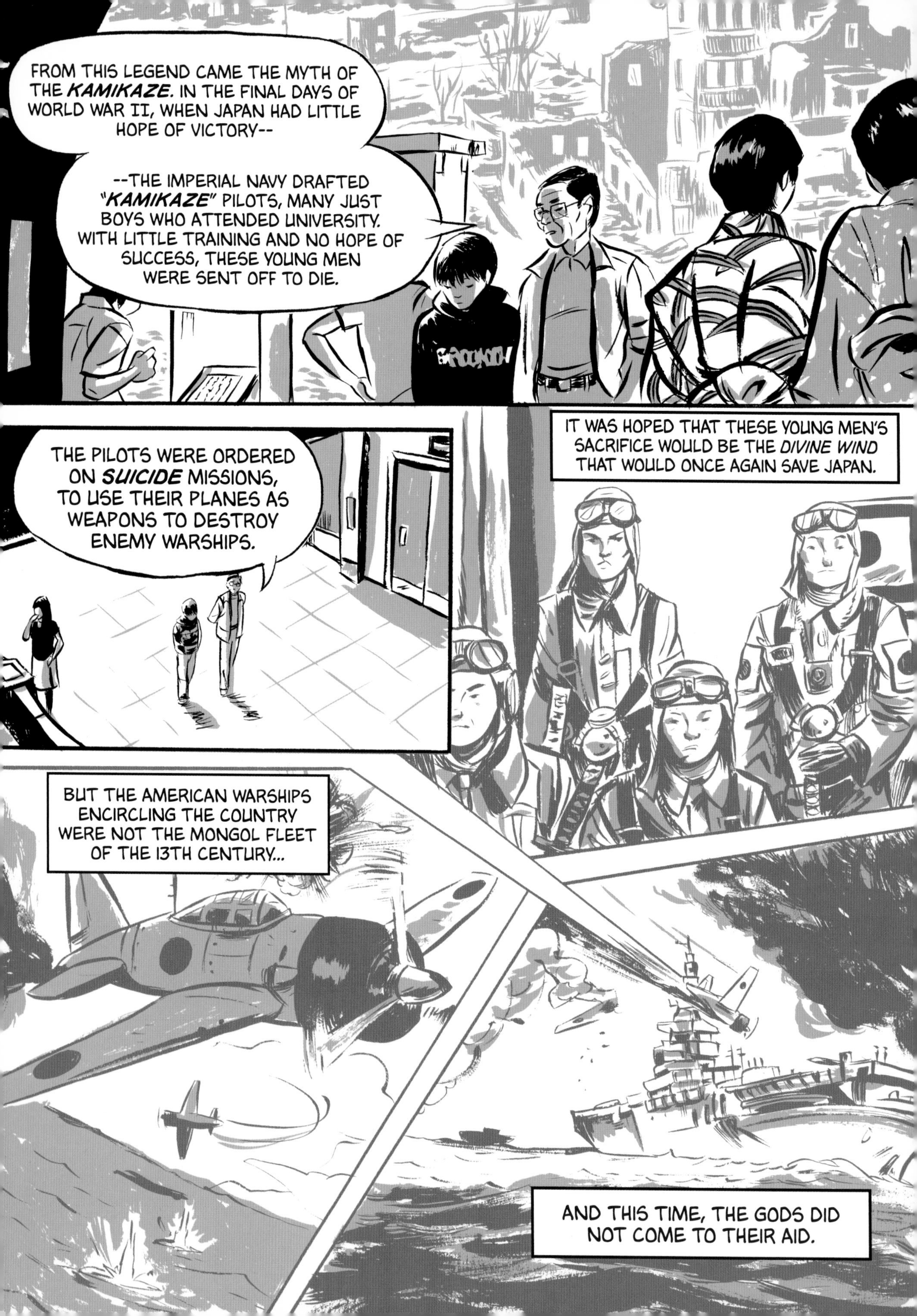
FROM THIS LEGEND CAME THE MYTH OF THE KAMIKAZE. IN THE FINAL DAYS OF WORLD WAR II, WHEN JAPAN HAD LITTLE HOPE OF VICTORY--
--THE IMPERIAL NAVY DRAFTED "KAMIKAZE" PILOTS, MANY JUST BOYS WHO ATTENDED UNIVERSITY. WITH LITTLE TRAINING AND NO HOPE OF SUCCESS, THESE YOUNG MEN WERE SENT OFF TO DIE.
THE PILOTS WERE ORDERED ON SUICIDE MISSIONS, TO USE THEIR PLANES AS WEAPONS TO DESTROY ENEMY WARSHIPS.
IT WAS HOPED THAT THESE YOUNG MEN'S SACRIFICE WOULD BE THE DIVINE WIND THAT WOULD ONCE AGAIN SAVE JAPAN.
BUT THE AMERICAN WARSHIPS ENCIRCLING THE COUNTRY WERE NOT THE MONGOL FLEET OF THE 13TH CENTURY...
AND THIS TIME, THE GODS DID NOT COME TO THEIR AID.

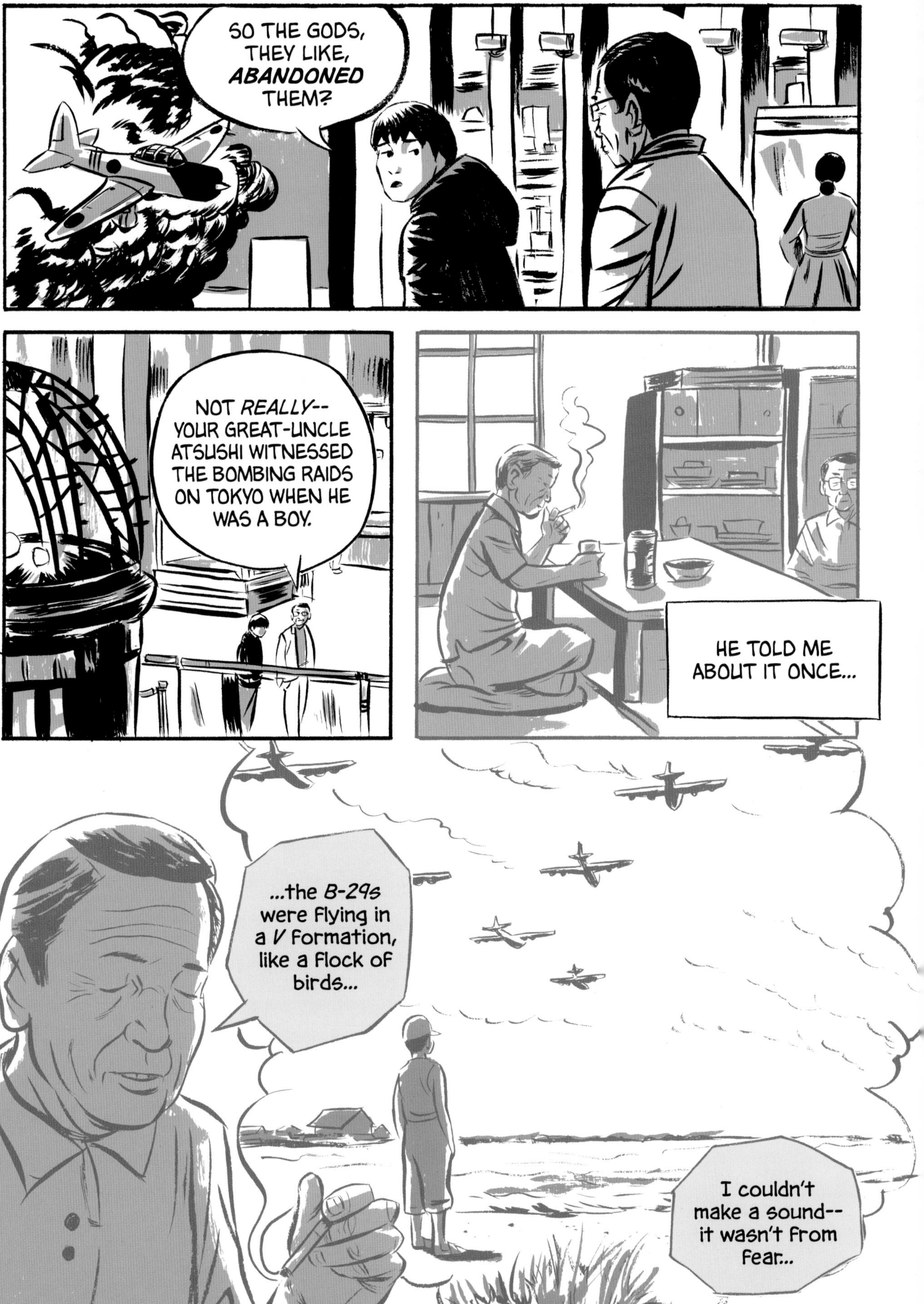
SO THE GODS, THEY LIKE, ABANDONED THEM?
NOT REALLY-- YOUR GREAT-UNCLE ATSUSHI WITNESSED THE BOMBING RAIDS ON TOKYO WHEN HE WAS A BOY.
HE TOLD ME ABOUT IT ONCE...
...the B-29s were flying in a V formation, like a flock of birds...
I couldn't make a sound-- it wasn't from fear...

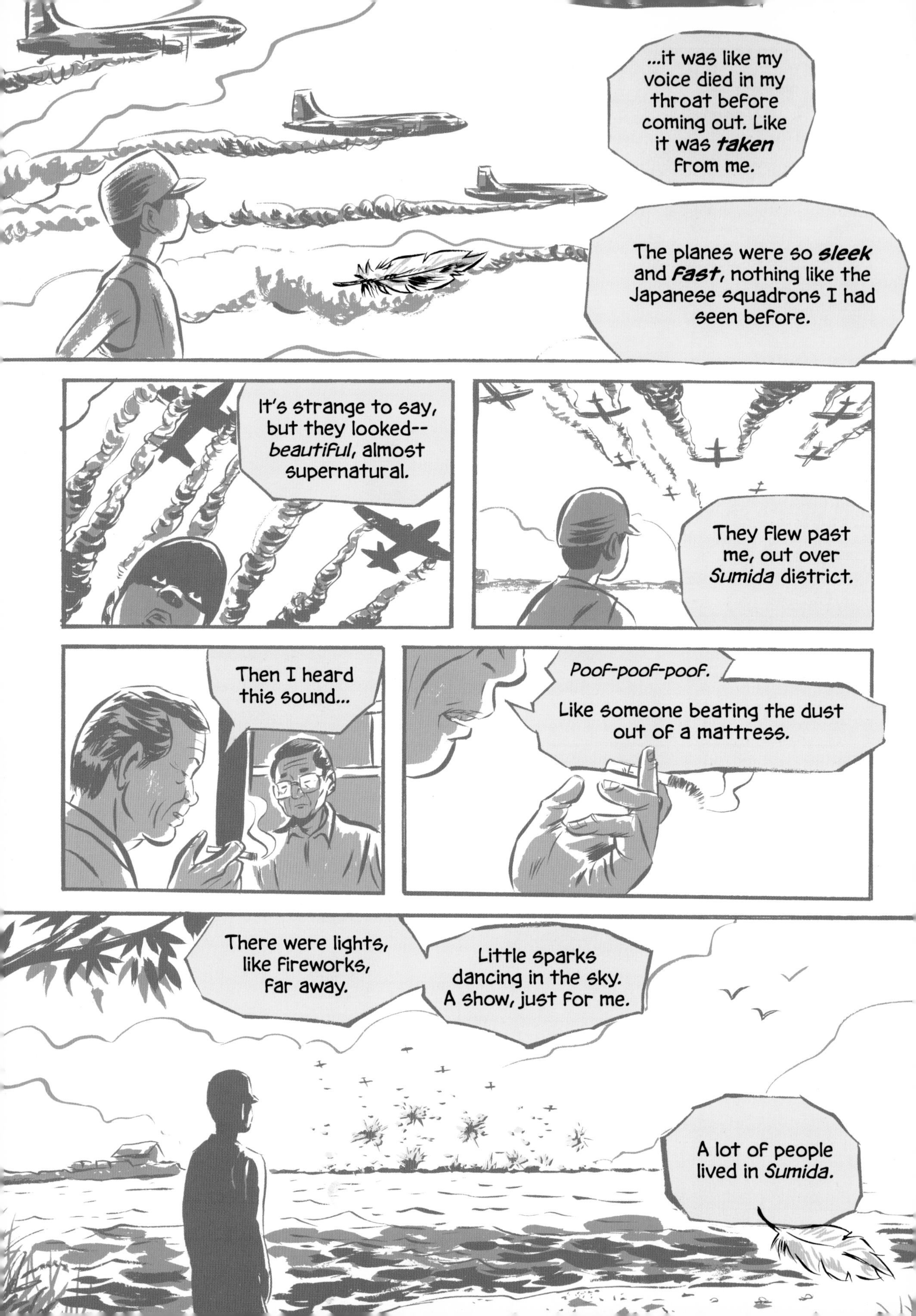
...it was like my voice died in my throat before coming out. Like it was *taken* from me.
The planes were so *sleek* and *fast*, nothing like the Japanese squadrons I had seen before.
It's strange to say, but they looked--*beautiful*, almost supernatural.
They flew past me, out over *Sumida* district.
Then I heard this sound...
Poof-poof-poof.
Like someone beating the dust out of a mattress.
There were lights, like fireworks, far away.
Little sparks dancing in the sky. A show, just for me.
A lot of people lived in *Sumida*.

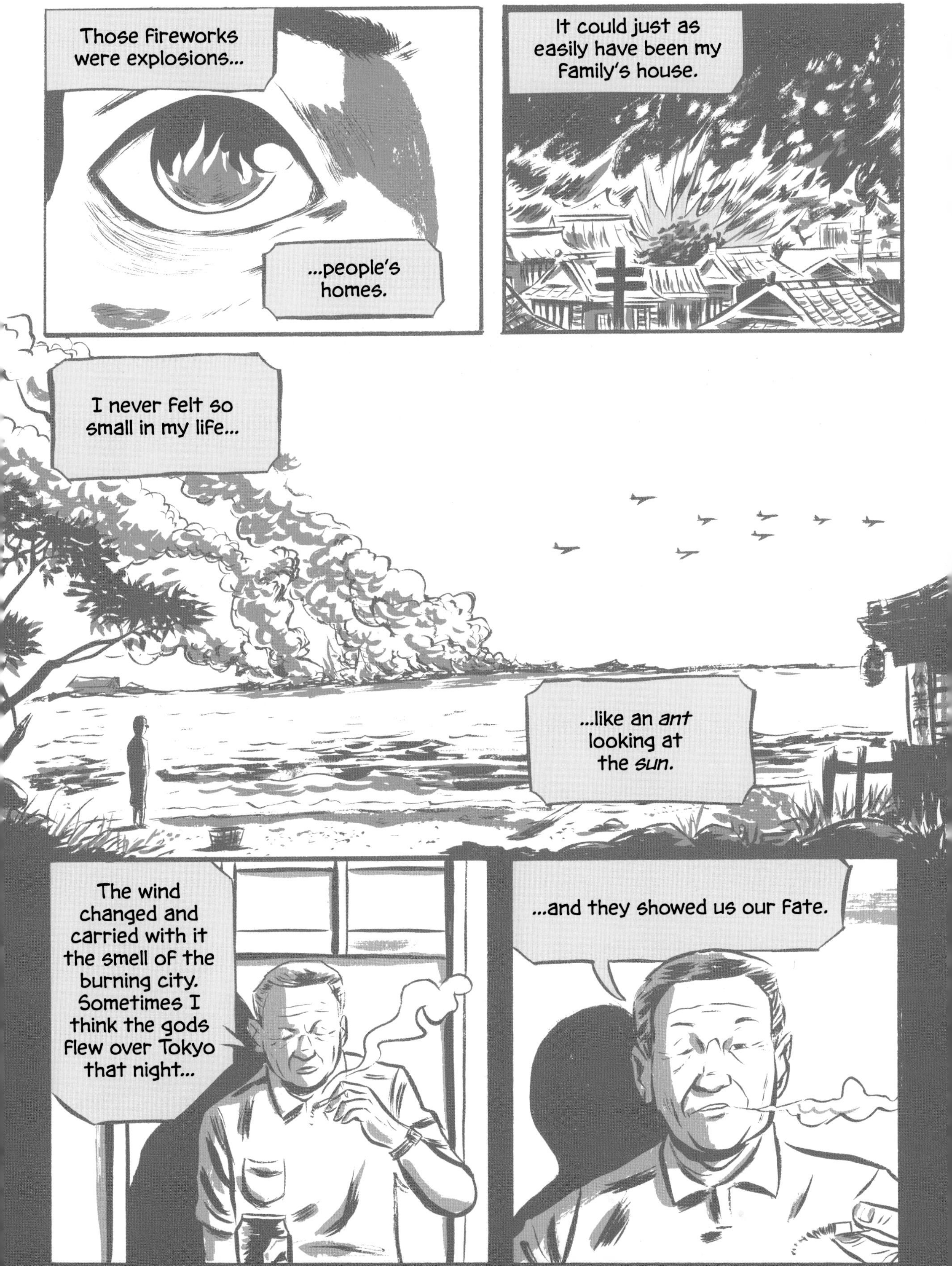
Those fireworks were explosions...
...people's homes.
It could just as easily have been my family's house.
I never felt so small in my life...
...like an *ant* looking at the *sun.*
The wind changed and carried with it the smell of the burning city. Sometimes I think the gods flew over Tokyo that night...
...and they showed us our fate.

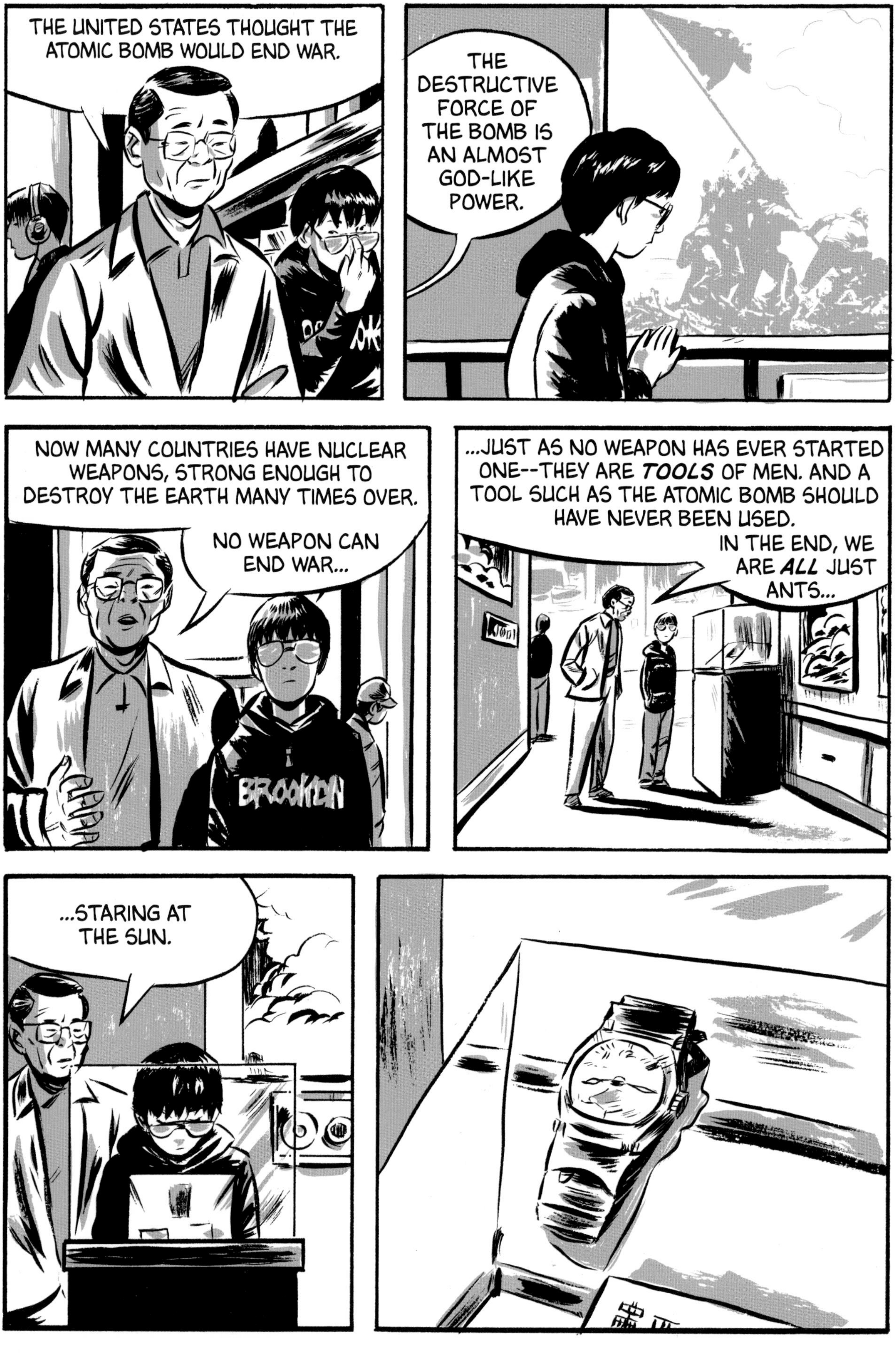
THE UNITED STATES THOUGHT THE ATOMIC BOMB WOULD END WAR.
THE DESTRUCTIVE FORCE OF THE BOMB IS AN ALMOST GOD-LIKE POWER.
NOW MANY COUNTRIES HAVE NUCLEAR WEAPONS, STRONG ENOUGH TO DESTROY THE EARTH MANY TIMES OVER.
NO WEAPON CAN END WAR...
BROOKLYN
...JUST AS NO WEAPON HAS EVER STARTED ONE--THEY ARE *TOOLS* OF MEN. AND A TOOL SUCH AS THE ATOMIC BOMB SHOULD HAVE NEVER BEEN USED.
IN THE END, WE ARE *ALL* JUST ANTS...
...STARING AT THE SUN.

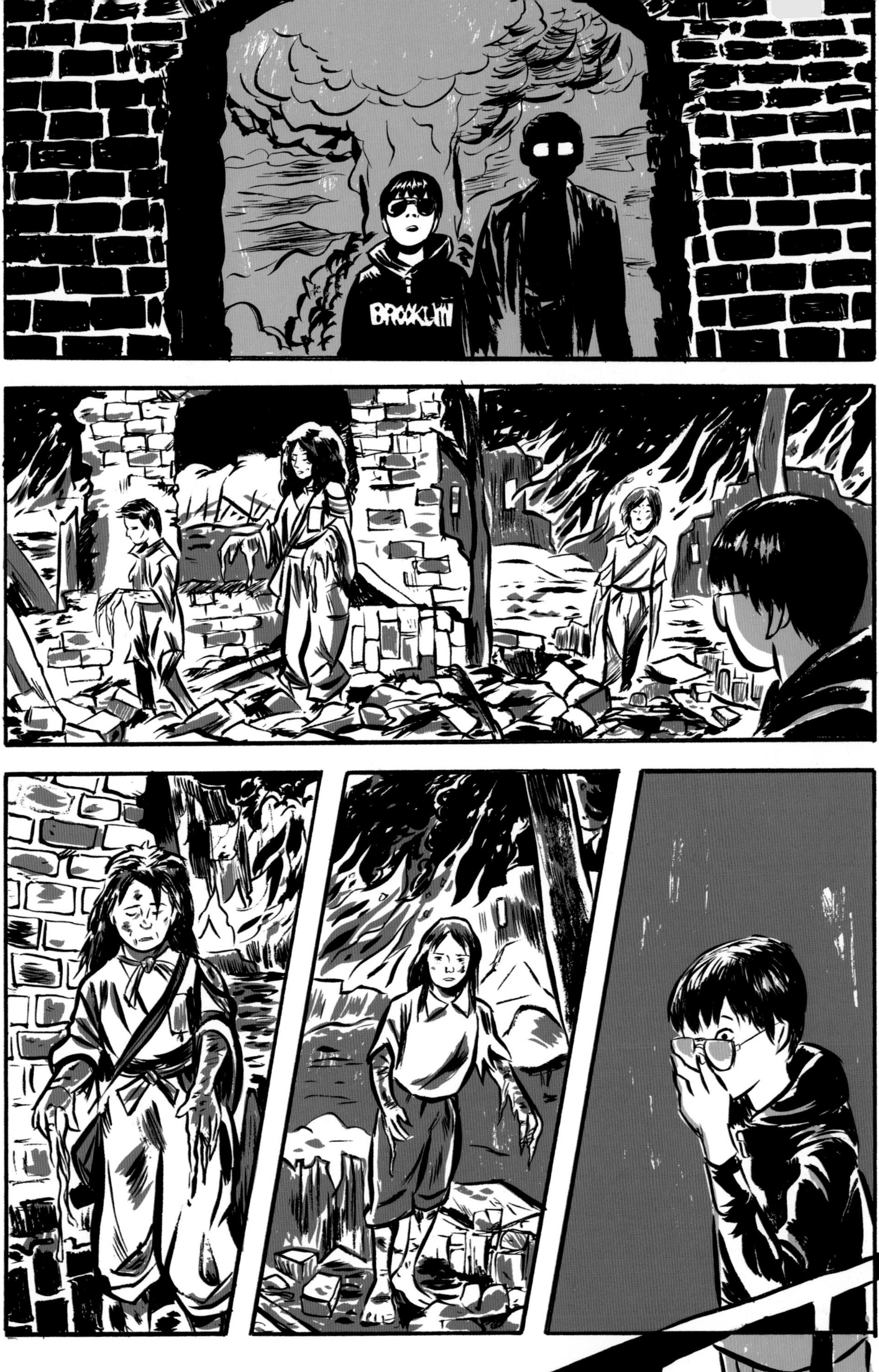
BROOKLYN

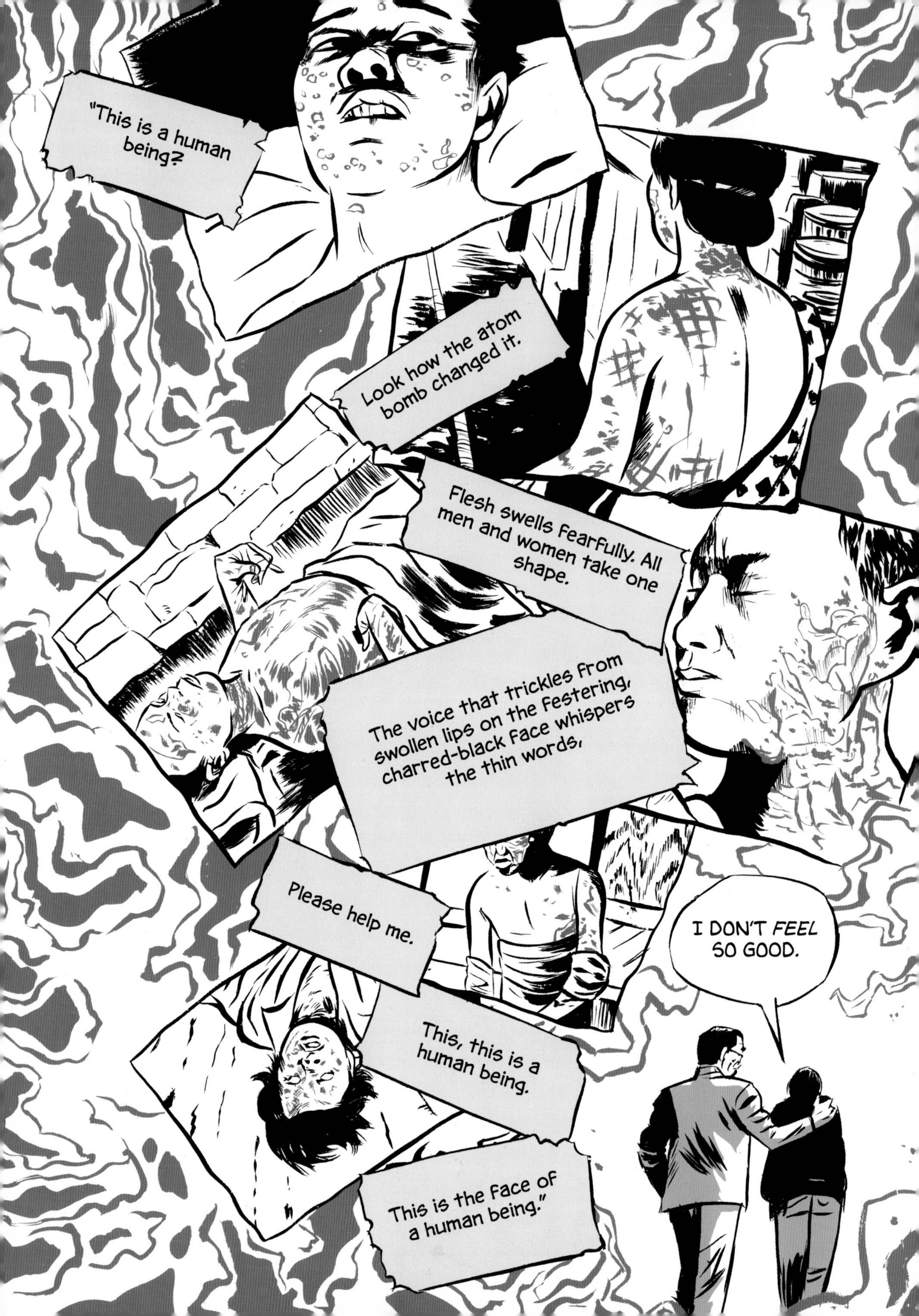
"This is a human being?
Look how the atom bomb changed it.
Flesh swells fearfully. All men and women take one shape.
The voice that trickles from swollen lips on the festering, charred-black face whispers the thin words,
Please help me.
This, this is a human being.
This is the face of a human being."
I DON'T *FEEL* SO GOOD.

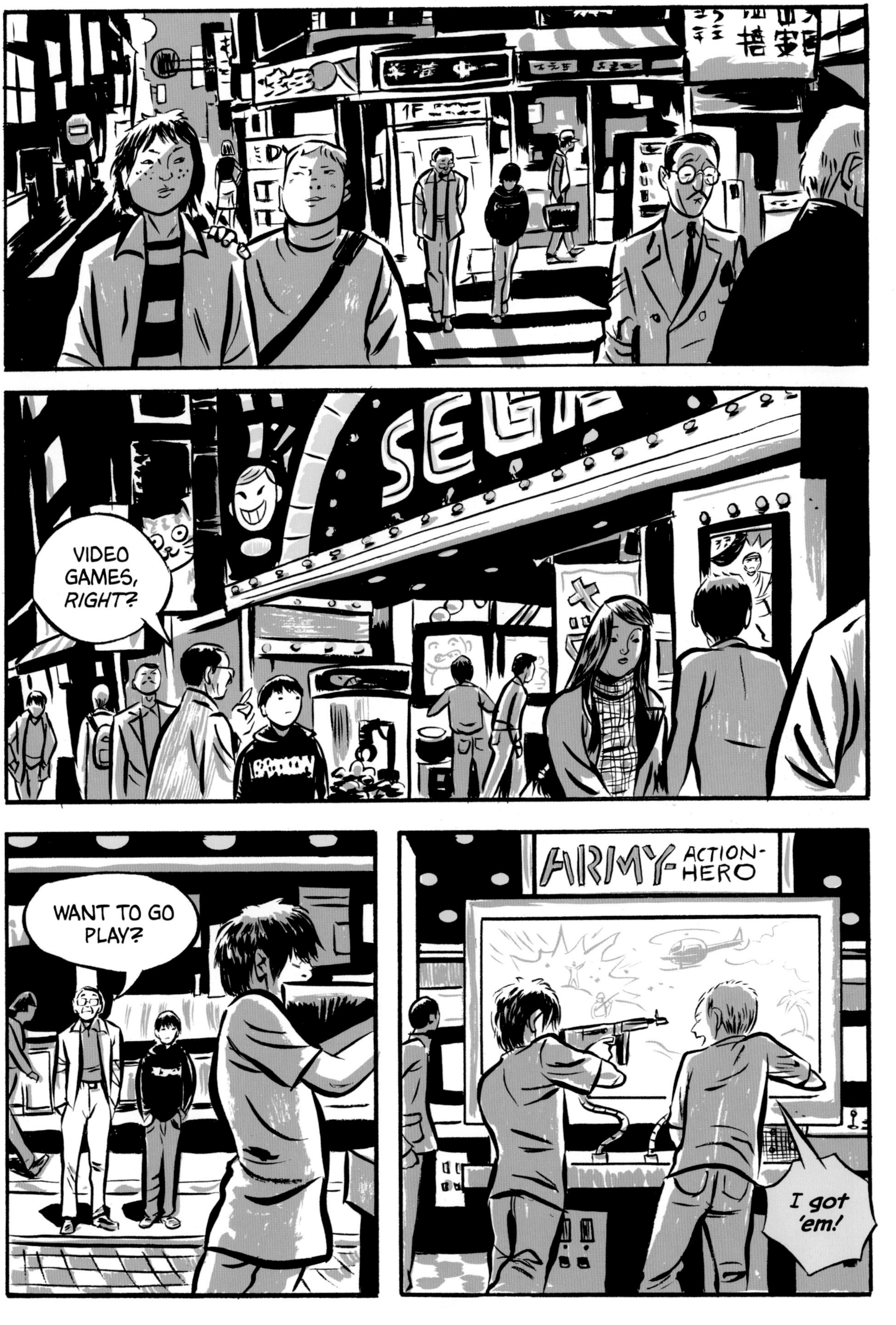
VIDEO GAMES, *RIGHT?*
WANT TO GO PLAY?
ARMY- ACTION-HERO
I got 'em!

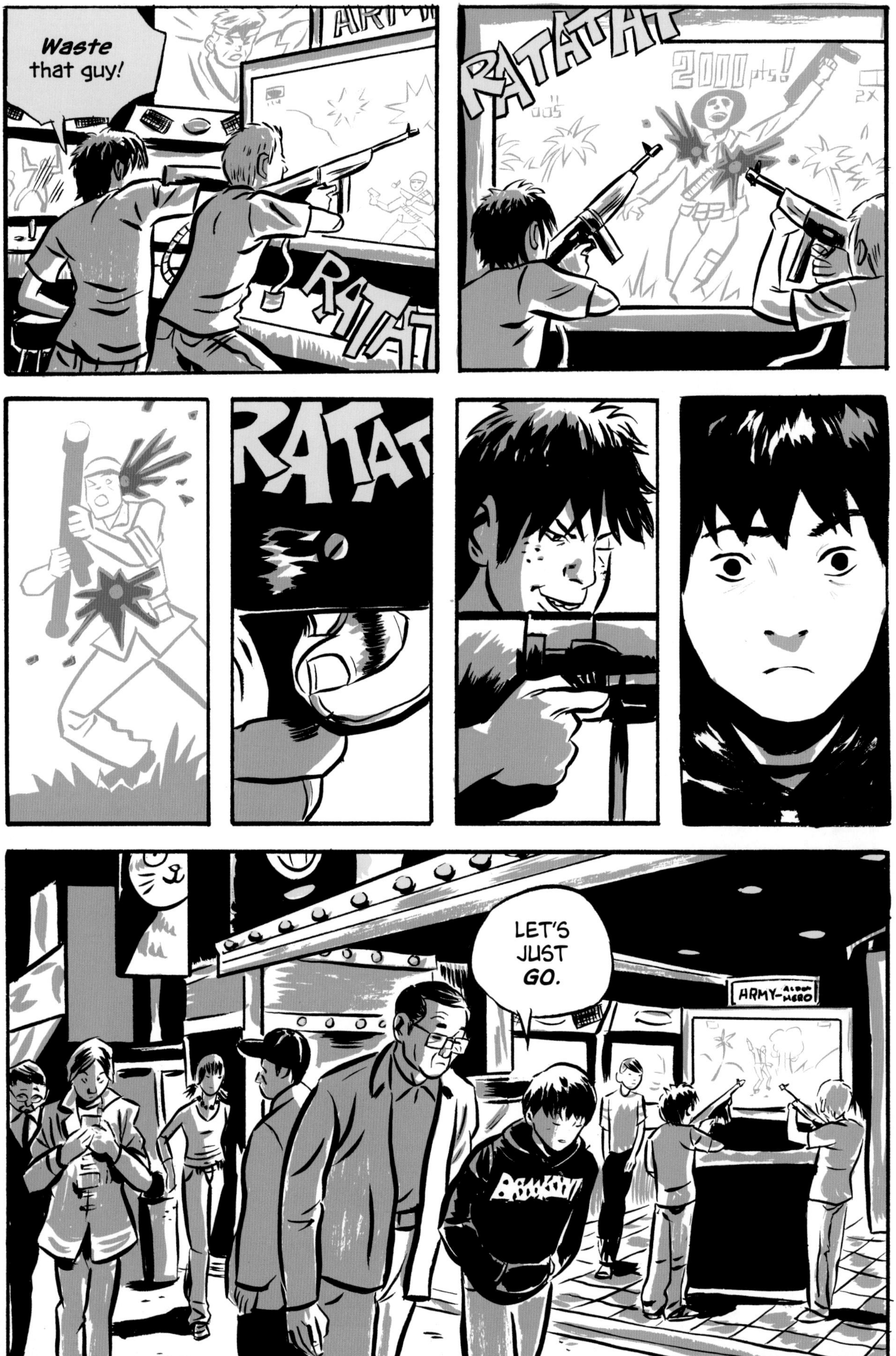
Waste that guy!
RATATAT
RATATAT
2000 pts!
RATAT
LET'S JUST GO.
ARMY-

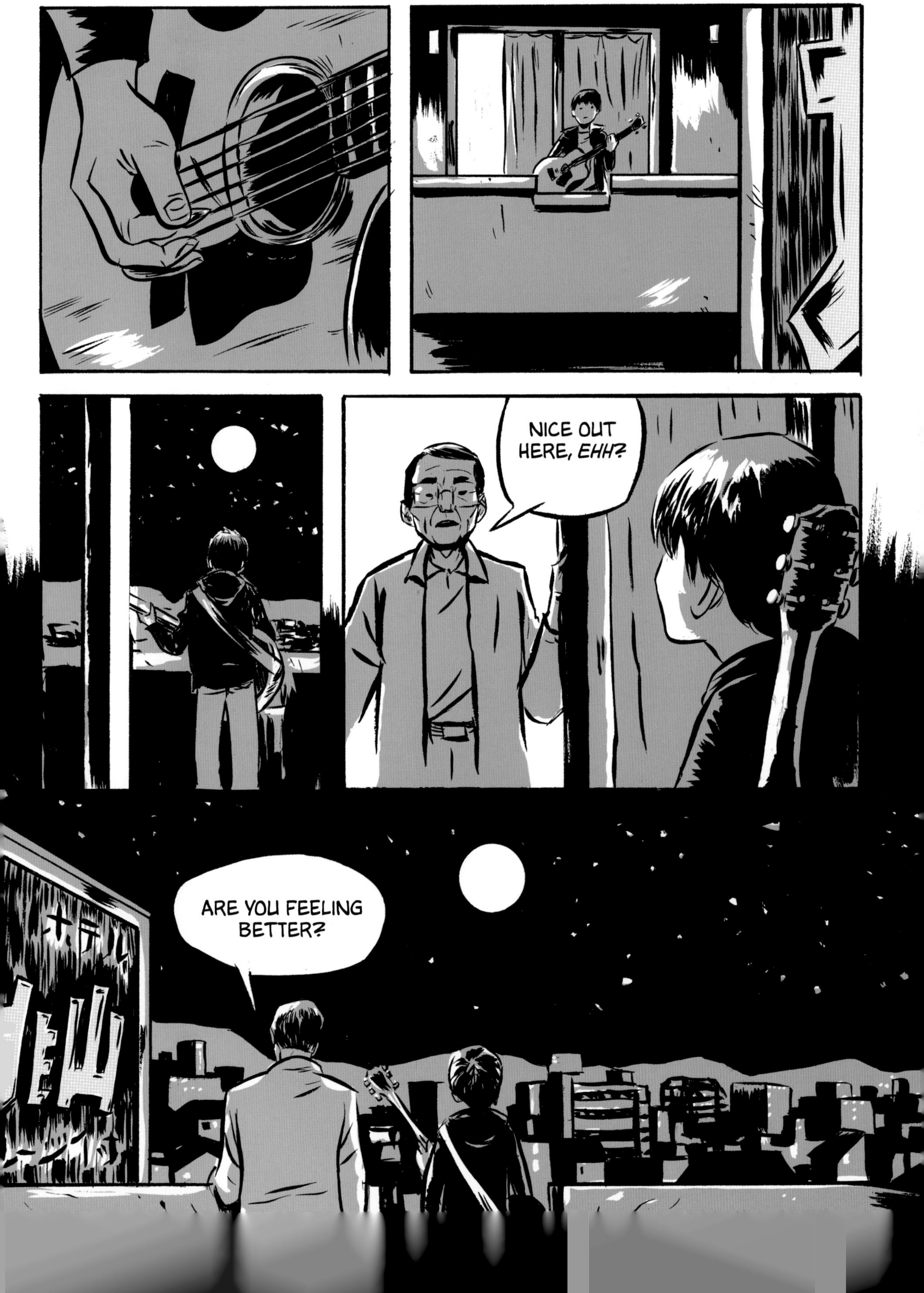
NICE OUT HERE, *EHH?*
ARE YOU FEELING BETTER?

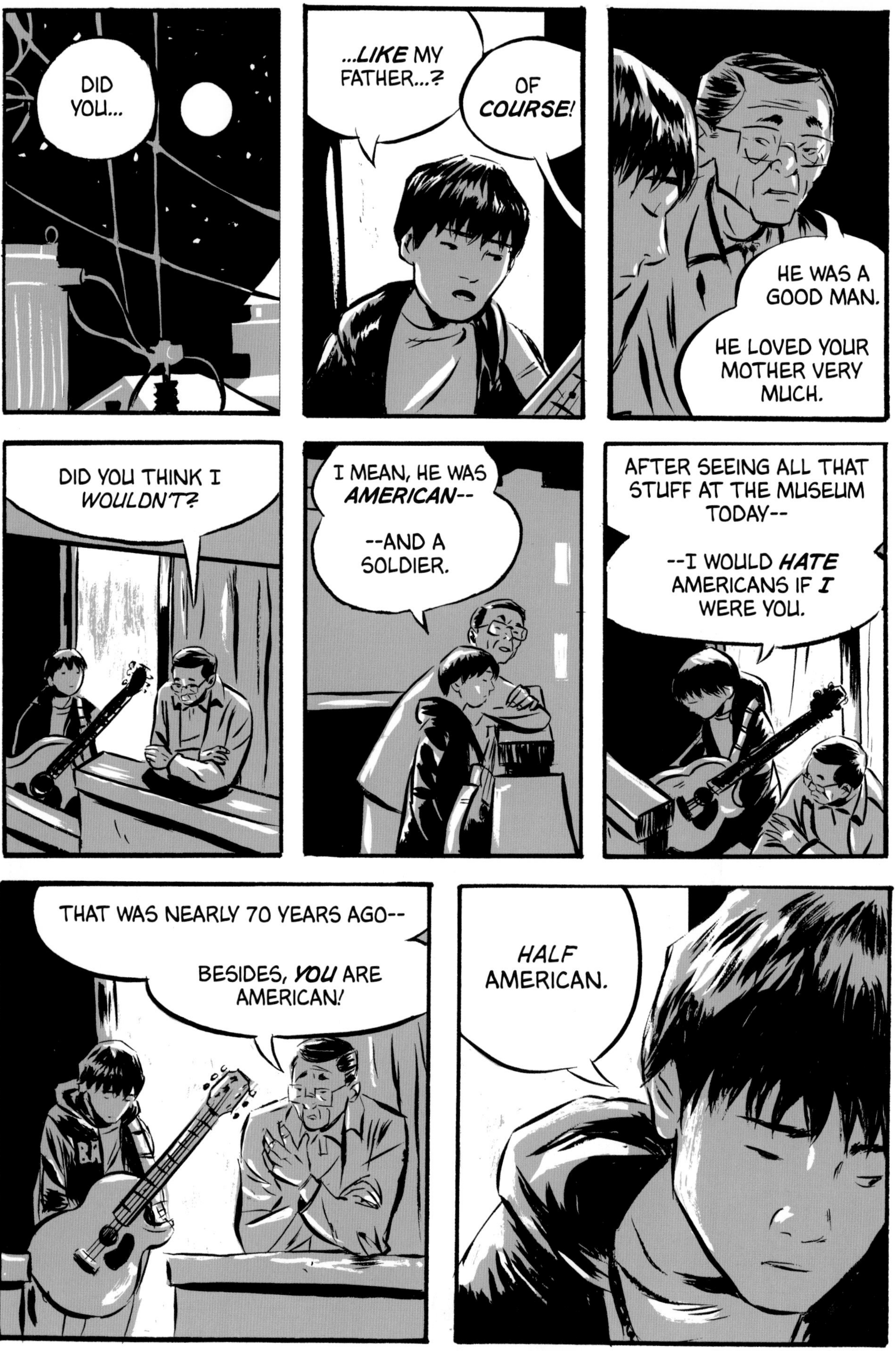
DID YOU...
...LIKE MY FATHER...?
OF COURSE!
HE WAS A GOOD MAN.
HE LOVED YOUR MOTHER VERY MUCH.
DID YOU THINK I WOULDN'T?
I MEAN, HE WAS AMERICAN--
--AND A SOLDIER.
AFTER SEEING ALL THAT STUFF AT THE MUSEUM TODAY--
--I WOULD HATE AMERICANS IF I WERE YOU.
THAT WAS NEARLY 70 YEARS AGO--
BESIDES, YOU ARE AMERICAN!
HALF AMERICAN.

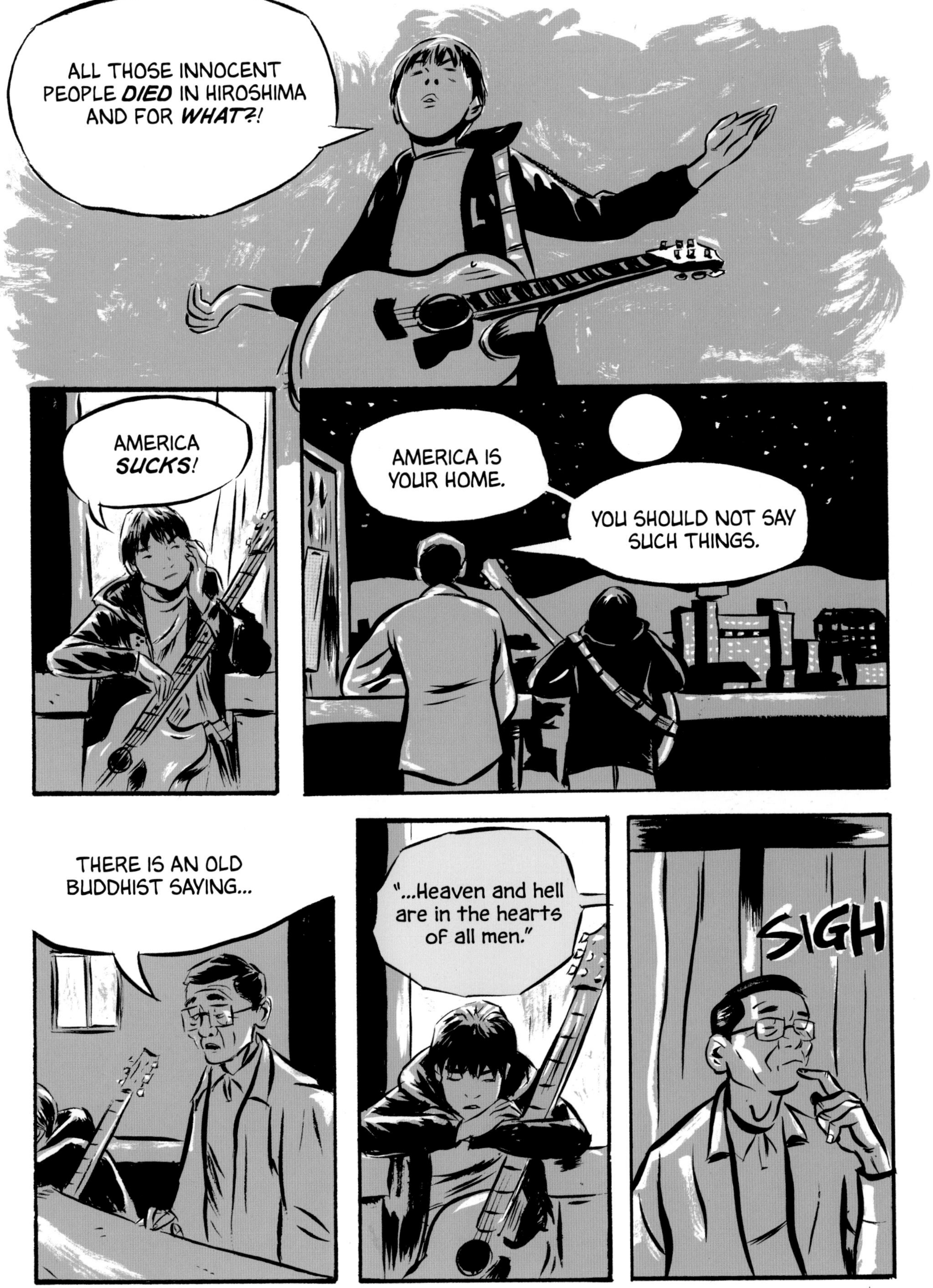
ALL THOSE INNOCENT PEOPLE DIED IN HIROSHIMA AND FOR WHAT?!
AMERICA SUCKS!
AMERICA IS YOUR HOME.
YOU SHOULD NOT SAY SUCH THINGS.
THERE IS AN OLD BUDDHIST SAYING...
"...Heaven and hell are in the hearts of all men."
SIGH

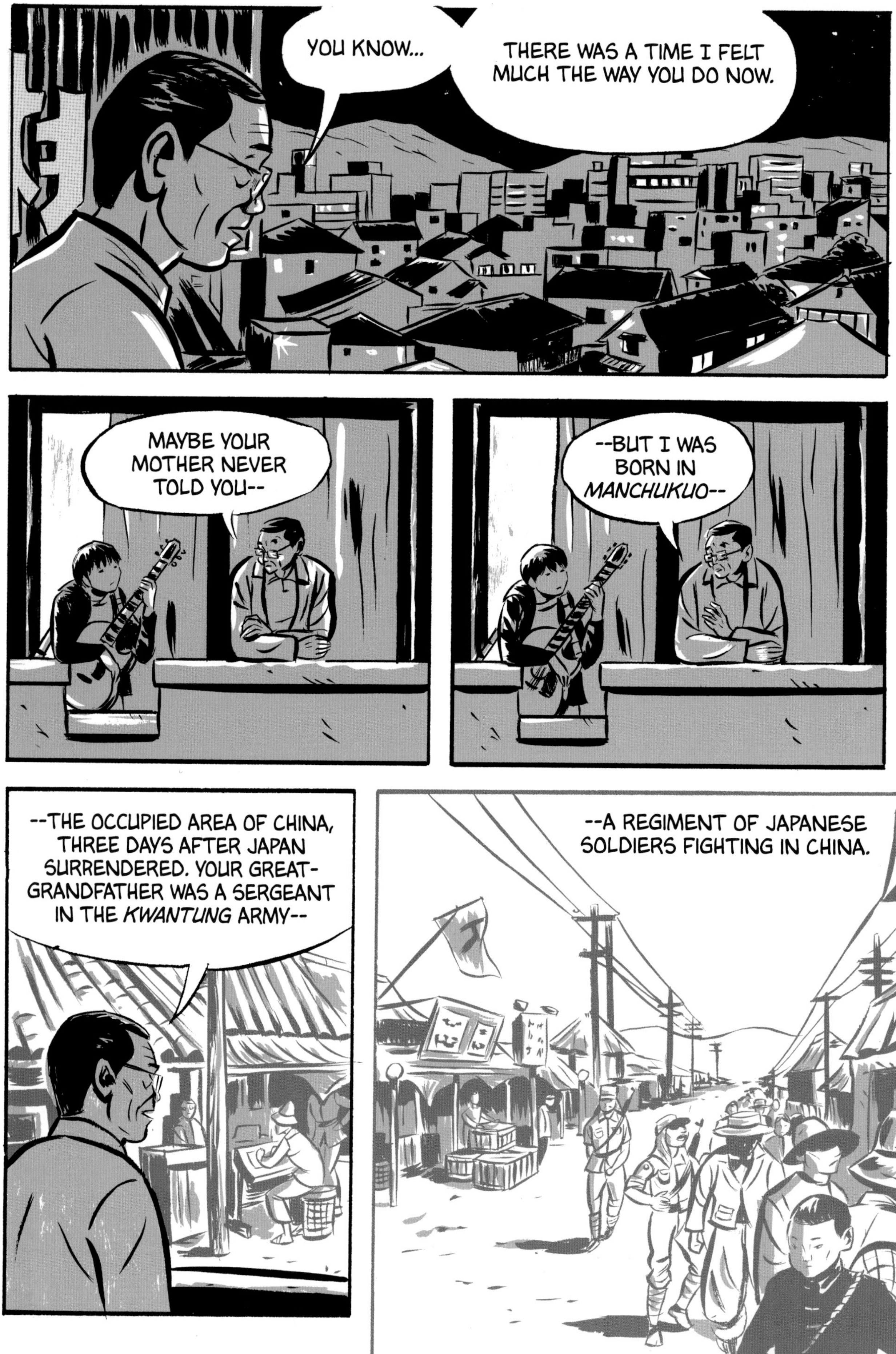
YOU KNOW...
THERE WAS A TIME I FELT MUCH THE WAY YOU DO NOW.
MAYBE YOUR MOTHER NEVER TOLD YOU--
--BUT I WAS BORN IN *MANCHUKUO*--
--THE OCCUPIED AREA OF CHINA, THREE DAYS AFTER JAPAN SURRENDERED. YOUR GREAT-GRANDFATHER WAS A SERGEANT IN THE *KWANTUNG* ARMY--
--A REGIMENT OF JAPANESE SOLDIERS FIGHTING IN CHINA.

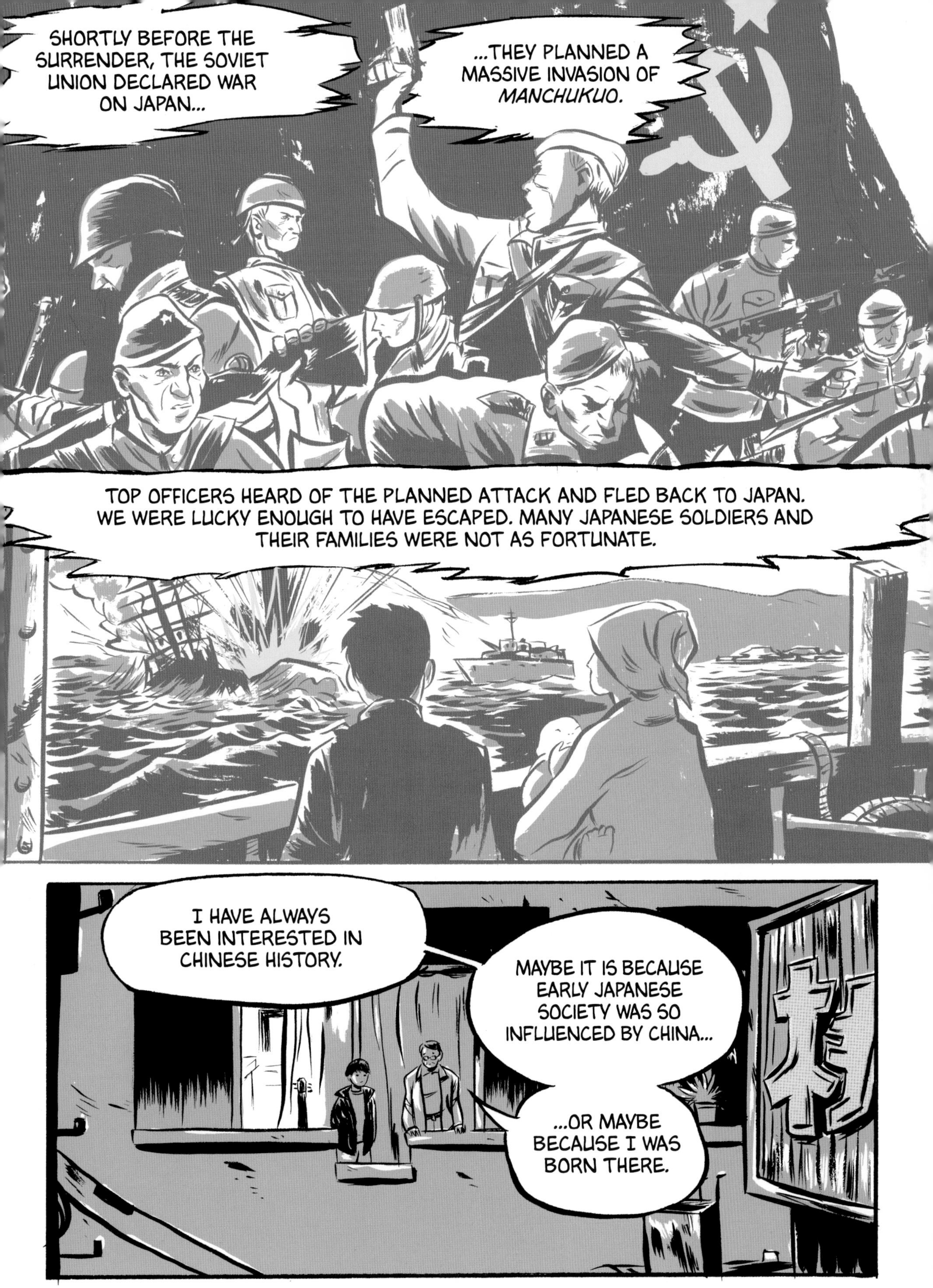

SHORTLY BEFORE THE SURRENDER, THE SOVIET UNION DECLARED WAR ON JAPAN...
...THEY PLANNED A MASSIVE INVASION OF *MANCHUKUO.*
TOP OFFICERS HEARD OF THE PLANNED ATTACK AND FLED BACK TO JAPAN. WE WERE LUCKY ENOUGH TO HAVE ESCAPED. MANY JAPANESE SOLDIERS AND THEIR FAMILIES WERE NOT AS FORTUNATE.
I HAVE ALWAYS BEEN INTERESTED IN CHINESE HISTORY.
MAYBE IT IS BECAUSE EARLY JAPANESE SOCIETY WAS SO INFLUENCED BY CHINA...
...OR MAYBE BECAUSE I WAS BORN THERE.

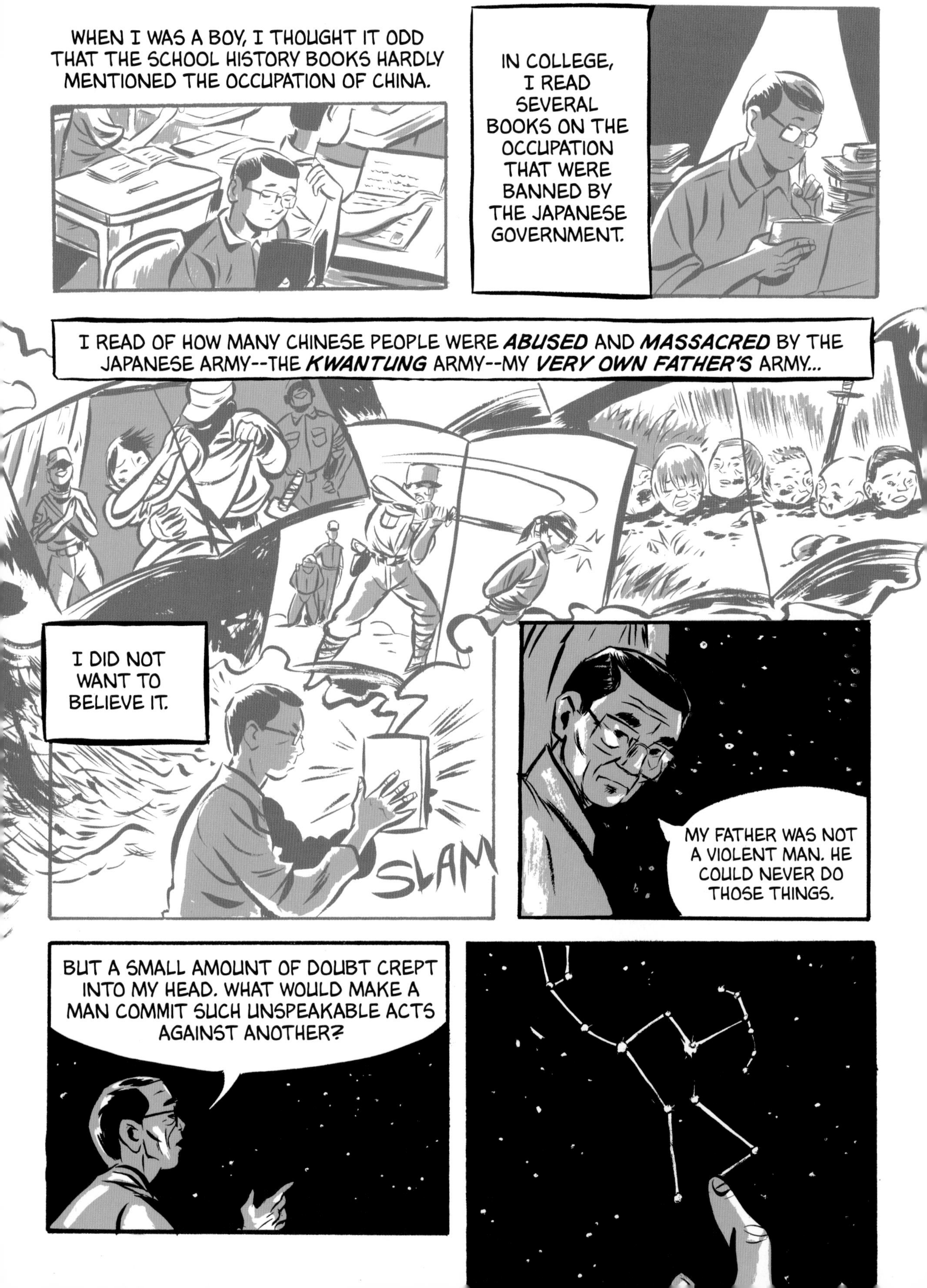
WHEN I WAS A BOY, I THOUGHT IT ODD THAT THE SCHOOL HISTORY BOOKS HARDLY MENTIONED THE OCCUPATION OF CHINA.
IN COLLEGE, I READ SEVERAL BOOKS ON THE OCCUPATION THAT WERE BANNED BY THE JAPANESE GOVERNMENT.
I READ OF HOW MANY CHINESE PEOPLE WERE ***ABUSED*** AND ***MASSACRED*** BY THE JAPANESE ARMY--THE ***KWANTUNG*** ARMY--MY ***VERY OWN FATHER'S*** ARMY...
I DID NOT WANT TO BELIEVE IT.
SLAM
MY FATHER WAS NOT A VIOLENT MAN. HE COULD NEVER DO THOSE THINGS.
BUT A SMALL AMOUNT OF DOUBT CREPT INTO MY HEAD. WHAT WOULD MAKE A MAN COMMIT SUCH UNSPEAKABLE ACTS AGAINST ANOTHER?

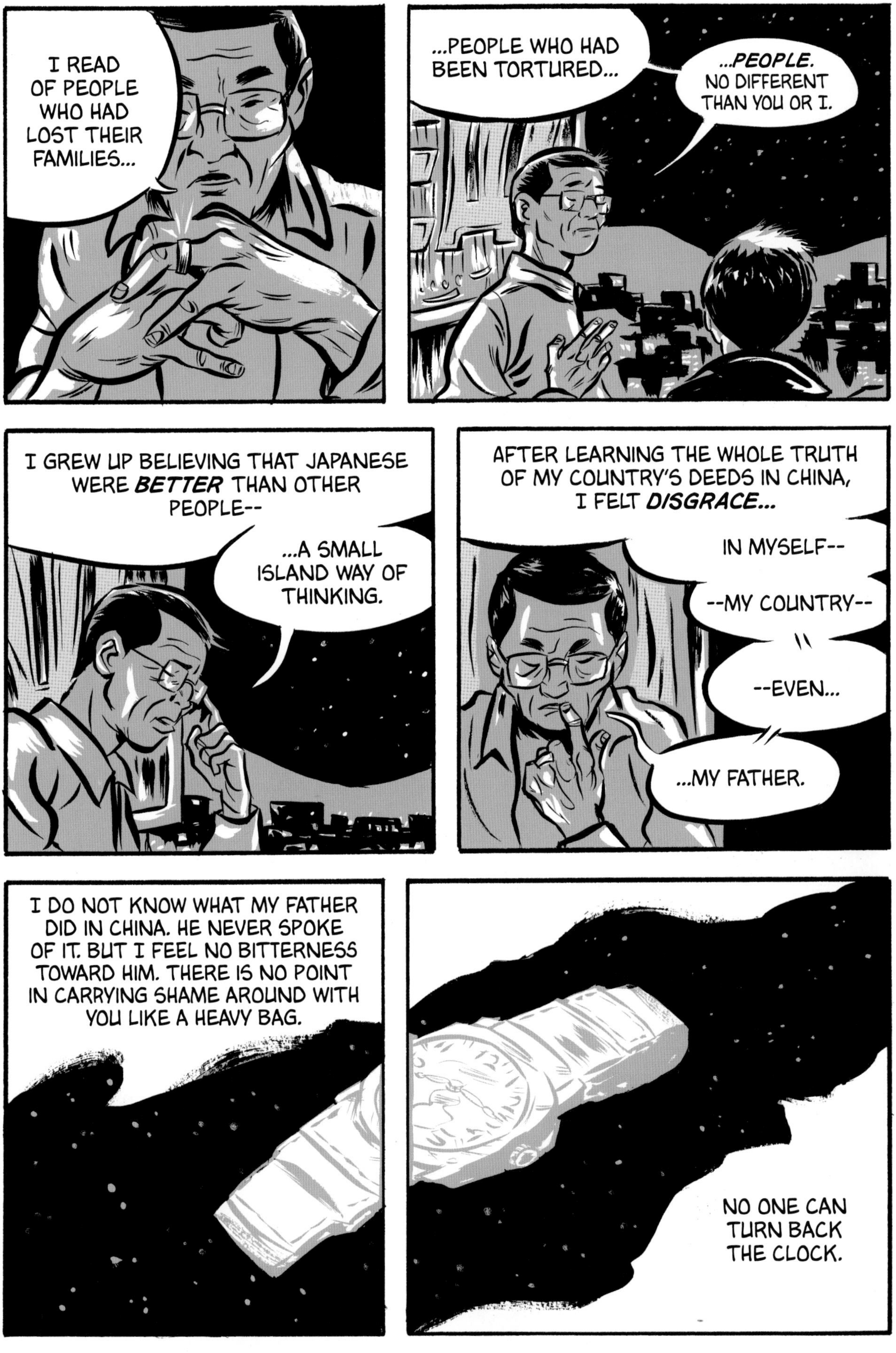
I READ OF PEOPLE WHO HAD LOST THEIR FAMILIES...
...PEOPLE WHO HAD BEEN TORTURED...
...PEOPLE. NO DIFFERENT THAN YOU OR I.
I GREW UP BELIEVING THAT JAPANESE WERE BETTER THAN OTHER PEOPLE--
...A SMALL ISLAND WAY OF THINKING.
AFTER LEARNING THE WHOLE TRUTH OF MY COUNTRY'S DEEDS IN CHINA, I FELT DISGRACE...
IN MYSELF--
--MY COUNTRY--
--EVEN...
...MY FATHER.
I DO NOT KNOW WHAT MY FATHER DID IN CHINA. HE NEVER SPOKE OF IT. BUT I FEEL NO BITTERNESS TOWARD HIM. THERE IS NO POINT IN CARRYING SHAME AROUND WITH YOU LIKE A HEAVY BAG.
NO ONE CAN TURN BACK THE CLOCK.

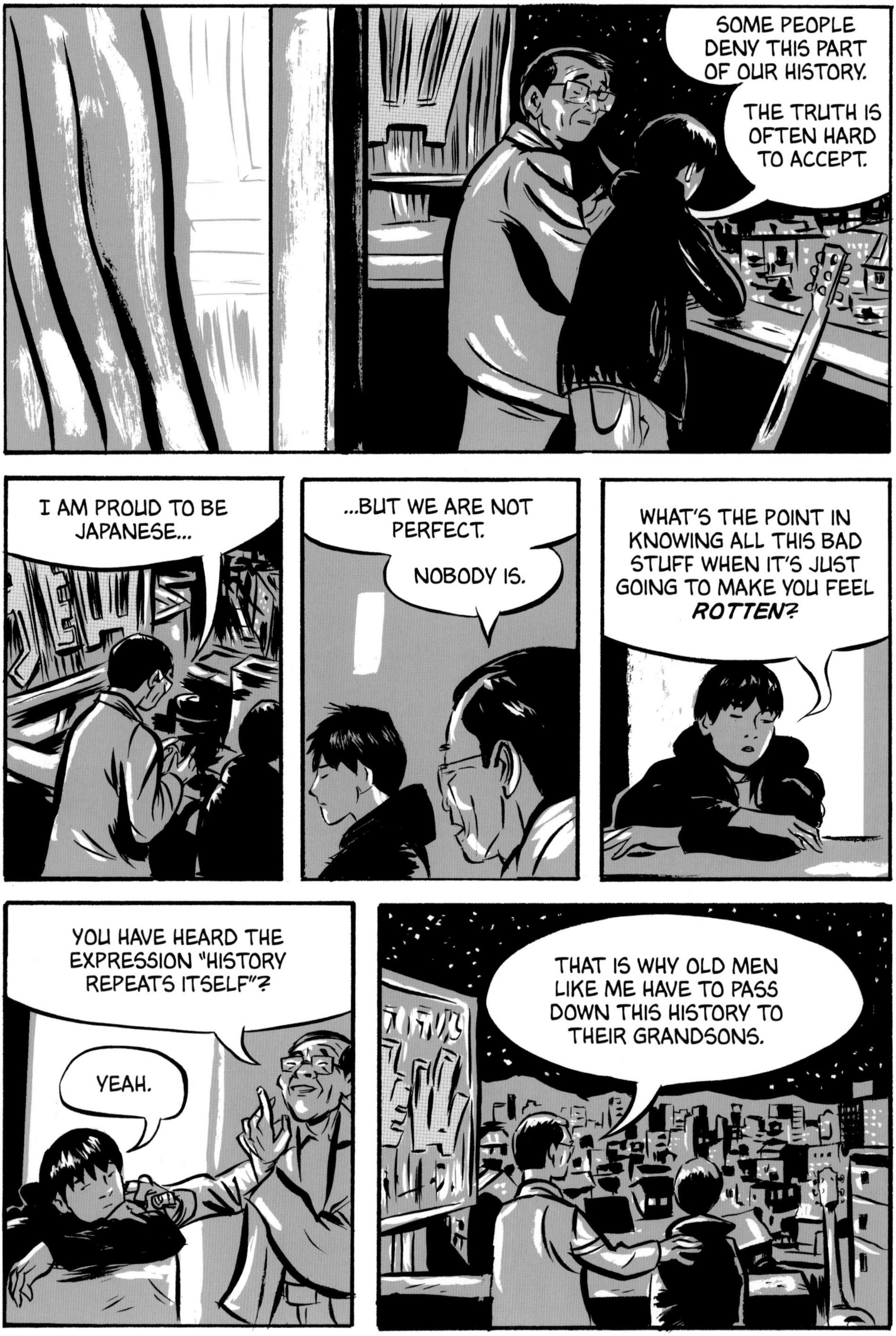

SOME PEOPLE DENY THIS PART OF OUR HISTORY.
THE TRUTH IS OFTEN HARD TO ACCEPT.
I AM PROUD TO BE JAPANESE...
...BUT WE ARE NOT PERFECT.
NOBODY IS.
WHAT'S THE POINT IN KNOWING ALL THIS BAD STUFF WHEN IT'S JUST GOING TO MAKE YOU FEEL ROTTEN?
YOU HAVE HEARD THE EXPRESSION "HISTORY REPEATS ITSELF"?
YEAH.
THAT IS WHY OLD MEN LIKE ME HAVE TO PASS DOWN THIS HISTORY TO THEIR GRANDSONS.

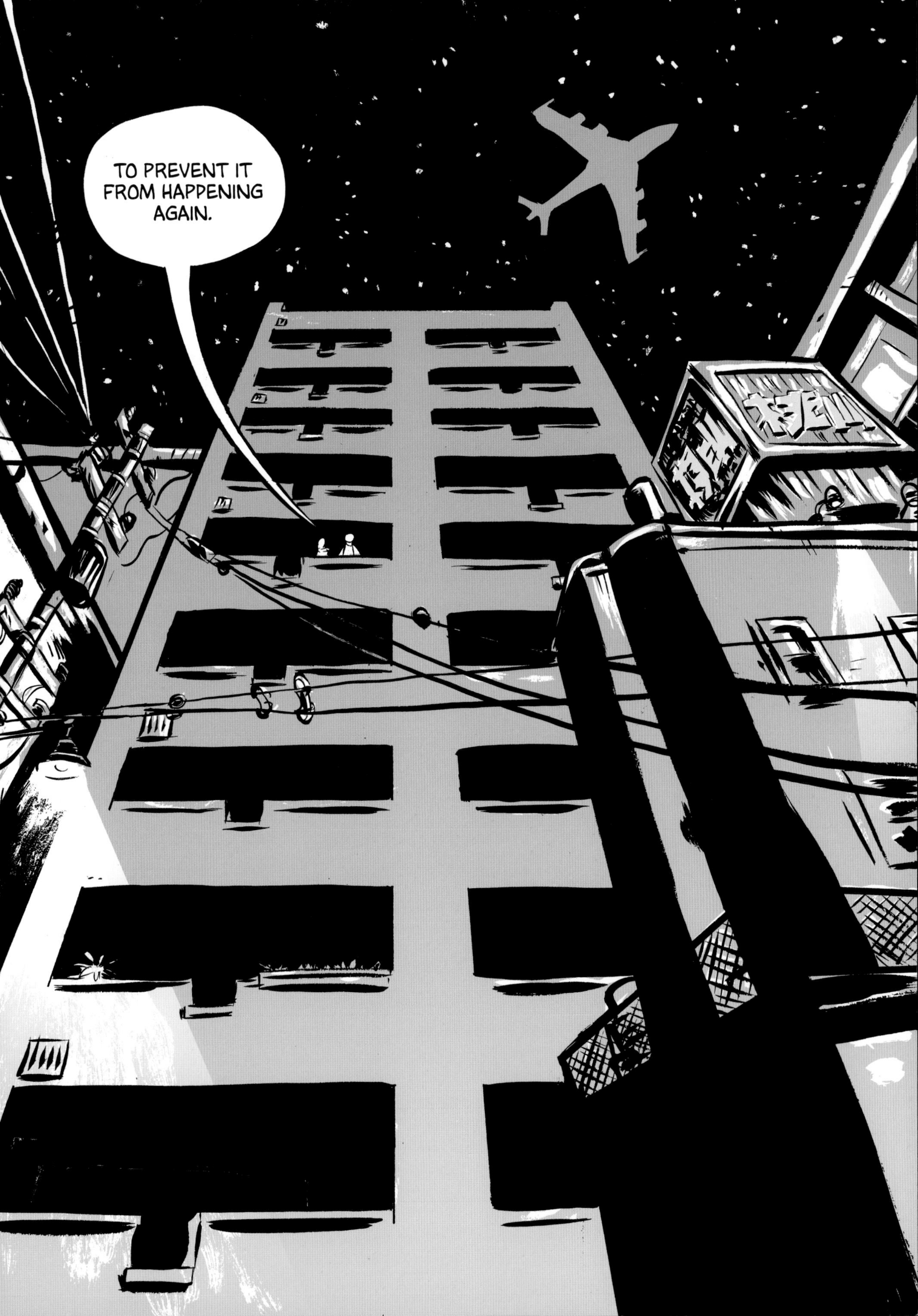
TO PREVENT IT FROM HAPPENING AGAIN.

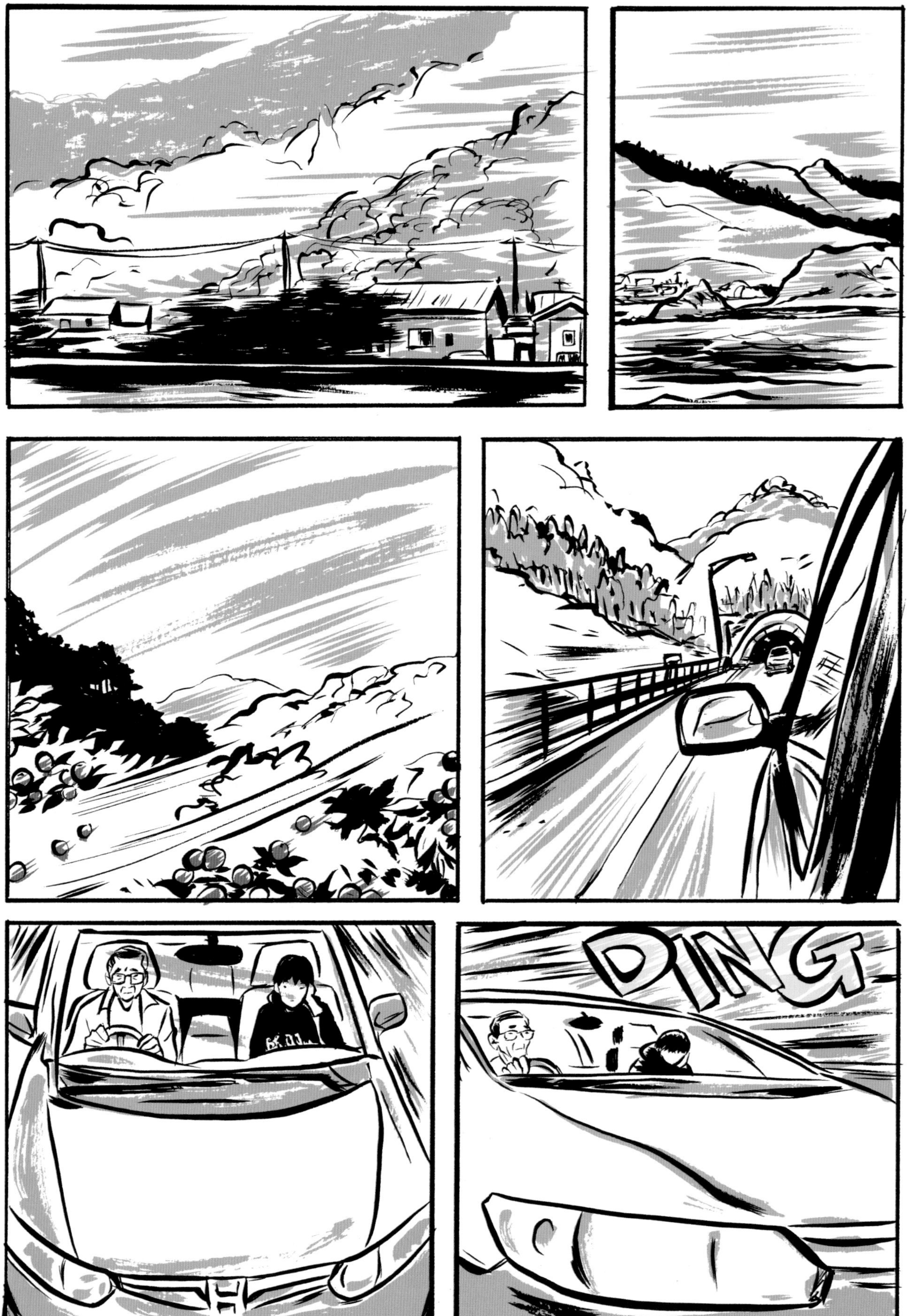
DING

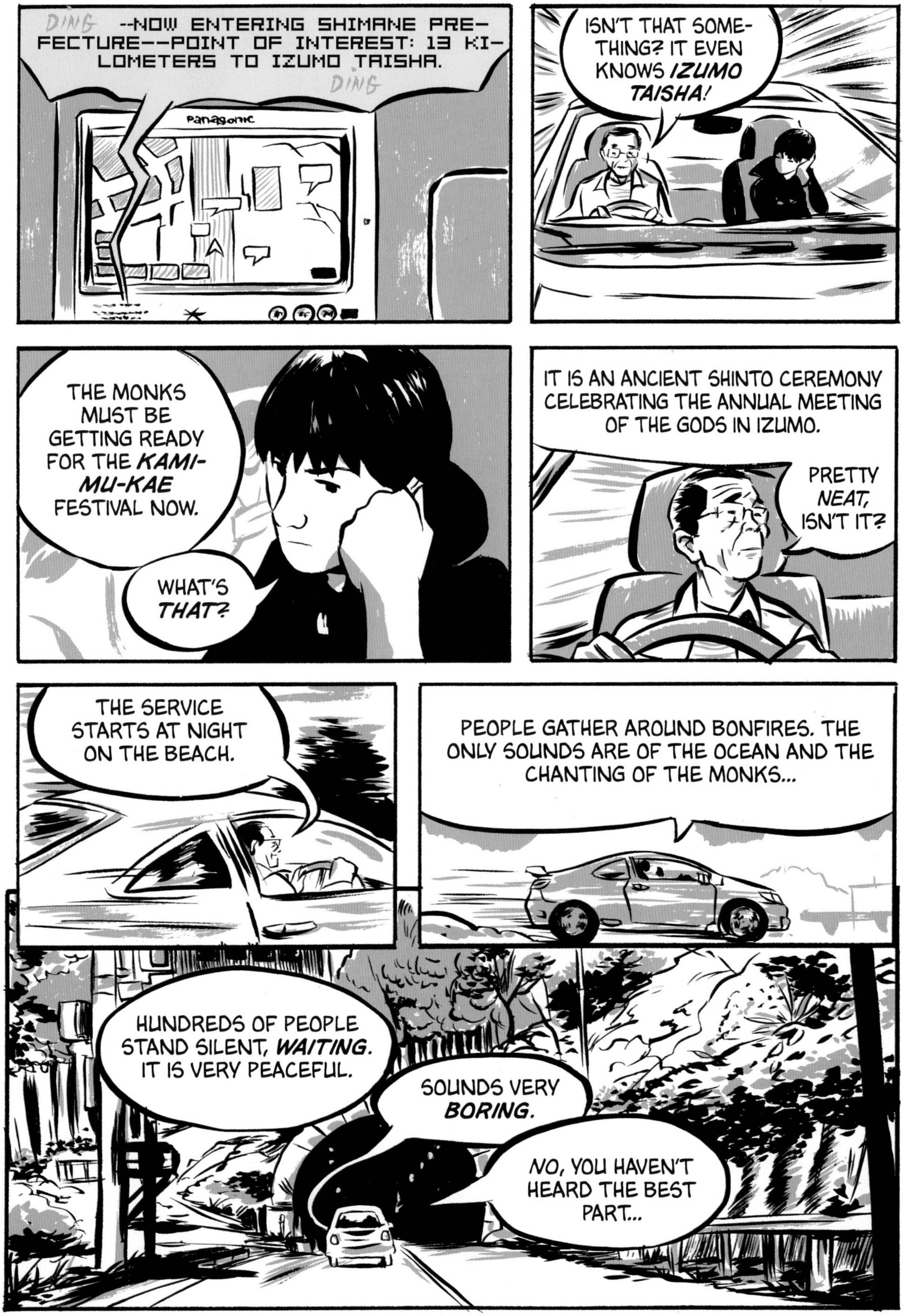
DING --NOW ENTERING SHIMANE PREFECTURE--POINT OF INTEREST: 13 KILOMETERS TO IZUMO TAISHA. DING
Panasonic
ISN'T THAT SOMETHING? IT EVEN KNOWS *IZUMO TAISHA!*
THE MONKS MUST BE GETTING READY FOR THE *KAMI-MU-KAE* FESTIVAL NOW.
WHAT'S *THAT?*
IT IS AN ANCIENT SHINTO CEREMONY CELEBRATING THE ANNUAL MEETING OF THE GODS IN IZUMO.
PRETTY *NEAT,* ISN'T IT?
THE SERVICE STARTS AT NIGHT ON THE BEACH.
PEOPLE GATHER AROUND BONFIRES. THE ONLY SOUNDS ARE OF THE OCEAN AND THE CHANTING OF THE MONKS...
HUNDREDS OF PEOPLE STAND SILENT, *WAITING.* IT IS VERY PEACEFUL.
SOUNDS VERY *BORING.*
NO, YOU HAVEN'T HEARD THE BEST PART...

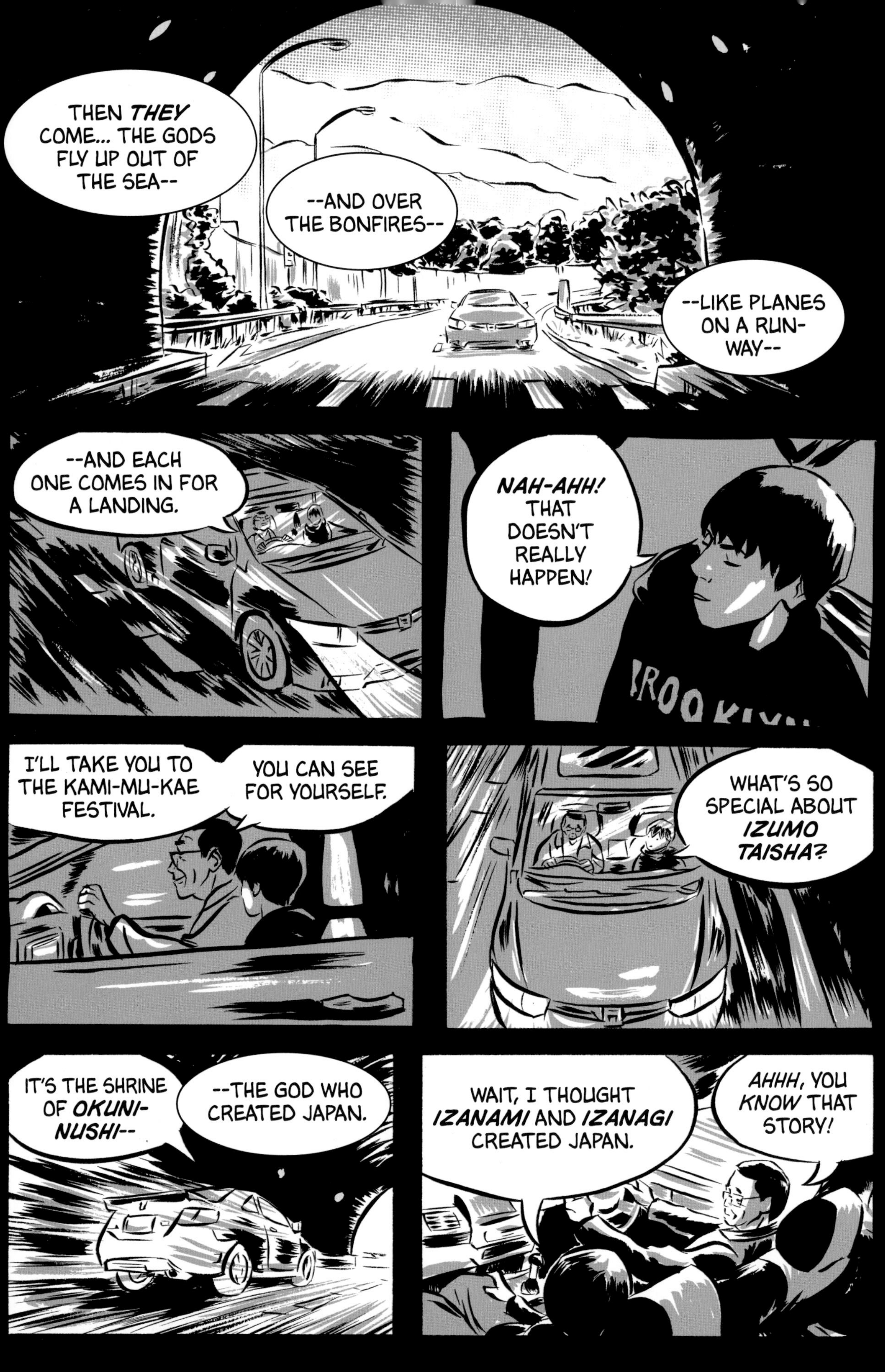
THEN *THEY* COME... THE GODS FLY UP OUT OF THE SEA--
--AND OVER THE BONFIRES--
--LIKE PLANES ON A RUN-WAY--
--AND EACH ONE COMES IN FOR A LANDING.
NAH-AHH! THAT DOESN'T REALLY HAPPEN!
BROOKLYN
I'LL TAKE YOU TO THE KAMI-MU-KAE FESTIVAL.
YOU CAN SEE FOR YOURSELF.
WHAT'S SO SPECIAL ABOUT *IZUMO TAISHA?*
IT'S THE SHRINE OF *OKUNI-NUSHI*--
--THE GOD WHO CREATED JAPAN.
WAIT, I THOUGHT *IZANAMI* AND *IZANAGI* CREATED JAPAN.
AHHH, YOU *KNOW* THAT STORY!

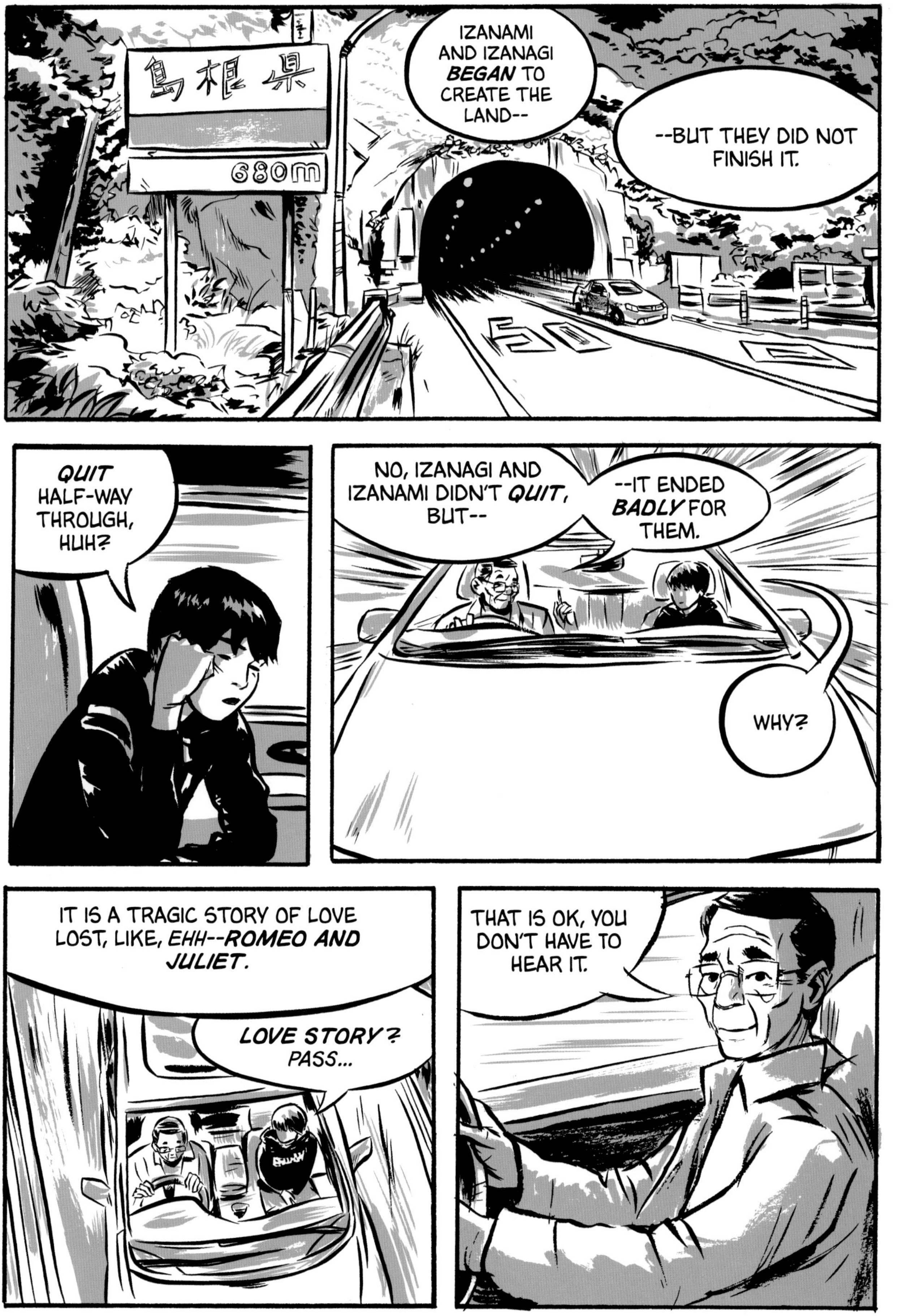

島根県
680m
IZANAMI AND IZANAGI *BEGAN* TO CREATE THE LAND--
--BUT THEY DID NOT FINISH IT.
QUIT HALF-WAY THROUGH, HUH?
NO, IZANAGI AND IZANAMI DIDN'T *QUIT*, BUT--
--IT ENDED *BADLY* FOR THEM.
WHY?
IT IS A TRAGIC STORY OF LOVE LOST, LIKE, *EHH*--***ROMEO AND JULIET***.
LOVE STORY? PASS...
THAT IS OK, YOU DON'T HAVE TO HEAR IT.

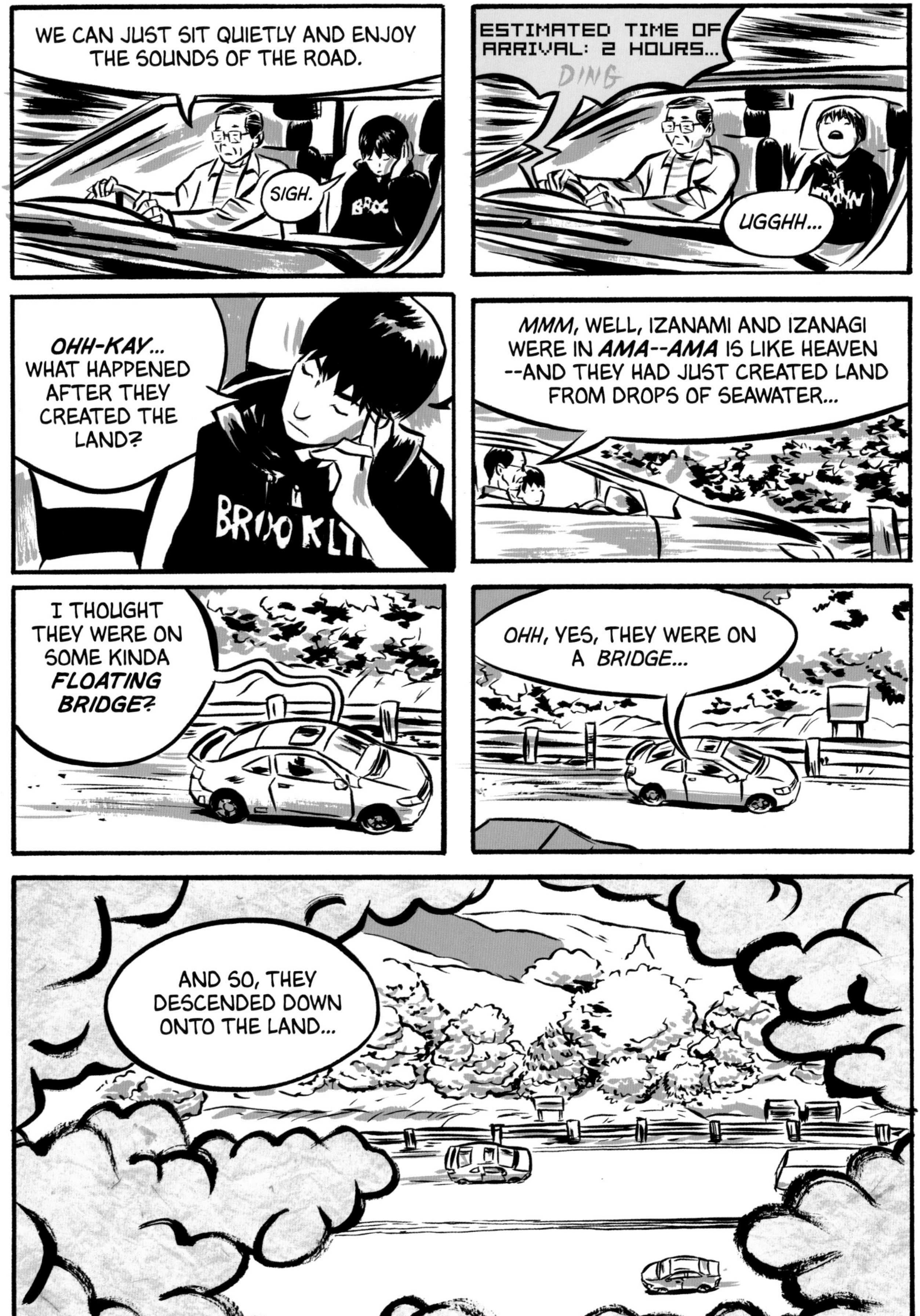
WE CAN JUST SIT QUIETLY AND ENJOY THE SOUNDS OF THE ROAD.
SIGH.
ESTIMATED TIME OF ARRIVAL: 2 HOURS...
DING
UGGHH...
OHH-KAY... WHAT HAPPENED AFTER THEY CREATED THE LAND?
MMM, WELL, IZANAMI AND IZANAGI WERE IN ***AMA--AMA*** IS LIKE HEAVEN --AND THEY HAD JUST CREATED LAND FROM DROPS OF SEAWATER...
I THOUGHT THEY WERE ON SOME KINDA ***FLOATING BRIDGE?***
OHH, YES, THEY WERE ON A *BRIDGE*...
AND SO, THEY DESCENDED DOWN ONTO THE LAND...

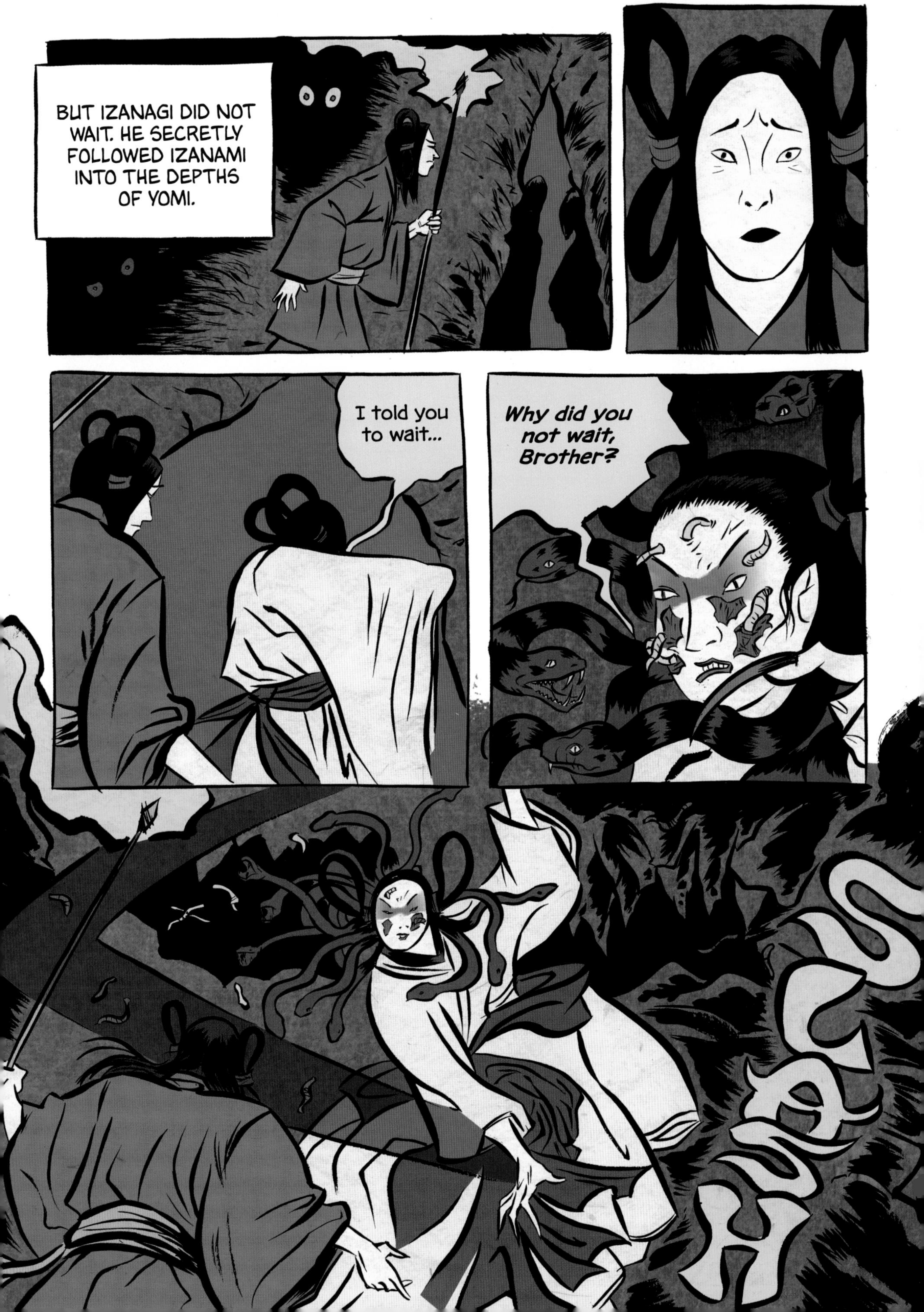

BUT IZANAGI DID NOT WAIT. HE SECRETLY FOLLOWED IZANAMI INTO THE DEPTHS OF YOMI.
I told you to wait...
Why did you not wait, Brother?

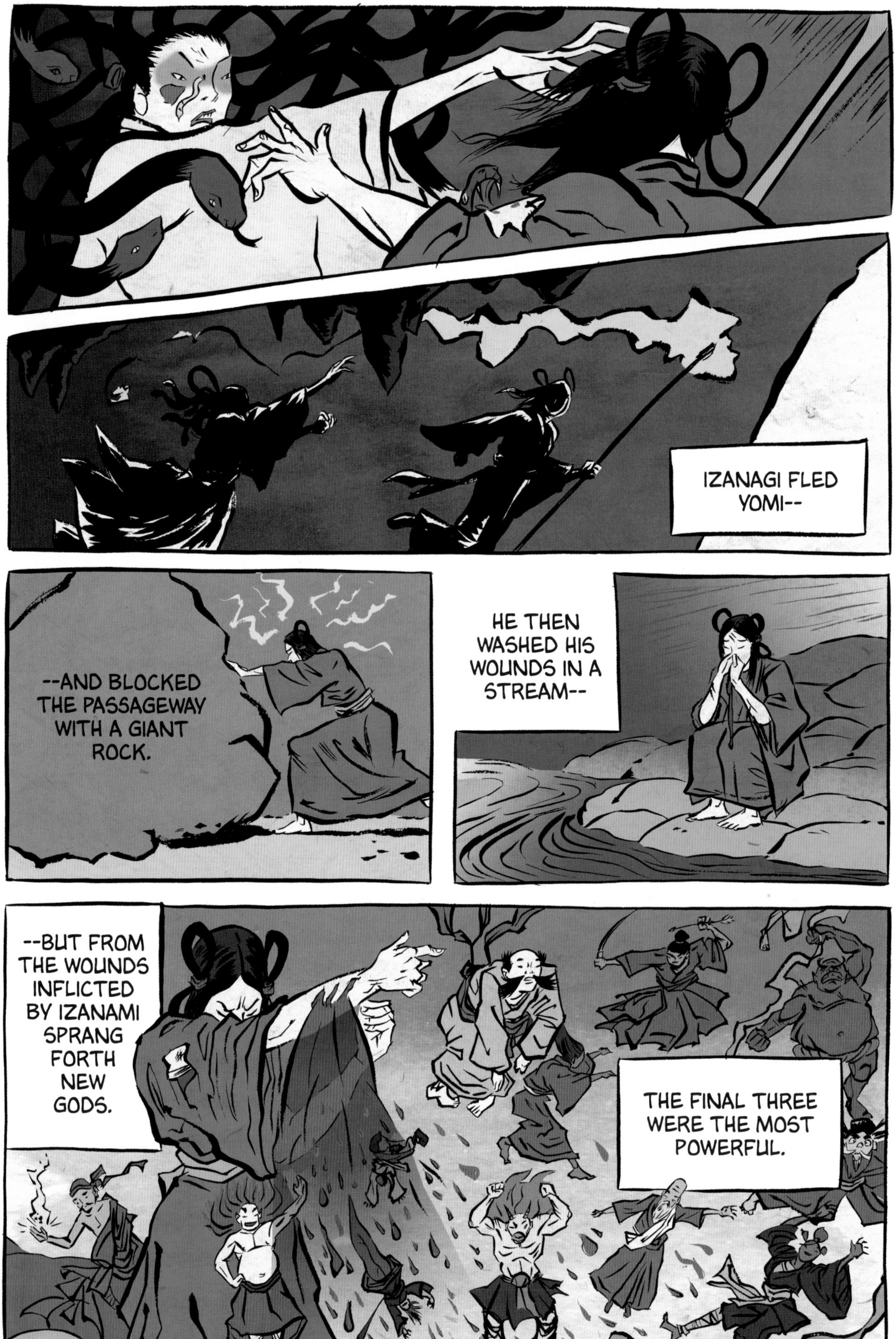
IZANAGI FLED YOMI--
--AND BLOCKED THE PASSAGEWAY WITH A GIANT ROCK.
HE THEN WASHED HIS WOUNDS IN A STREAM--
--BUT FROM THE WOUNDS INFLICTED BY IZANAMI SPRANG FORTH NEW GODS.
THE FINAL THREE WERE THE MOST POWERFUL.

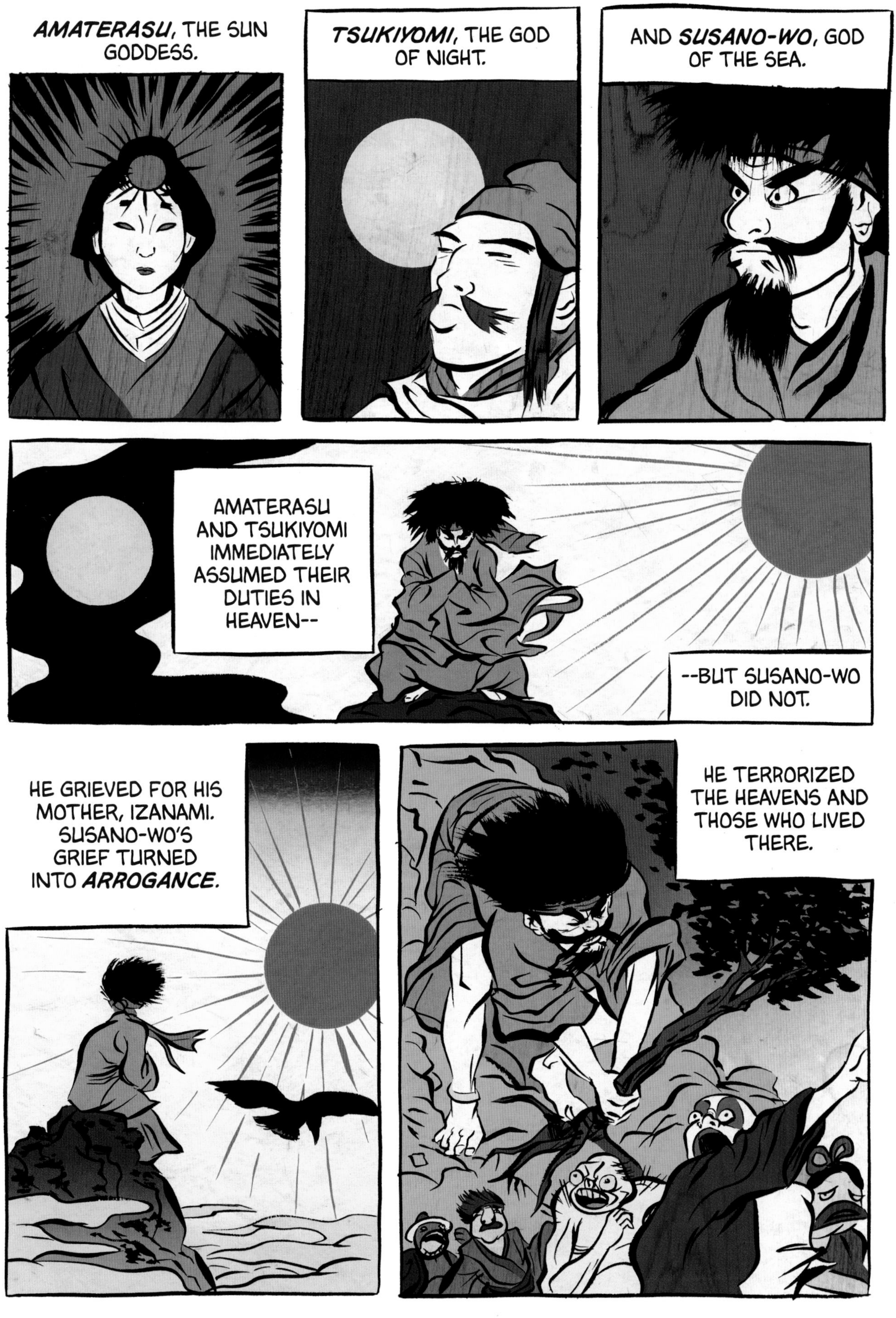

AMATERASU, THE SUN GODDESS.
TSUKIYOMI, THE GOD OF NIGHT.
AND SUSANO-WO, GOD OF THE SEA.
AMATERASU AND TSUKIYOMI IMMEDIATELY ASSUMED THEIR DUTIES IN HEAVEN--
--BUT SUSANO-WO DID NOT.
HE GRIEVED FOR HIS MOTHER, IZANAMI. SUSANO-WO'S GRIEF TURNED INTO ARROGANCE.
HE TERRORIZED THE HEAVENS AND THOSE WHO LIVED THERE.

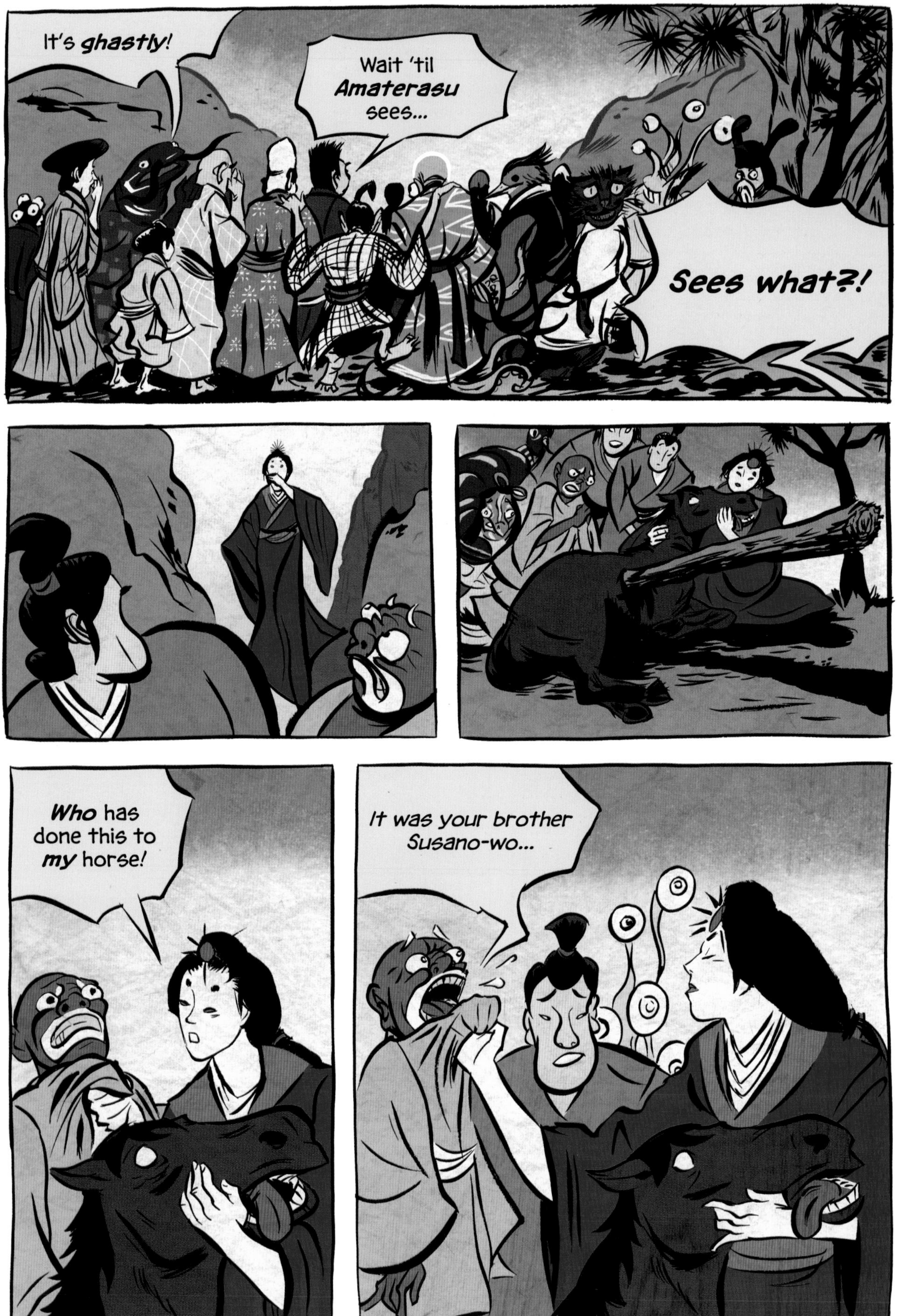
It's *ghastly!*
Wait 'til *Amaterasu* sees...
Sees what?!
Who has done this to *my* horse!
It was your brother Susano-wo...

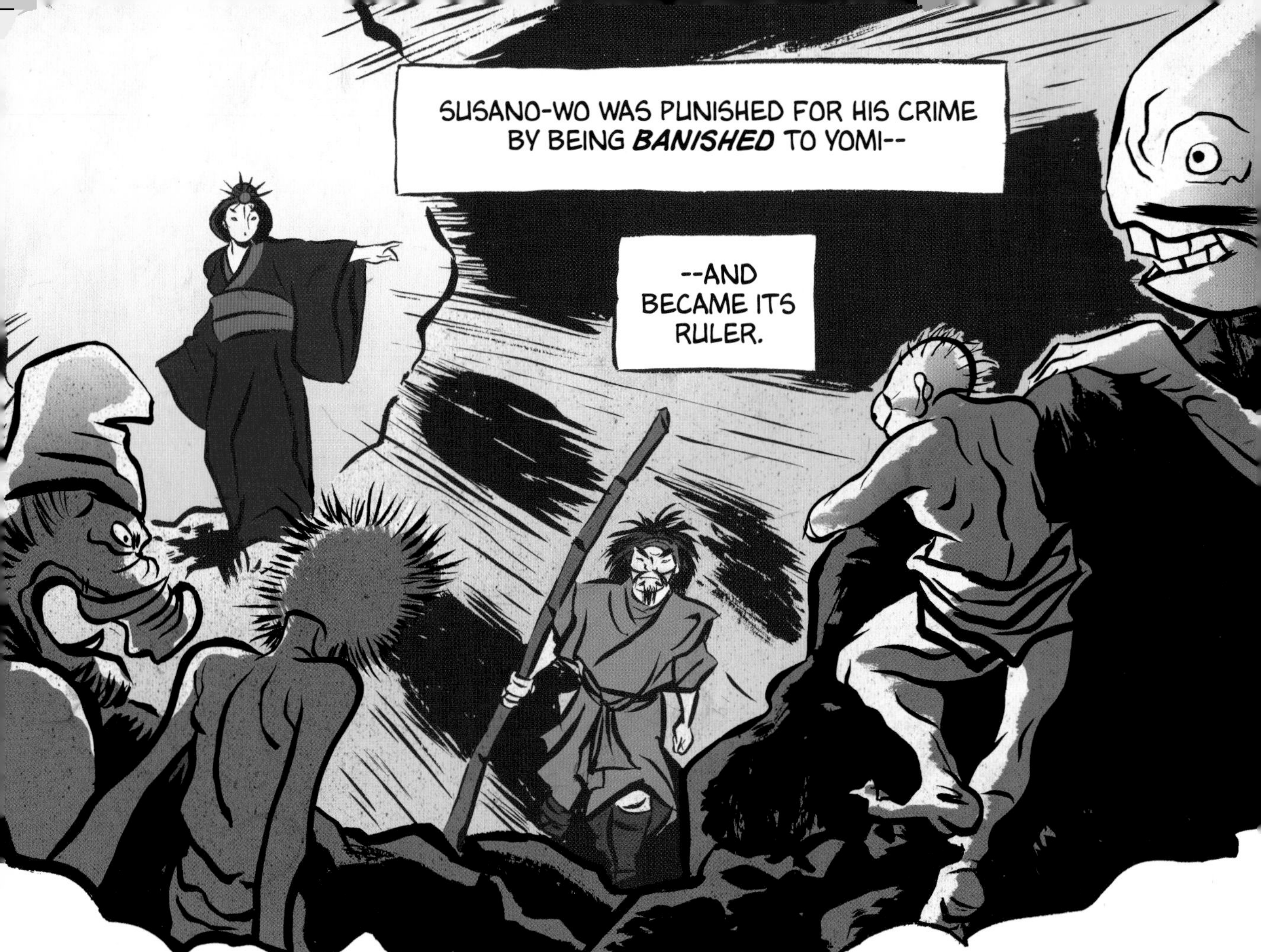
SUSANO-WO WAS PUNISHED FOR HIS CRIME BY BEING BANISHED TO YOMI--
--AND BECAME ITS RULER.

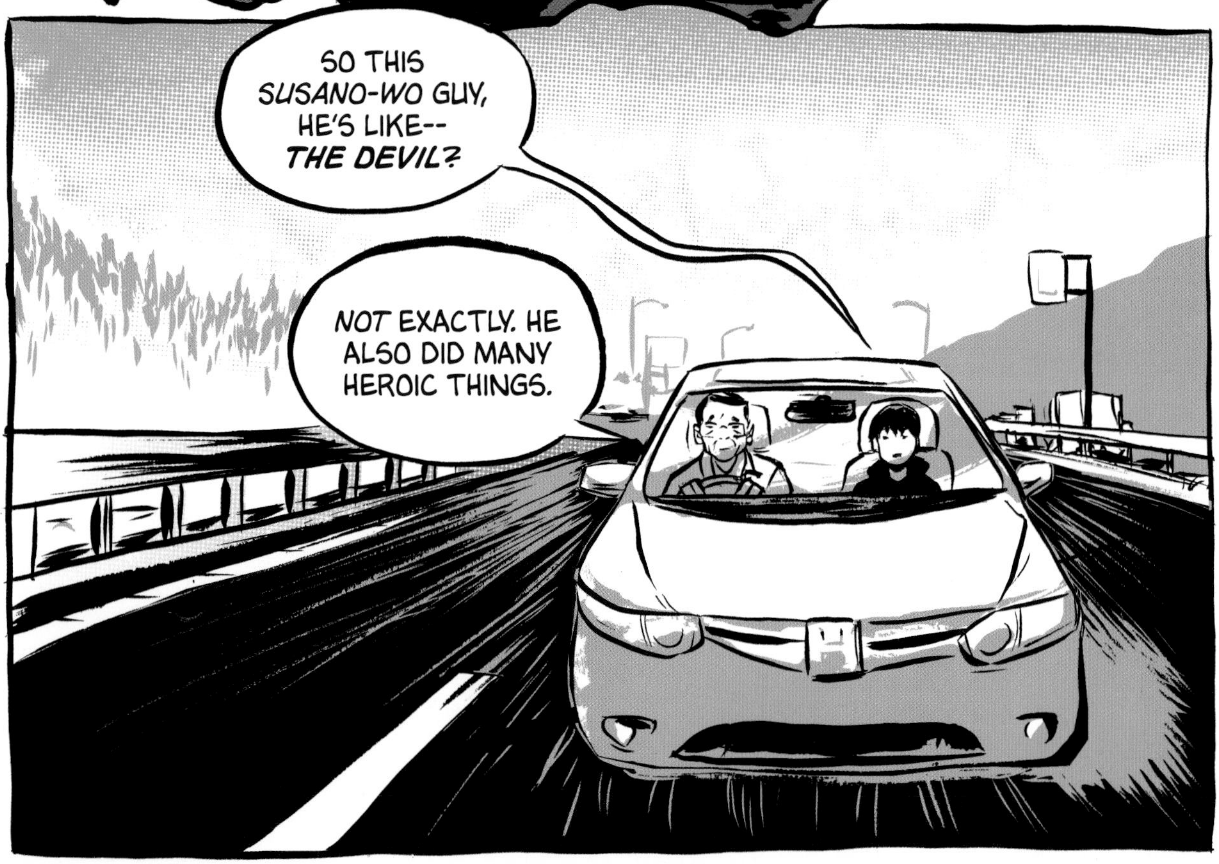
SO THIS SUSANO-WO GUY, HE'S LIKE-- THE DEVIL?
NOT EXACTLY. HE ALSO DID MANY HEROIC THINGS.

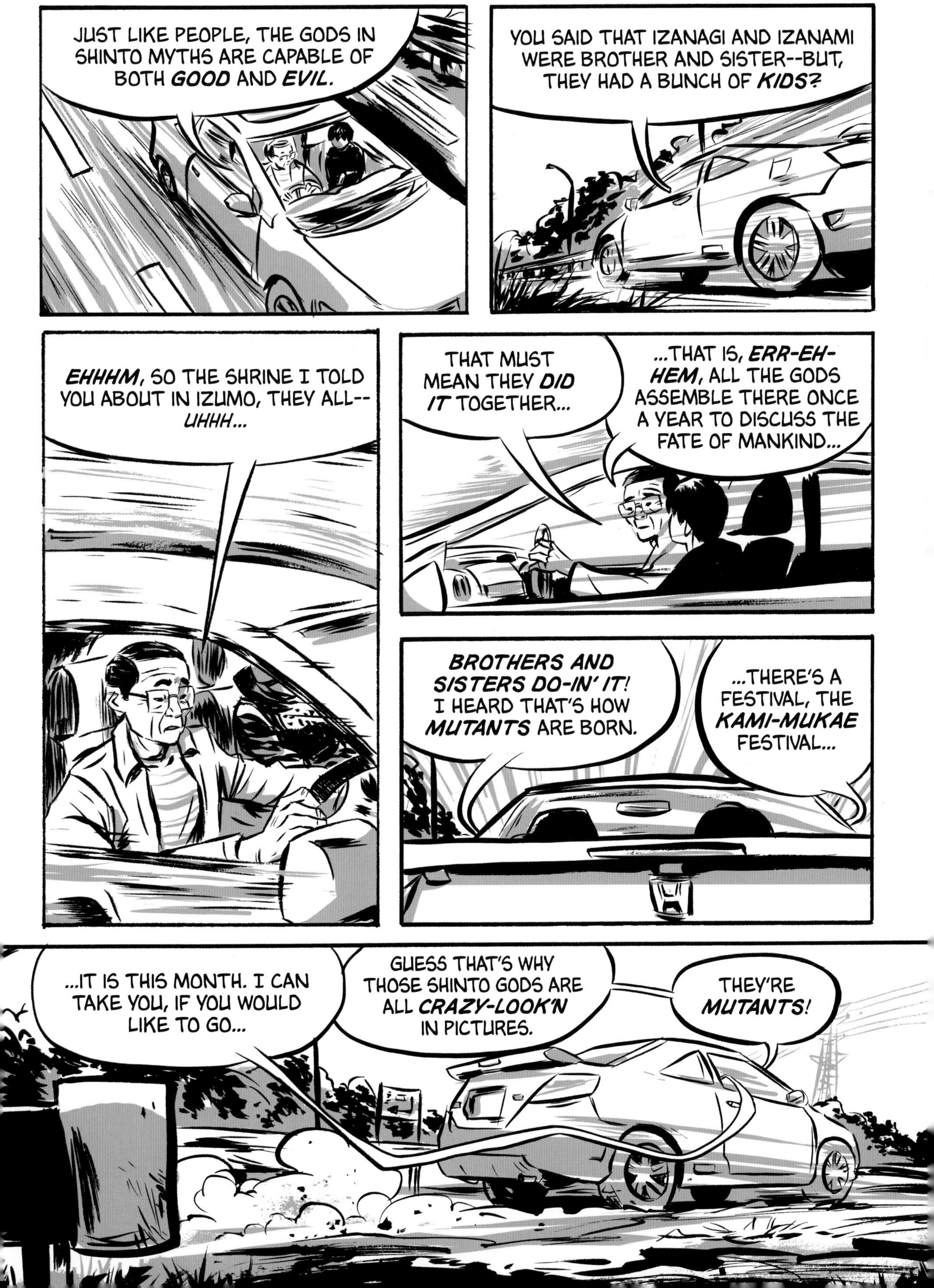

JUST LIKE PEOPLE, THE GODS IN SHINTO MYTHS ARE CAPABLE OF BOTH ***GOOD*** AND ***EVIL.***
YOU SAID THAT IZANAGI AND IZANAMI WERE BROTHER AND SISTER--BUT, THEY HAD A BUNCH OF ***KIDS?***
EHHHM, SO THE SHRINE I TOLD YOU ABOUT IN IZUMO, THEY ALL-- ***UHHH...***
THAT MUST MEAN THEY ***DID IT*** TOGETHER...
...THAT IS, ***ERR-EH-HEM,*** ALL THE GODS ASSEMBLE THERE ONCE A YEAR TO DISCUSS THE FATE OF MANKIND...
BROTHERS AND SISTERS DO-IN' IT! I HEARD THAT'S HOW ***MUTANTS*** ARE BORN.
...THERE'S A FESTIVAL, THE ***KAMI-MUKAE*** FESTIVAL...
...IT IS THIS MONTH. I CAN TAKE YOU, IF YOU WOULD LIKE TO GO...
GUESS THAT'S WHY THOSE SHINTO GODS ARE ALL ***CRAZY-LOOK'N*** IN PICTURES.
THEY'RE ***MUTANTS!***

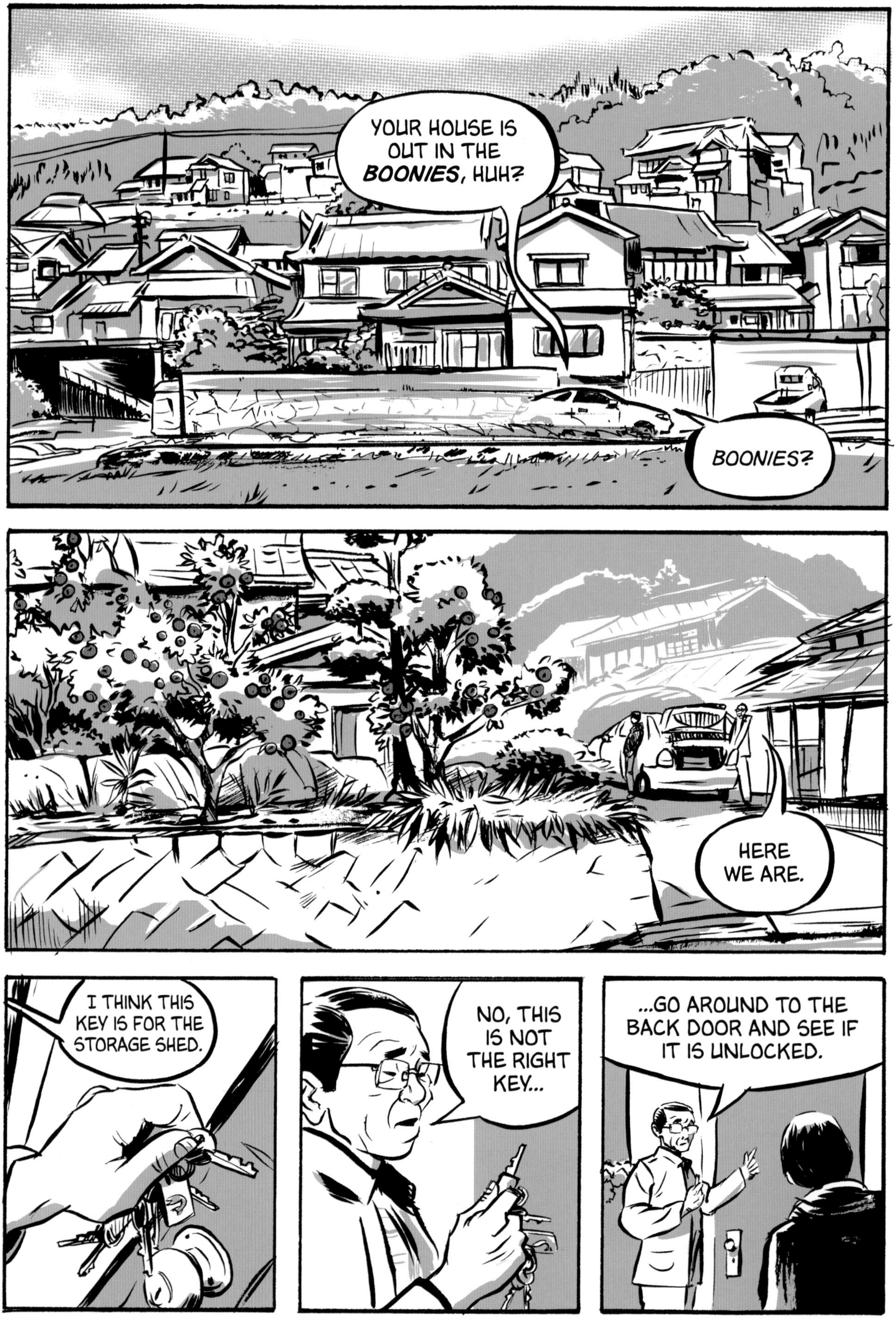

YOUR HOUSE IS OUT IN THE *BOONIES*, HUH?
BOONIES?
HERE WE ARE.
I THINK THIS KEY IS FOR THE STORAGE SHED.
NO, THIS IS NOT THE RIGHT KEY...
...GO AROUND TO THE BACK DOOR AND SEE IF IT IS UNLOCKED.

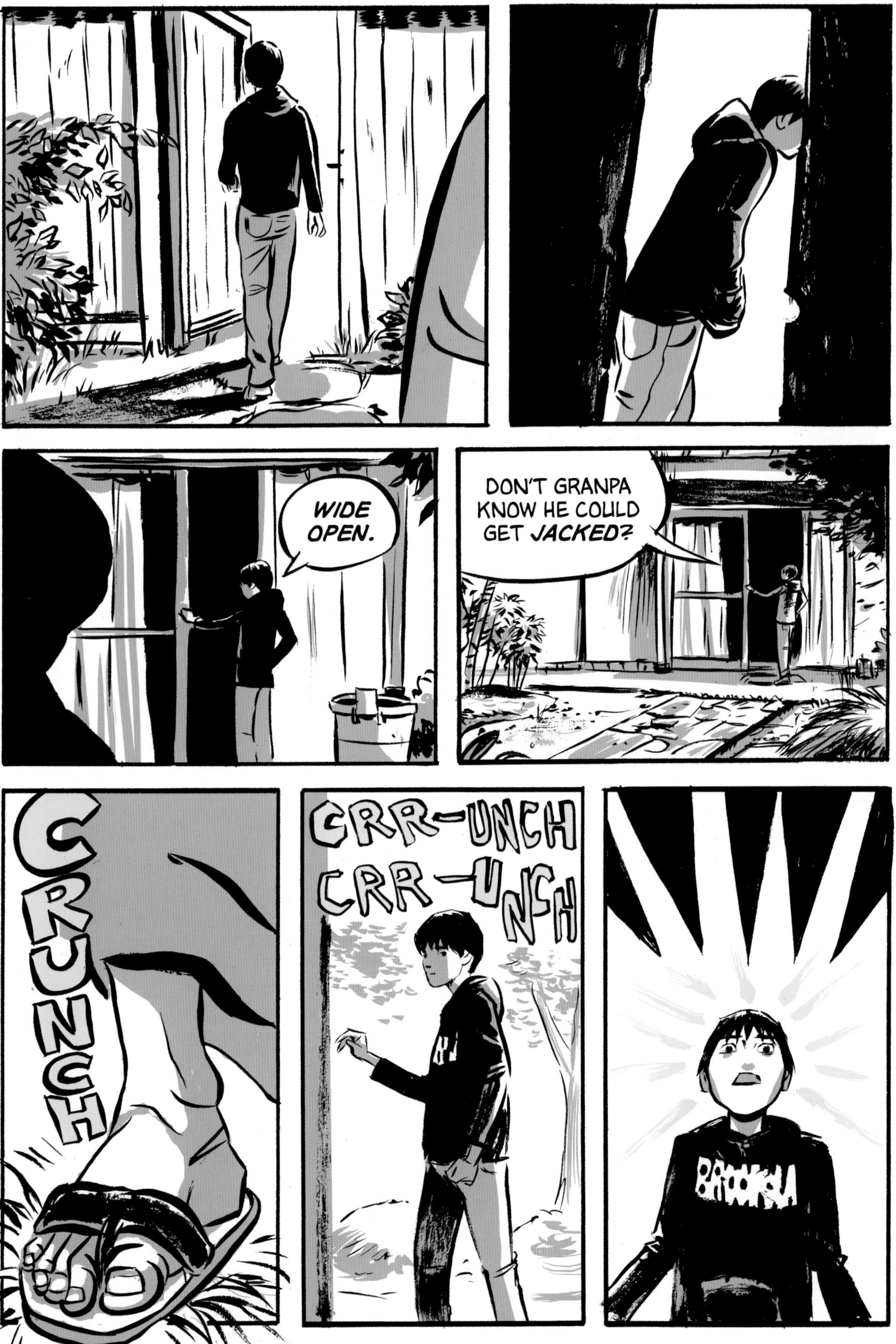
WIDE OPEN.
DON'T GRANPA KNOW HE COULD GET JACKED?
CRUNCH
CRR-UNCH CRR-UNCH

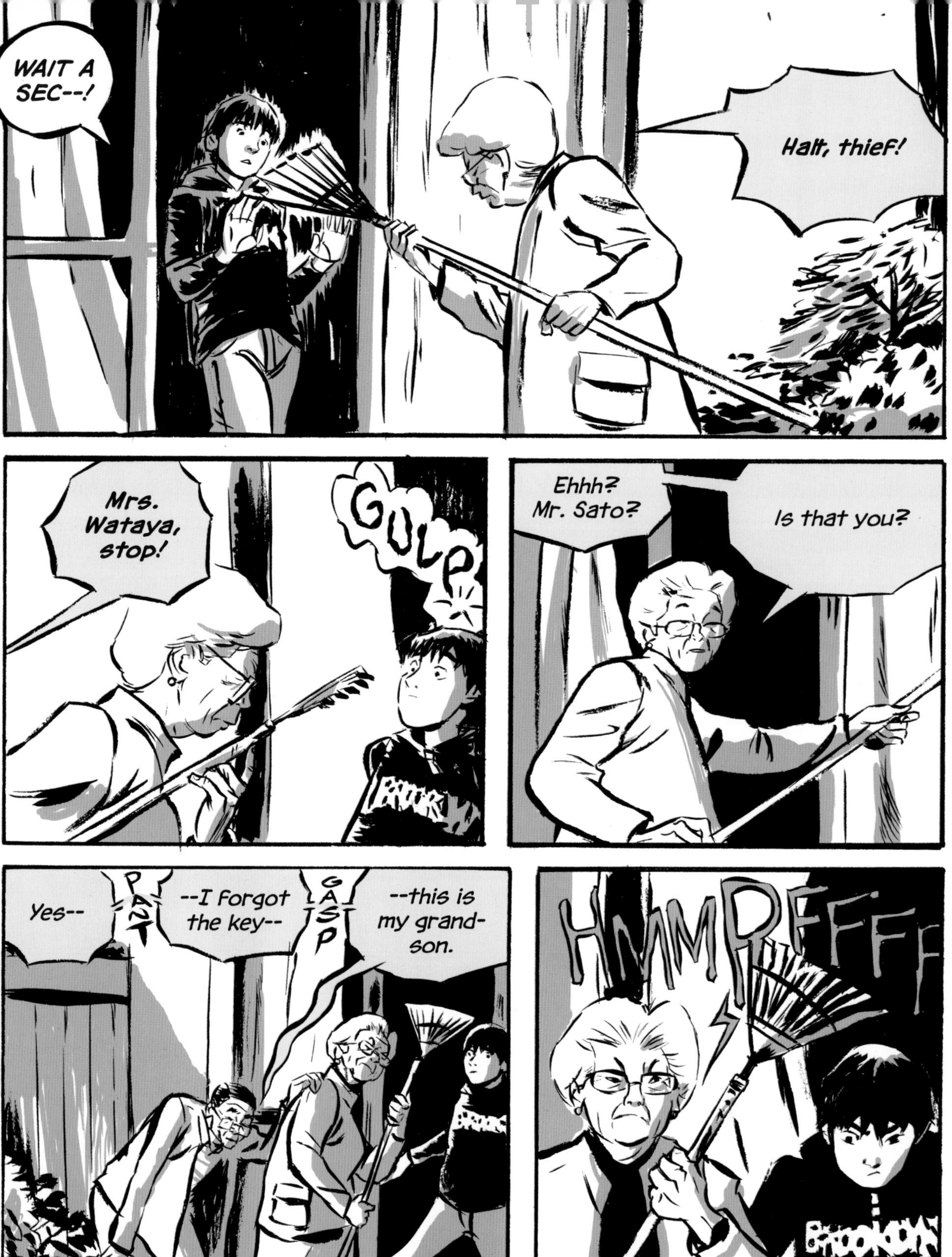
WAIT A SEC--!
Halt, thief!
Mrs. Wataya, stop!
GULP
Ehhh? Mr. Sato?
Is that you?
Yes--
PANT
--I forgot the key--
GASP
--this is my grand-son.
HMMPFFFF

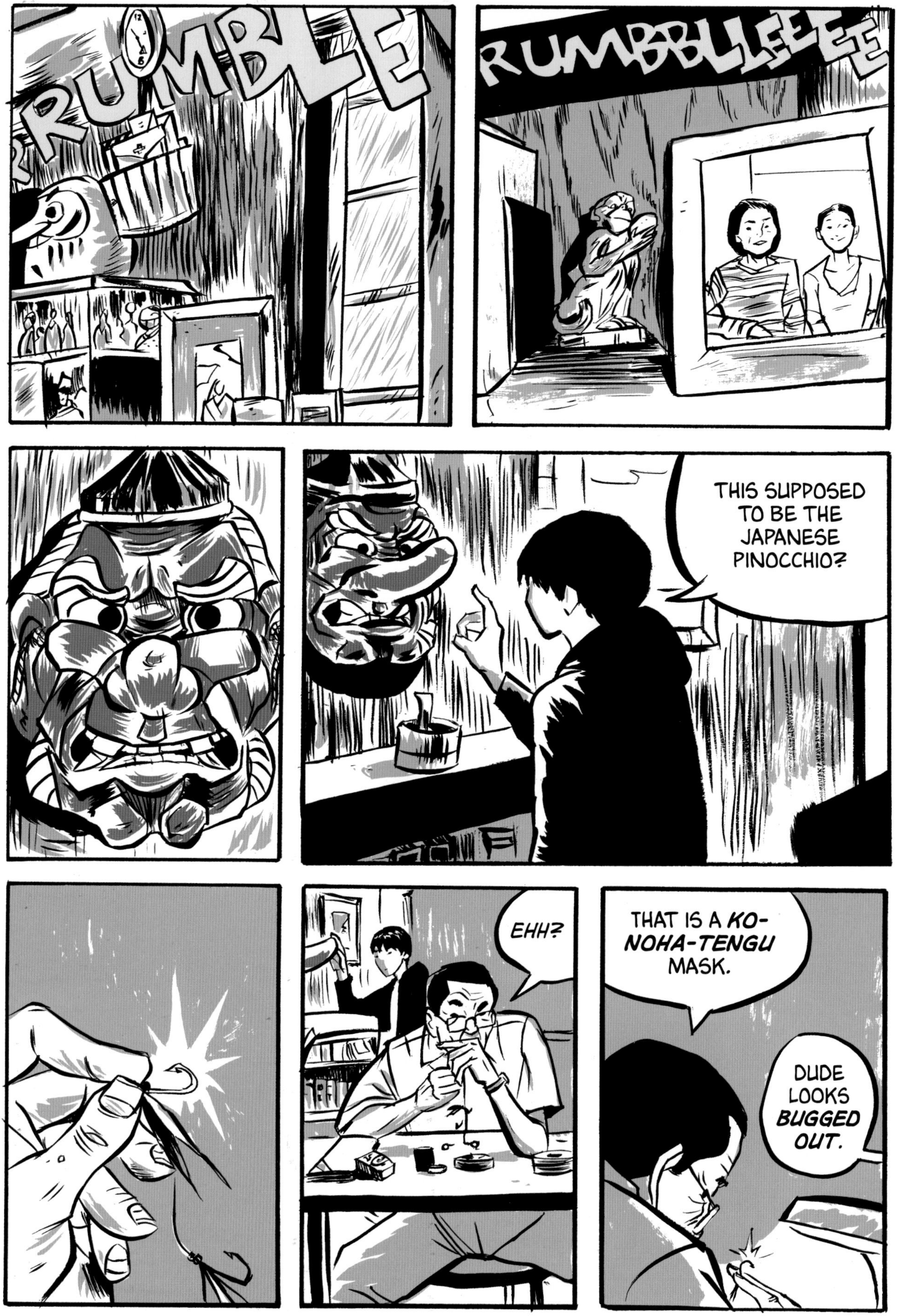
RUMBLE
RUMBBLLEEEE
THIS SUPPOSED TO BE THE JAPANESE PINOCCHIO?
EHH?
THAT IS A *KO-NOHA-TENGU* MASK.
DUDE LOOKS *BUGGED OUT.*

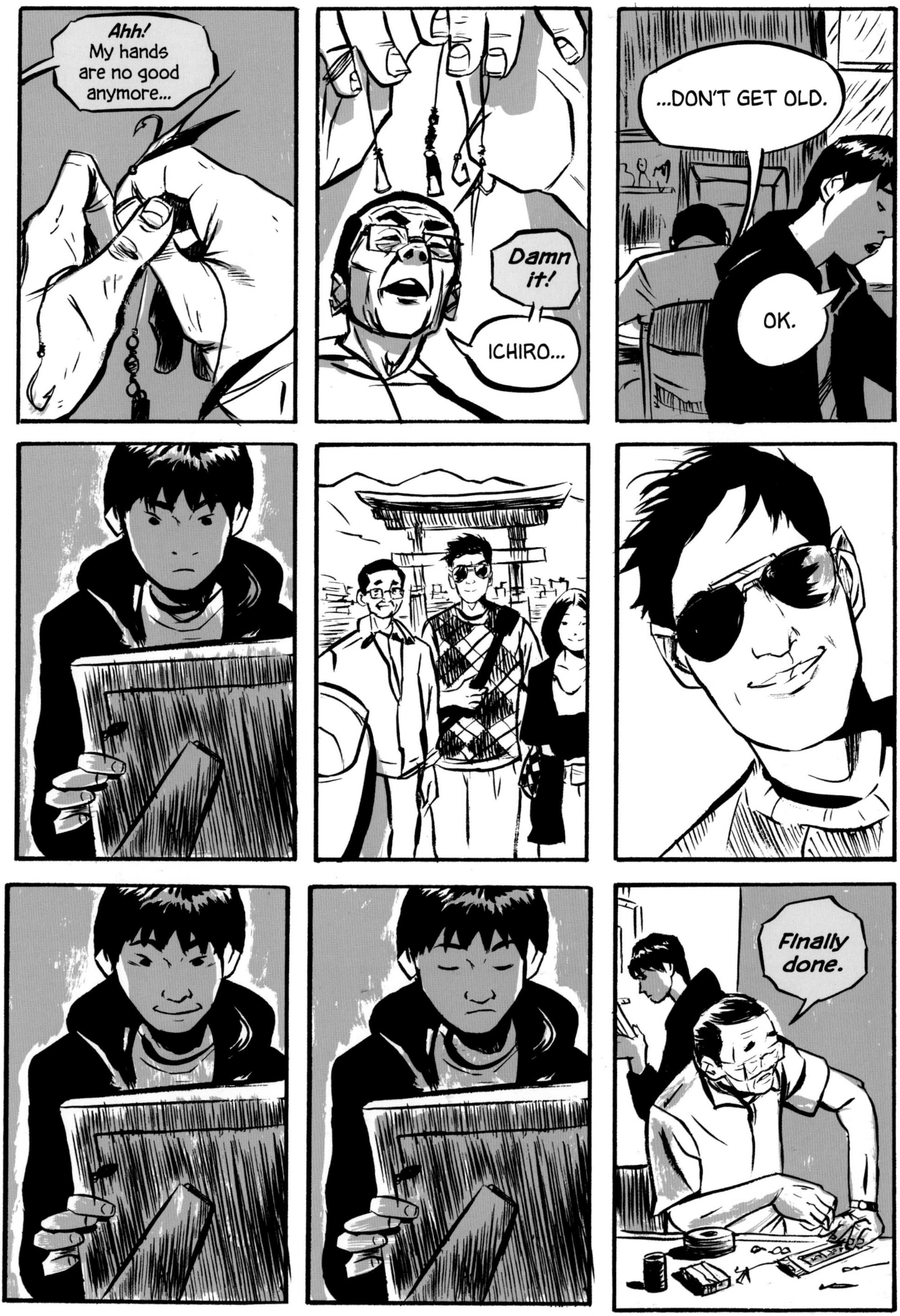
Ahh! My hands are no good anymore...
Damn it!
ICHIRO...
...DON'T GET OLD.
OK.
Finally done.

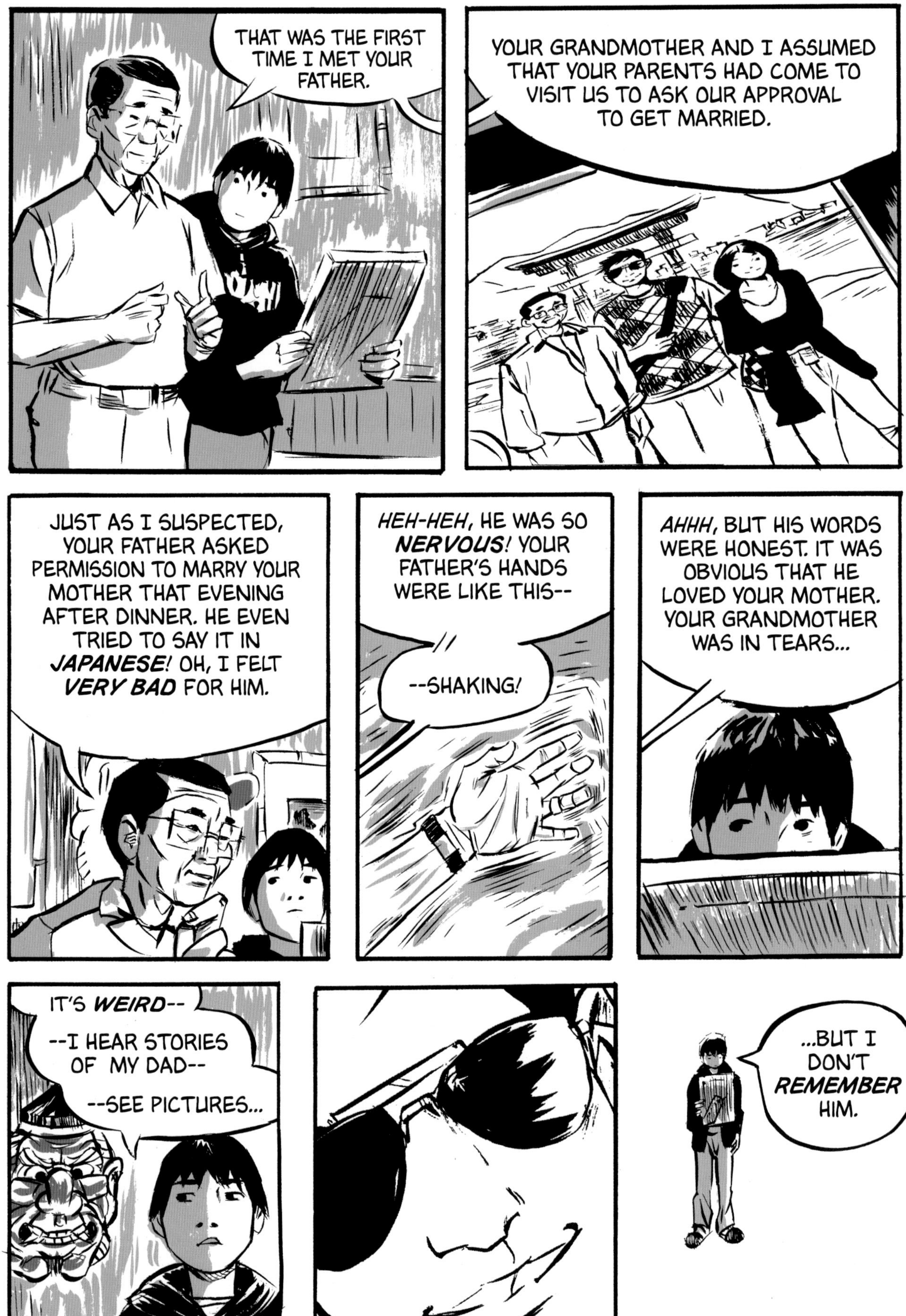
THAT WAS THE FIRST TIME I MET YOUR FATHER.
YOUR GRANDMOTHER AND I ASSUMED THAT YOUR PARENTS HAD COME TO VISIT US TO ASK OUR APPROVAL TO GET MARRIED.
JUST AS I SUSPECTED, YOUR FATHER ASKED PERMISSION TO MARRY YOUR MOTHER THAT EVENING AFTER DINNER. HE EVEN TRIED TO SAY IT IN JAPANESE! OH, I FELT VERY BAD FOR HIM.
HEH-HEH, HE WAS SO NERVOUS! YOUR FATHER'S HANDS WERE LIKE THIS--
--SHAKING!
AHHH, BUT HIS WORDS WERE HONEST. IT WAS OBVIOUS THAT HE LOVED YOUR MOTHER. YOUR GRANDMOTHER WAS IN TEARS...
IT'S WEIRD--
--I HEAR STORIES OF MY DAD--
--SEE PICTURES...
...BUT I DON'T REMEMBER HIM.

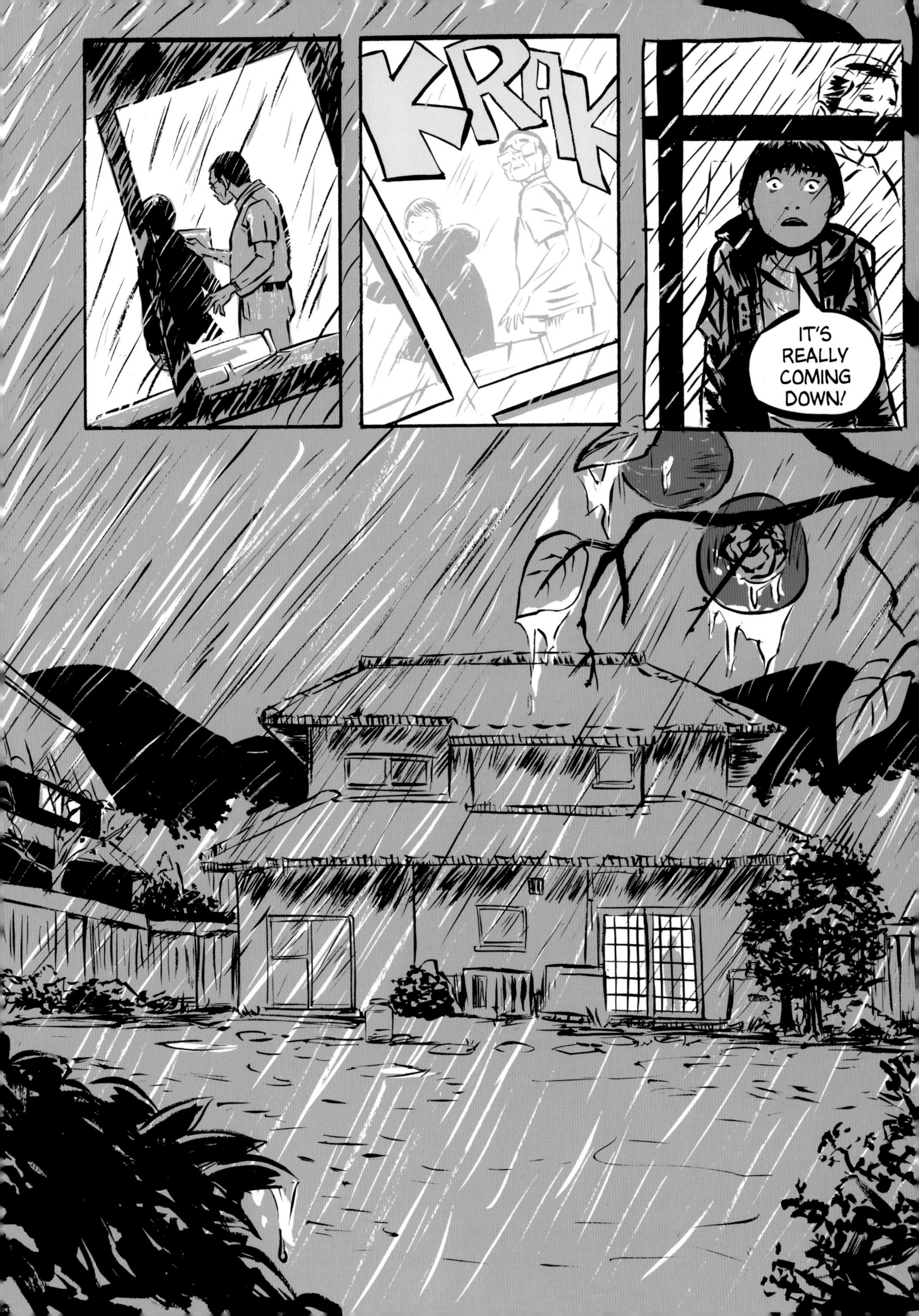
KRAK
IT'S REALLY COMING DOWN!

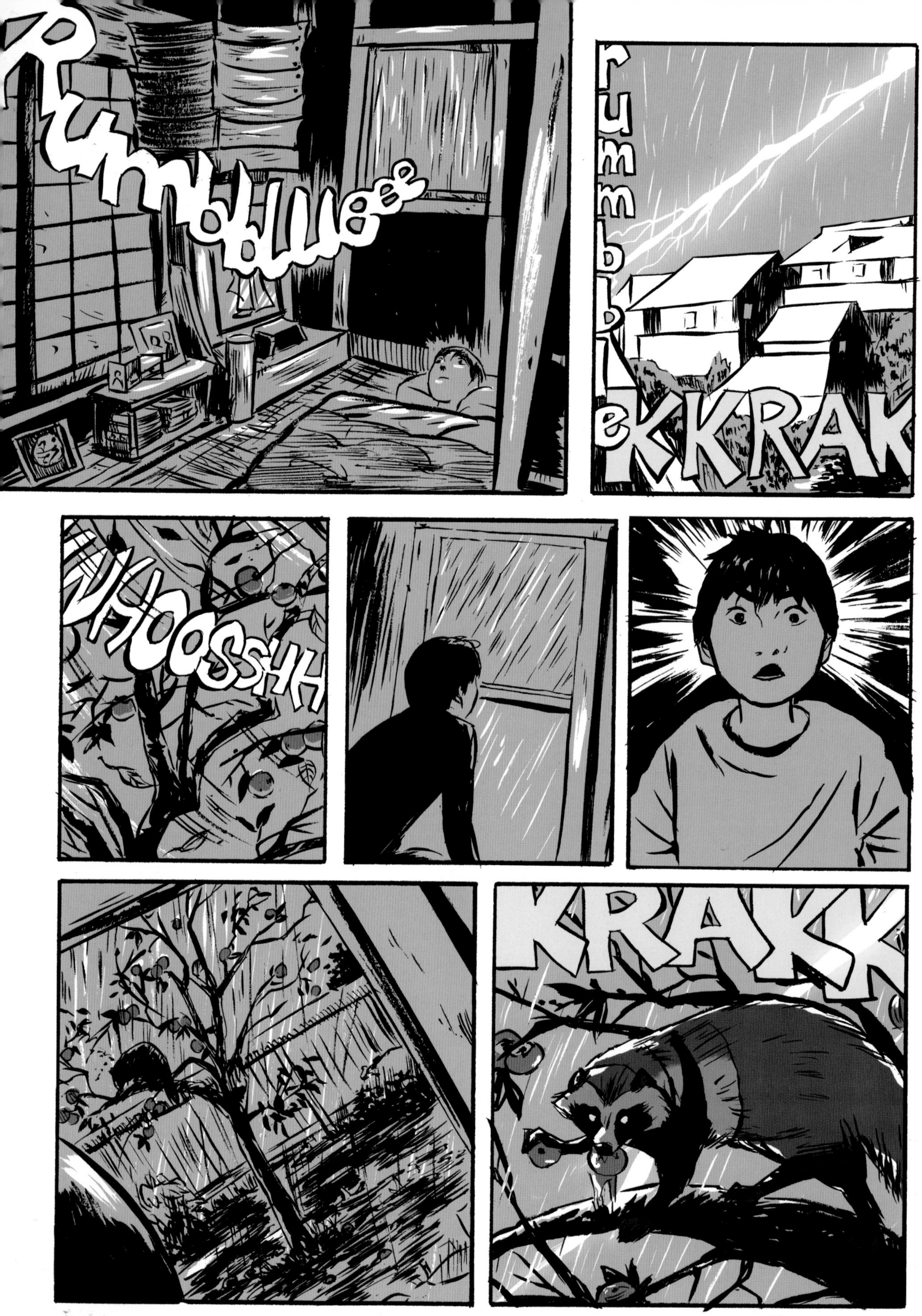
Rumbblugee
rummbble
KKRAK
WHOOSSHH
KRAKK

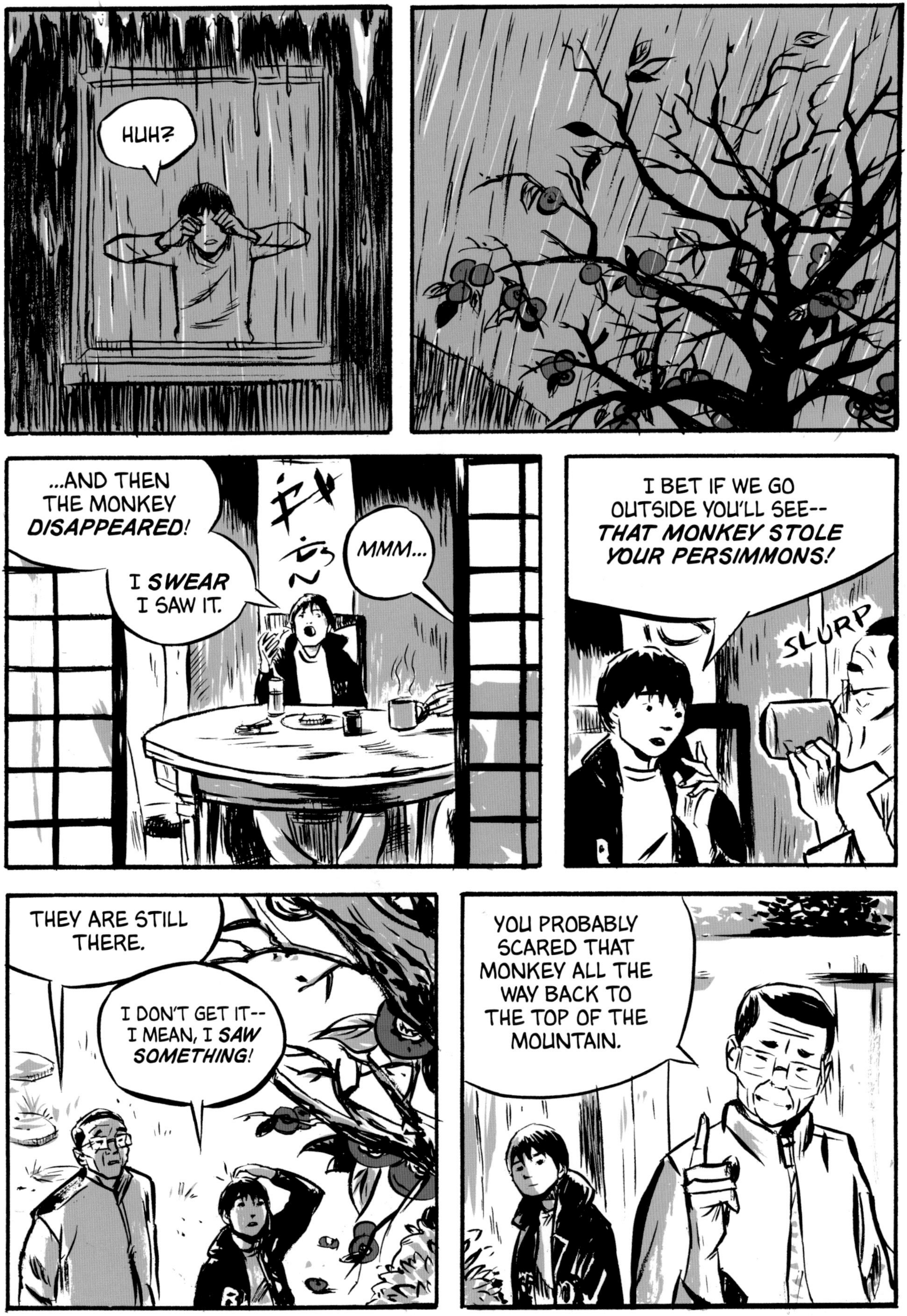
HUH?
...AND THEN THE MONKEY DISAPPEARED!
I SWEAR I SAW IT.
MMM...
I BET IF WE GO OUTSIDE YOU'LL SEE-- THAT MONKEY STOLE YOUR PERSIMMONS!
SLURP
THEY ARE STILL THERE.
I DON'T GET IT-- I MEAN, I SAW SOMETHING!
YOU PROBABLY SCARED THAT MONKEY ALL THE WAY BACK TO THE TOP OF THE MOUNTAIN.

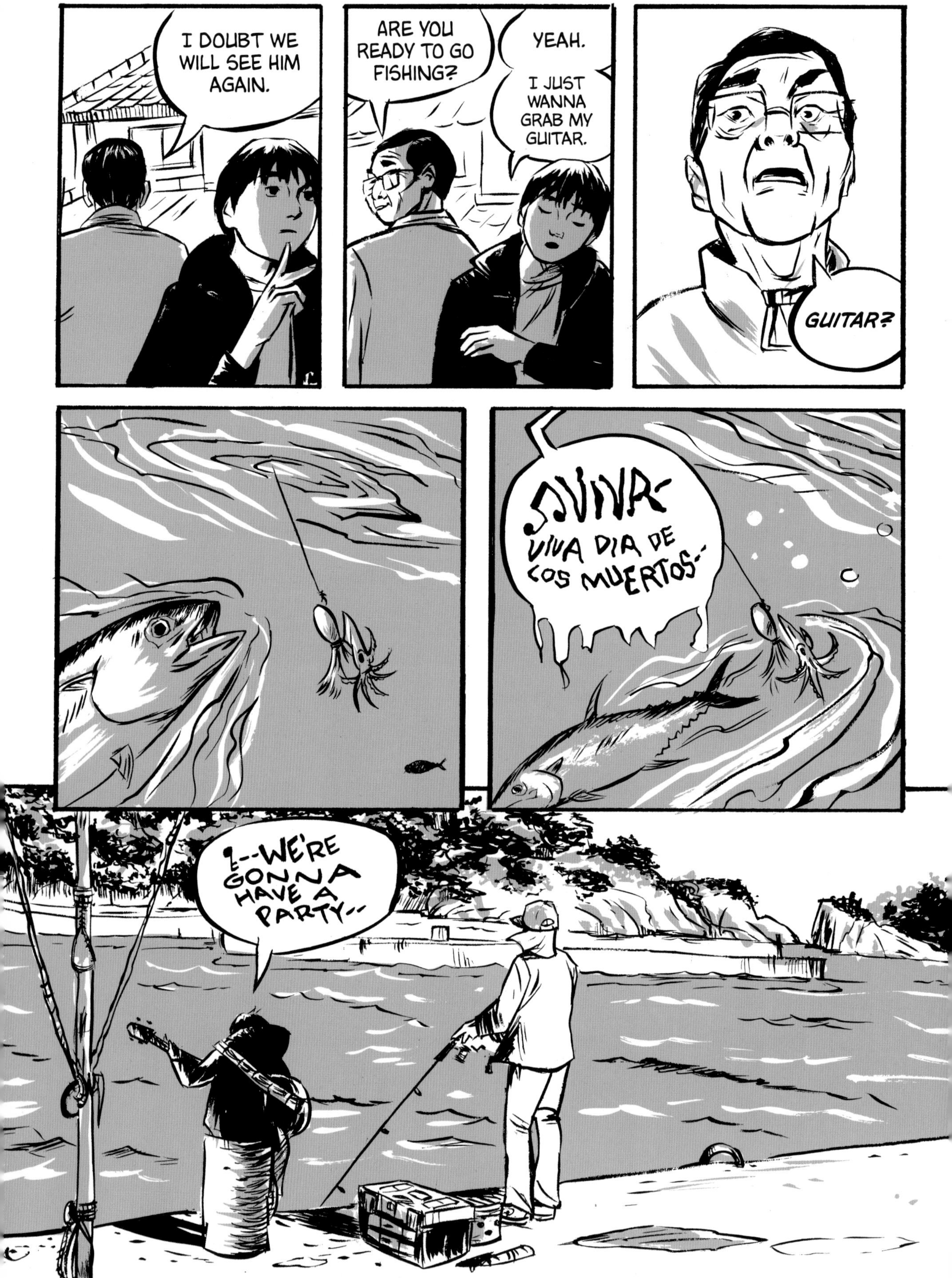
I DOUBT WE WILL SEE HIM AGAIN.
ARE YOU READY TO GO FISHING?
YEAH.
I JUST WANNA GRAB MY GUITAR.
GUITAR?
VIVA-
VIVA DIA DE LOS MUERTOS-
--WE'RE GONNA HAVE A PARTY--

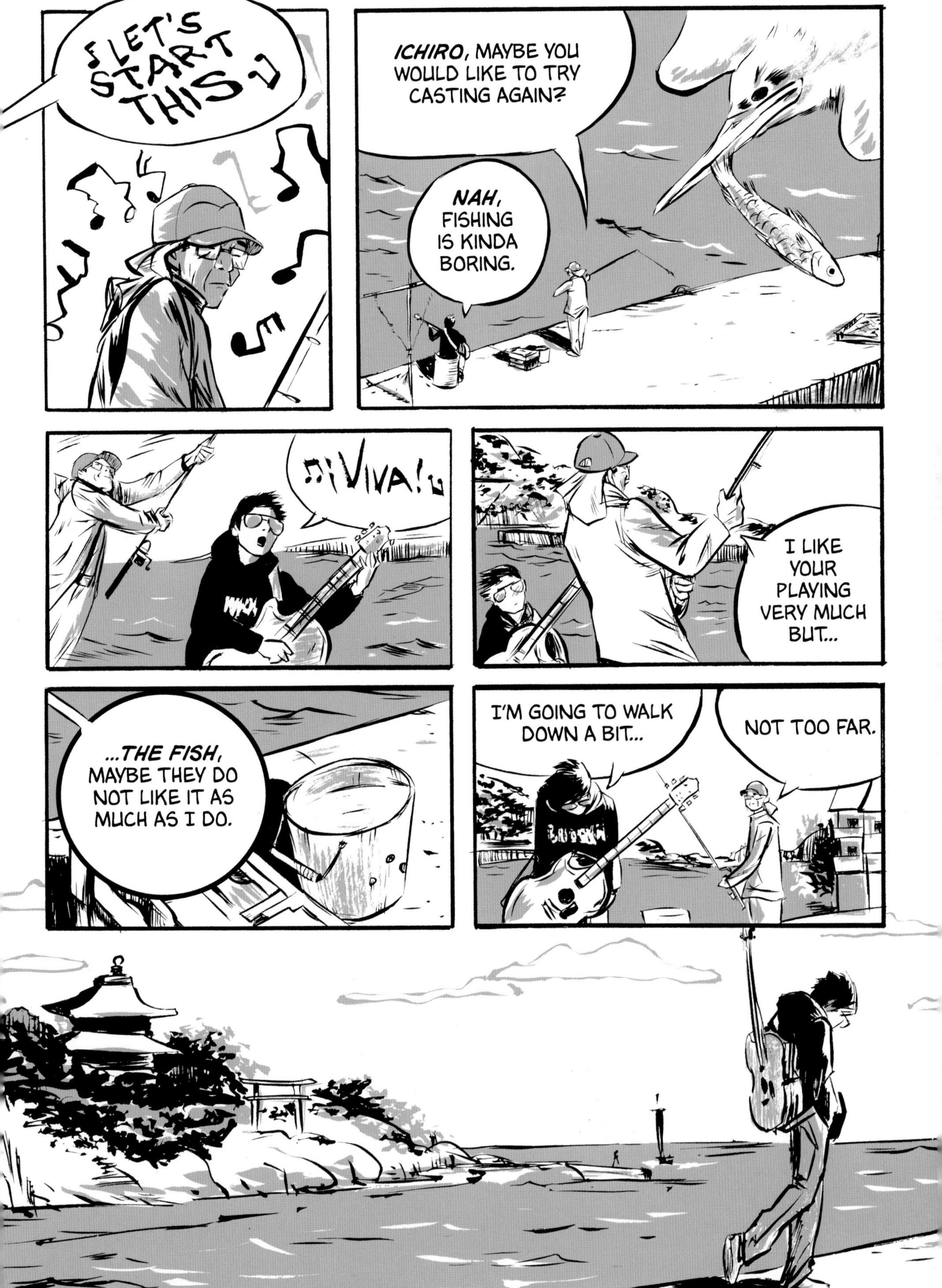
LET'S START THIS
ICHIRO, MAYBE YOU WOULD LIKE TO TRY CASTING AGAIN?
NAH, FISHING IS KINDA BORING.
¡VIVA!
I LIKE YOUR PLAYING VERY MUCH BUT...
...THE FISH, MAYBE THEY DO NOT LIKE IT AS MUCH AS I DO.
I'M GOING TO WALK DOWN A BIT...
NOT TOO FAR.

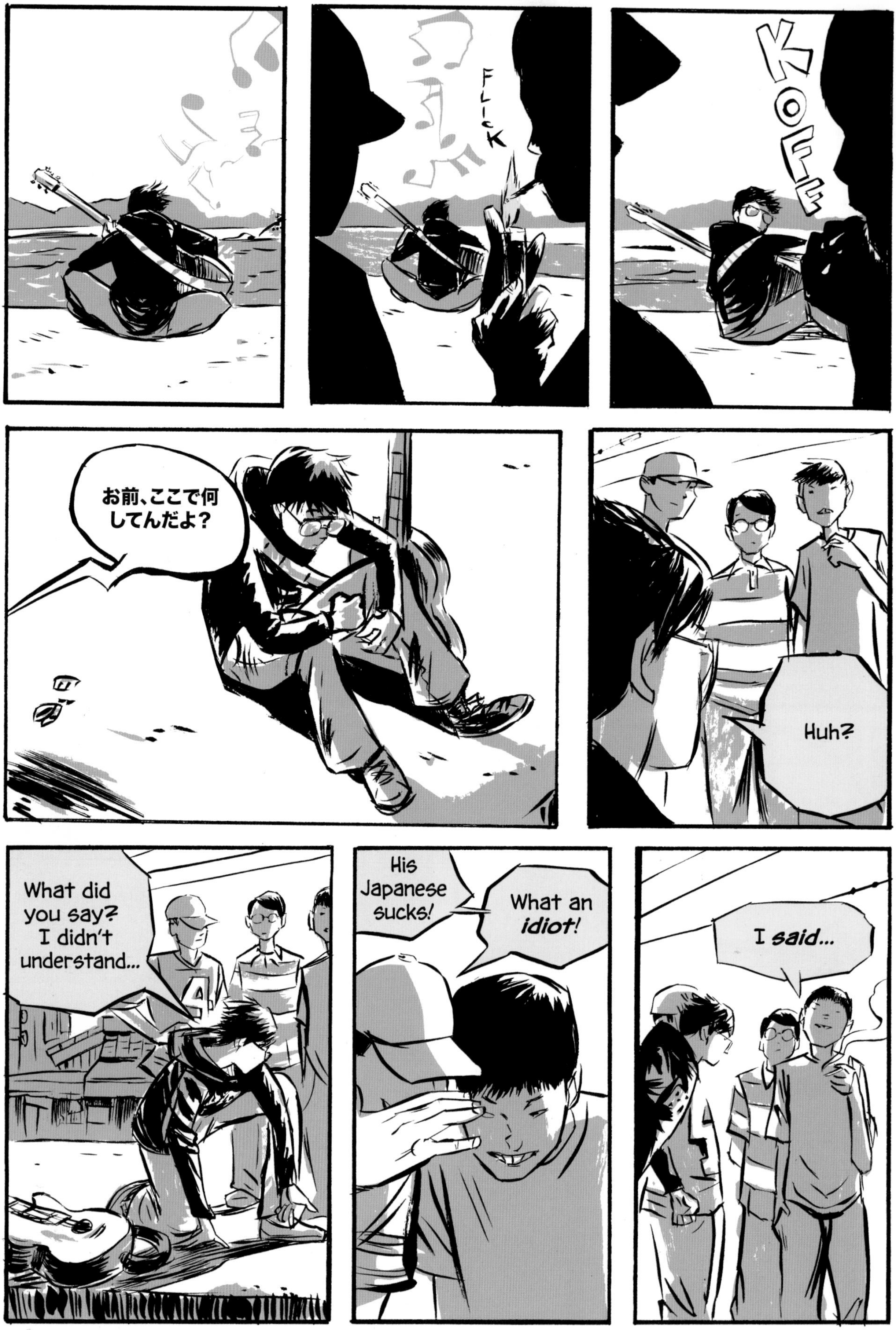
FLICK
KOFF
お前、ここで何
してんだよ？
Huh?
What did you say? I didn't understand...
His Japanese sucks!
What an *idiot*!
I *said*...

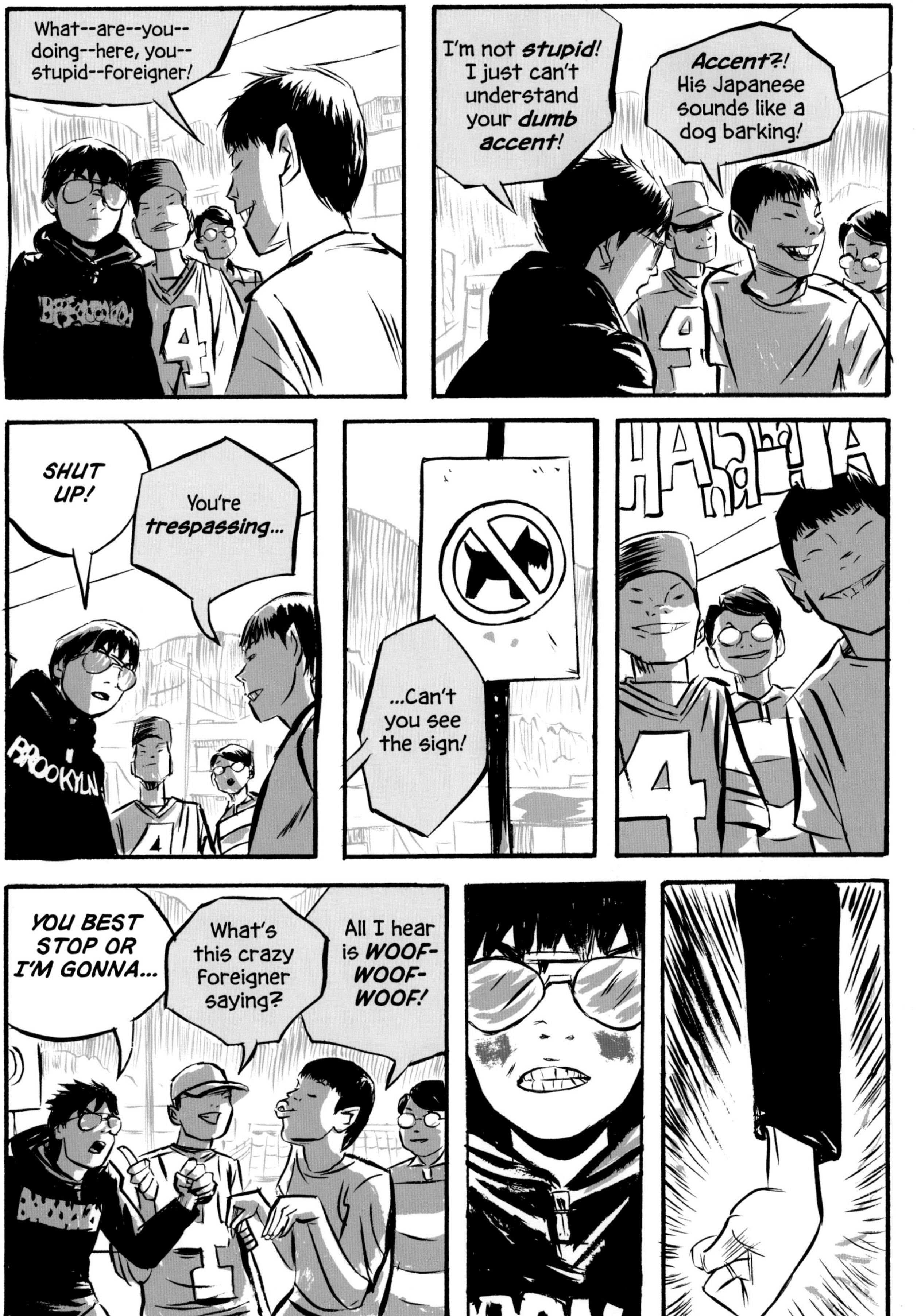

What--are--you--doing--here, you--stupid--foreigner!
I'm not stupid! I just can't understand your dumb accent!
Accent?! His Japanese sounds like a dog barking!
SHUT UP!
You're trespassing...
...Can't you see the sign!
HA ha HA
YOU BEST STOP OR I'M GONNA...
What's this crazy foreigner saying?
All I hear is WOOF-WOOF-WOOF!

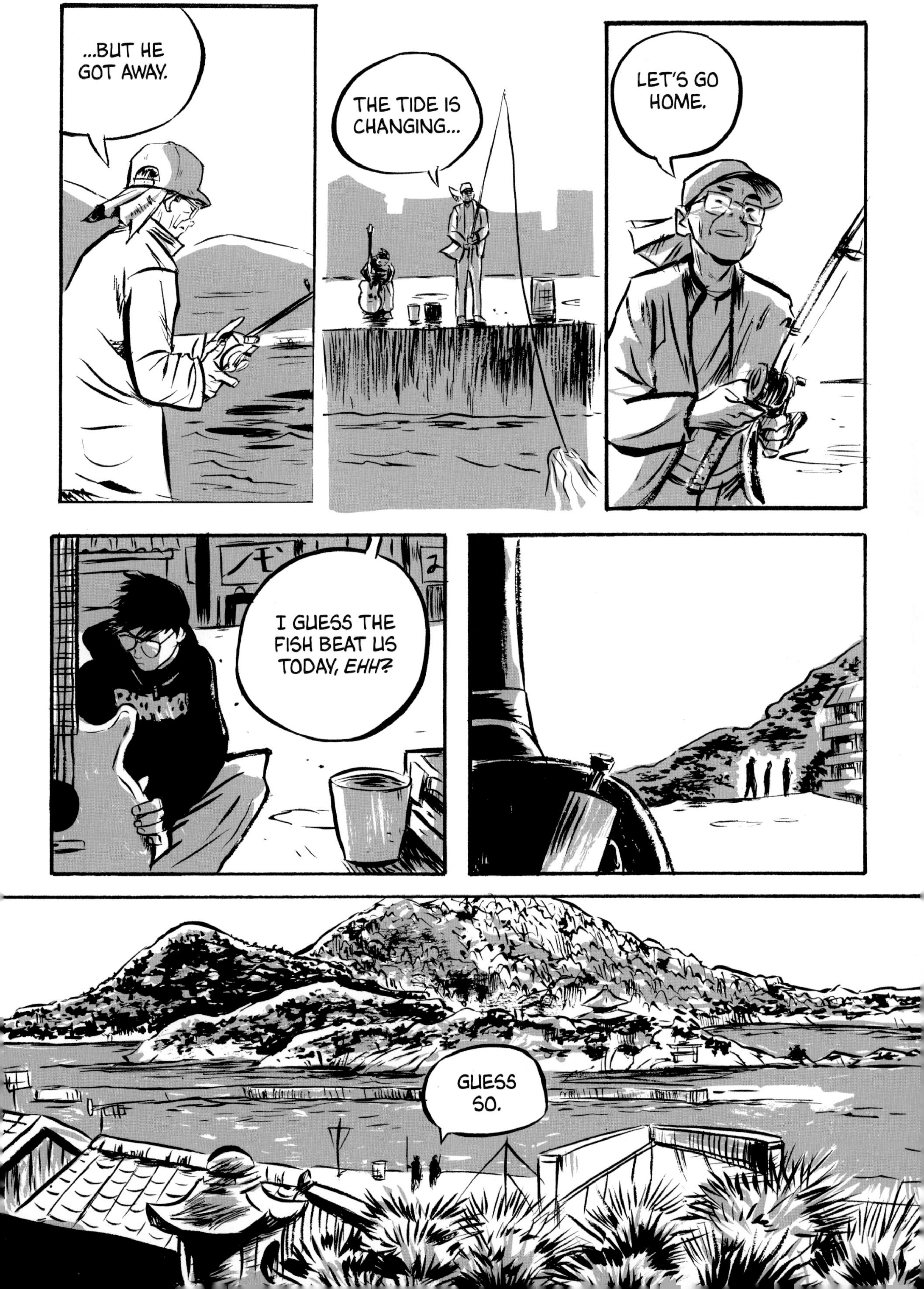
...BUT HE GOT AWAY.
THE TIDE IS CHANGING...
LET'S GO HOME.
I GUESS THE FISH BEAT US TODAY, *EHH?*
GUESS SO.

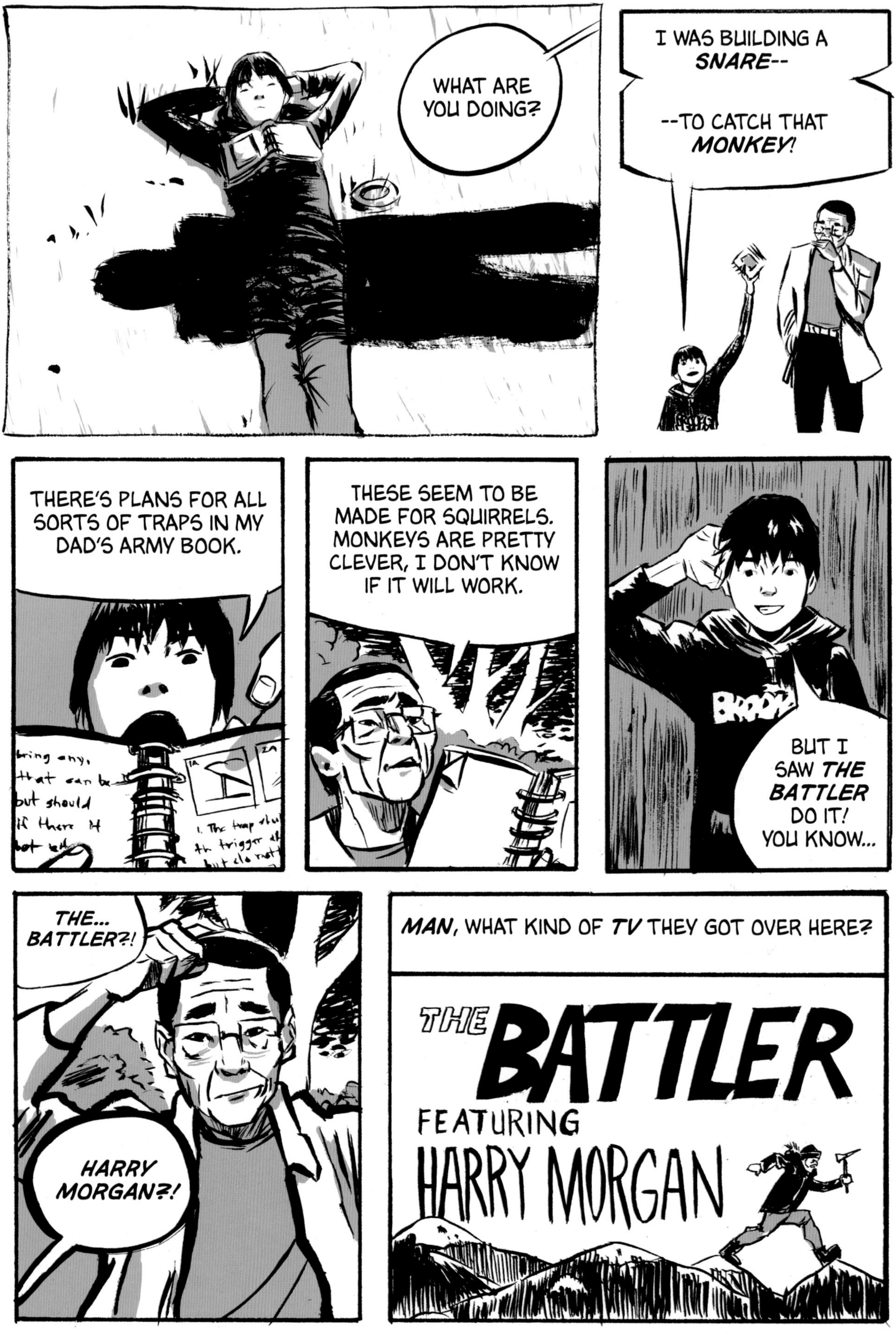
WHAT ARE YOU DOING?
I WAS BUILDING A *SNARE*--
--TO CATCH THAT *MONKEY*!
THERE'S PLANS FOR ALL SORTS OF TRAPS IN MY DAD'S ARMY BOOK.
THESE SEEM TO BE MADE FOR SQUIRRELS. MONKEYS ARE PRETTY CLEVER, I DON'T KNOW IF IT WILL WORK.
BUT I SAW *THE BATTLER* DO IT! YOU KNOW...
THE... BATTLER?!
HARRY MORGAN?!
MAN, WHAT KIND OF *TV* THEY GOT OVER HERE?
THE BATTLER
FEATURING
HARRY MORGAN

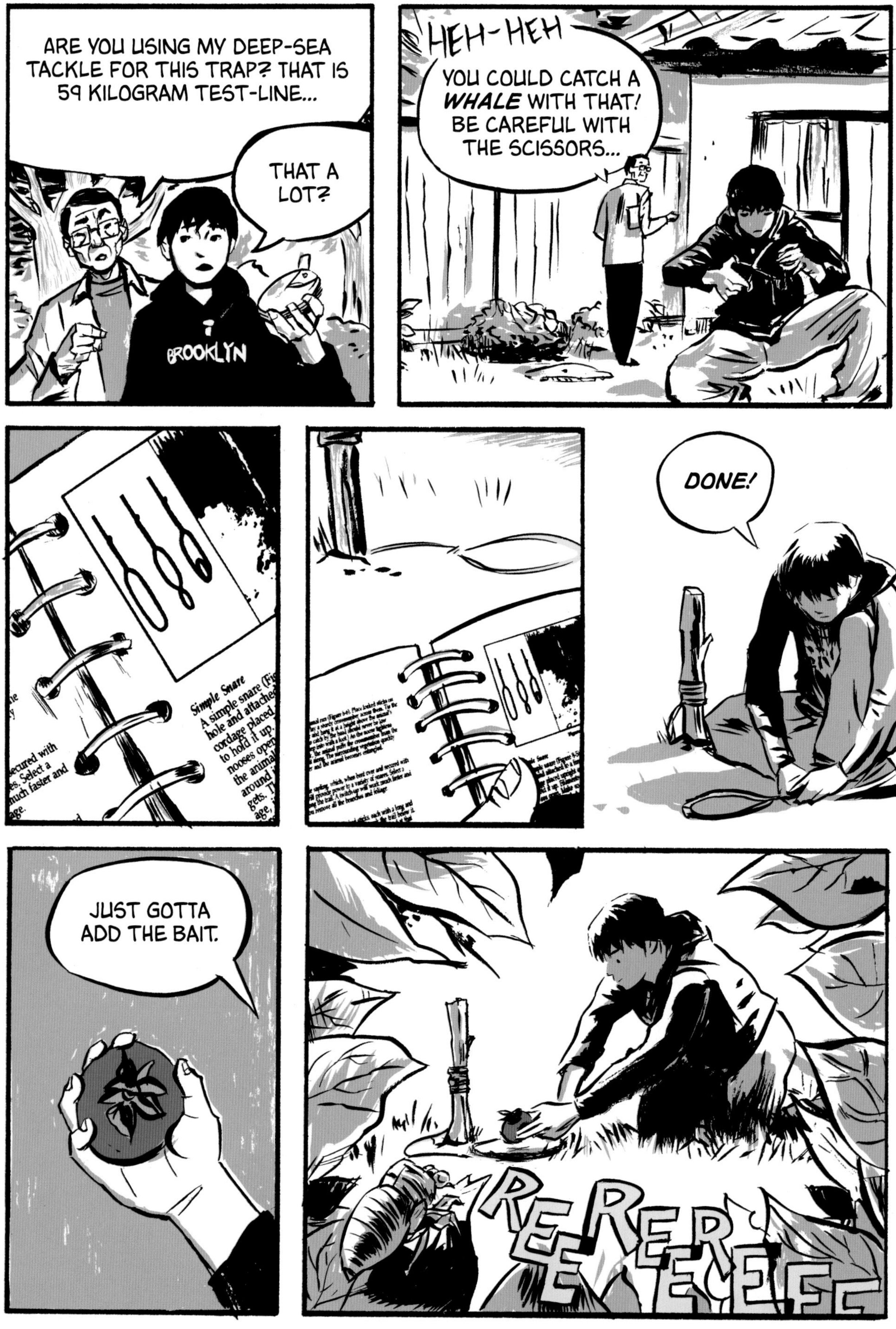
ARE YOU USING MY DEEP-SEA TACKLE FOR THIS TRAP? THAT IS 59 KILOGRAM TEST-LINE...
THAT A LOT?
HEH-HEH
YOU COULD CATCH A *WHALE* WITH THAT! BE CAREFUL WITH THE SCISSORS...
BROOKLYN
Simple Snare
DONE!
JUST GOTTA ADD THE BAIT.

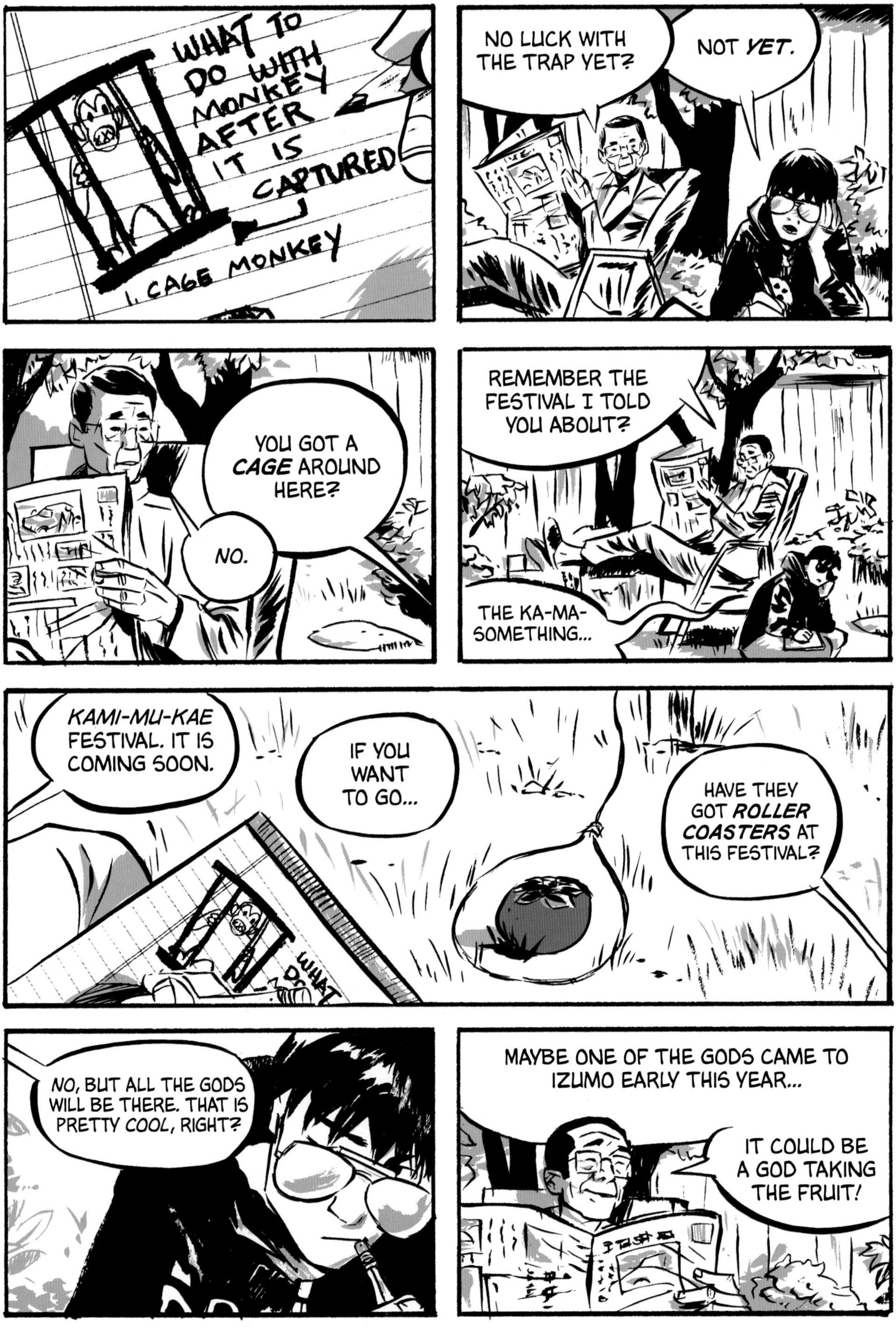
WHAT TO DO WITH MONKEY AFTER IT IS CAPTURED
1. CAGE MONKEY
NO LUCK WITH THE TRAP YET?
NOT *YET*.
YOU GOT A *CAGE* AROUND HERE?
NO.
REMEMBER THE FESTIVAL I TOLD YOU ABOUT?
THE KA-MA-SOMETHING...
KAMI-MU-KAE FESTIVAL. IT IS COMING SOON.
IF YOU WANT TO GO...
HAVE THEY GOT *ROLLER COASTERS* AT THIS FESTIVAL?
NO, BUT ALL THE GODS WILL BE THERE. THAT IS PRETTY *COOL*, RIGHT?
MAYBE ONE OF THE GODS CAME TO IZUMO EARLY THIS YEAR...
IT COULD BE A GOD TAKING THE FRUIT!

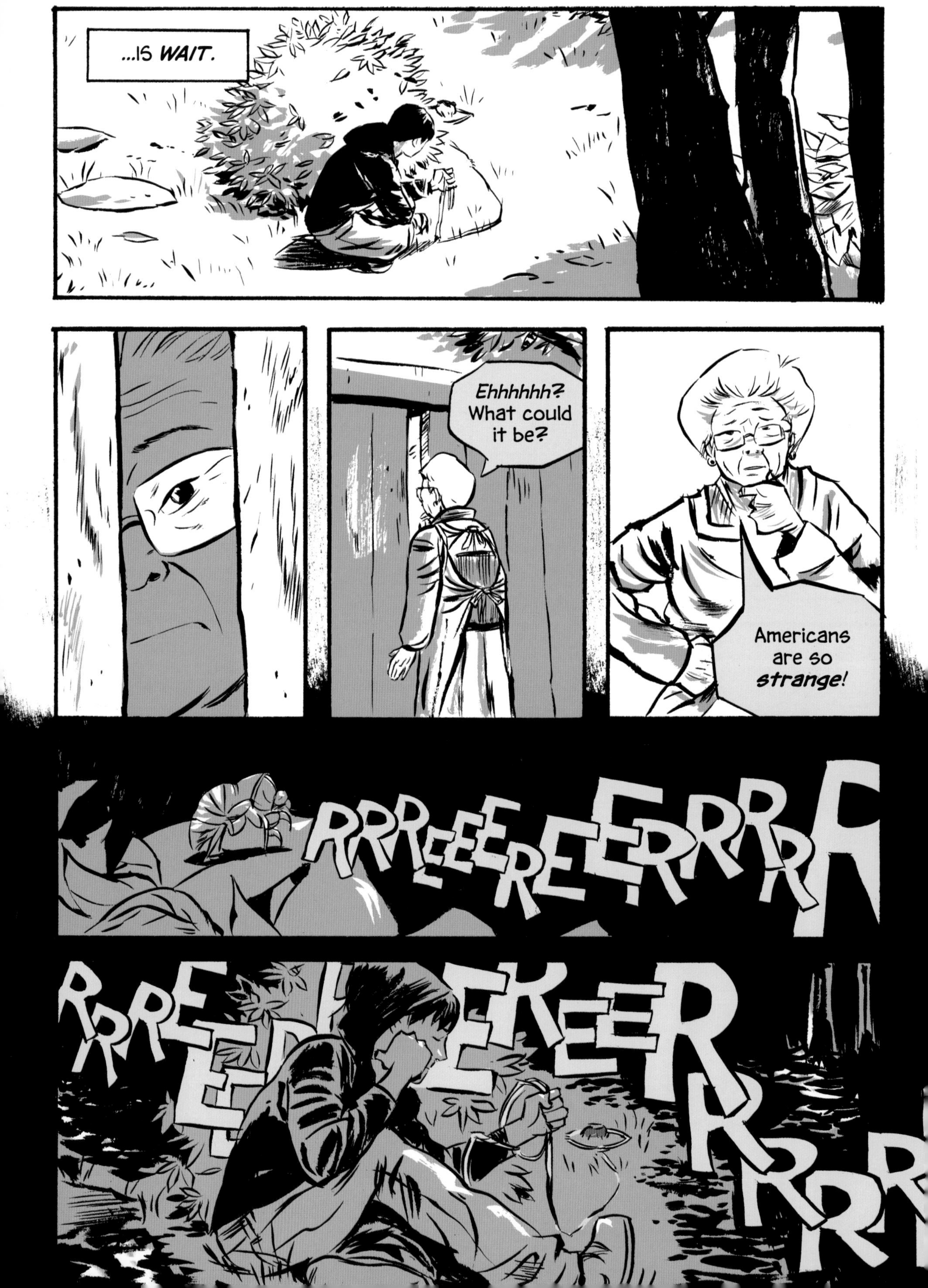
...IS WAIT.
Ehhhhhh? What could it be?
Americans are so strange!
RRRREEEREEERRRRR
RRREEEEKEERRRRR

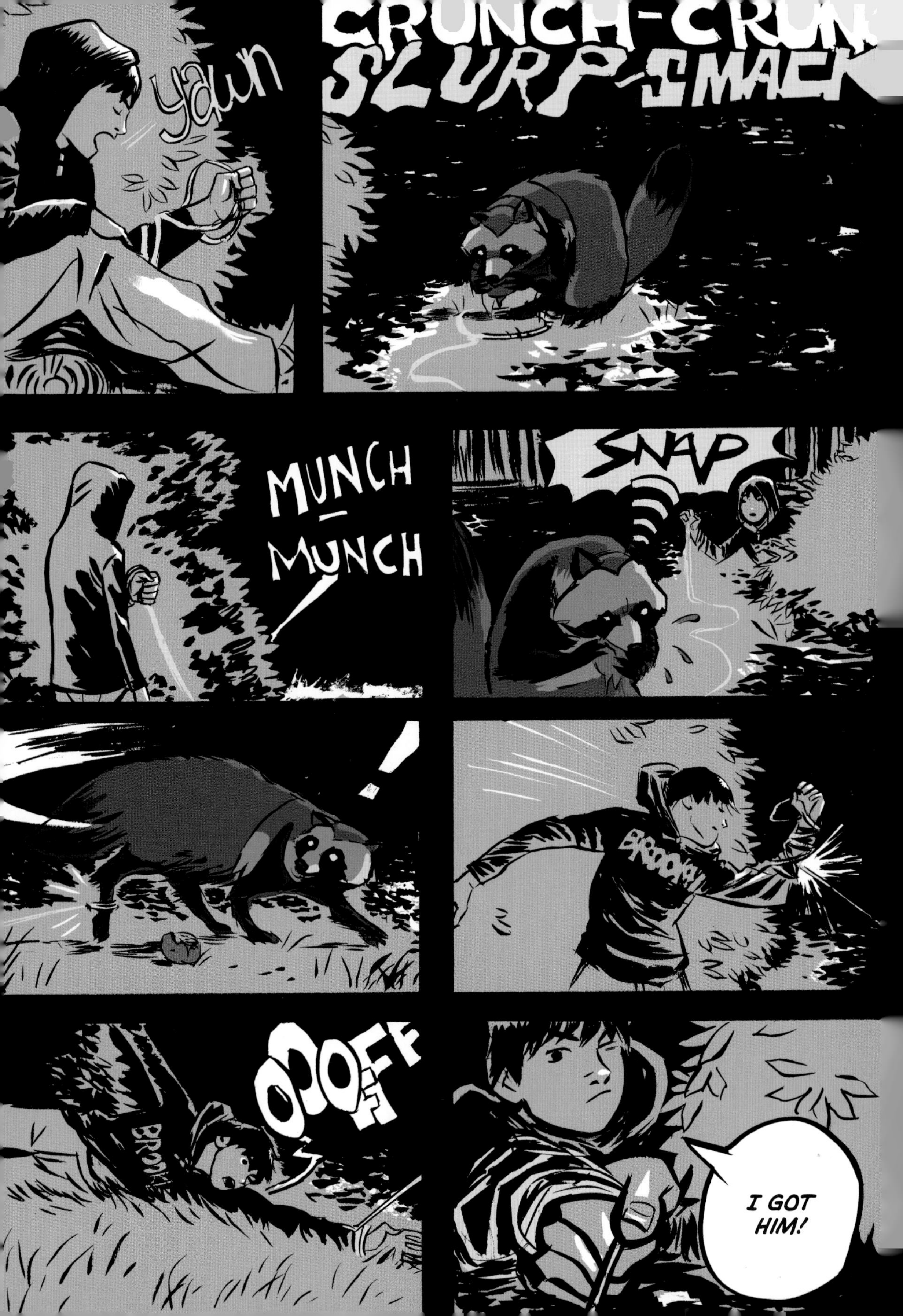
yawn
CRUNCH-CRUN
SLURP-SMACK
MUNCH
MUNCH
SNAP
!
OOOFF
I GOT HIM!

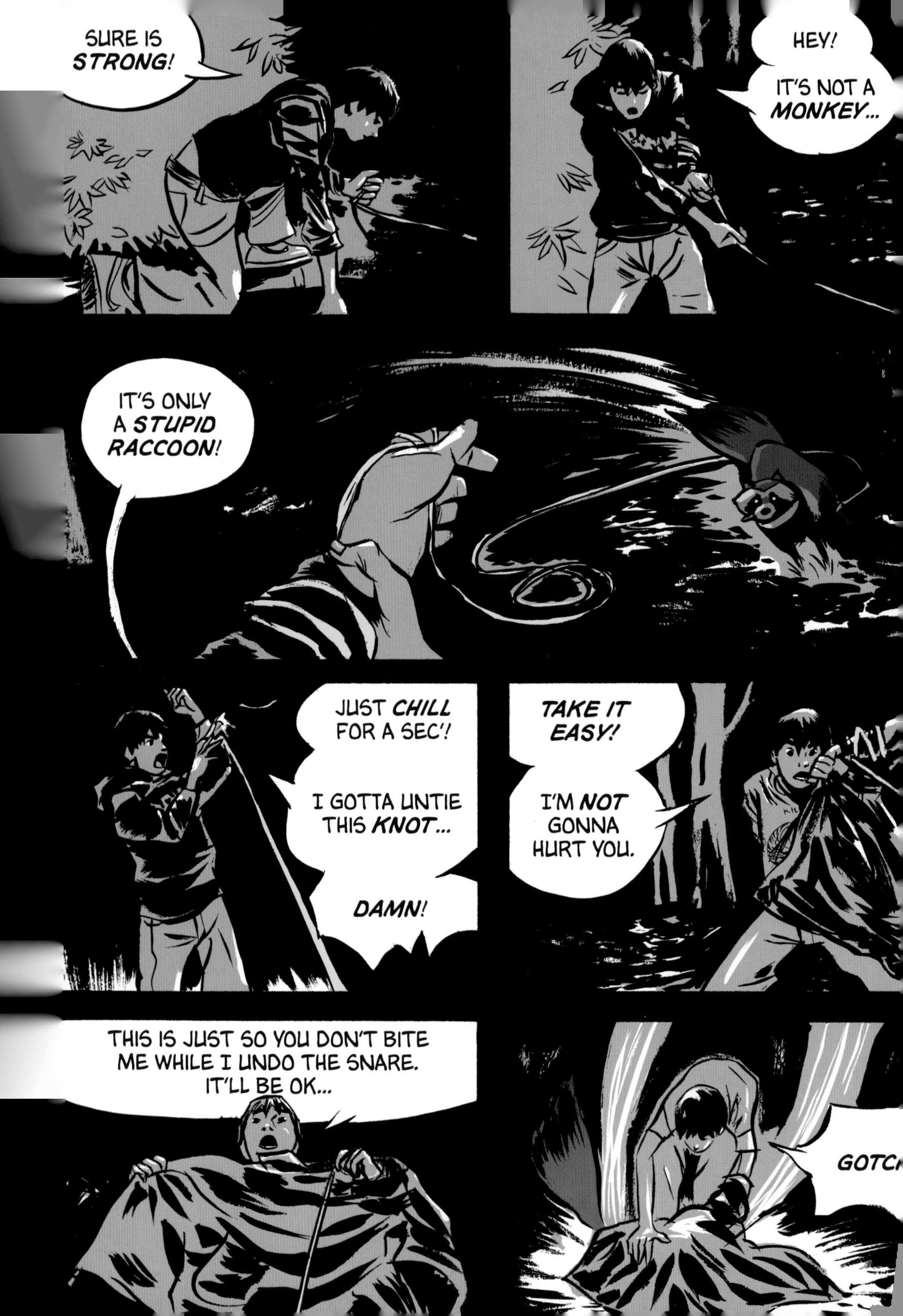
SURE IS STRONG!
HEY!
IT'S NOT A MONKEY...
IT'S ONLY A STUPID RACCOON!
JUST CHILL FOR A SEC'!
I GOTTA UNTIE THIS KNOT...
DAMN!
TAKE IT EASY!
I'M NOT GONNA HURT YOU.
THIS IS JUST SO YOU DON'T BITE ME WHILE I UNDO THE SNARE. IT'LL BE OK...

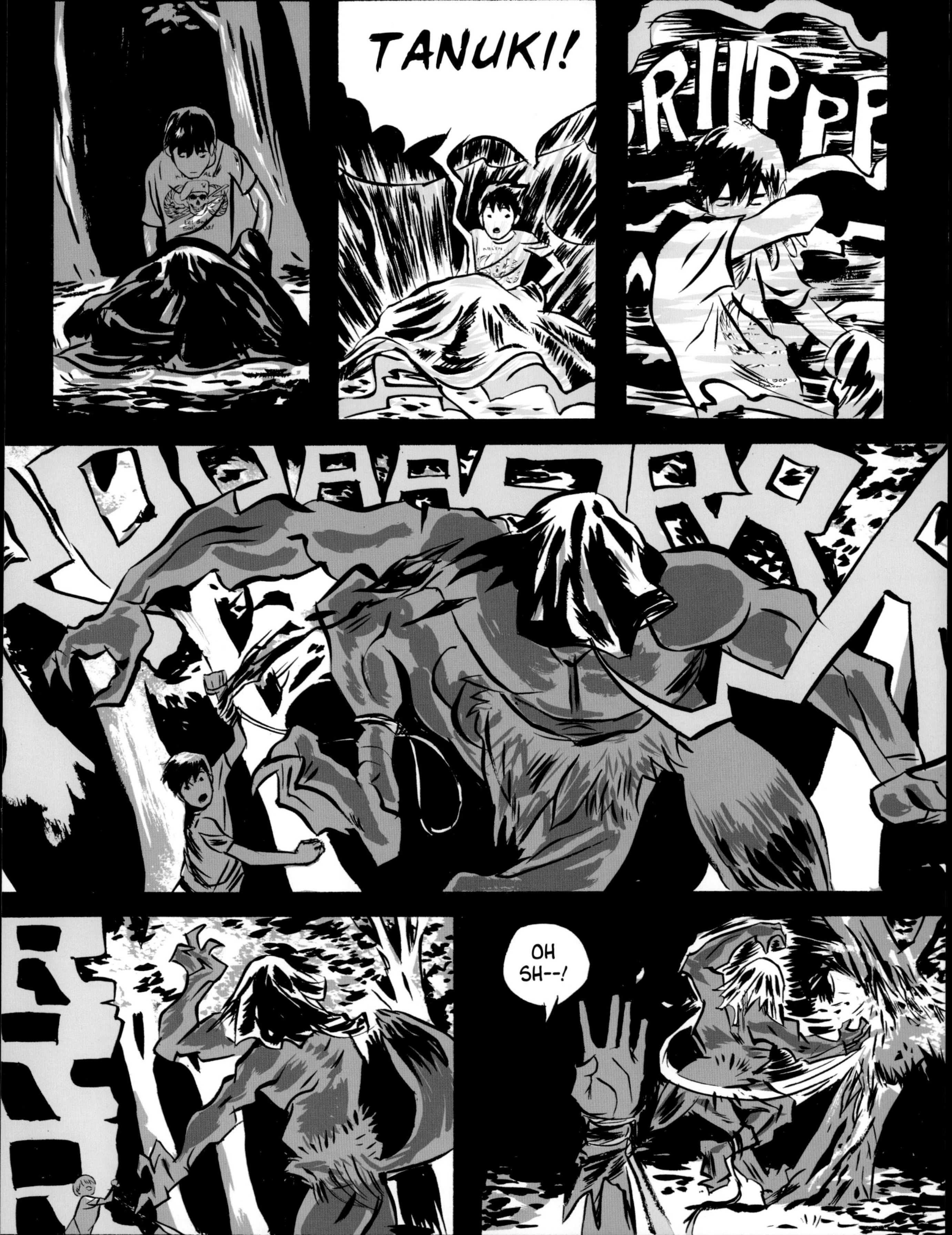
TANUKI!
RIIPPP
OH SH--!

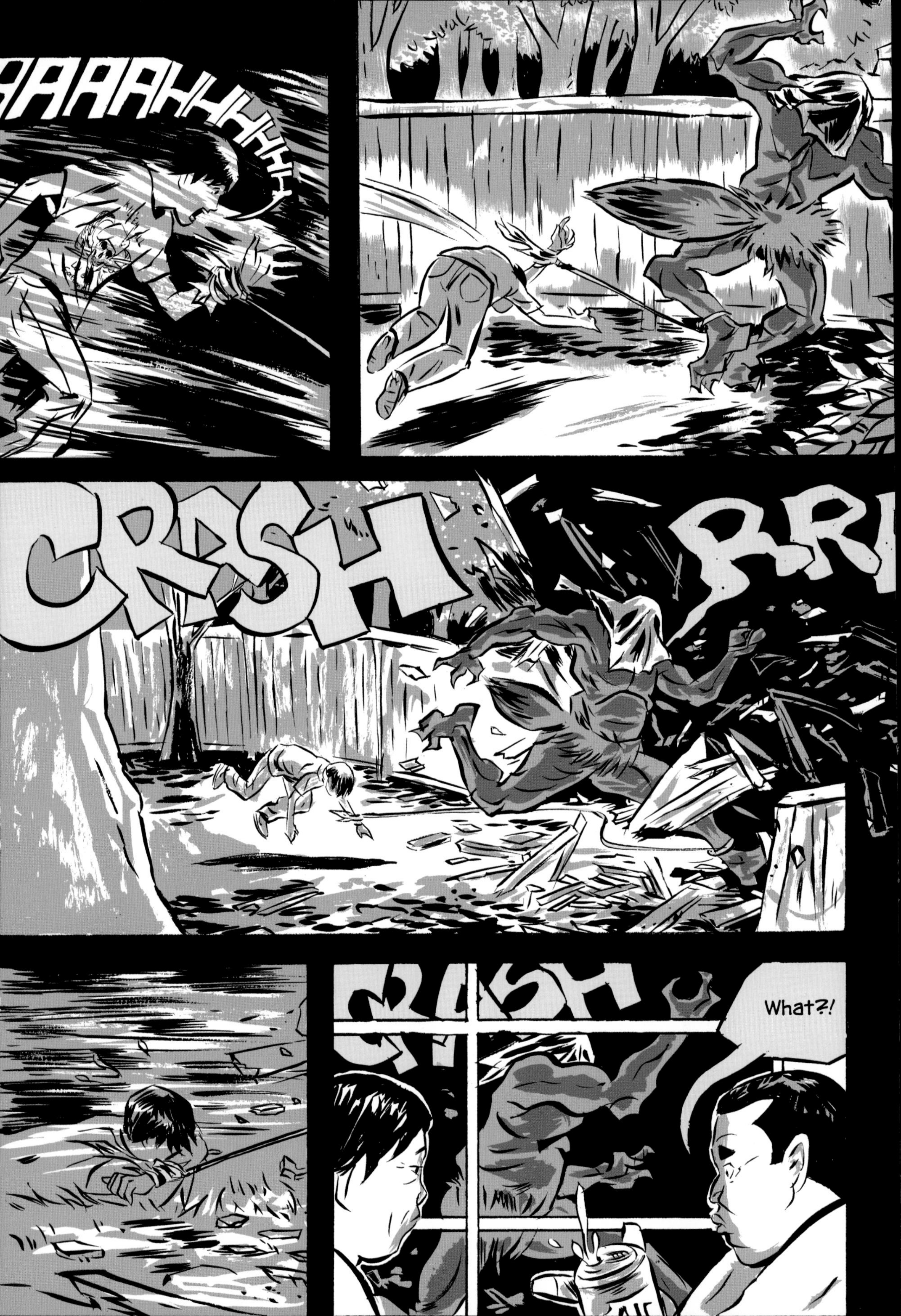

AAAAHHHHH
CRASH
CRASH
What?!

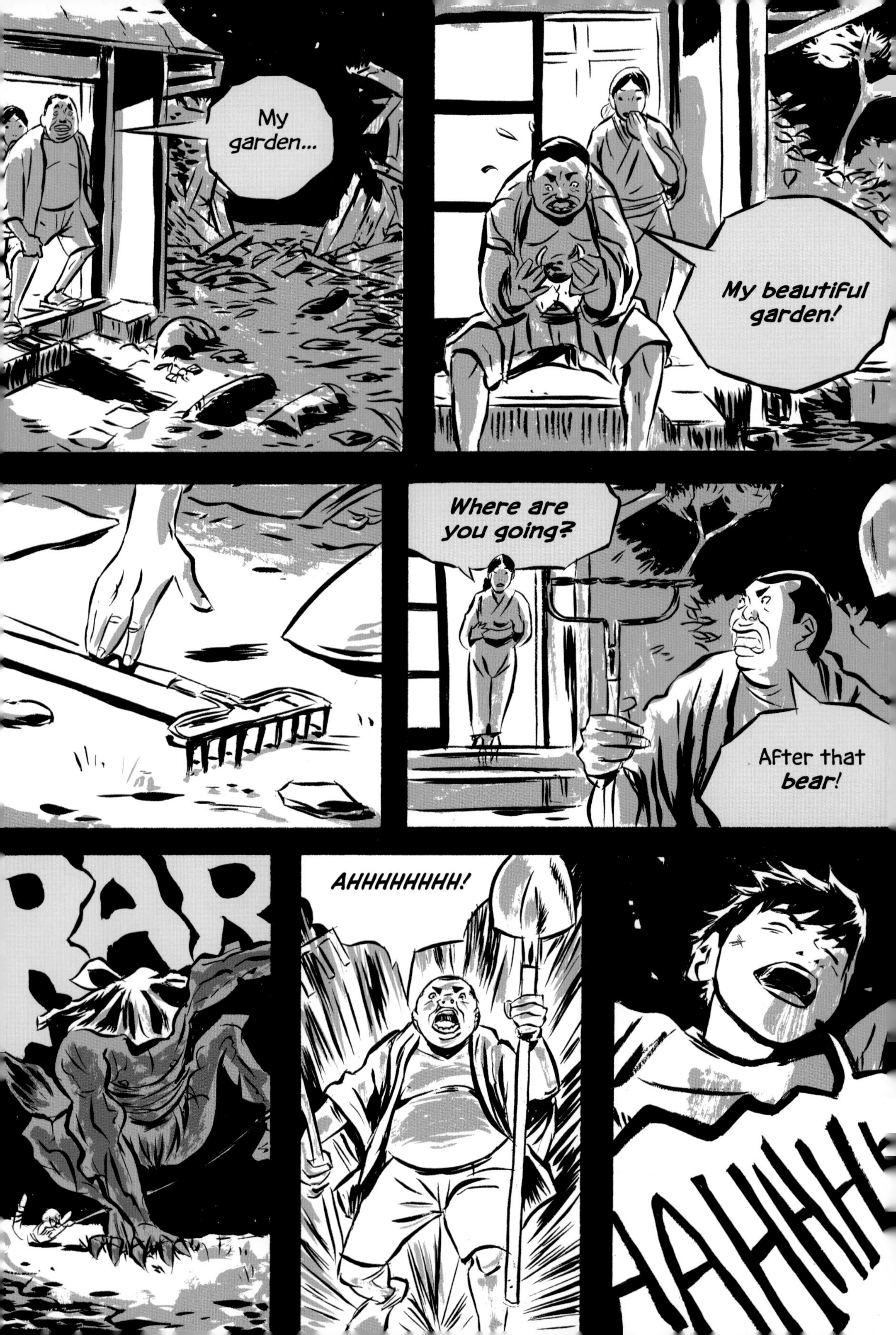
My garden...
My beautiful garden!
Where are you going?
After that bear!
AHHHHHHHH!

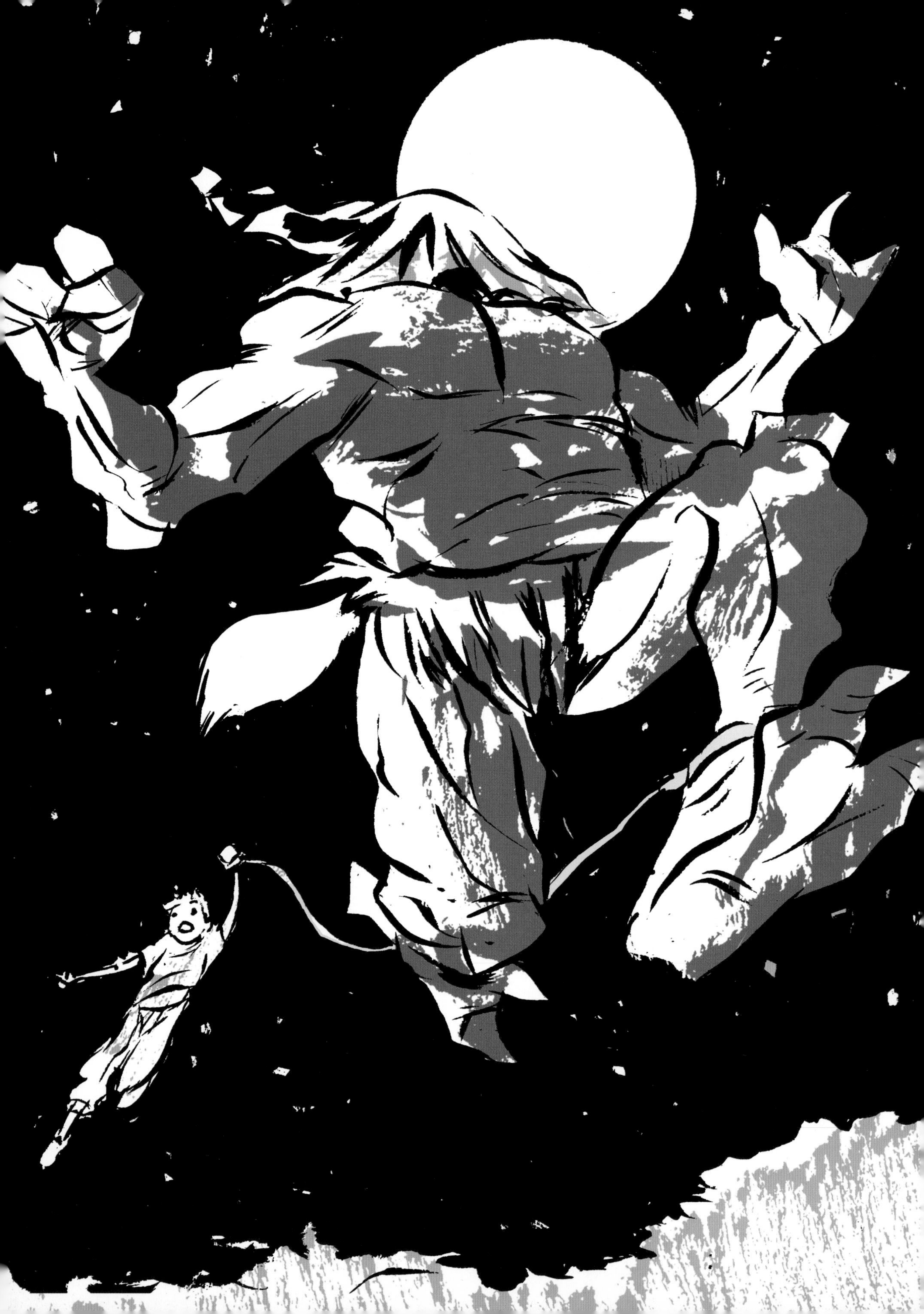

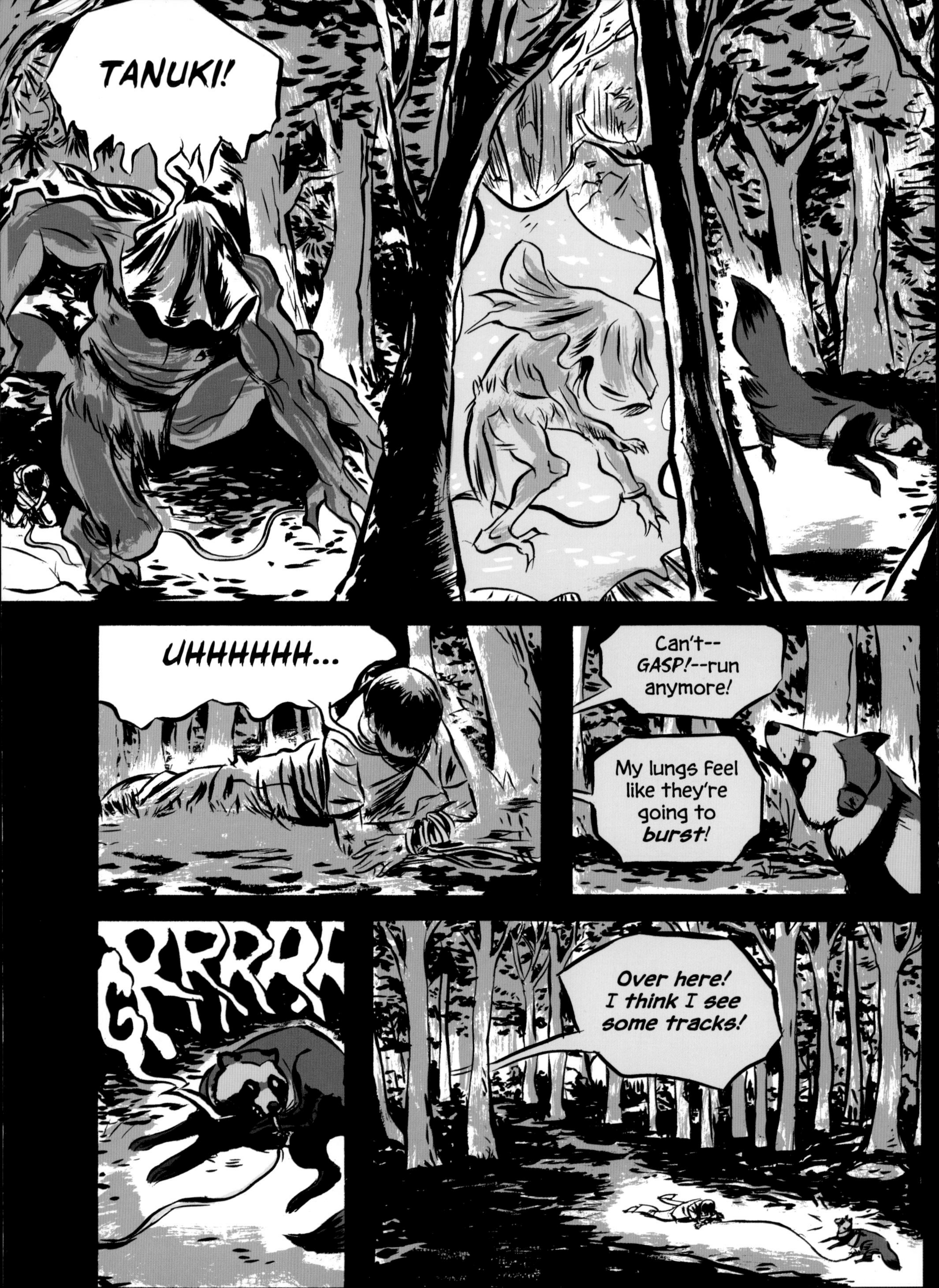
TANUKI!
UHHHHHH...
Can't--GASP!--run anymore!
My lungs feel like they're going to burst!
GRRR
Over here! I think I see some tracks!

SCRTCH
SCRTCH
SCRTCH
SCRTCH
SCRTC
WAIT, WHUT ARE YA DOIN'?
SCRTCH
SCRTCH
SCRTCH
SCRTCH
CRUNCH

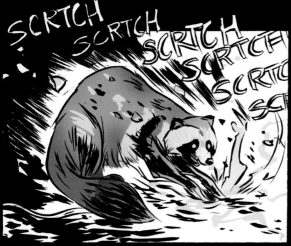

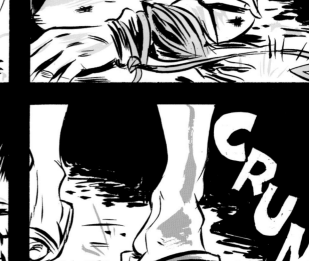

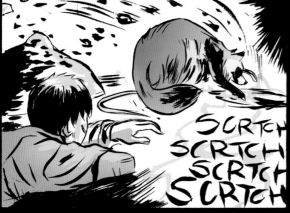

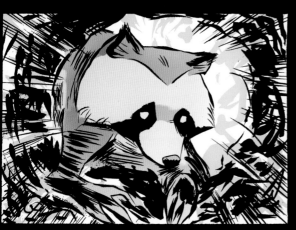

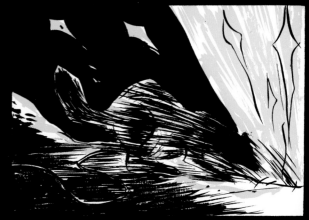

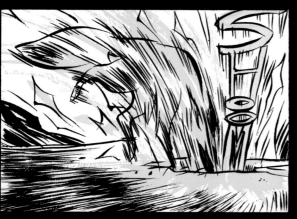

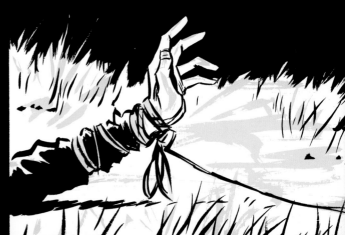

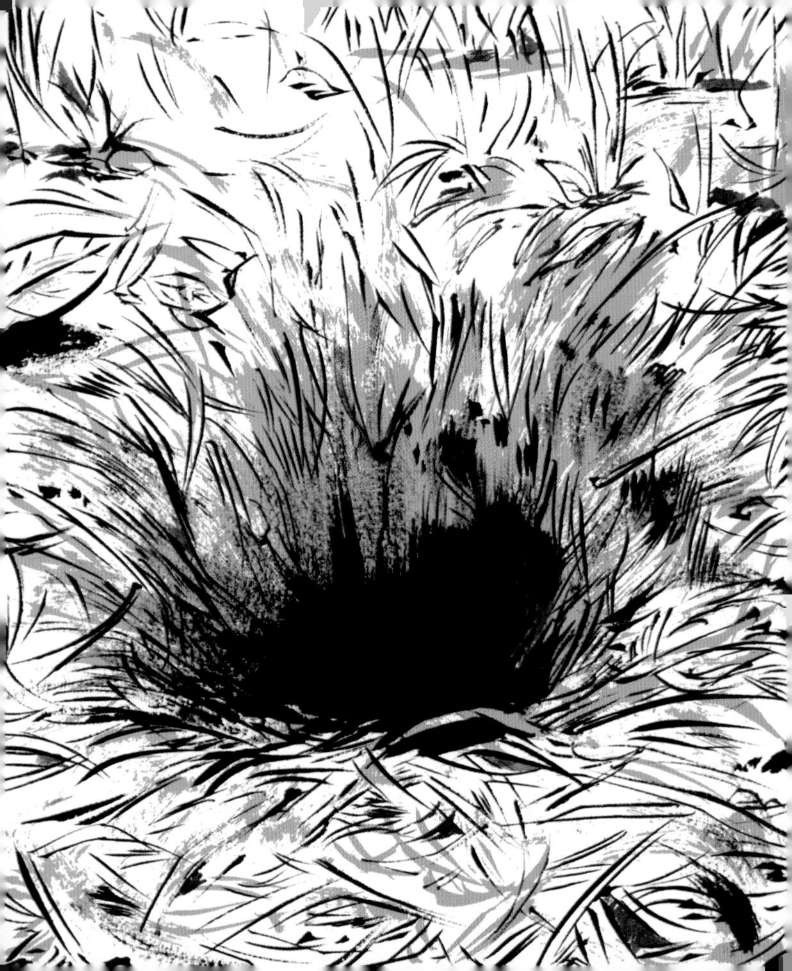

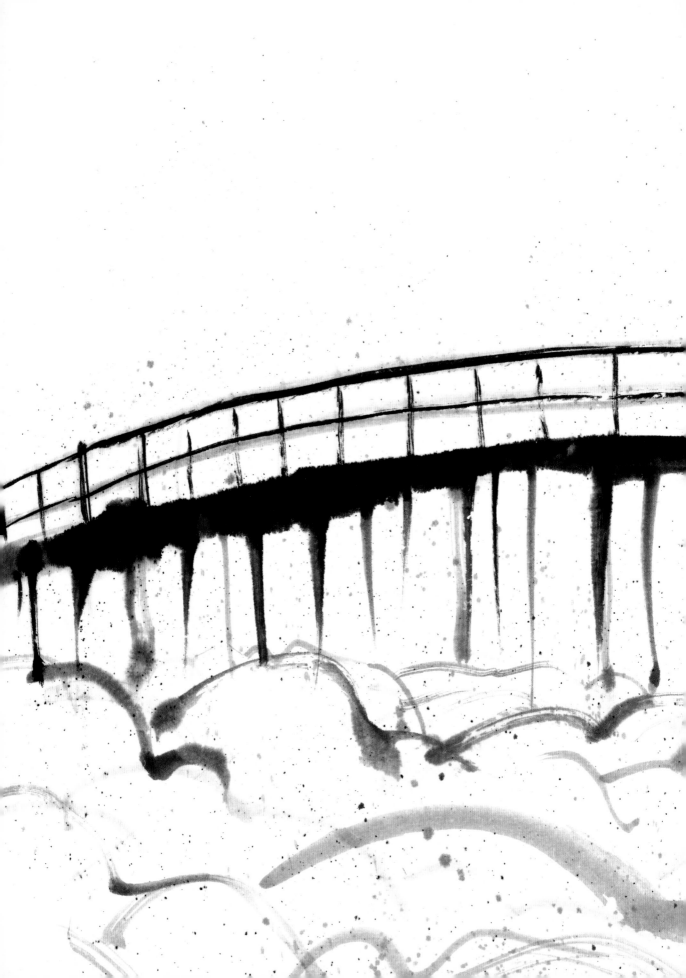

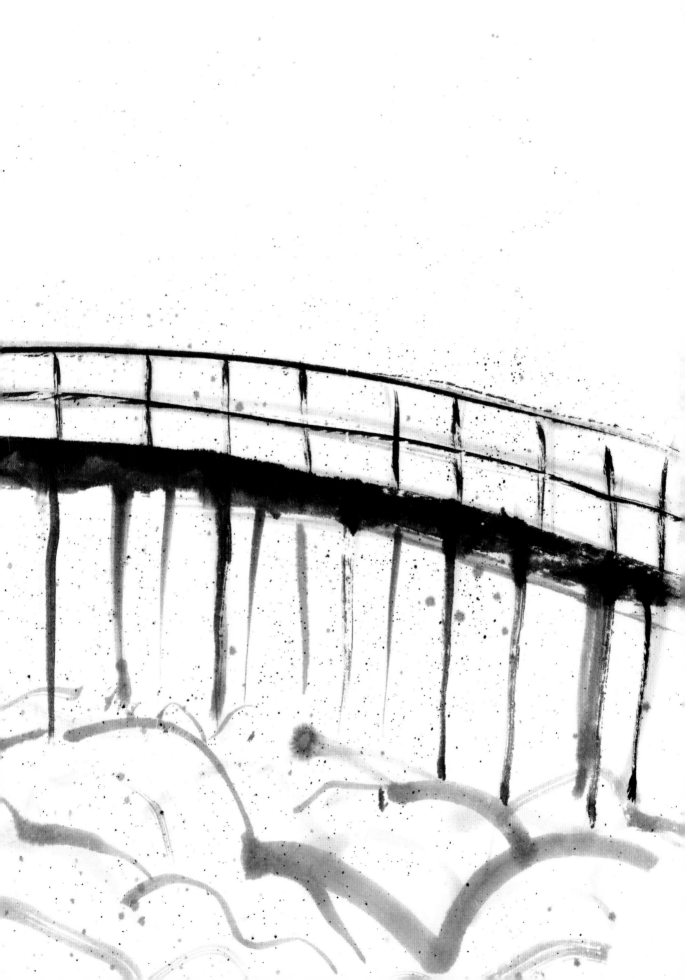

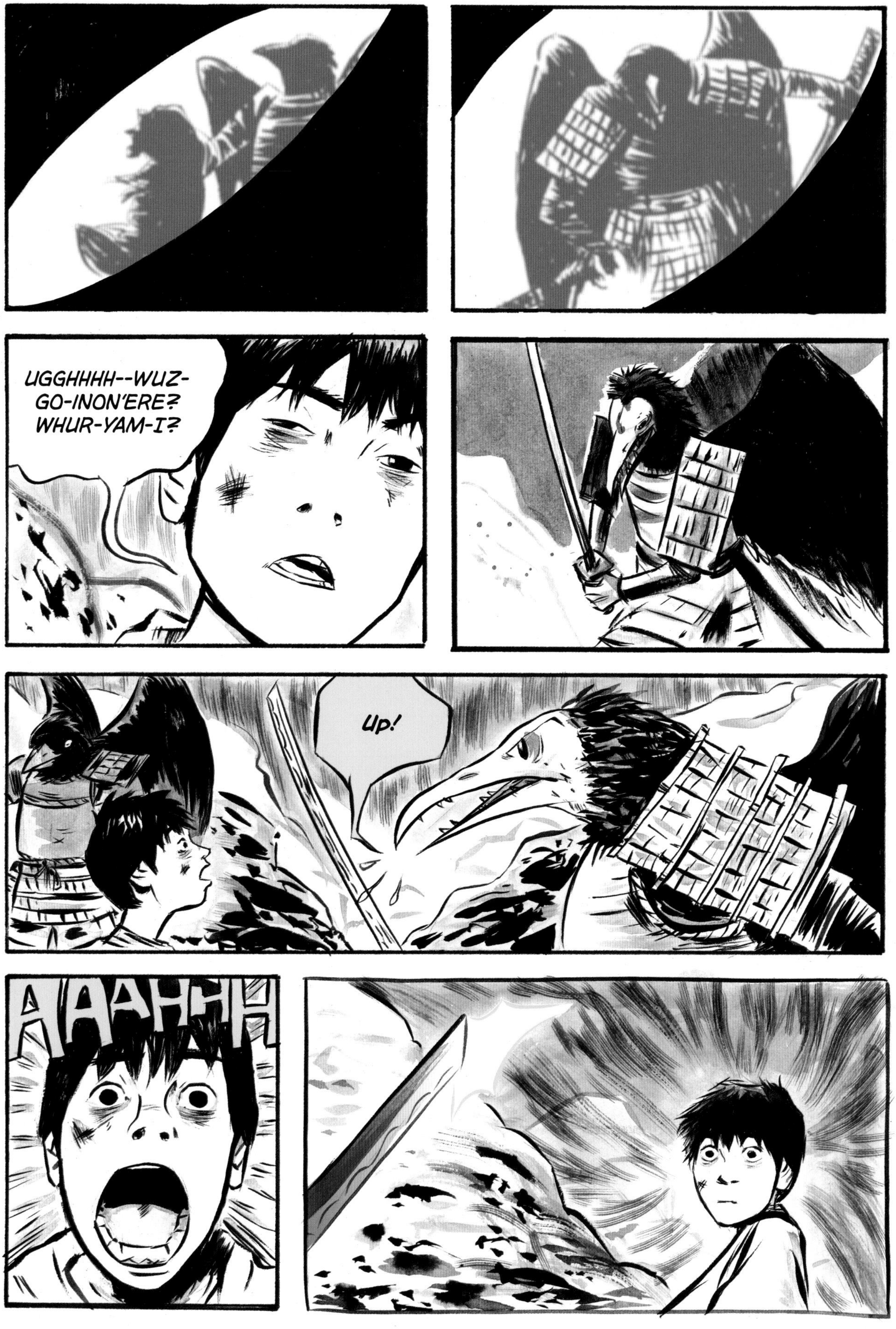
UGGHHHH--WUZ-
GO-INON'ERE?
WHUR-YAM-I?
Up!
AAAHHH

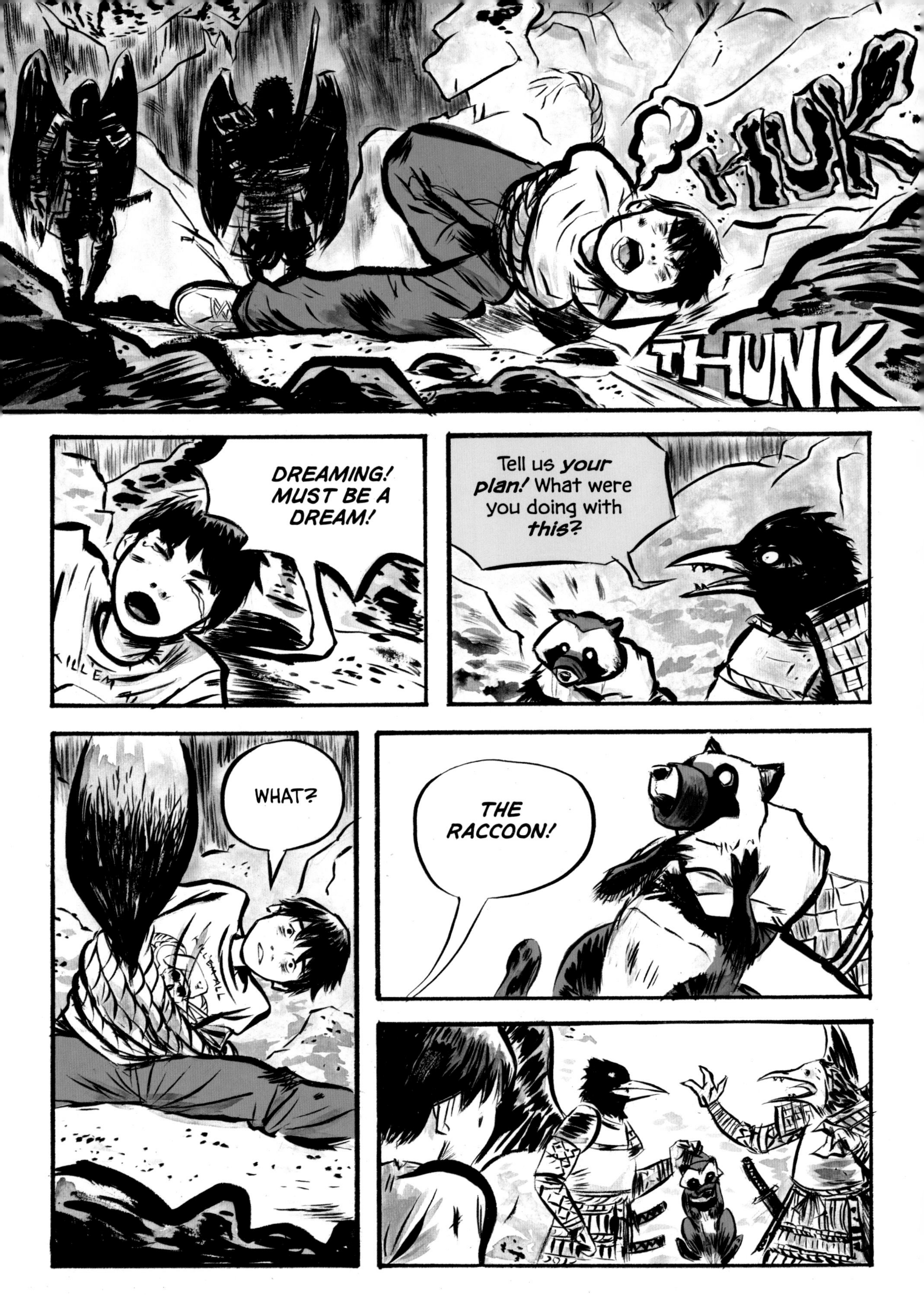
HUK
THUNK
DREAMING! MUST BE A DREAM!
Tell us *your plan!* What were you doing with *this?*
WHAT?
THE RACCOON!

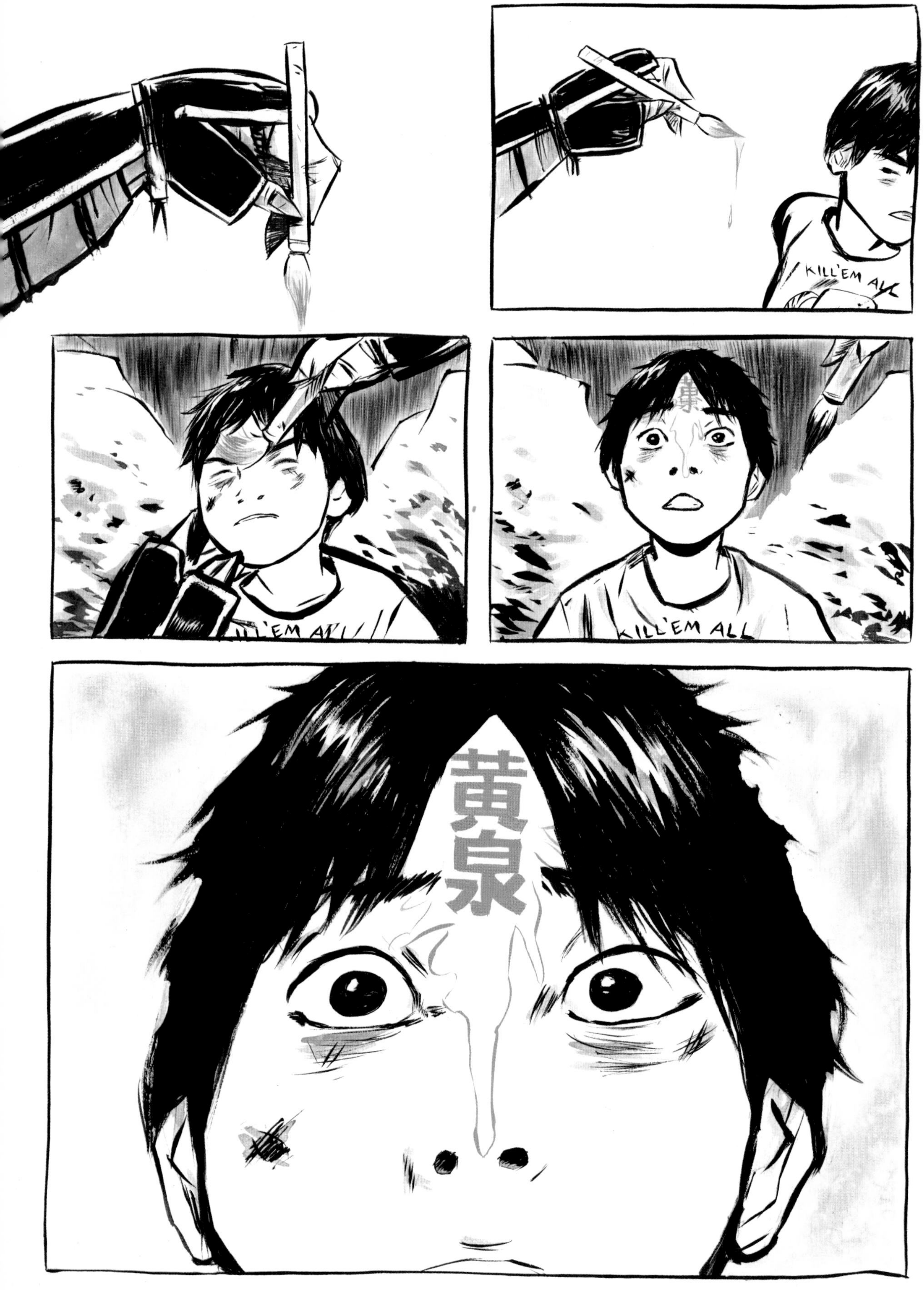
KILL'EM ALL
KILL'EM ALL
黄泉

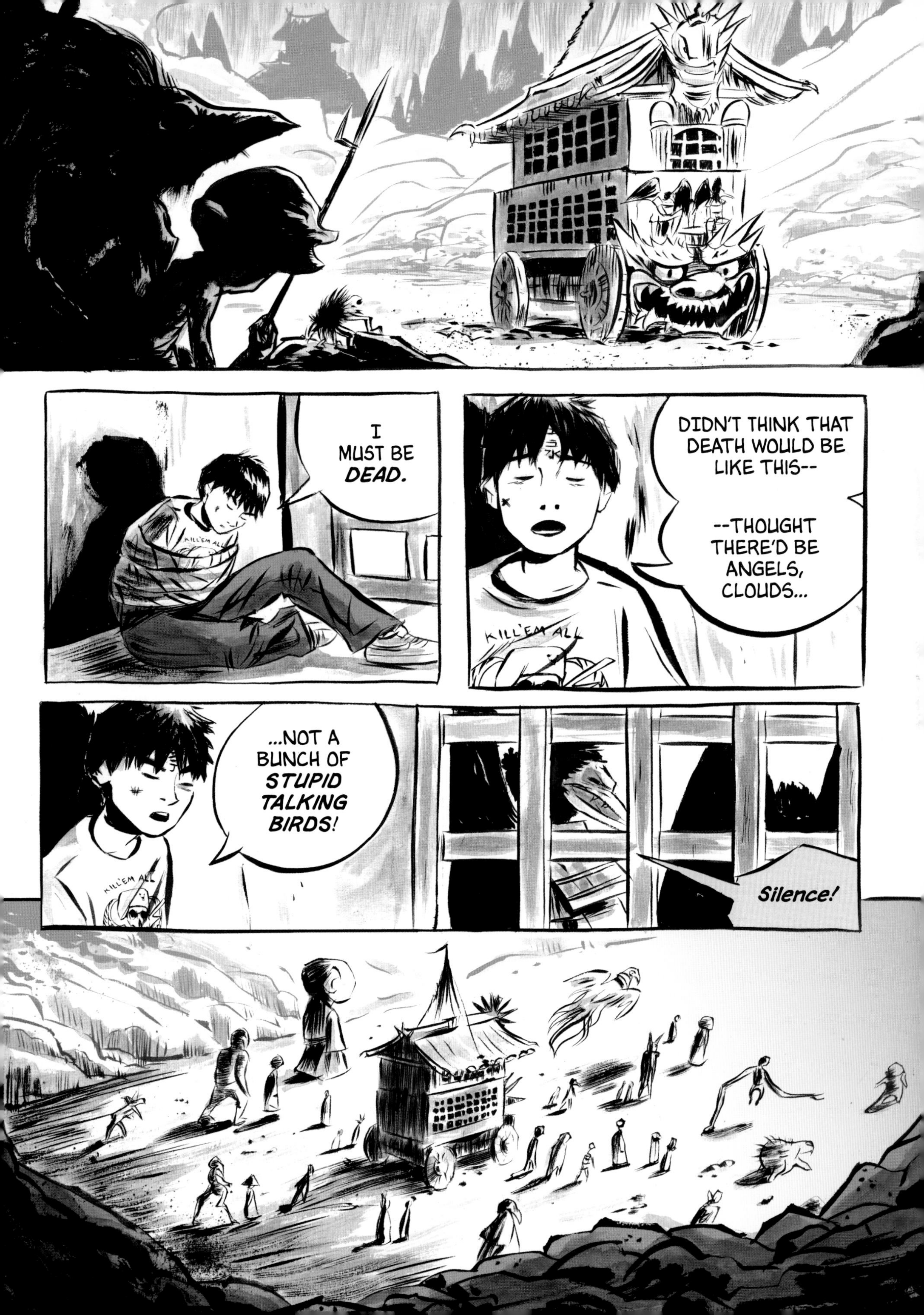

KILL'EM ALL
I MUST BE DEAD.
DIDN'T THINK THAT DEATH WOULD BE LIKE THIS--
--THOUGHT THERE'D BE ANGELS, CLOUDS...
KILL'EM ALL
...NOT A BUNCH OF STUPID TALKING BIRDS!
KILL'EM ALL
Silence!

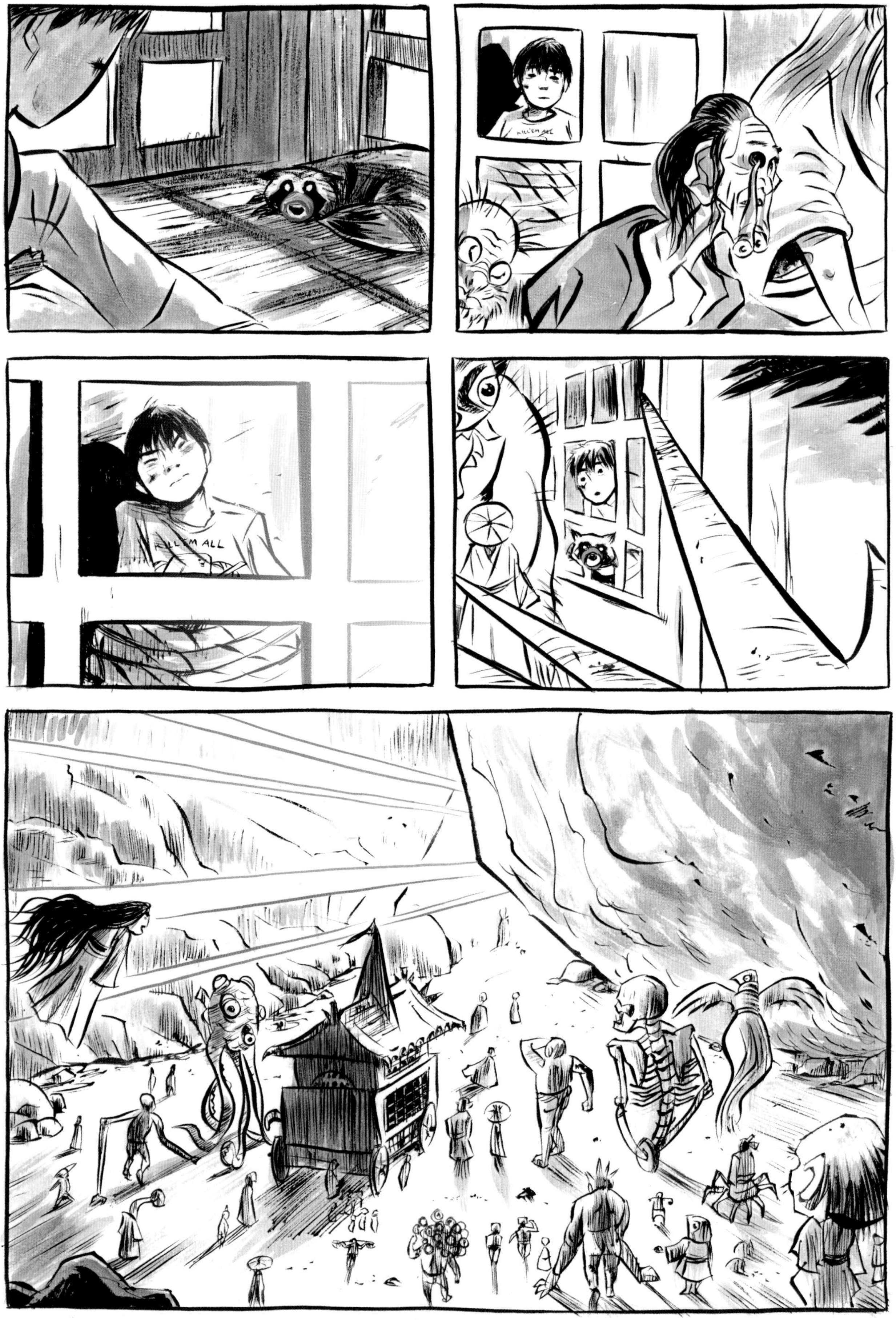
KILL'EM ALL
KILL'EM ALL

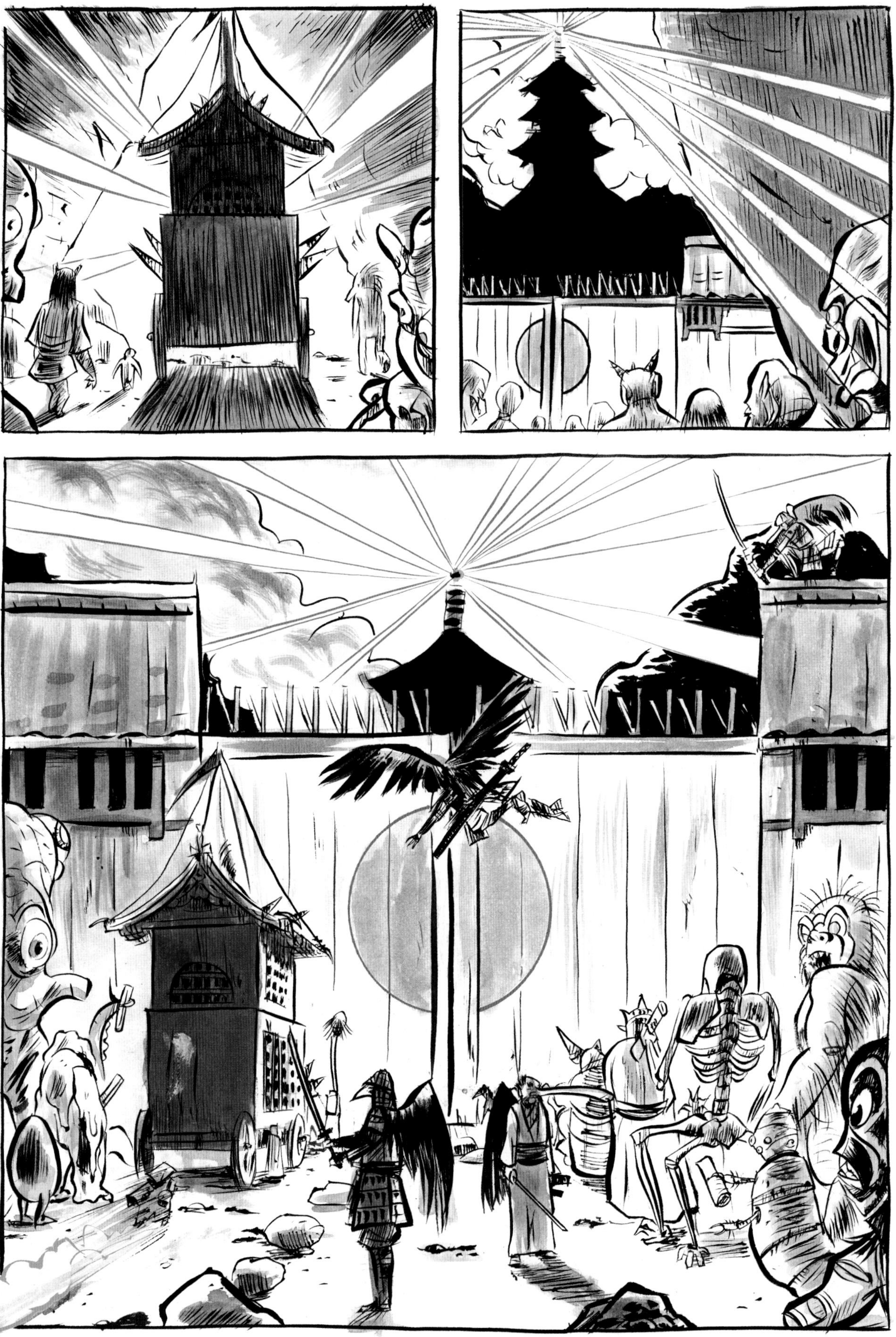

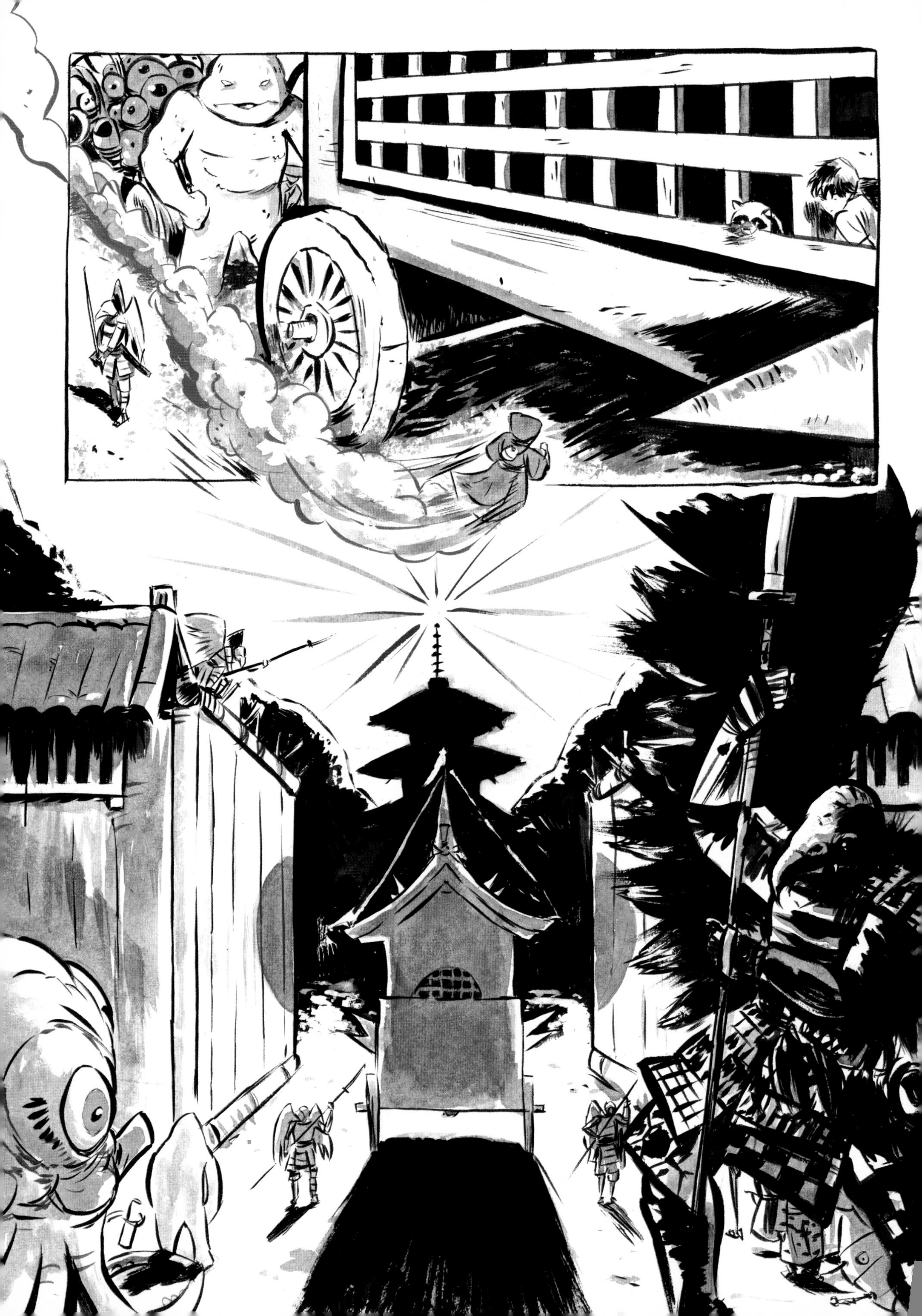

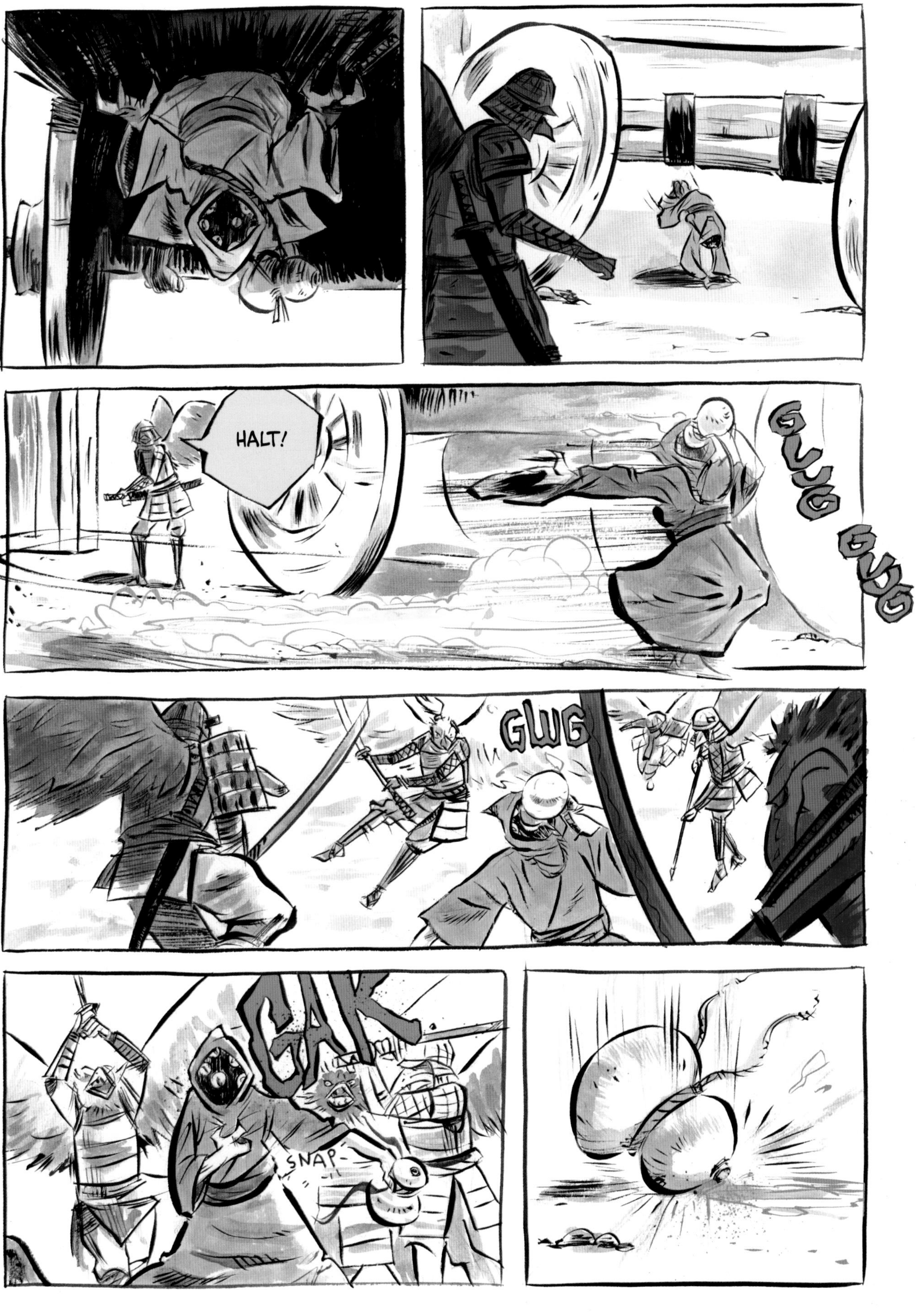
HALT!
GLUG GLUG
GLUG
CAK
SNAP

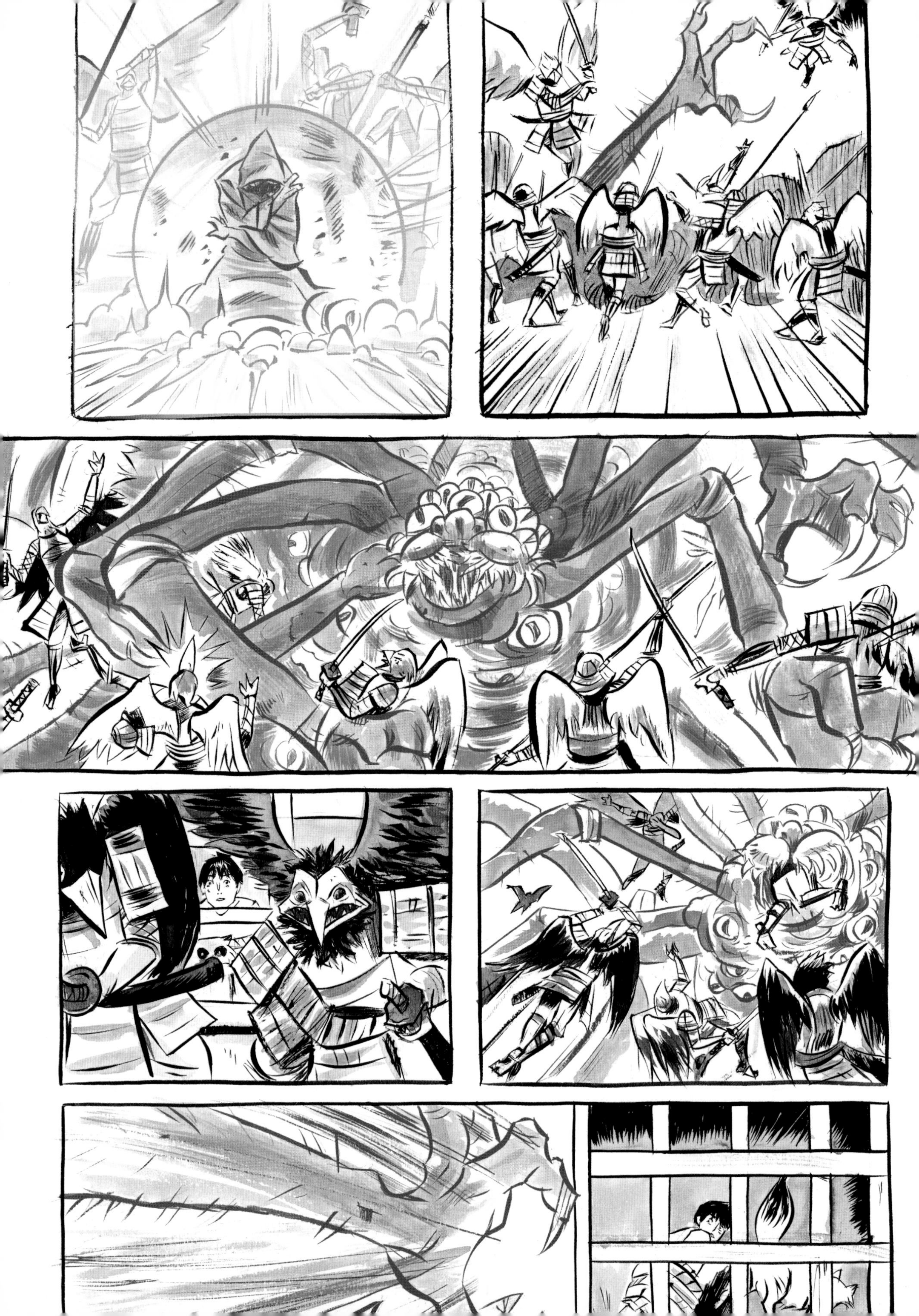

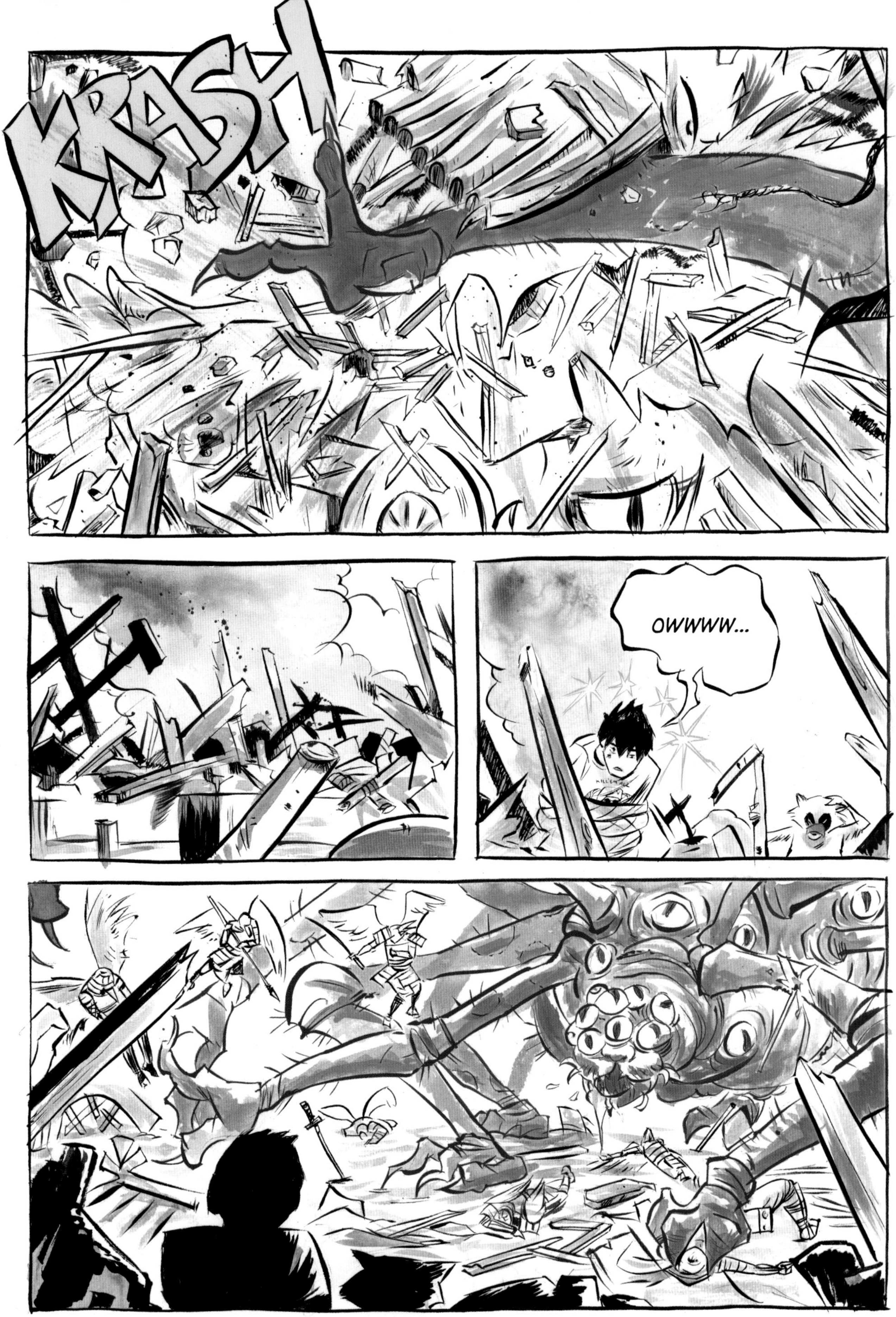
KRASH
OWWWW...

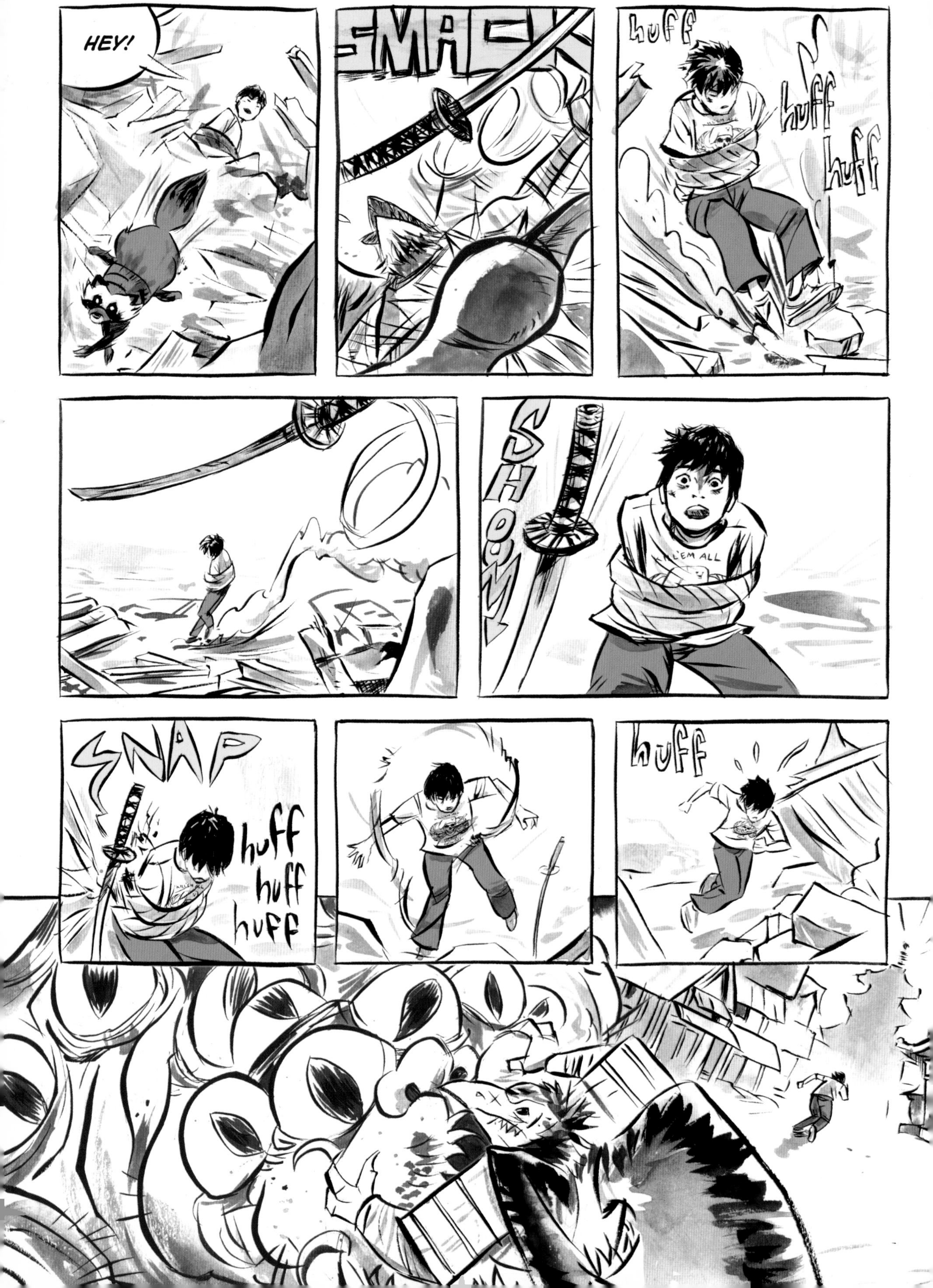
HEY!
SMACK
huff
huff
huff
SHOOM
SNAP
huff
huff
huff
huff

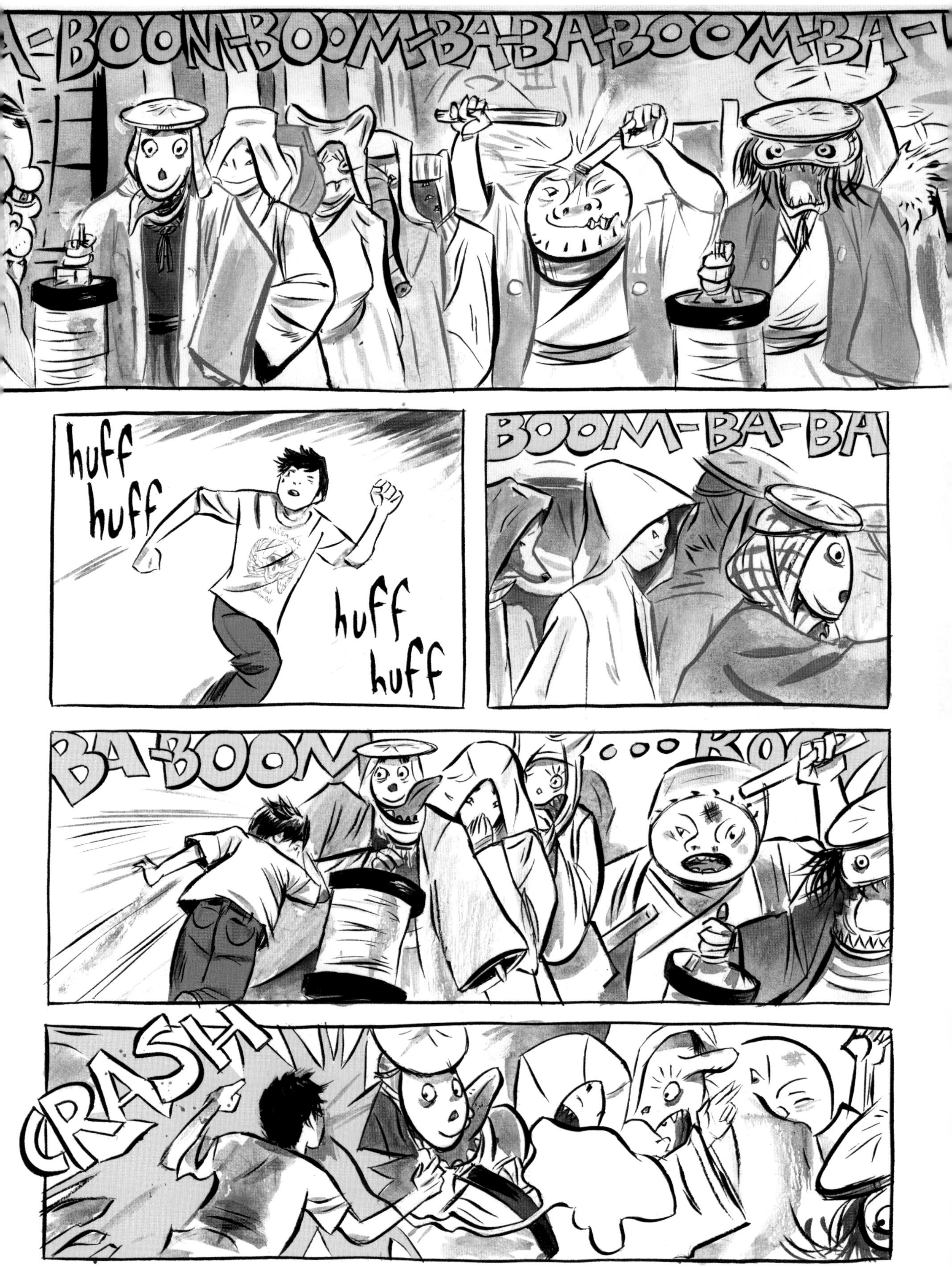
A-BOOM-BOOM-BA-BA-BOOM-BA-
huff
huff
huff
huff
BOOM-BA-BA
BA-BOOM
CRASH

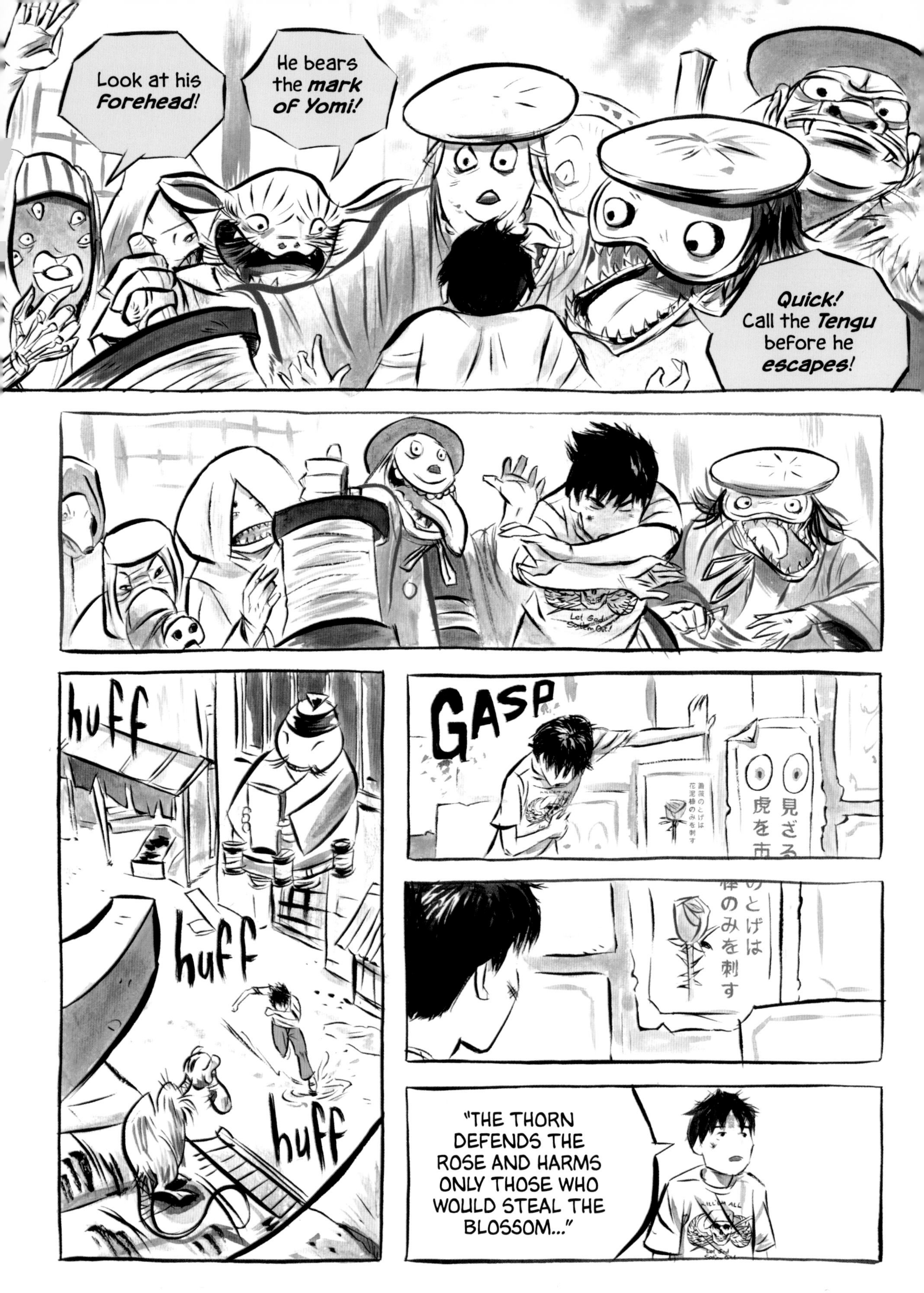
Look at his *forehead*!
He bears the *mark of Yomi*!
Quick! Call the *Tengu* before he *escapes*!
huff
huff
huff
GASP
"THE THORN DEFENDS THE ROSE AND HARMS ONLY THOSE WHO WOULD STEAL THE BLOSSOM..."

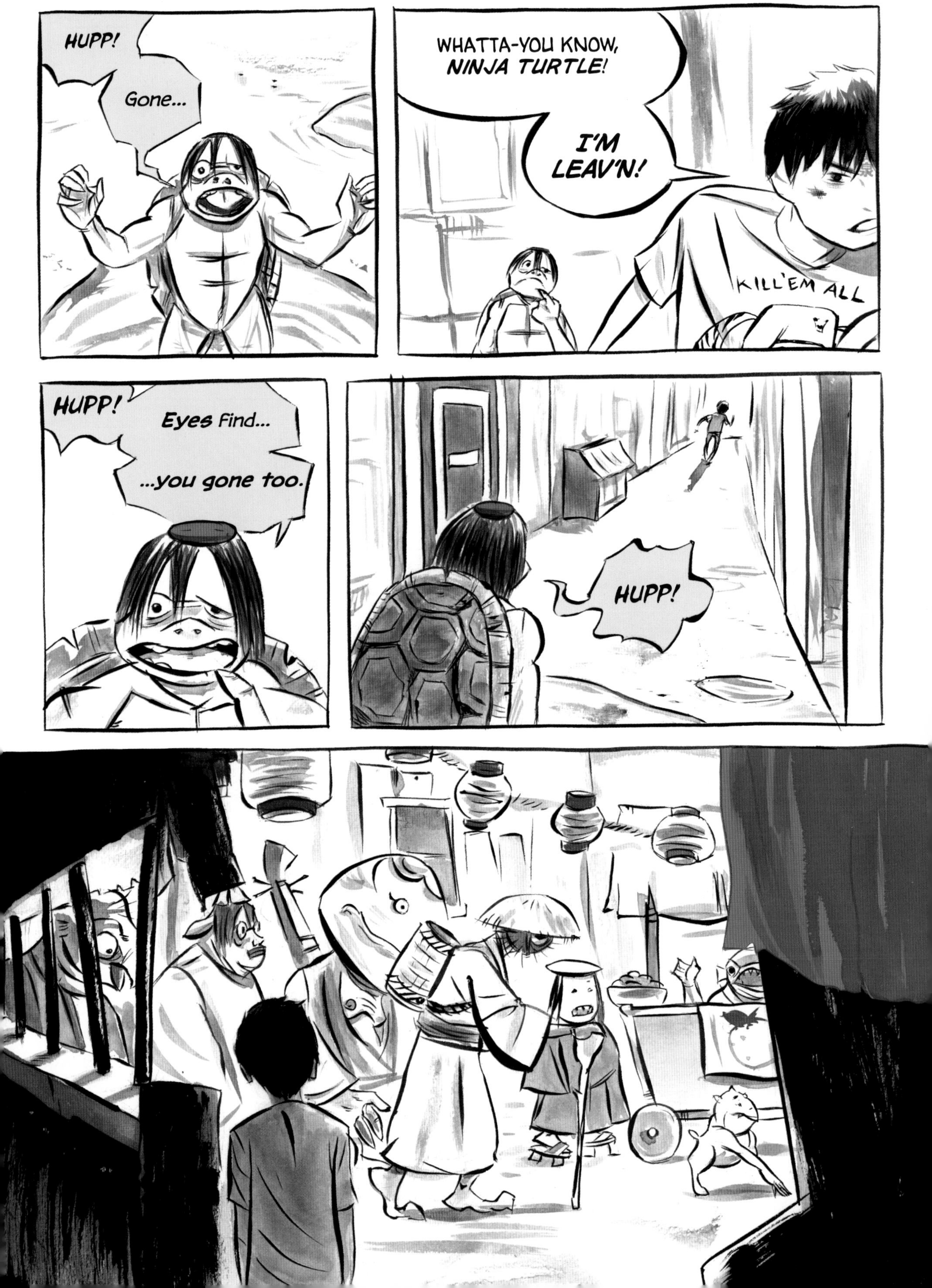
HUPP!
Gone...
WHATTA-YOU KNOW, NINJA TURTLE!
I'M LEAV'N!
KILL'EM ALL
HUPP!
Eyes find...
...you gone too.
HUPP!

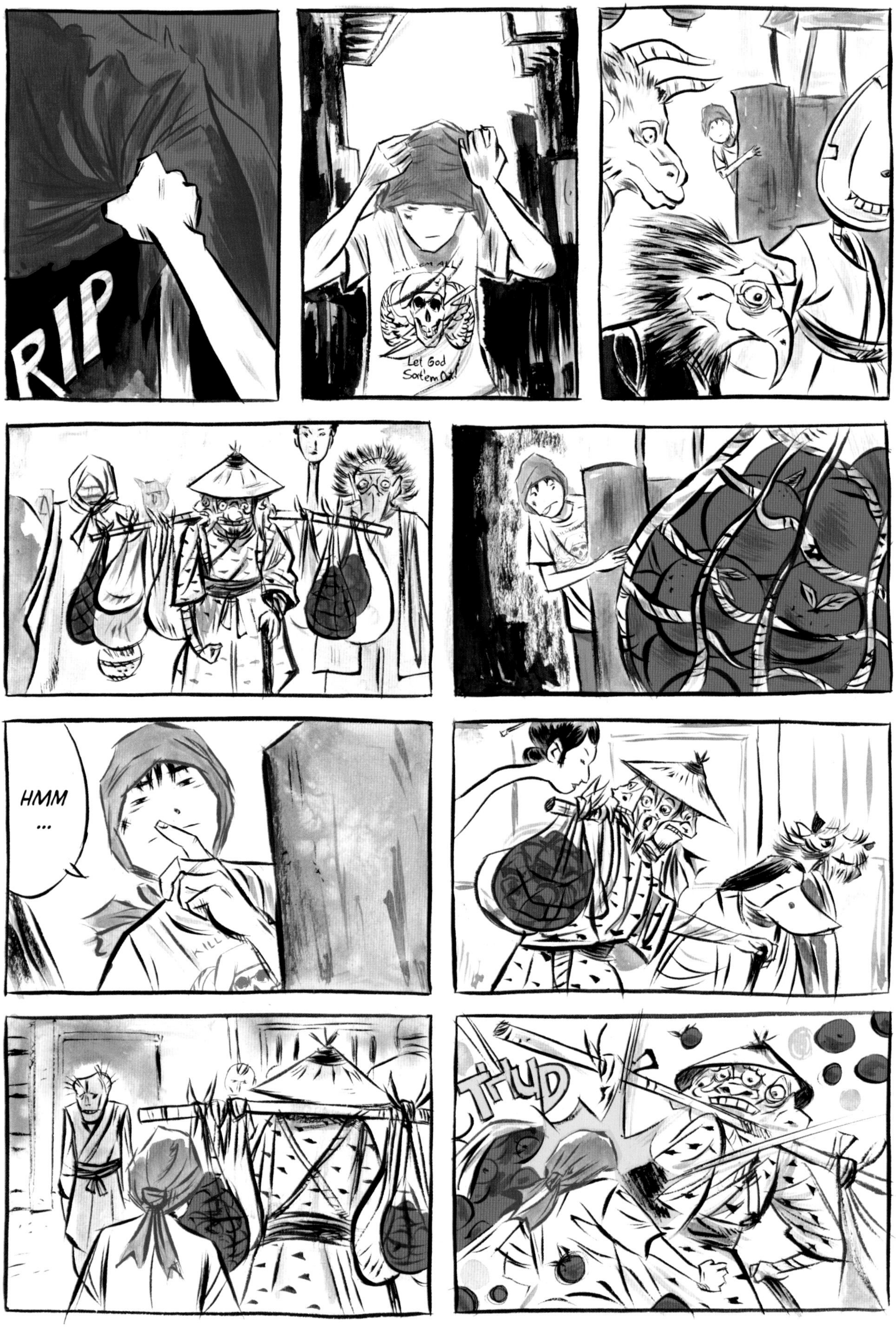
RIP
KILL 'EM ALL
Let God Sort'em Out!
HMM ...
THUD

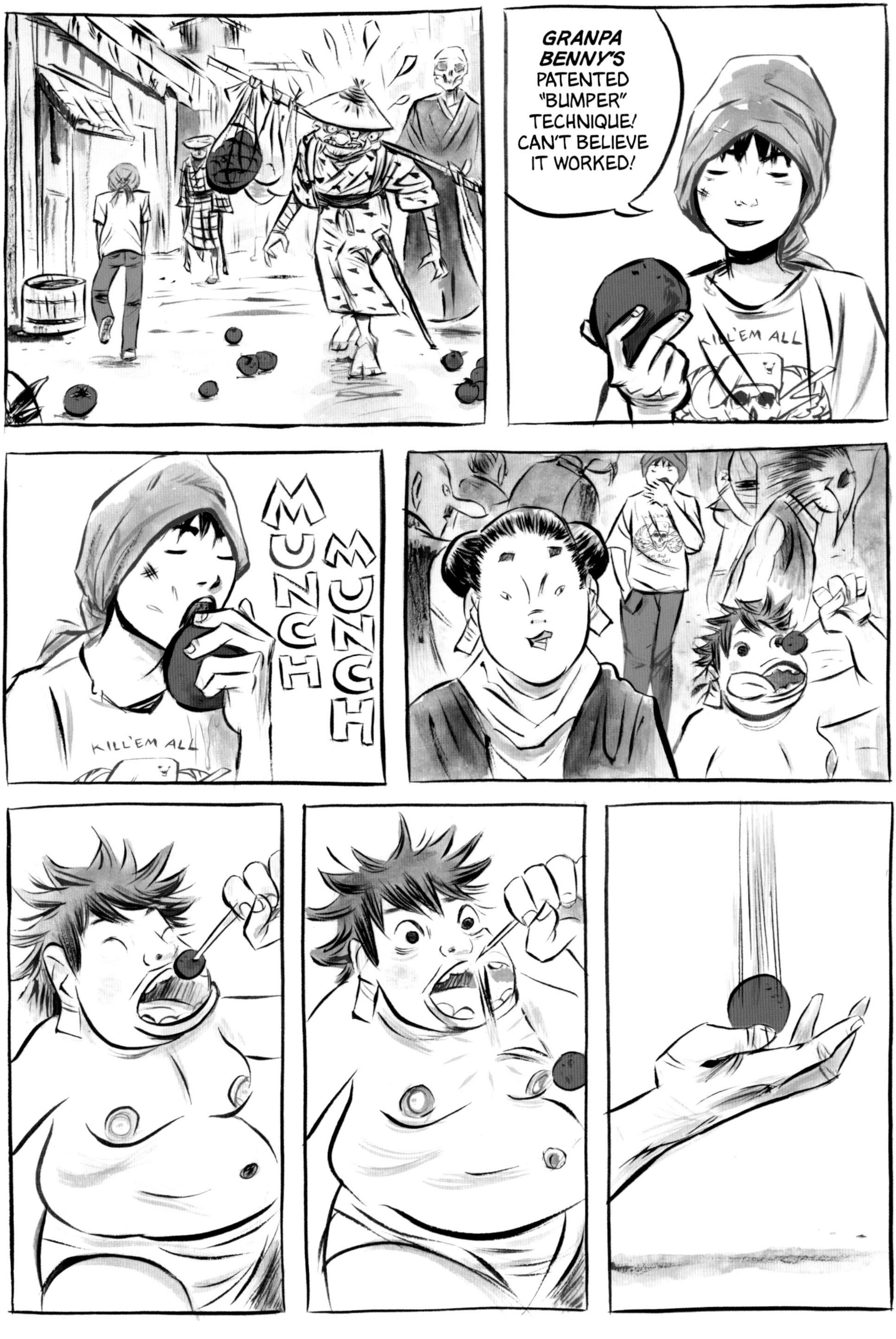
GRANPA BENNY'S PATENTED "BUMPER" TECHNIQUE! CAN'T BELIEVE IT WORKED!
KILL'EM ALL
KILL'EM ALL
MUNCH MUNCH

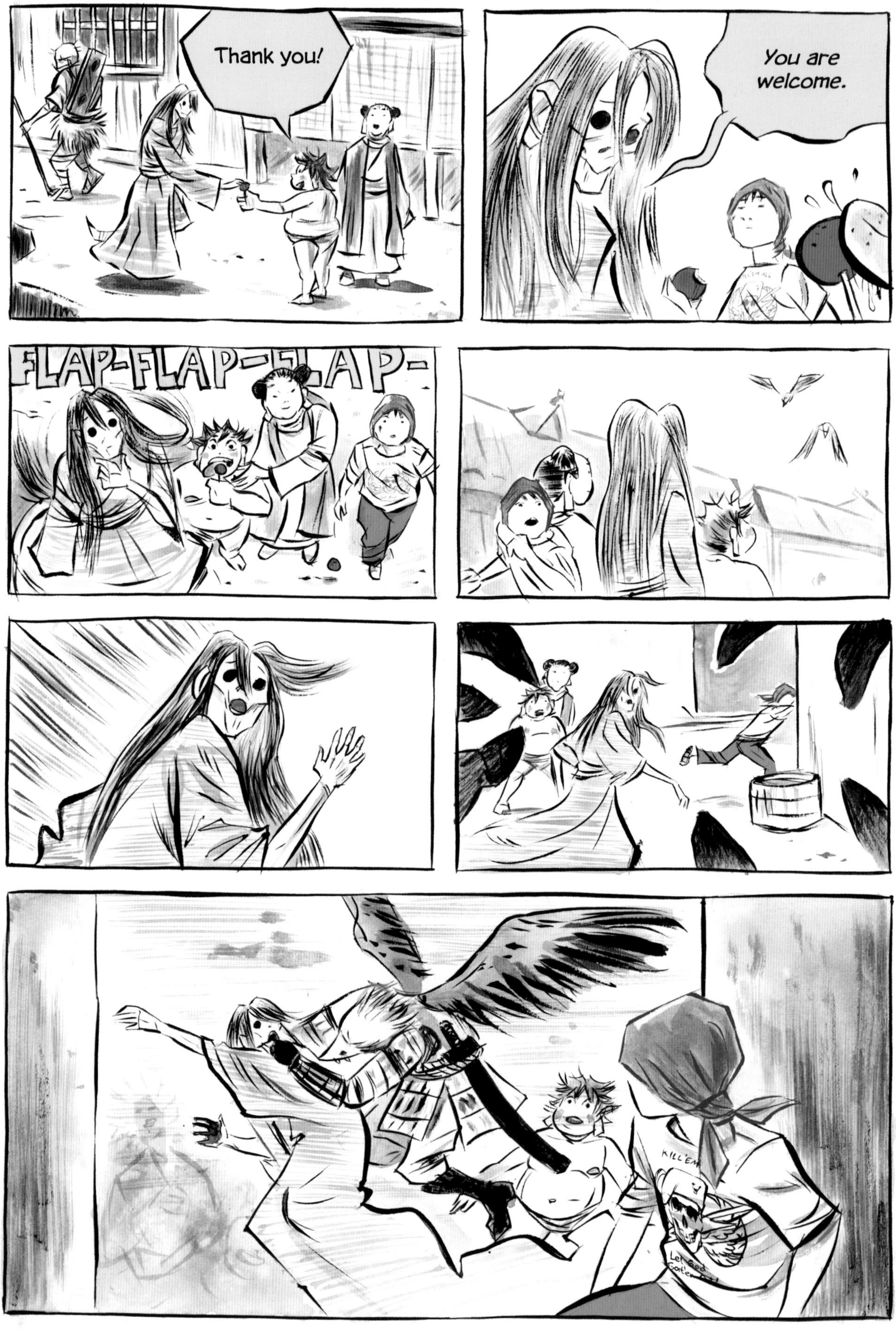
Thank you!
You are welcome.
FLAP-FLAP-FLAP-
KILL'EM

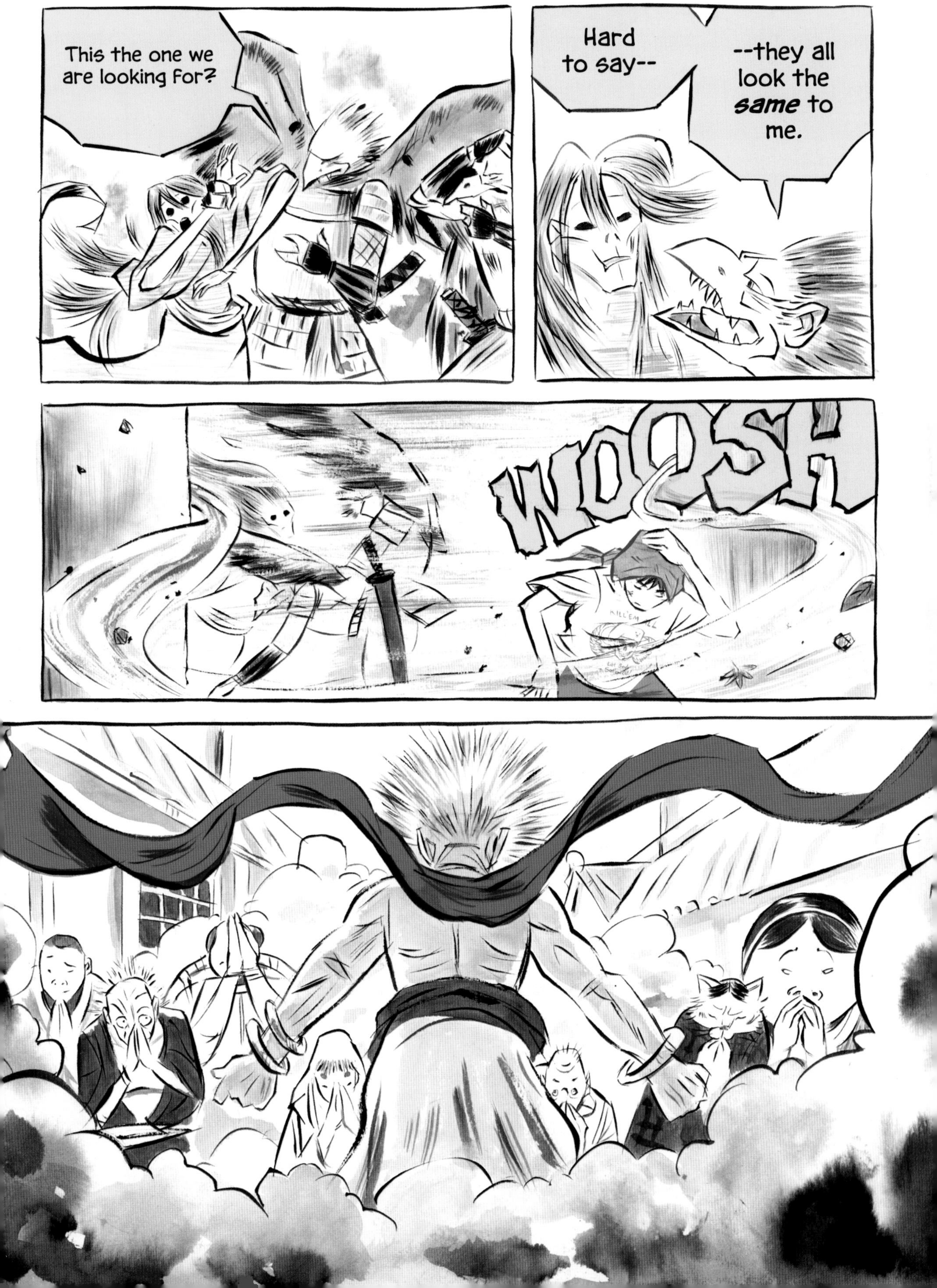
This the one we are looking for?
Hard to say--
--they all look the *same* to me.
WOOSH

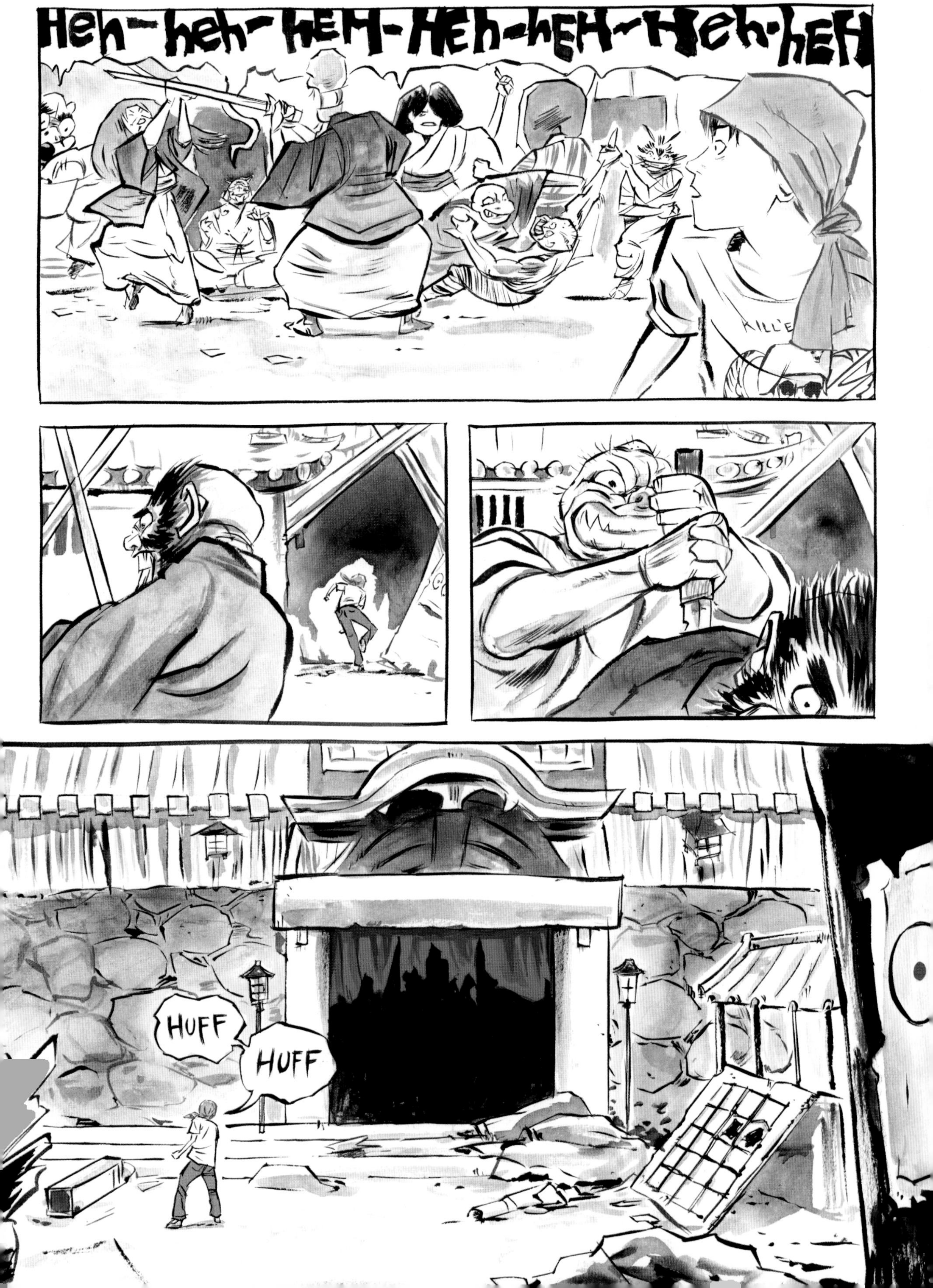
HEH-HEH-HEH-HEH-HEH-HEH-HEH
HUFF
HUFF

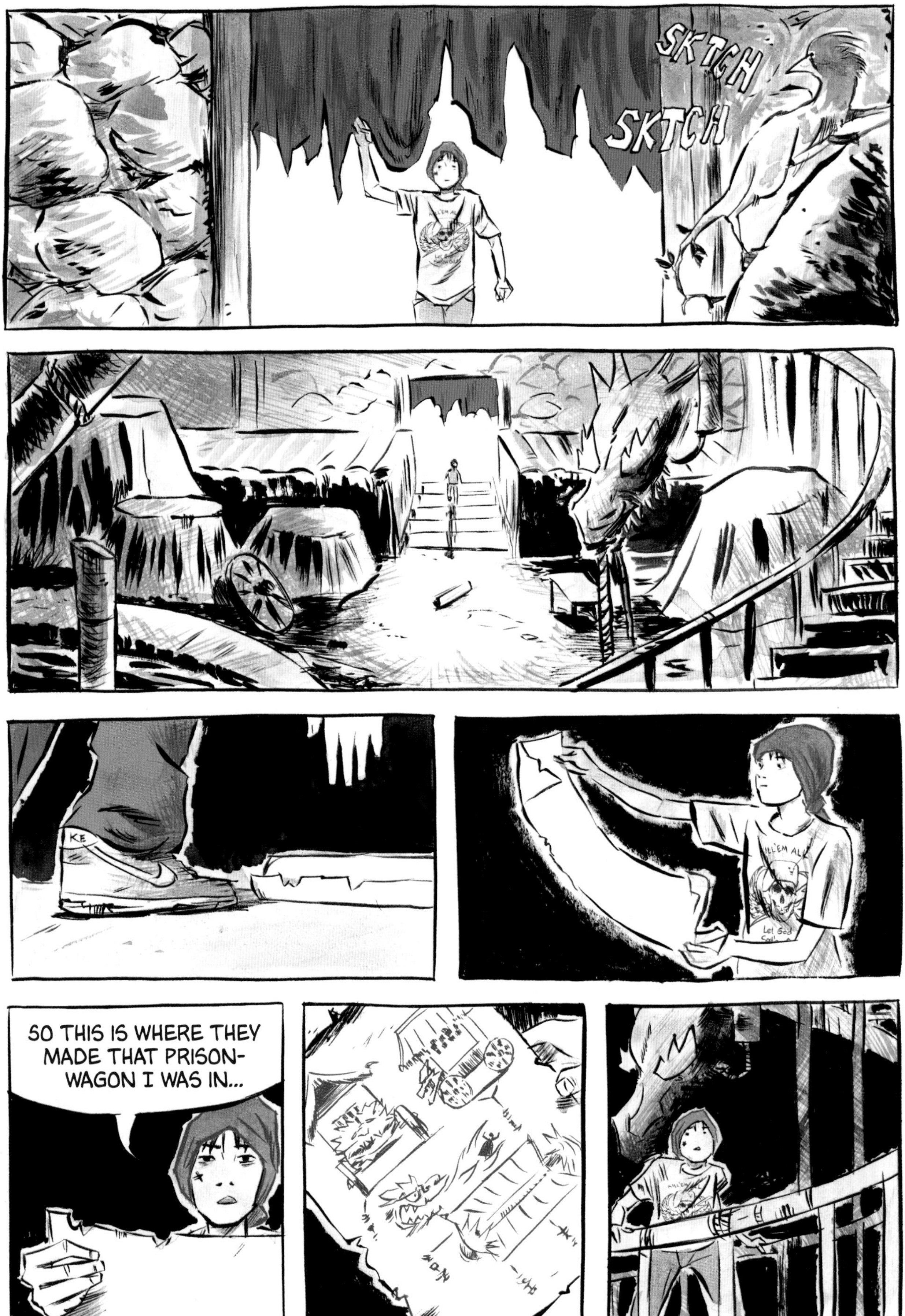
SKTCH
SKTCH
K.E.
SO THIS IS WHERE THEY MADE THAT PRISON-WAGON I WAS IN...

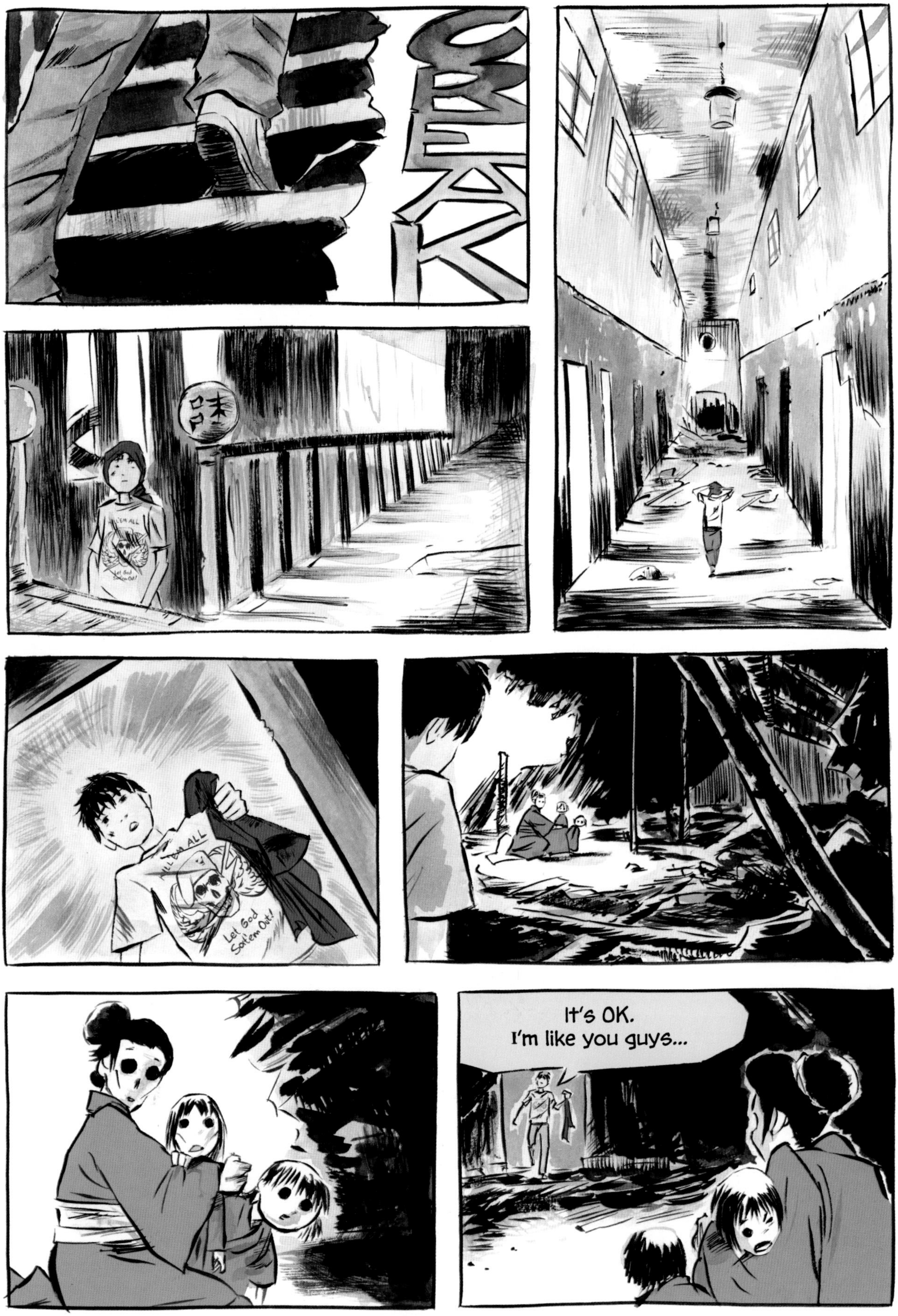
CREAK
Let God Sort'em Out!
It's OK.
I'm like you guys...

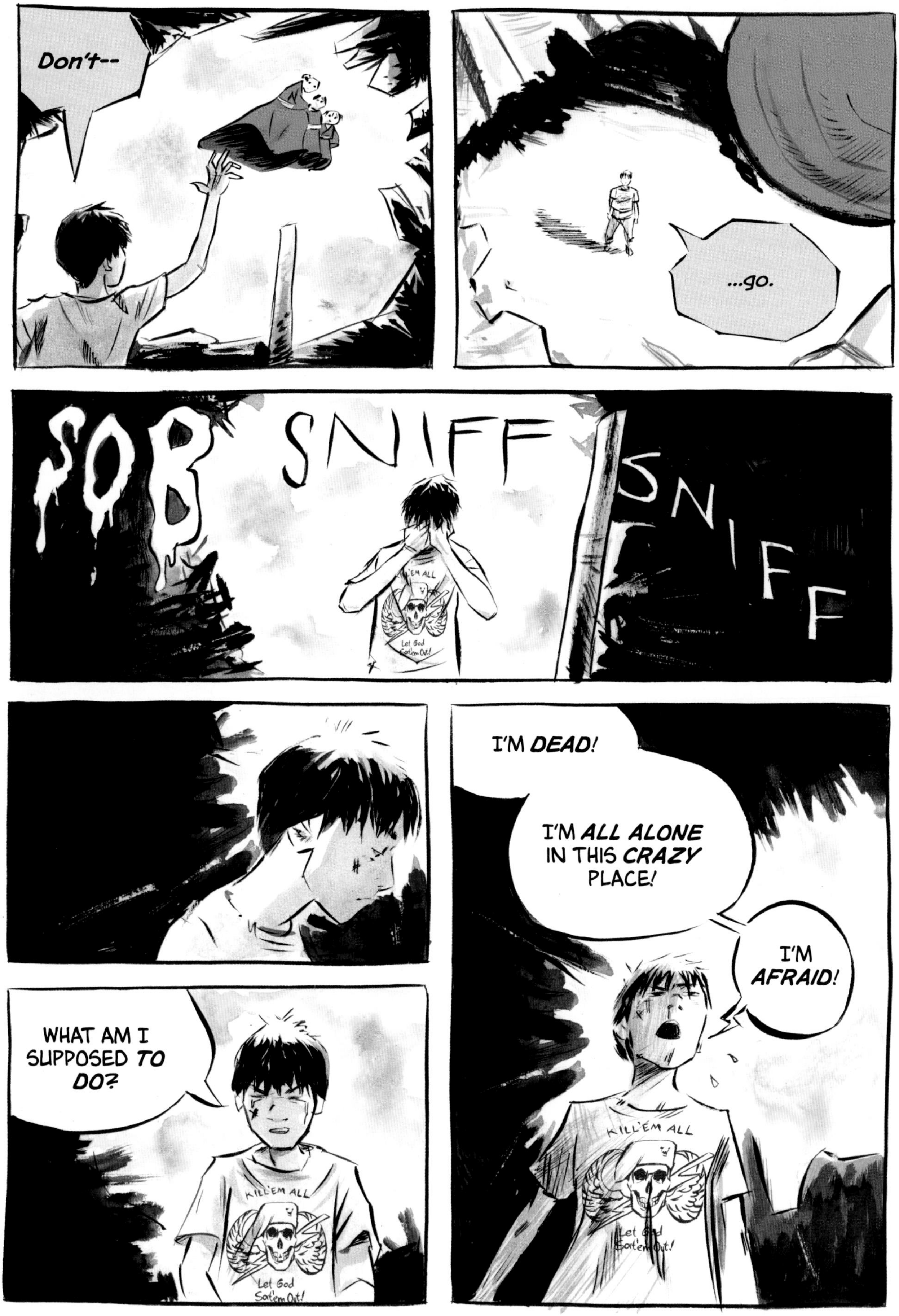
Don't--
...go.
SOB
SNIFF
SNIFF
KILL'EM ALL
Let God Sort'em Out!
I'M DEAD!
I'M ALL ALONE IN THIS CRAZY PLACE!
WHAT AM I SUPPOSED TO DO?
I'M AFRAID!

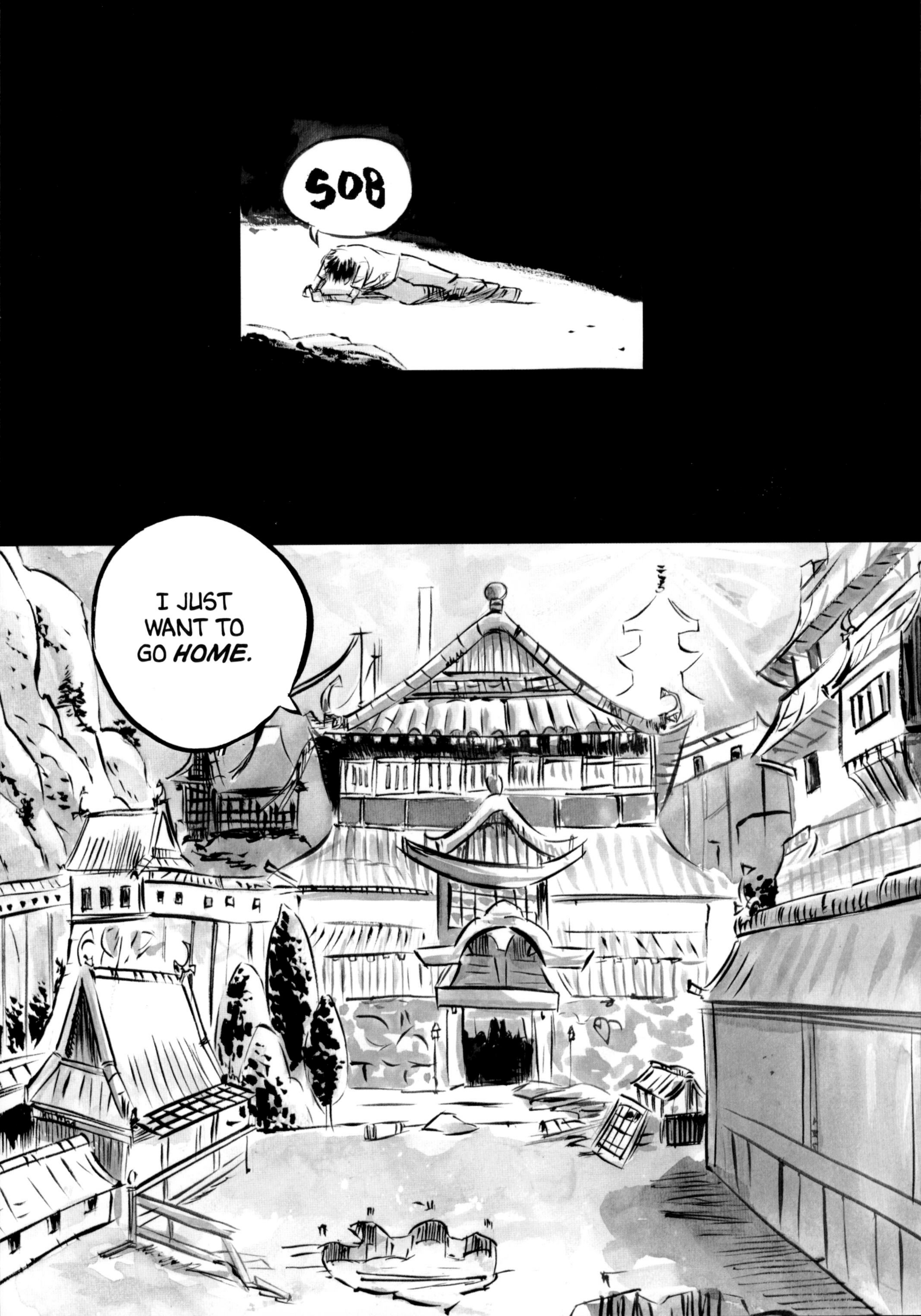
SOB
I JUST WANT TO GO *HOME.*

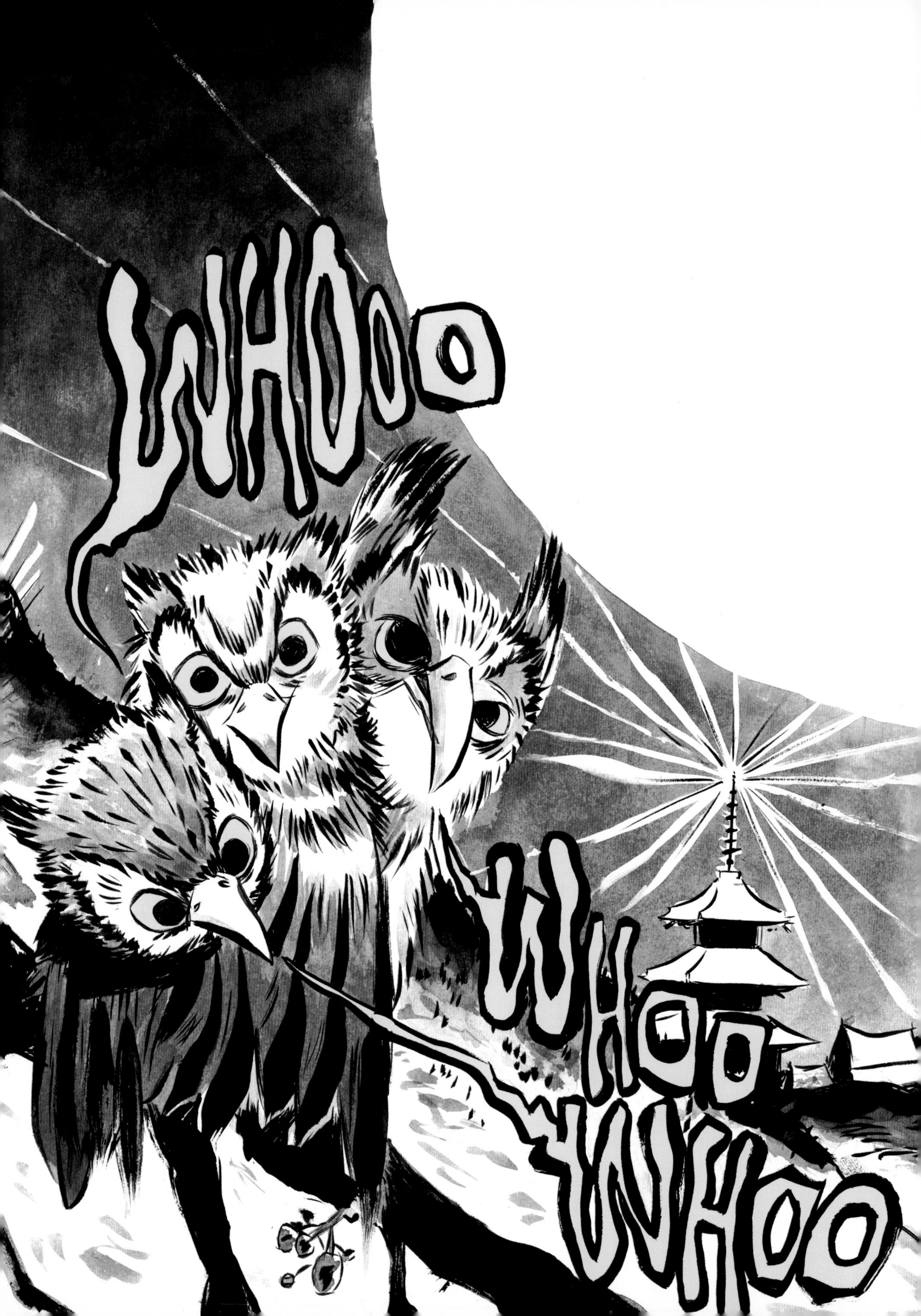
WHOoo
WHOO WHOO

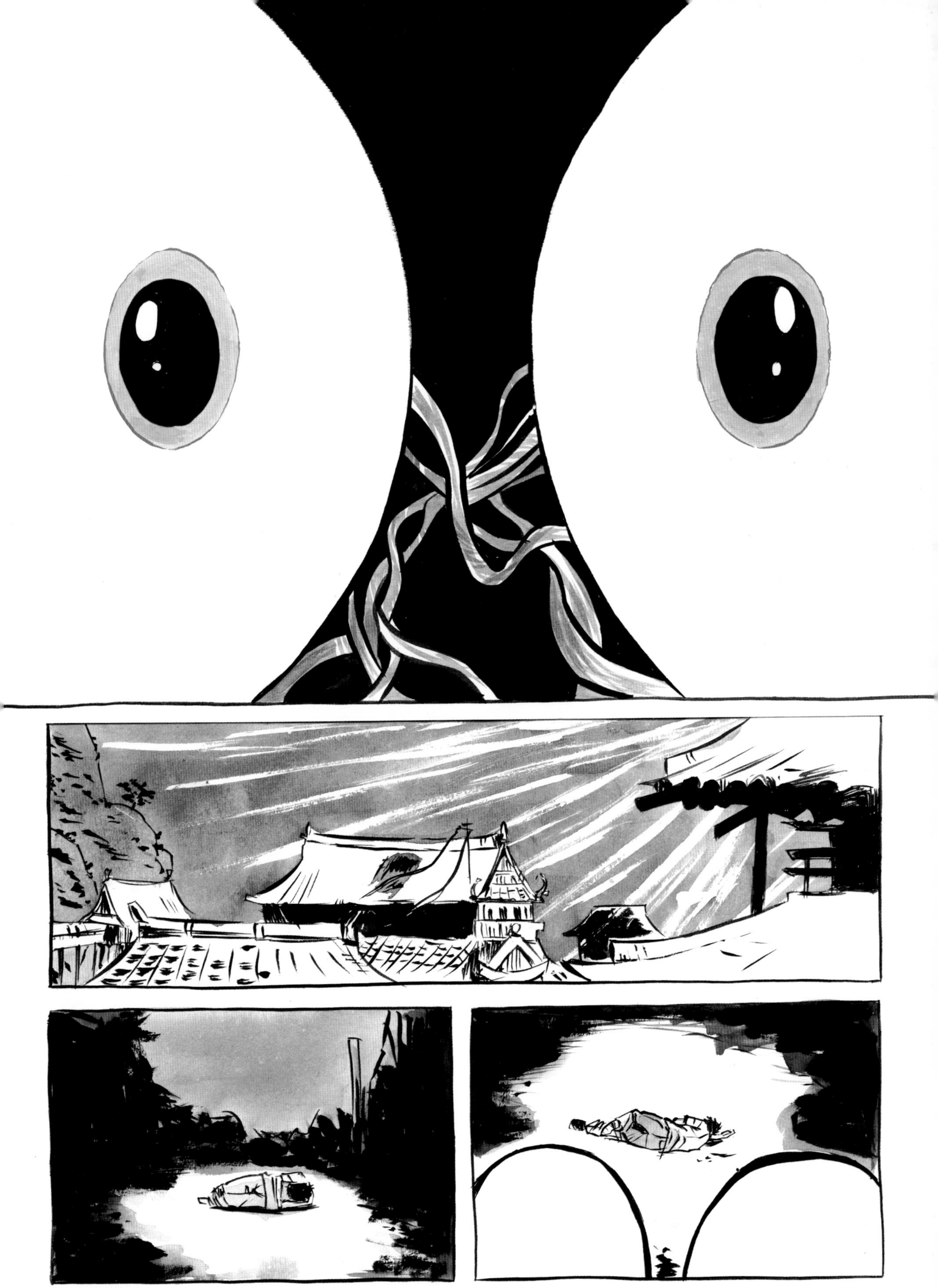

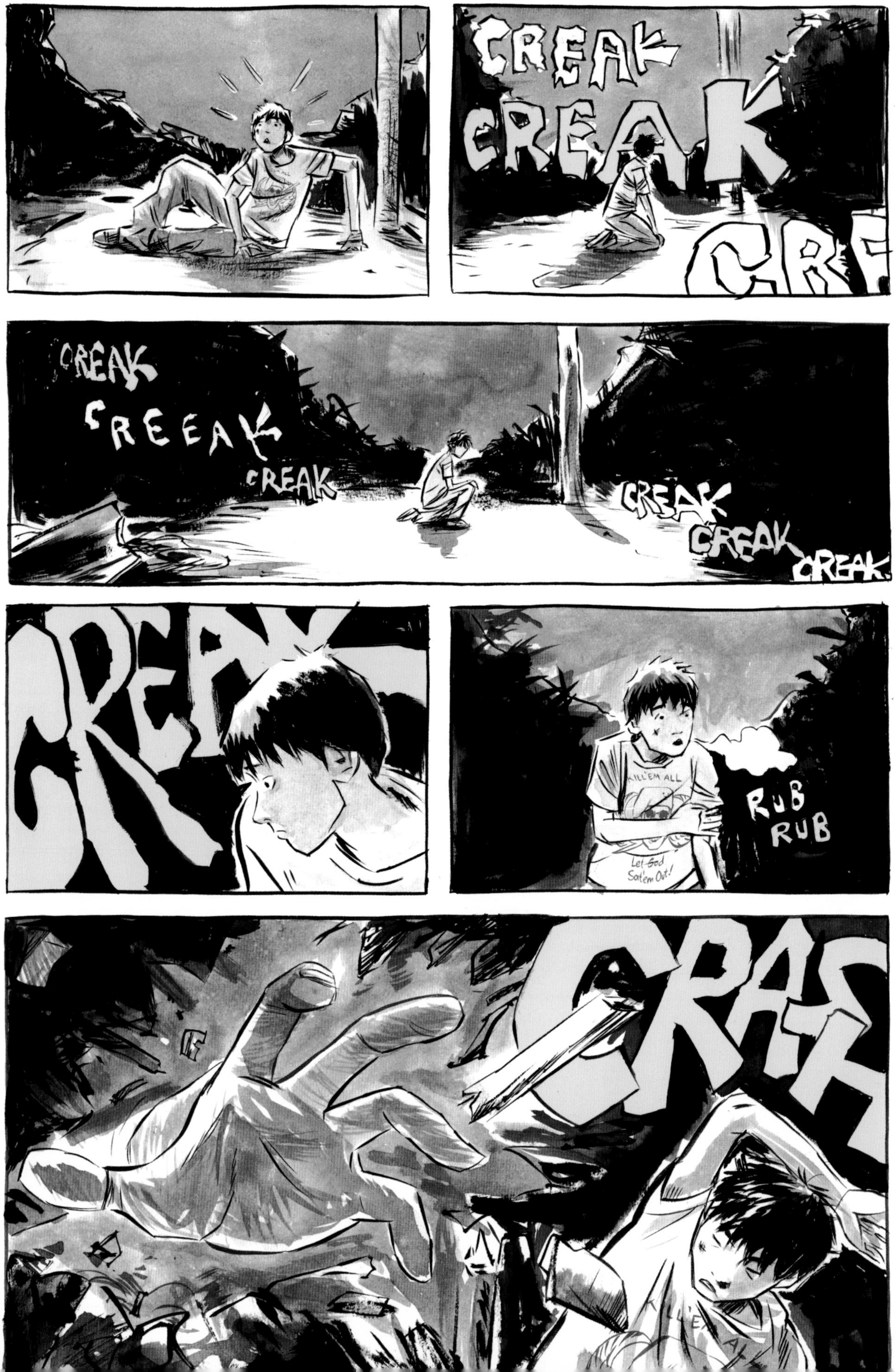
CREAK
CREAK
CREAK
CREEAK
CREAK
CREAK
CREAK
CREAK
RUB
RUB
KILL'EM ALL
Let God Sort'em Out!

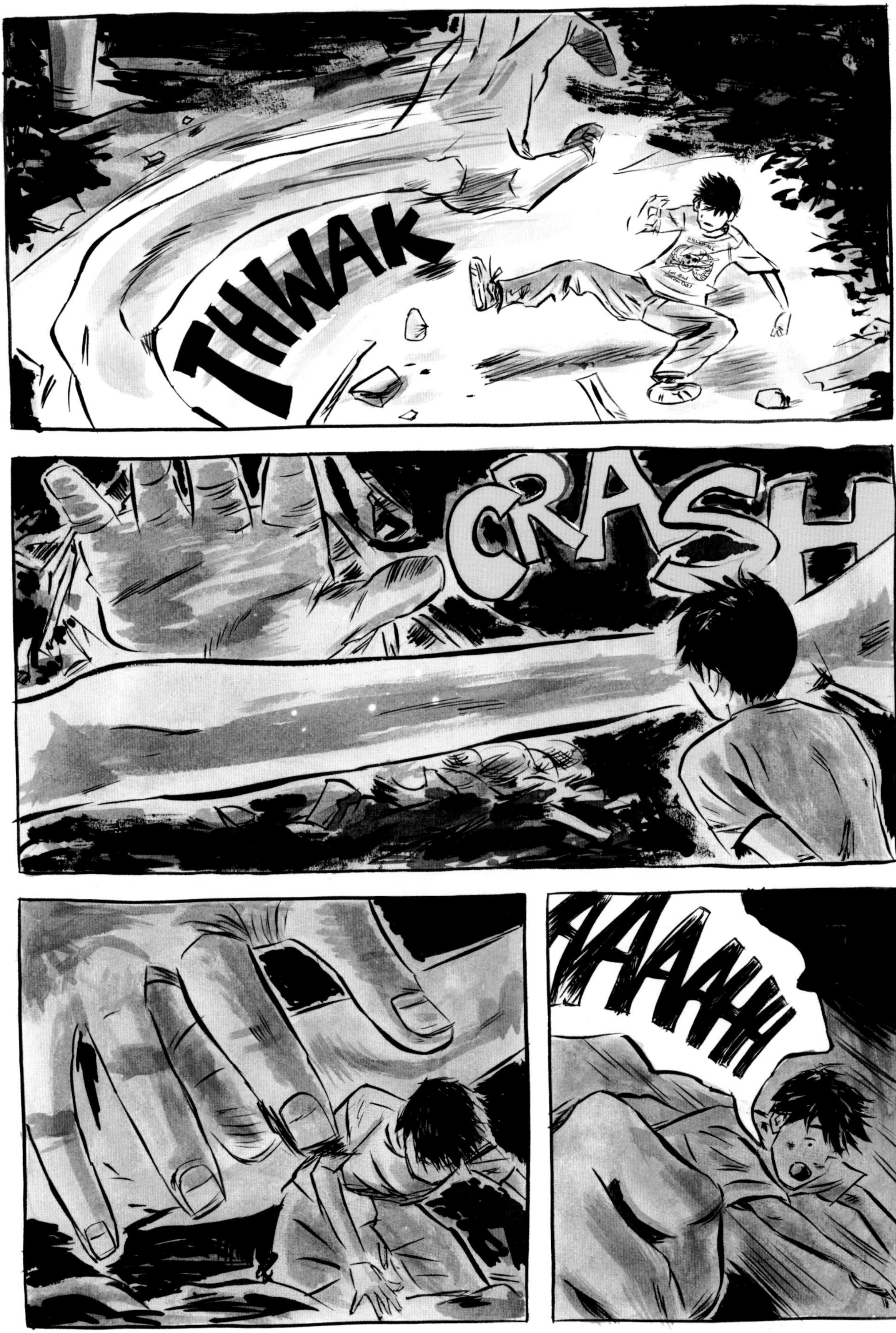
THWAK
CRASH
AAAAHH

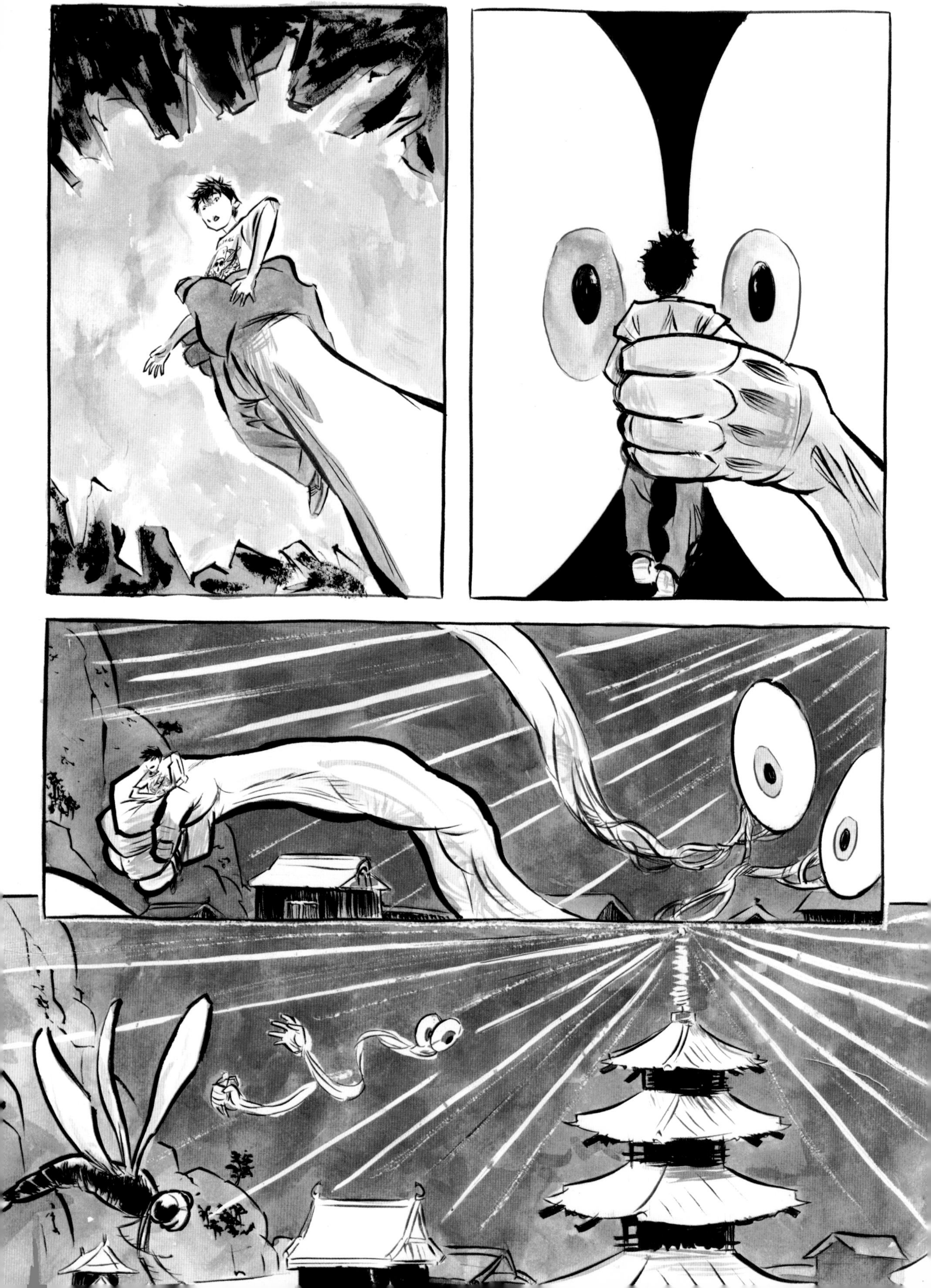

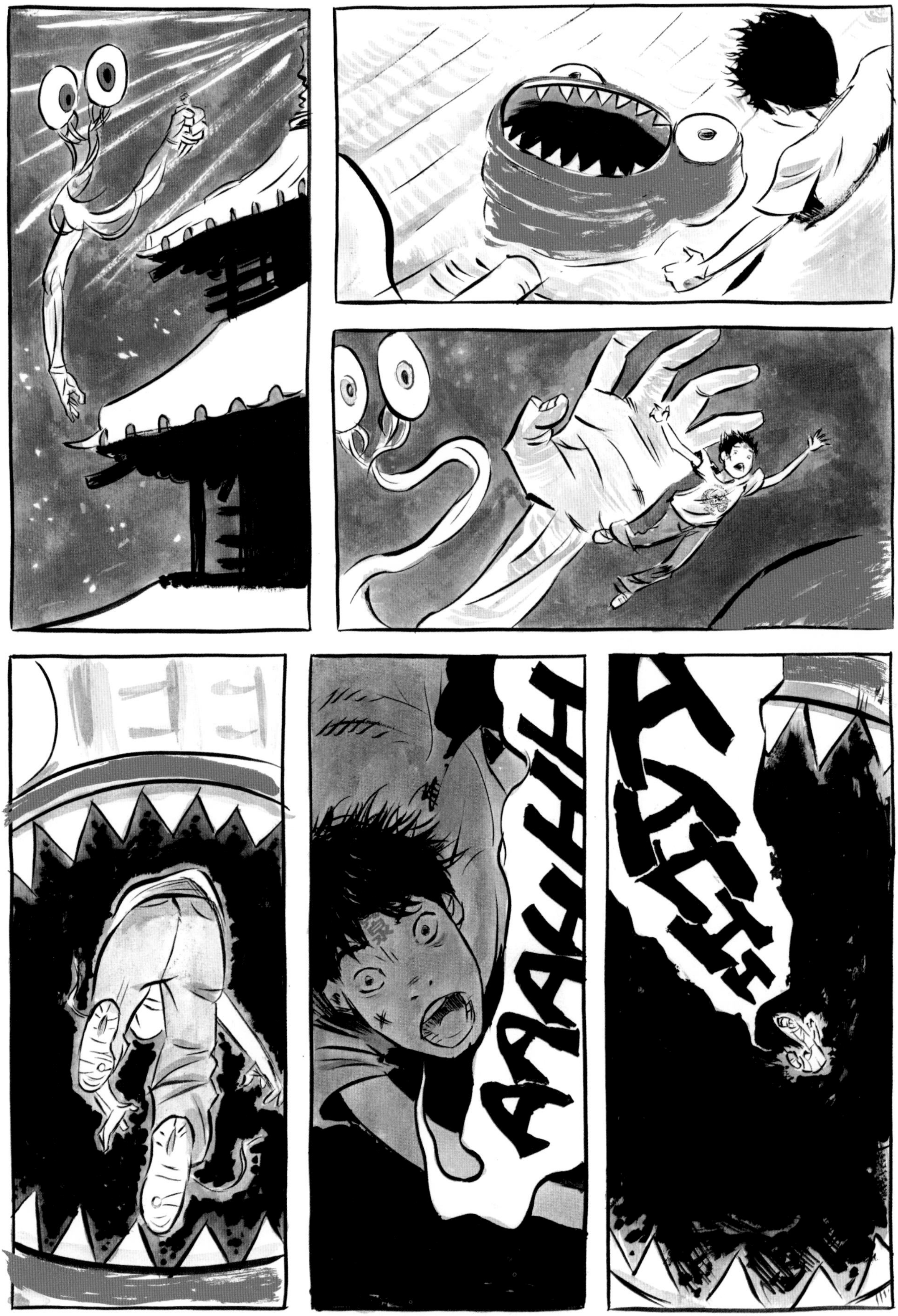
AAAAHHH
AHHHH

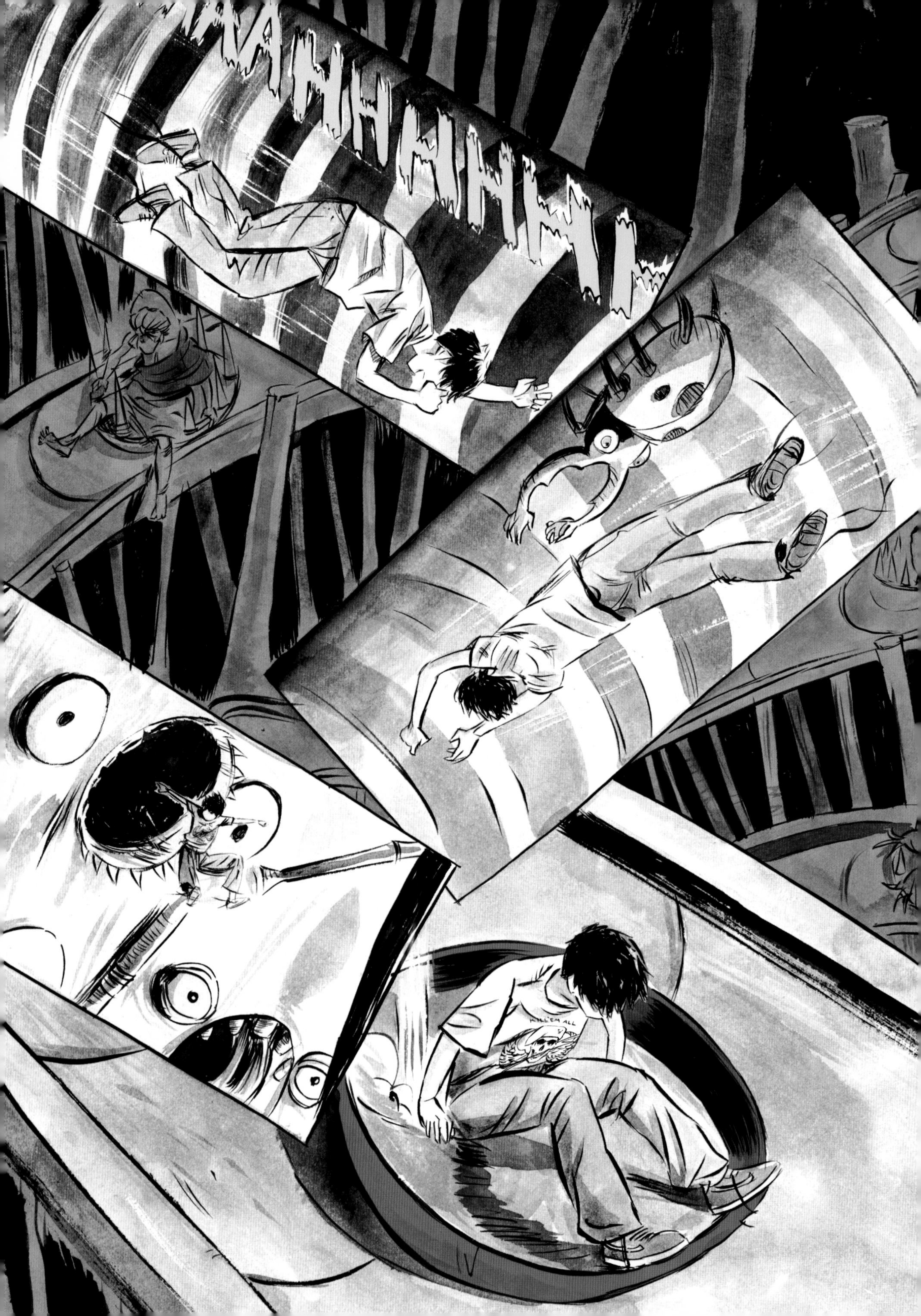

KILL'EM ALL

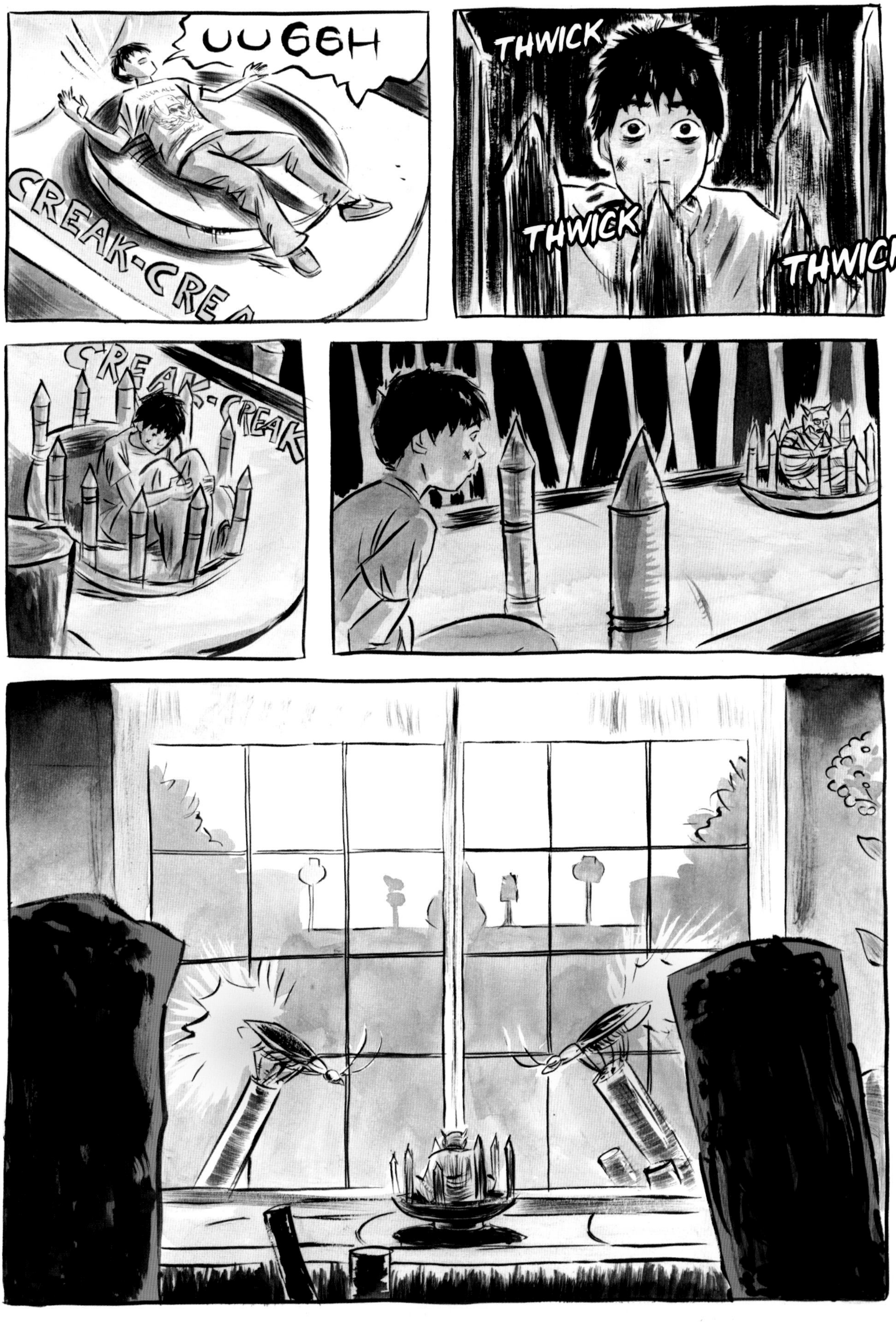
UUGGH
CREAK-CREA
THWICK
THWICK
THWICK
CREAK-CREAK

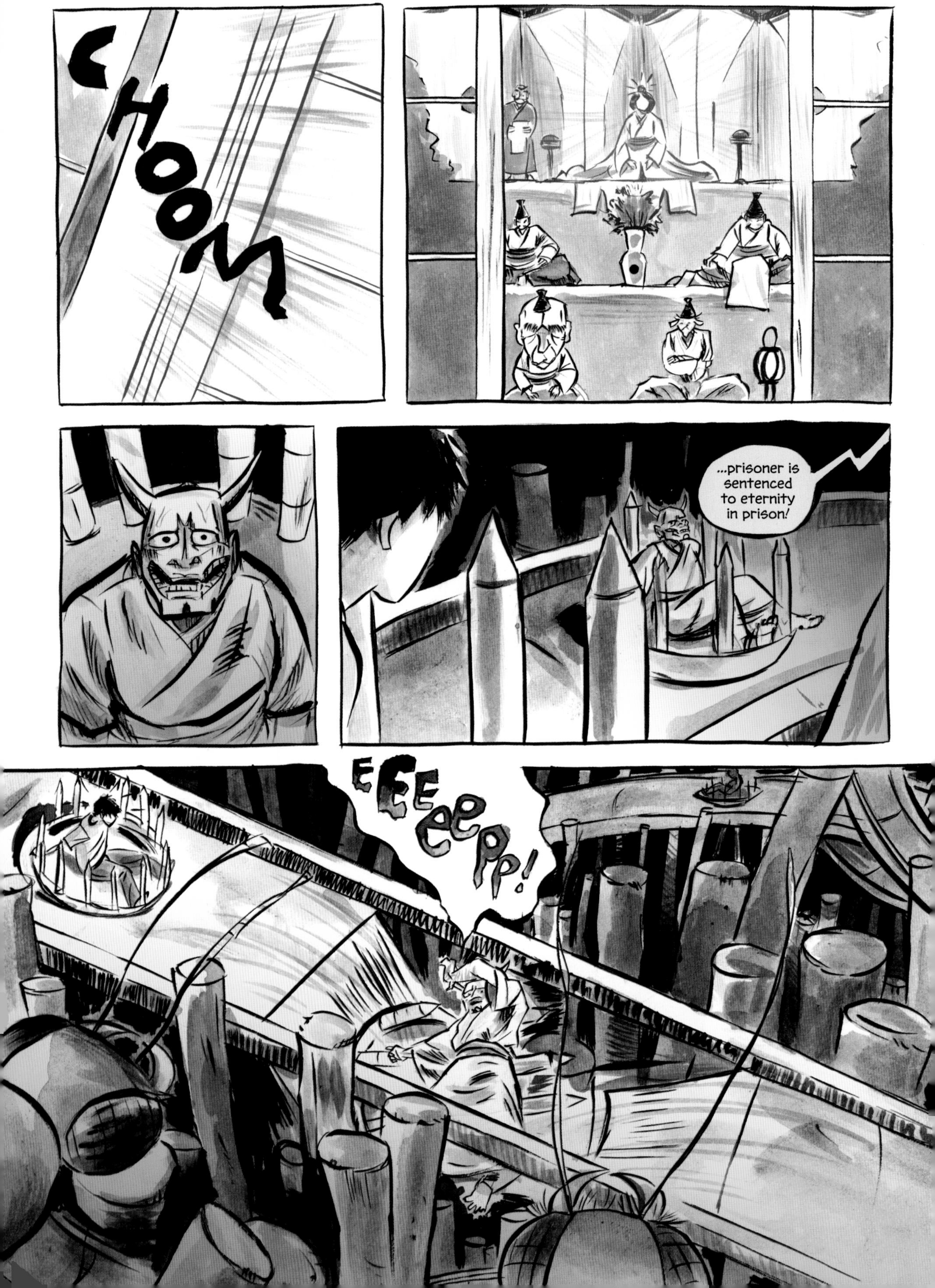
CHOOM
...prisoner is sentenced to eternity in prison!
EEEeePP!

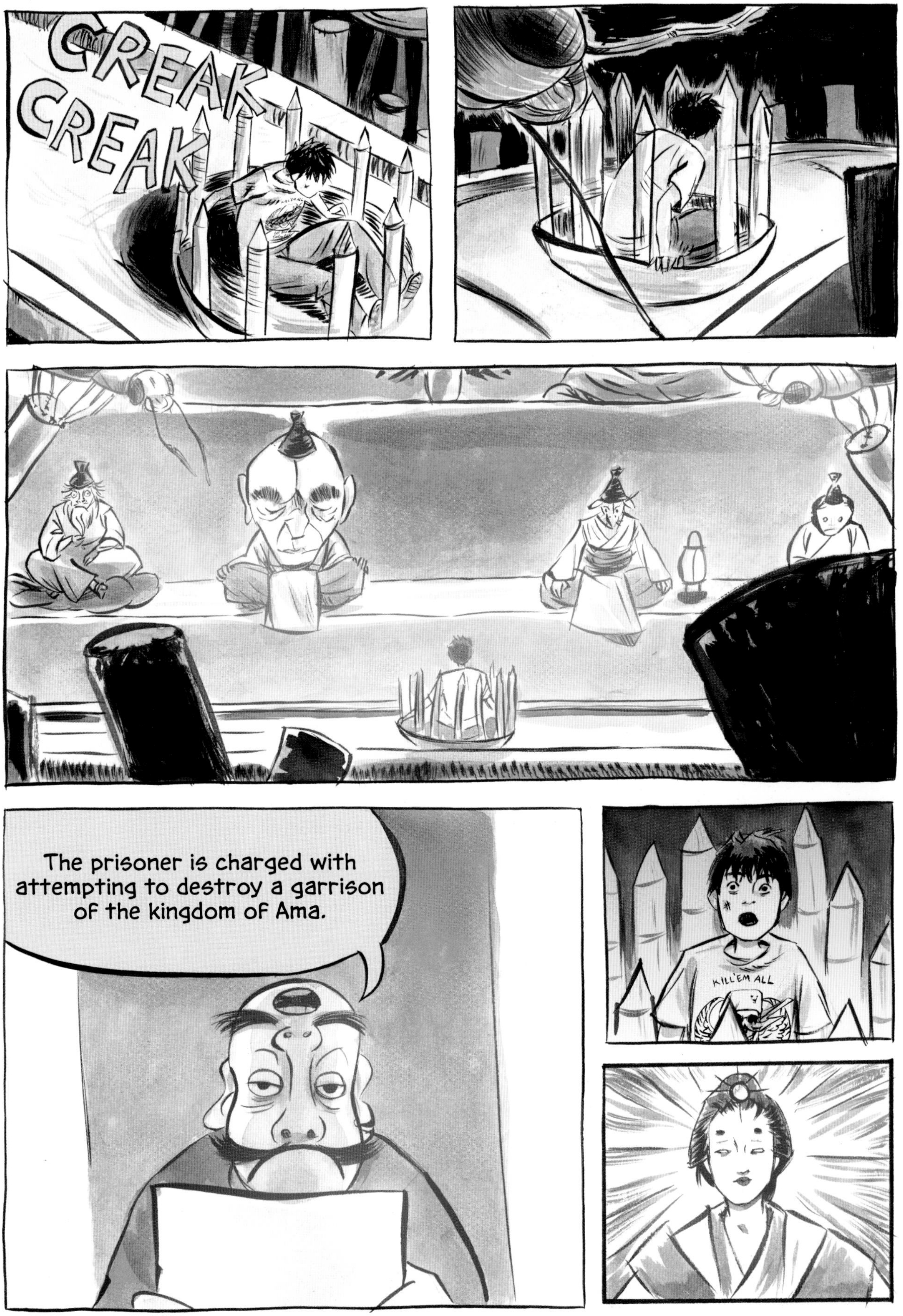
CREAK
CREAK
The prisoner is charged with attempting to destroy a garrison of the kingdom of Ama.
KILL'EM ALL

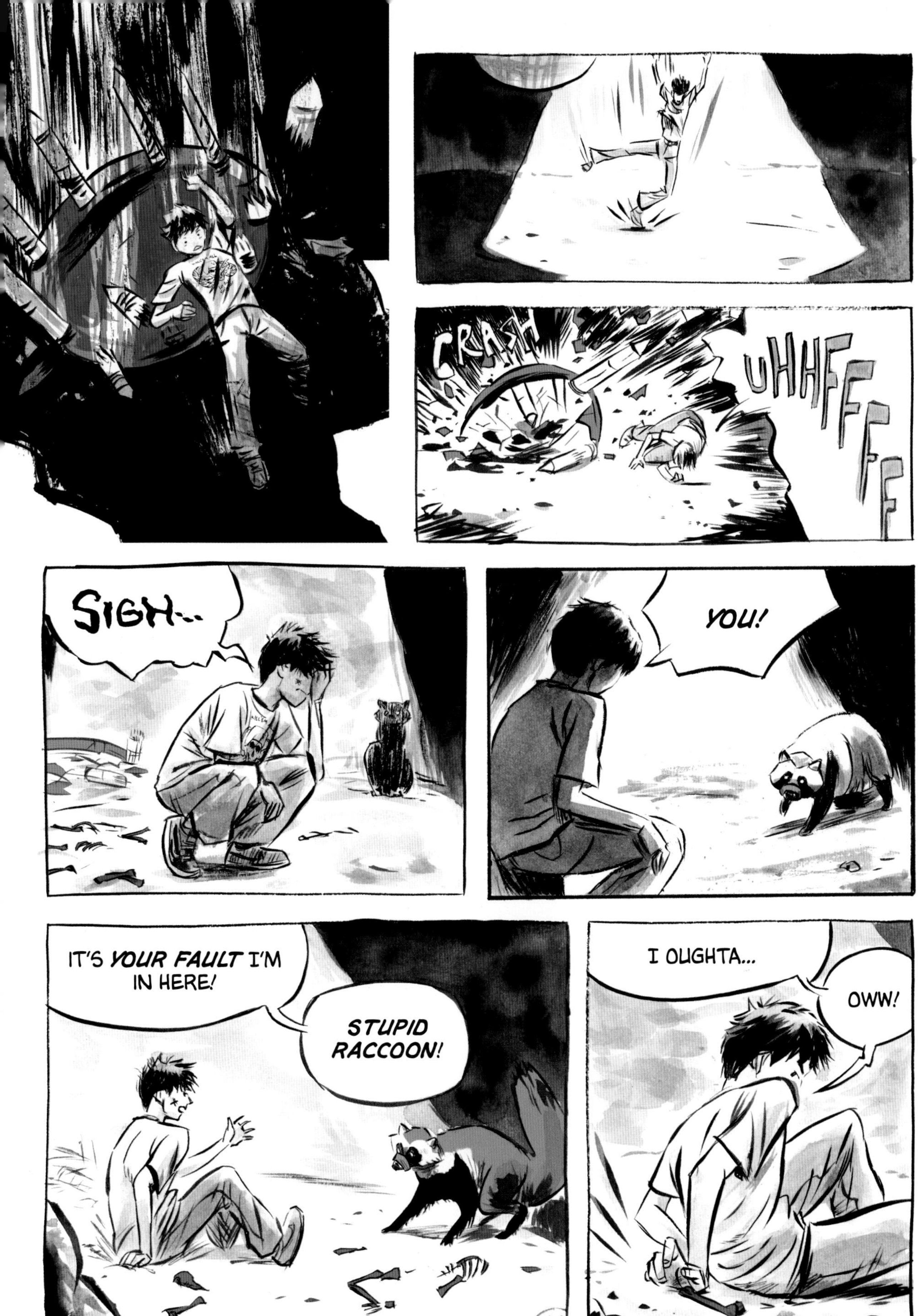
CRASH
UHHFFFFFF
SIGH...
YOU!
IT'S *YOUR FAULT* I'M IN HERE!
STUPID RACCOON!
I OUGHTA...
OWW!

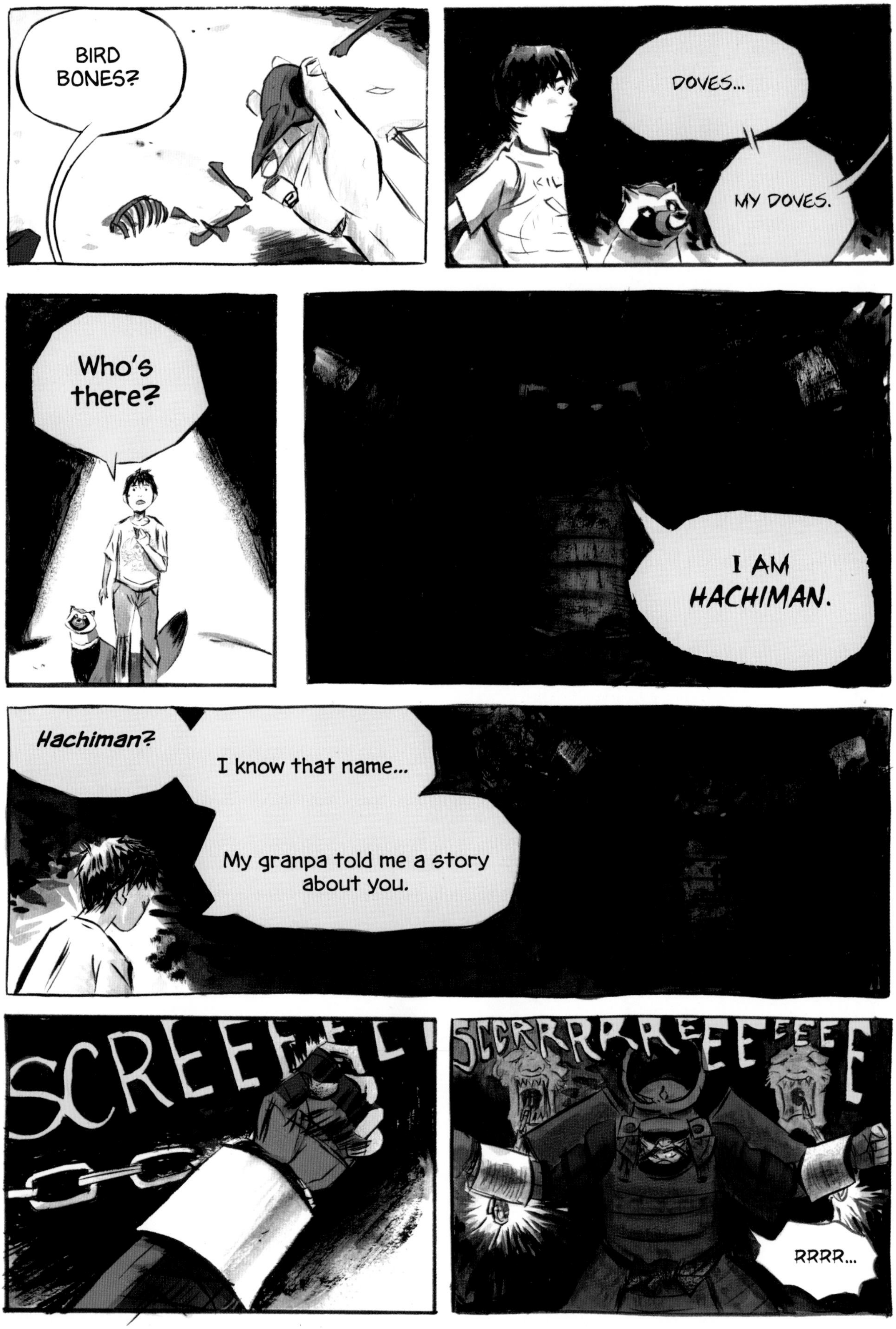
BIRD BONES?
DOVES...
MY DOVES.
Who's there?
I AM HACHIMAN.
Hachiman?
I know that name...
My granpa told me a story about you.
SCREEE
SCRRRRRREEEEEE
RRRR...

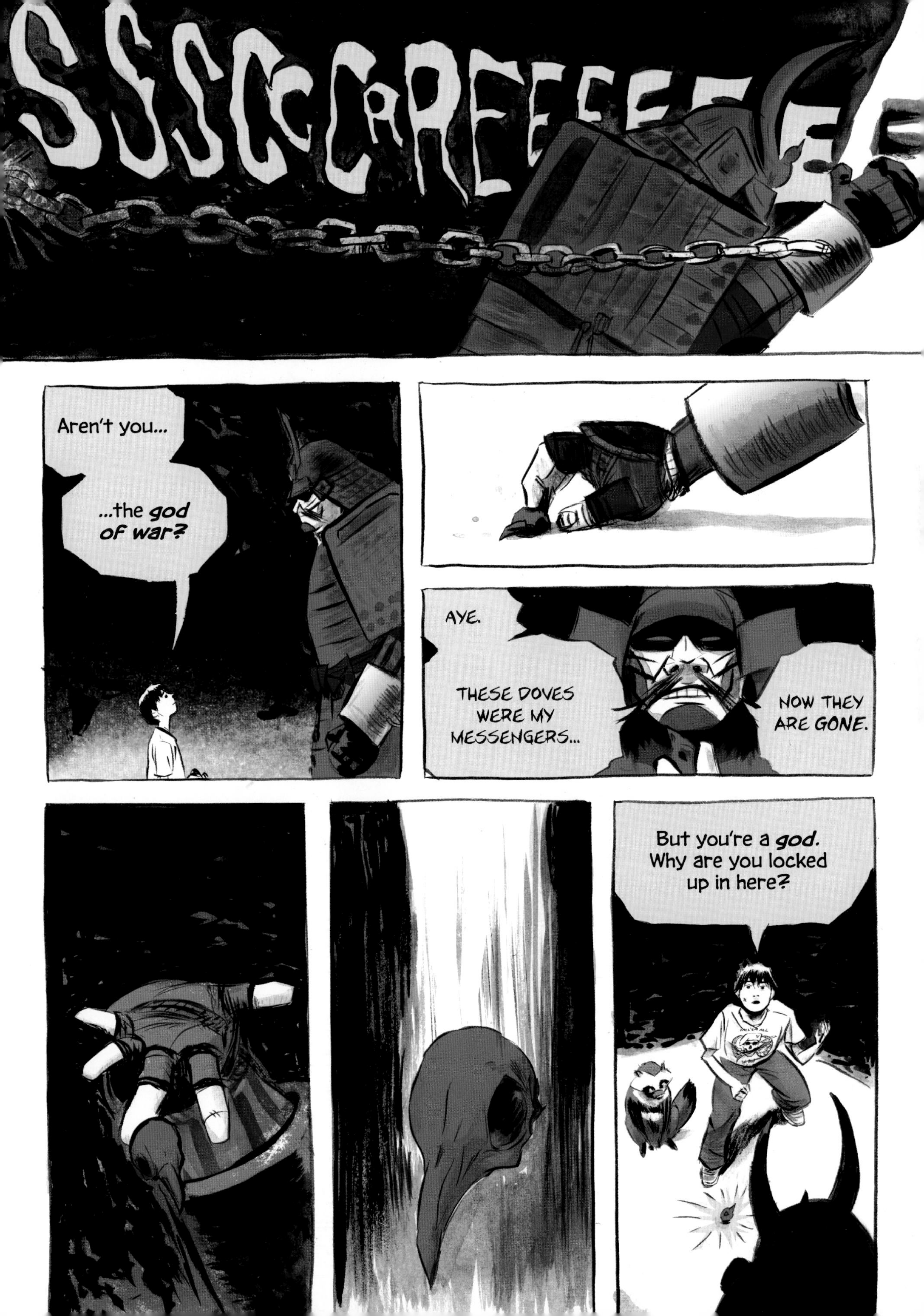
SSSCCRREEEEEE
Aren't you...
...the *god* of war?
AYE.
THESE DOVES WERE MY MESSENGERS...
NOW THEY ARE GONE.
But you're a *god*. Why are you locked up in here?

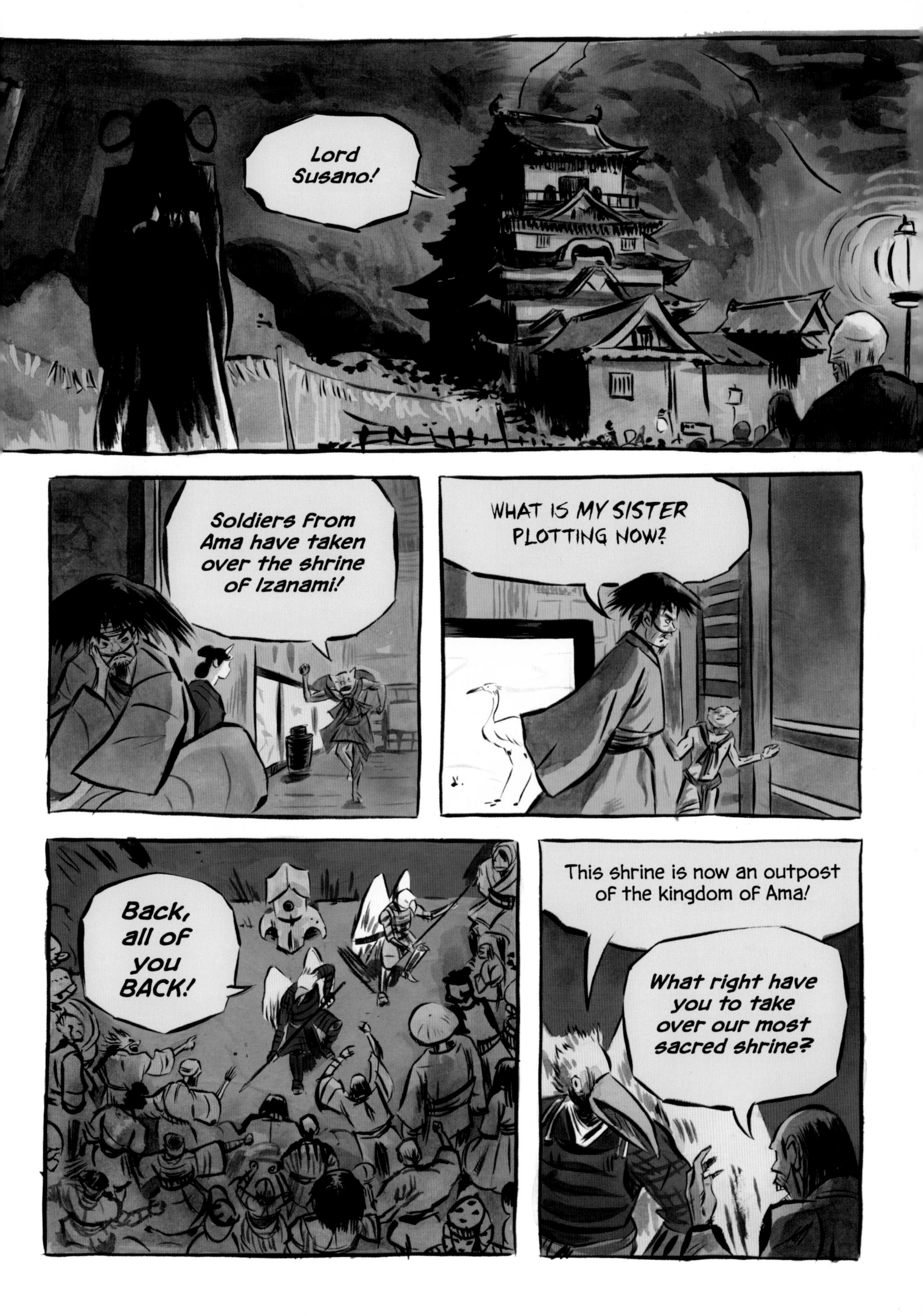
Lord Susano!
Soldiers from Ama have taken over the shrine of Izanami!
WHAT IS MY SISTER PLOTTING NOW?
Back, all of you BACK!
This shrine is now an outpost of the kingdom of Ama!
What right have you to take over our most sacred shrine?

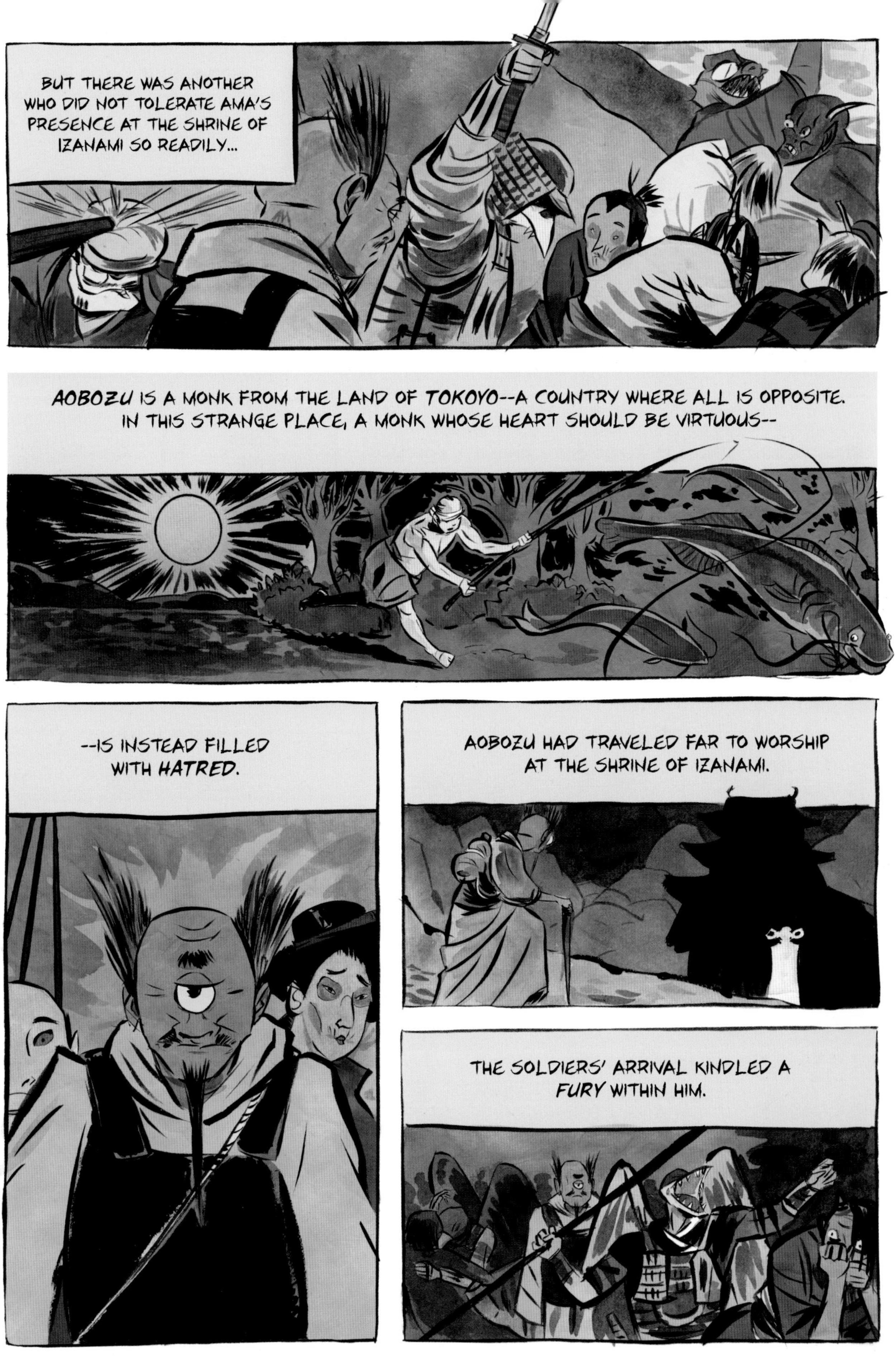
BUT THERE WAS ANOTHER WHO DID NOT TOLERATE AMA'S PRESENCE AT THE SHRINE OF IZANAMI SO READILY...
AOBOZU IS A MONK FROM THE LAND OF TOKOYO--A COUNTRY WHERE ALL IS OPPOSITE. IN THIS STRANGE PLACE, A MONK WHOSE HEART SHOULD BE VIRTUOUS--
--IS INSTEAD FILLED WITH HATRED.
AOBOZU HAD TRAVELED FAR TO WORSHIP AT THE SHRINE OF IZANAMI.
THE SOLDIERS' ARRIVAL KINDLED A FURY WITHIN HIM.

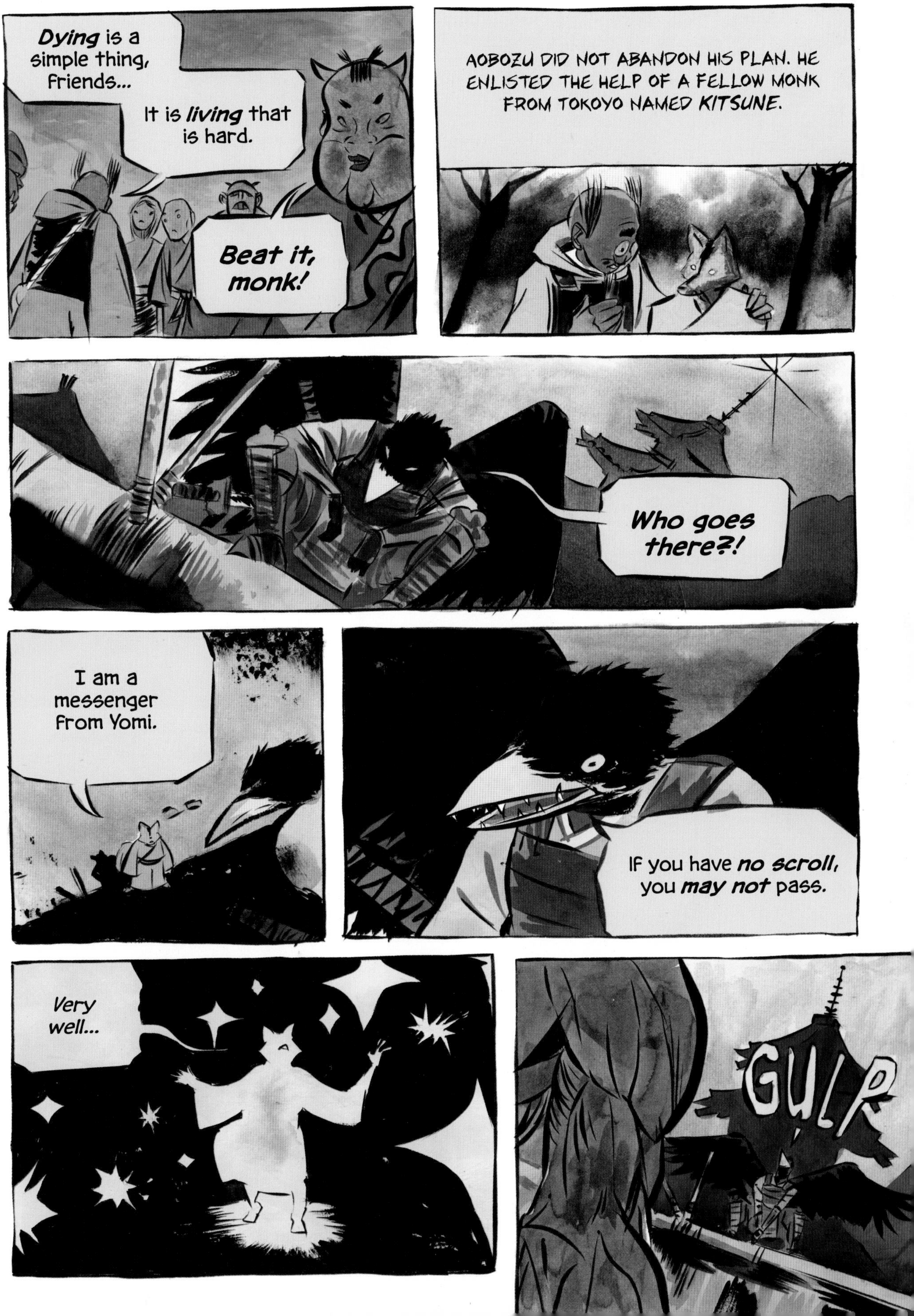
Dying is a simple thing, friends...
It is living that is hard.
Beat it, monk!
AOBOZU DID NOT ABANDON HIS PLAN. HE ENLISTED THE HELP OF A FELLOW MONK FROM TOKOYO NAMED KITSUNE.
Who goes there?!
I am a messenger from Yomi.
If you have no scroll, you may not pass.
Very well...
GULP

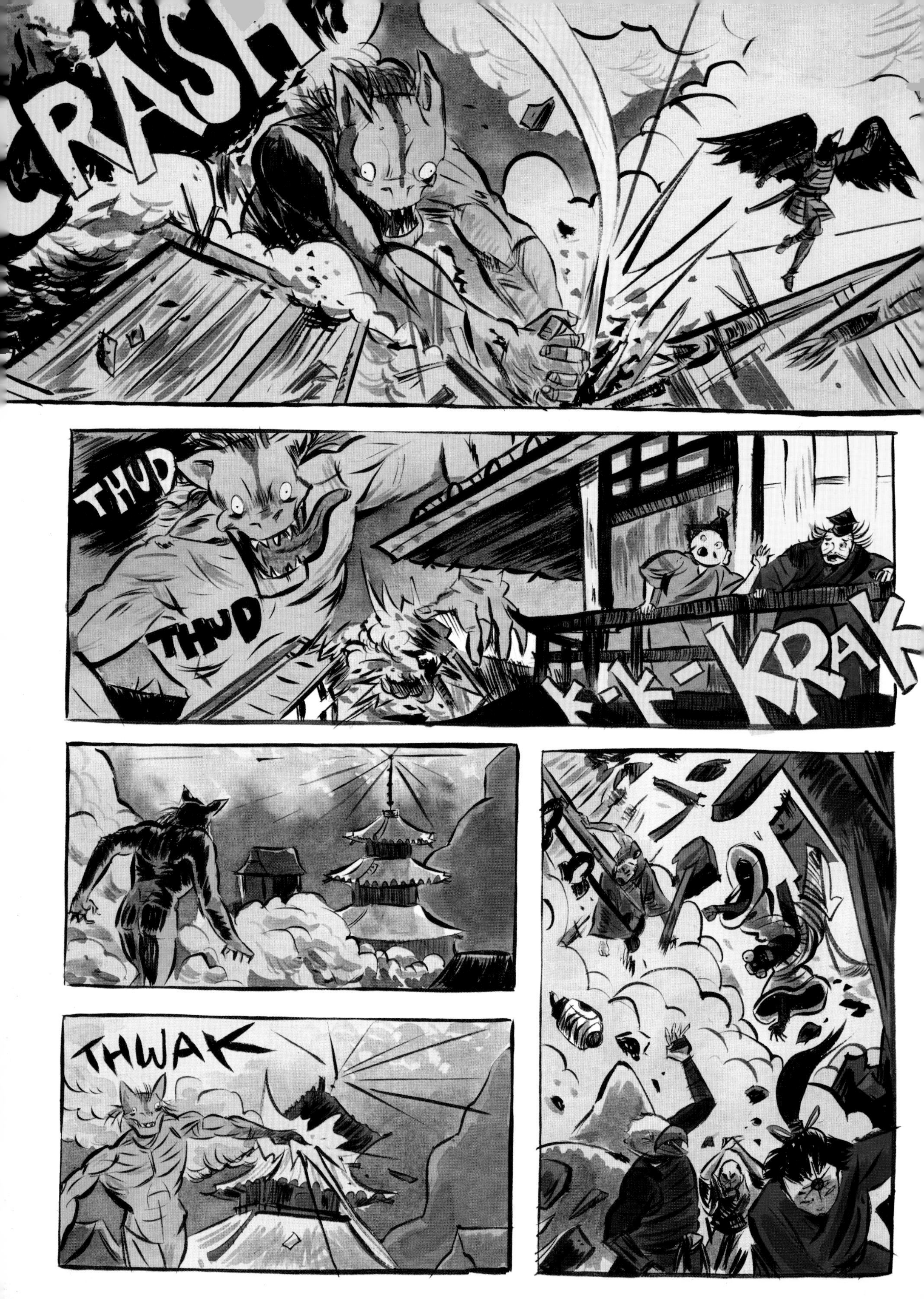
CRASH
THUD
THUD
K-K-KRAK
THWAK

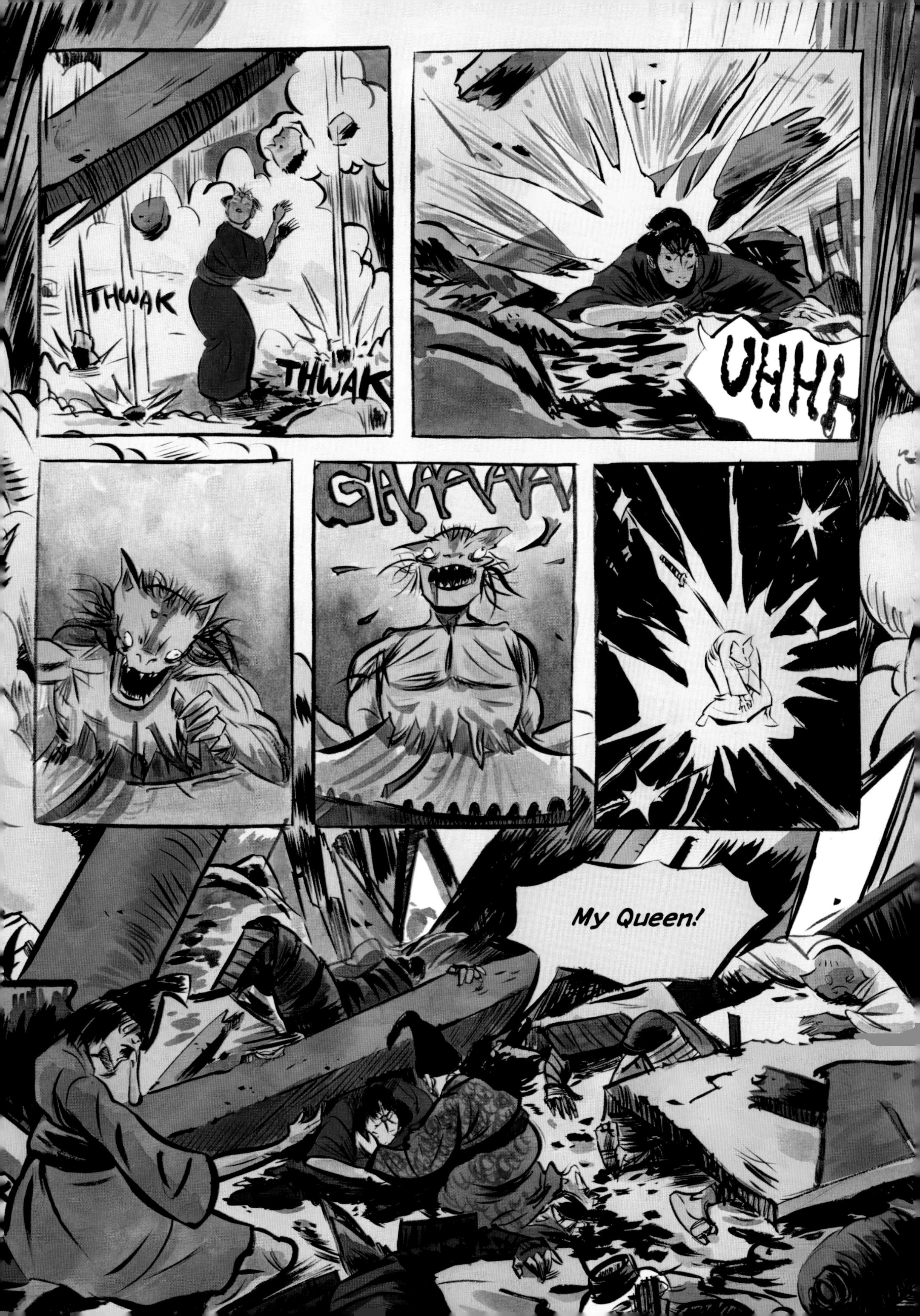
THWAK
THWAK
UHHH
GAAAAA
My Queen!

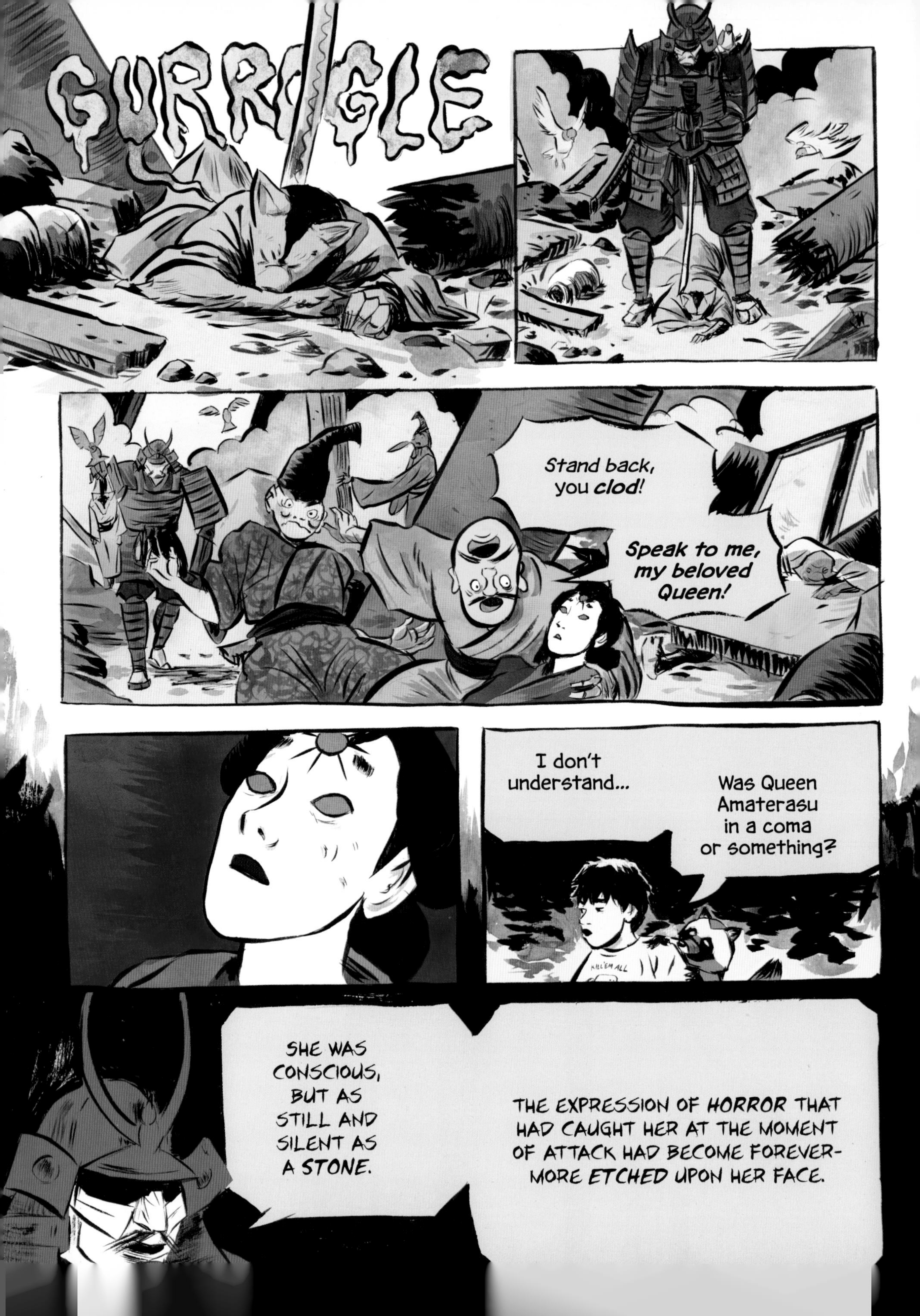
GURRGGLE
Stand back, you *clod!*
Speak to me, my beloved Queen!
I don't understand...
Was Queen Amaterasu in a coma or something?
KILL'EM ALL
SHE WAS CONSCIOUS, BUT AS STILL AND SILENT AS A *STONE*.
THE EXPRESSION OF *HORROR* THAT HAD CAUGHT HER AT THE MOMENT OF ATTACK HAD BECOME FOREVER-MORE *ETCHED* UPON HER FACE.

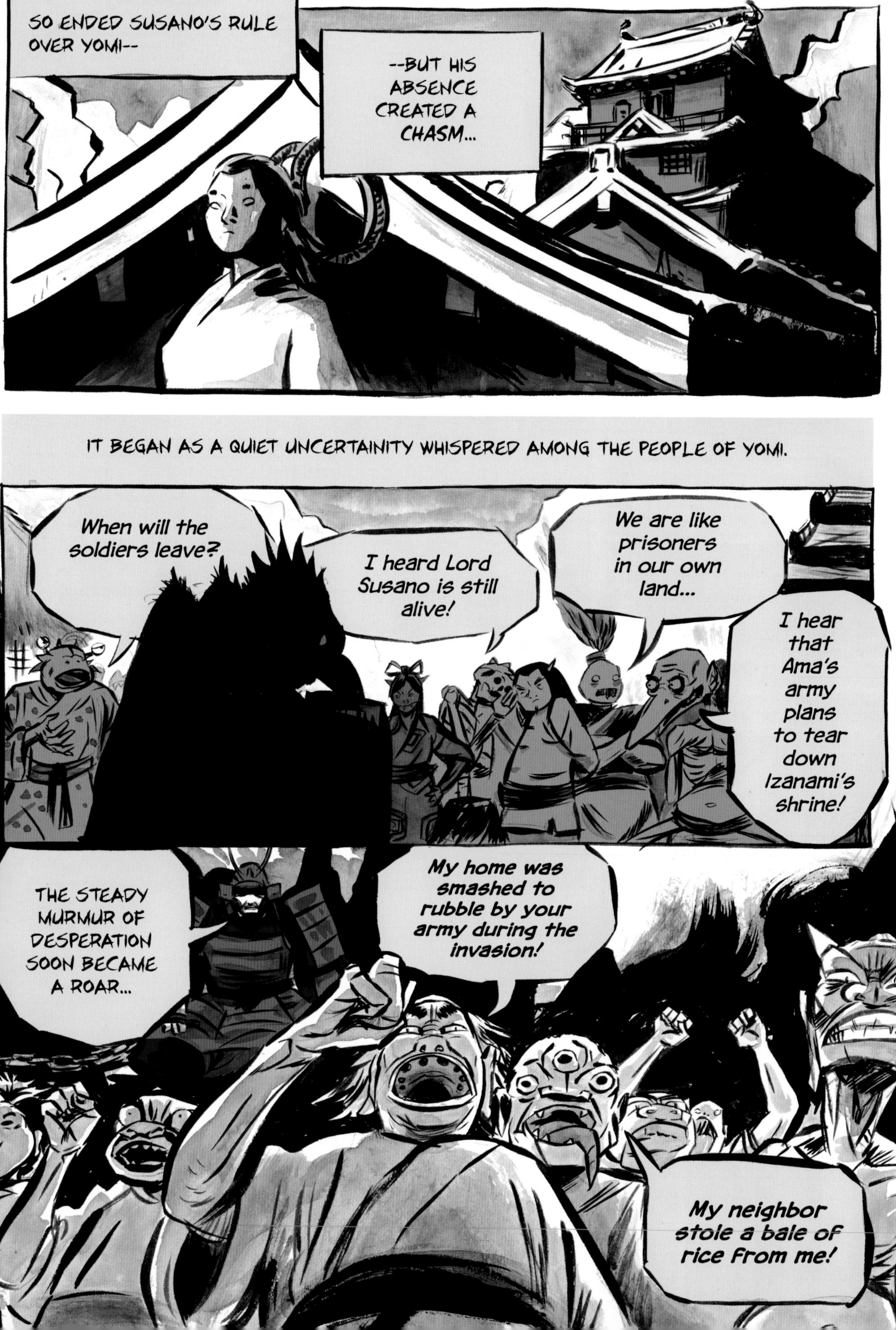
SO ENDED SUSANO'S RULE OVER YOMI--
--BUT HIS ABSENCE CREATED A CHASM...
IT BEGAN AS A QUIET UNCERTAINITY WHISPERED AMONG THE PEOPLE OF YOMI.
When will the soldiers leave?
I heard Lord Susano is still alive!
We are like prisoners in our own land...
I hear that Ama's army plans to tear down Izanami's shrine!
THE STEADY MURMUR OF DESPERATION SOON BECAME A ROAR...
My home was smashed to rubble by your army during the invasion!
My neighbor stole a bale of rice from me!

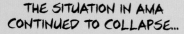

THE SITUATION IN AMA CONTINUED TO COLLAPSE...

HAVING LONG SINCE LOST THEIR TASTE FOR WAR, THE PEOPLE OF AMA DEMANDED ANSWERS FROM THEIR NEW RULER...

These shape-shifters may stand among us even now!

How can our safety be guaranteed?

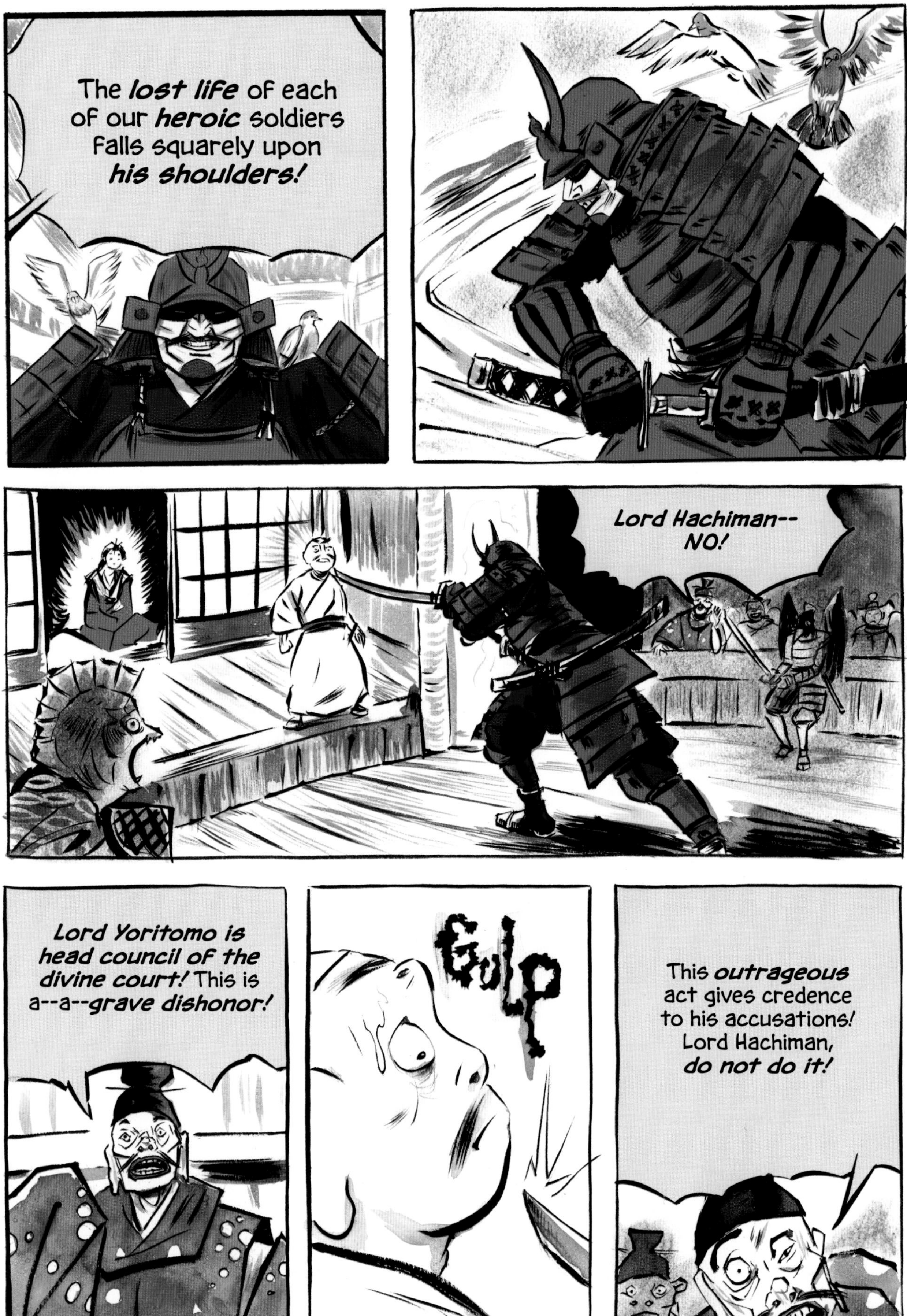

The *lost life* of each of our *heroic* soldiers falls squarely upon *his shoulders!*
Lord Hachiman--NO!
Lord Yoritomo is head council of the divine court! This is a--a--*grave dishonor!*
Gulp
This *outrageous* act gives credence to his accusations! Lord Hachiman, *do not do it!*

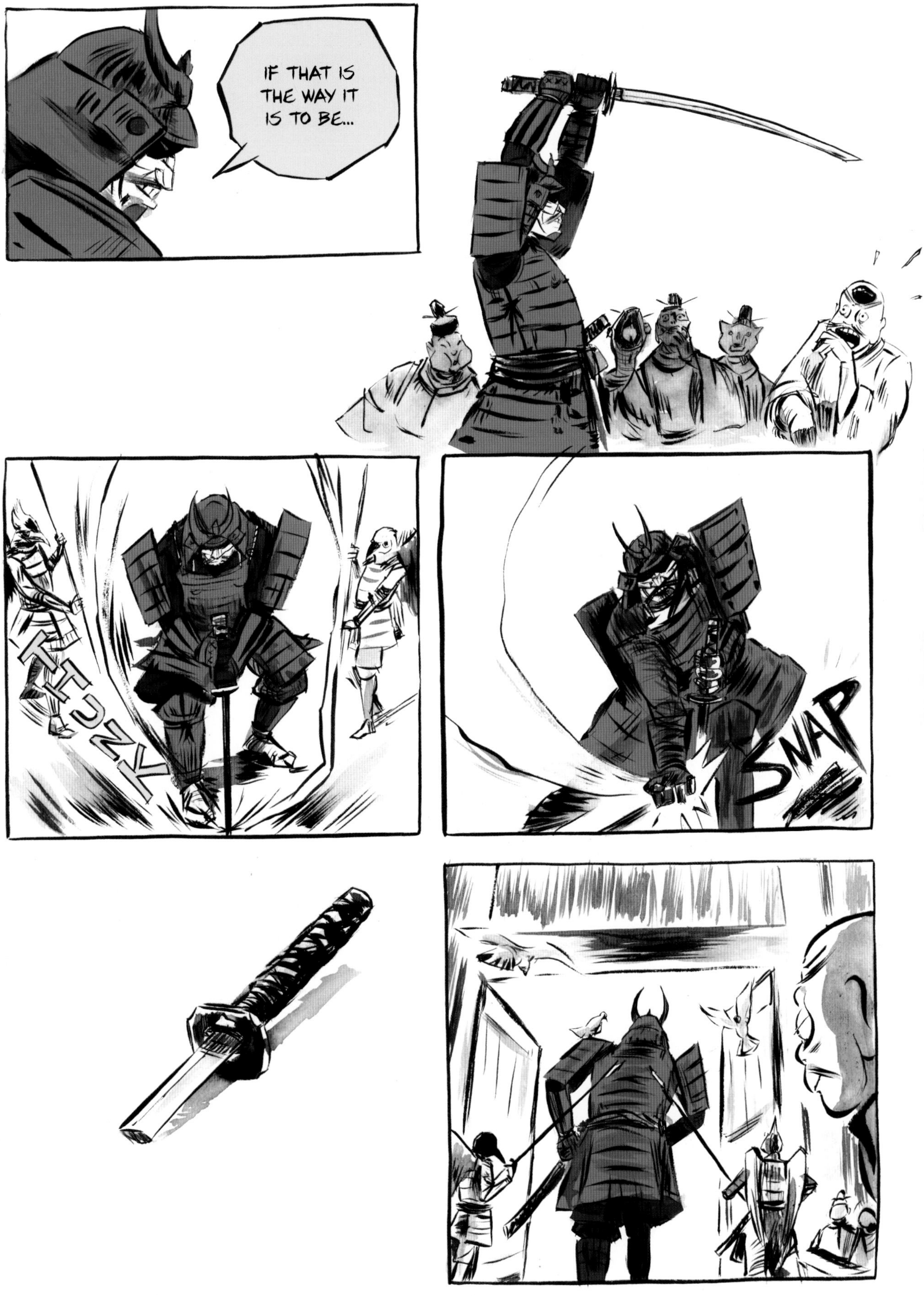

IF THAT IS THE WAY IT IS TO BE...
KHUNK
SNAP

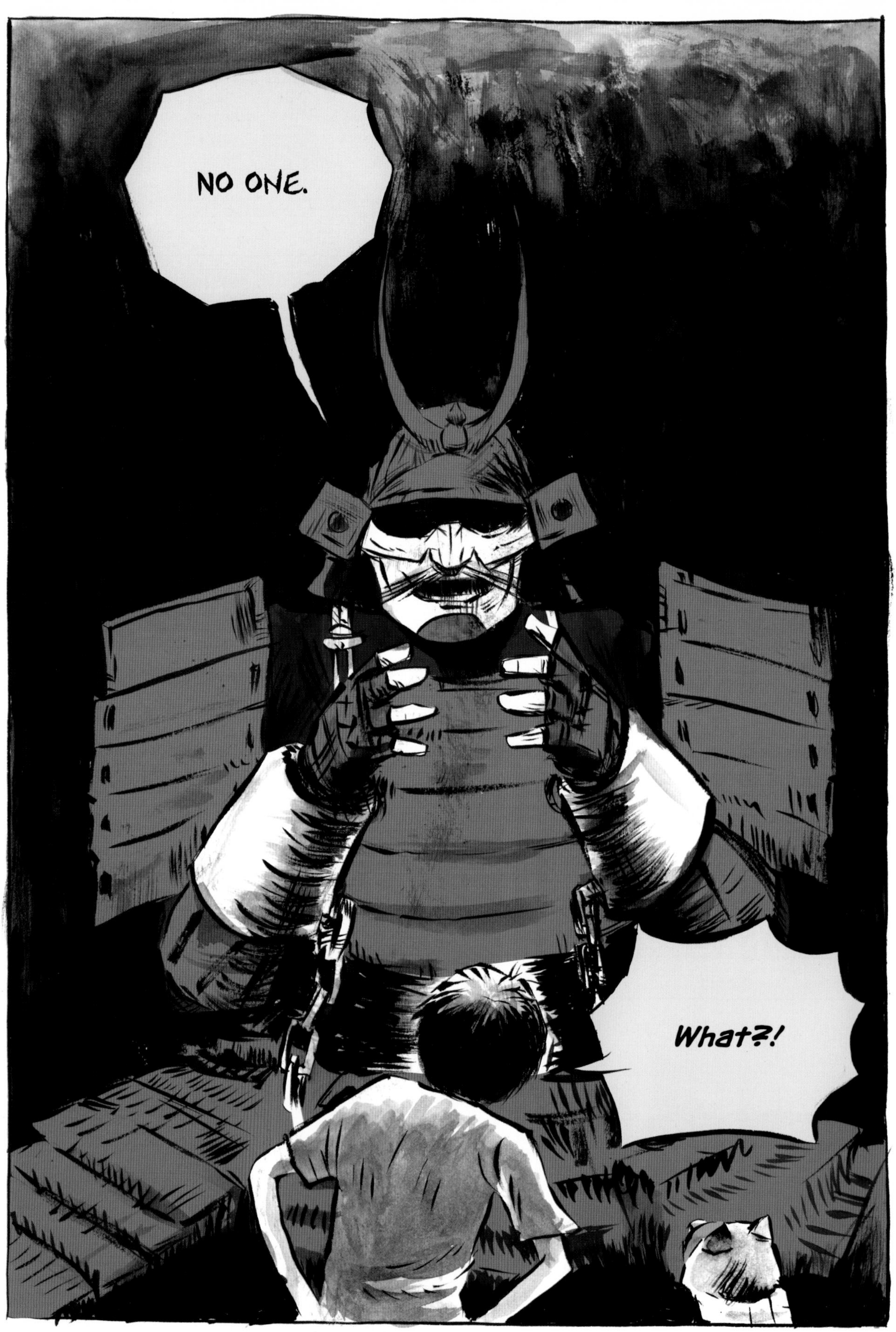
NO ONE.
What?!

I HAVE THOUGHT LONG AND HARD ON THIS QUESTION. THE BRIDGE HAS STOOD SINCE TIME IMMEMORIAL AS A BOND BETWEEN THE PLAINS OF HEAVEN AND EARTH. NO WEAPON OF MAN NOR HAND OF GOD COULD HAVE CREATED SO MUCH AS A SCRATCH ON ITS SURFACE. THE BRIDGE CRACKED...
...BECAUSE IT **RESOLVED ITSELF** TO CRACK.
BUT THAT IS NOT WHY IT **COLLAPSED.**
FOR IF WE HAD PATCHED THE CRACK WHEN IT WAS ONLY A SMALL FISSURE, THE BRIDGE MIGHT HAVE BEEN **SAVED.**
WHEN THE GREAT ARCH OF THE BRIDGE BEGAN TO **CRUMBLE,** AND ITS PILINGS **SPLINTERED** AND **TUMBLED** INTO THE ABYSS...

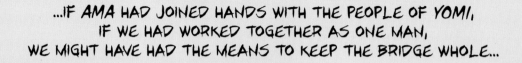

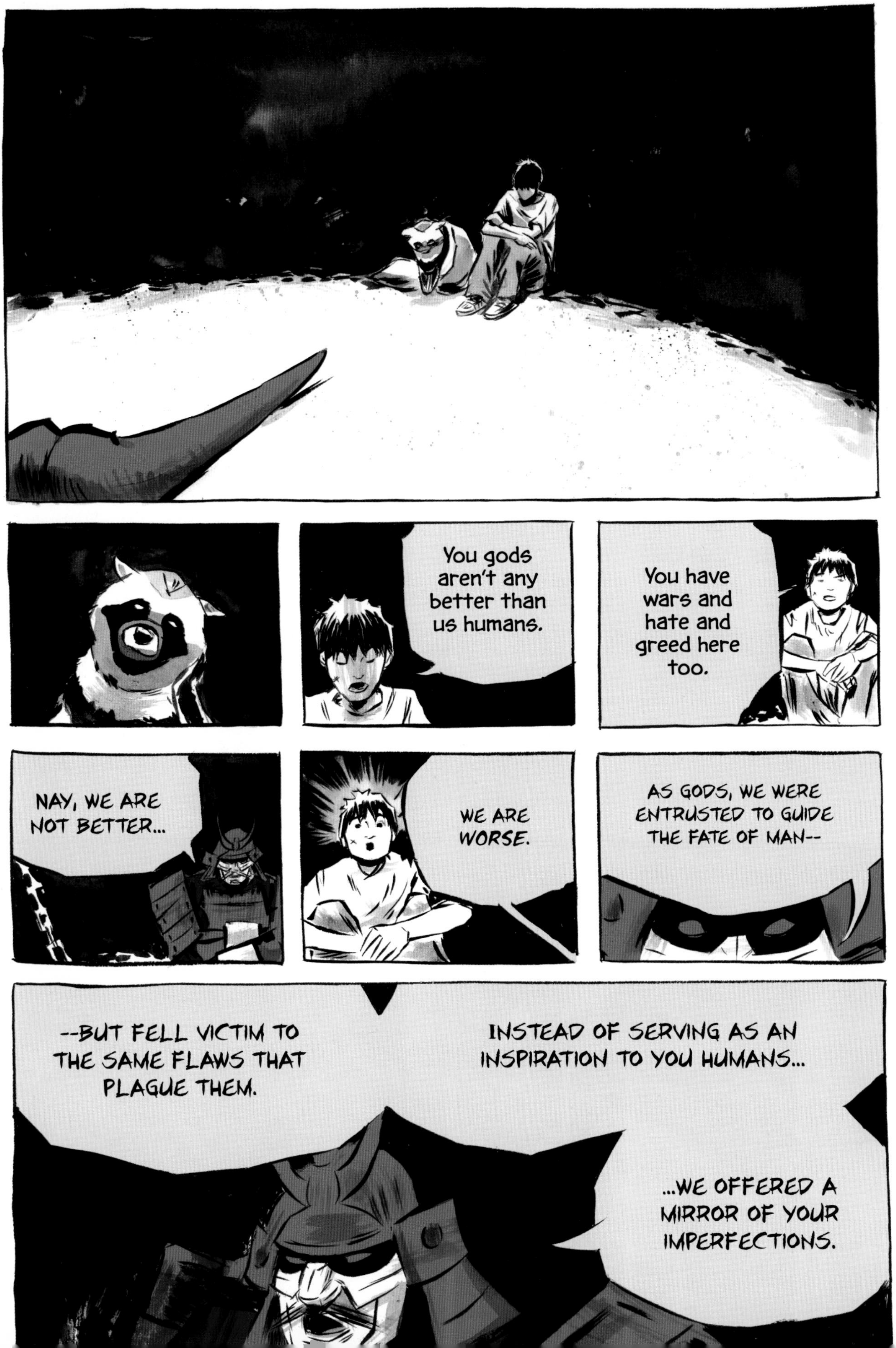
You gods aren't any better than us humans.
You have wars and hate and greed here too.
NAY, WE ARE NOT BETTER...
WE ARE WORSE.
AS GODS, WE WERE ENTRUSTED TO GUIDE THE FATE OF MAN--
--BUT FELL VICTIM TO THE SAME FLAWS THAT PLAGUE THEM.
INSTEAD OF SERVING AS AN INSPIRATION TO YOU HUMANS...
...WE OFFERED A MIRROR OF YOUR IMPERFECTIONS.

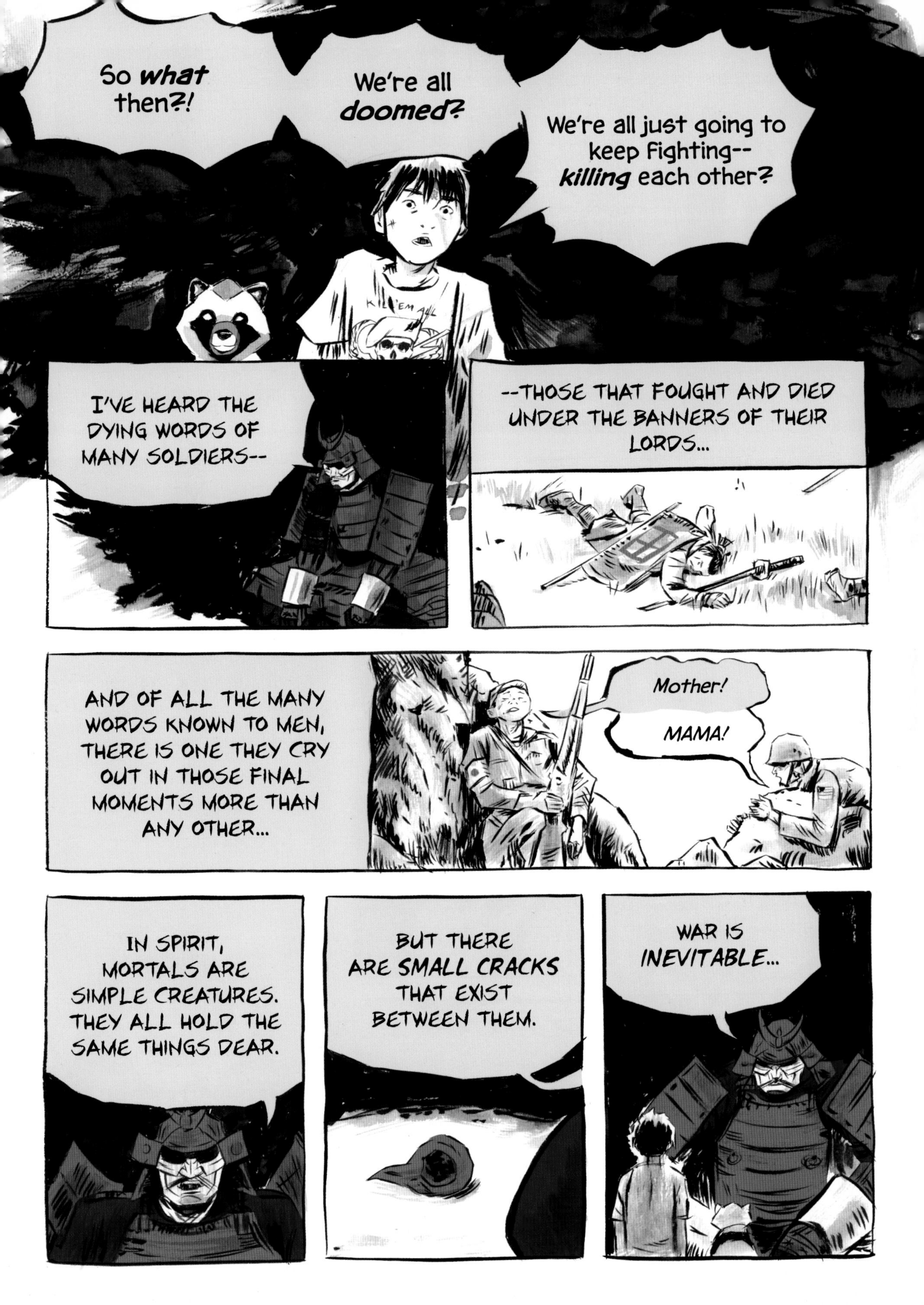
So what then?!
We're all doomed?
We're all just going to keep fighting-- killing each other?
KILL 'EM ALL
I'VE HEARD THE DYING WORDS OF MANY SOLDIERS--
--THOSE THAT FOUGHT AND DIED UNDER THE BANNERS OF THEIR LORDS...
AND OF ALL THE MANY WORDS KNOWN TO MEN, THERE IS ONE THEY CRY OUT IN THOSE FINAL MOMENTS MORE THAN ANY OTHER...
Mother!
MAMA!
IN SPIRIT, MORTALS ARE SIMPLE CREATURES. THEY ALL HOLD THE SAME THINGS DEAR.
BUT THERE ARE SMALL CRACKS THAT EXIST BETWEEN THEM.
WAR IS INEVITABLE...

Why don't you come with me?

IT IS MORE THAN THESE CHAINS THAT BIND ME.

IT IS NO MATTER. YOU WILL BE BETTER OFF WITHOUT ME.

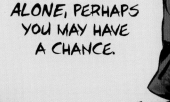

ALONE, PERHAPS YOU MAY HAVE A CHANCE.

BUT IF I CAME WITH YOU, YORITOMO WOULD NEVER REST UNTIL WE WERE BOTH CAPTURED. BUT LET US NOT TALK OF SUCH THINGS...

KILL 'EM ALL

I DO NOT KNOW IF YOU WILL EVER RETURN TO EARTH. IT IS A PLACE I REMEMBER FONDLY...

NOW THAT THE BRIDGE IS GONE, I CAN PICTURE YOUR WORLD IN MY MIND AND RECOLLECT ITS BEAUTY--

--BUT I DID NOT SEE IT BEFORE.

TO LOOK UPON A MOUNTAIN WAS TO SEE A MILLION QUESTIONS...

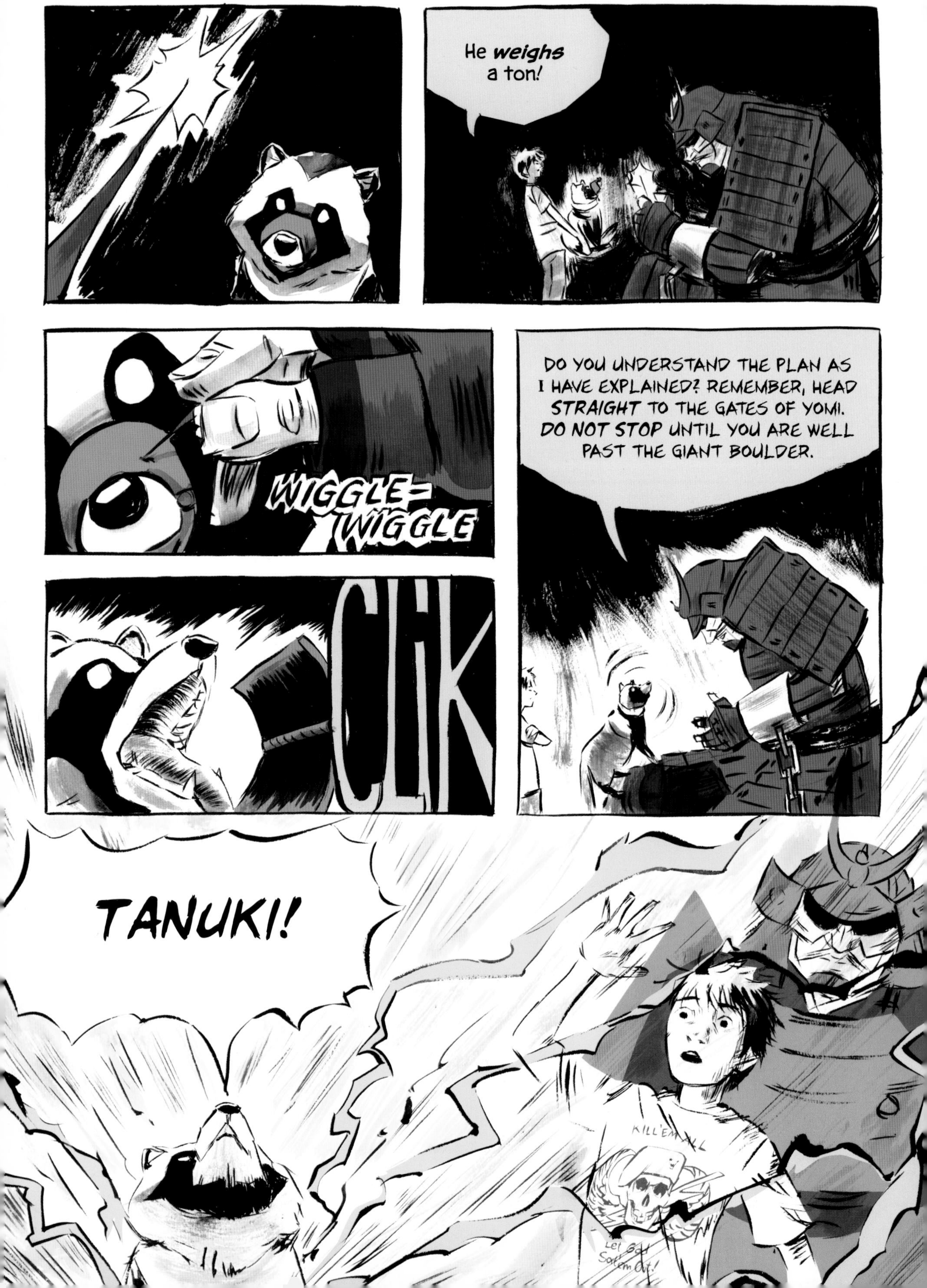

He *weighs* a ton!
WIGGLE-WIGGLE
DO YOU UNDERSTAND THE PLAN AS I HAVE EXPLAINED? REMEMBER, HEAD **STRAIGHT** TO THE GATES OF YOMI. **DO NOT STOP** UNTIL YOU ARE WELL PAST THE GIANT BOULDER.
CLIK
TANUKI!
KILL 'EM ALL

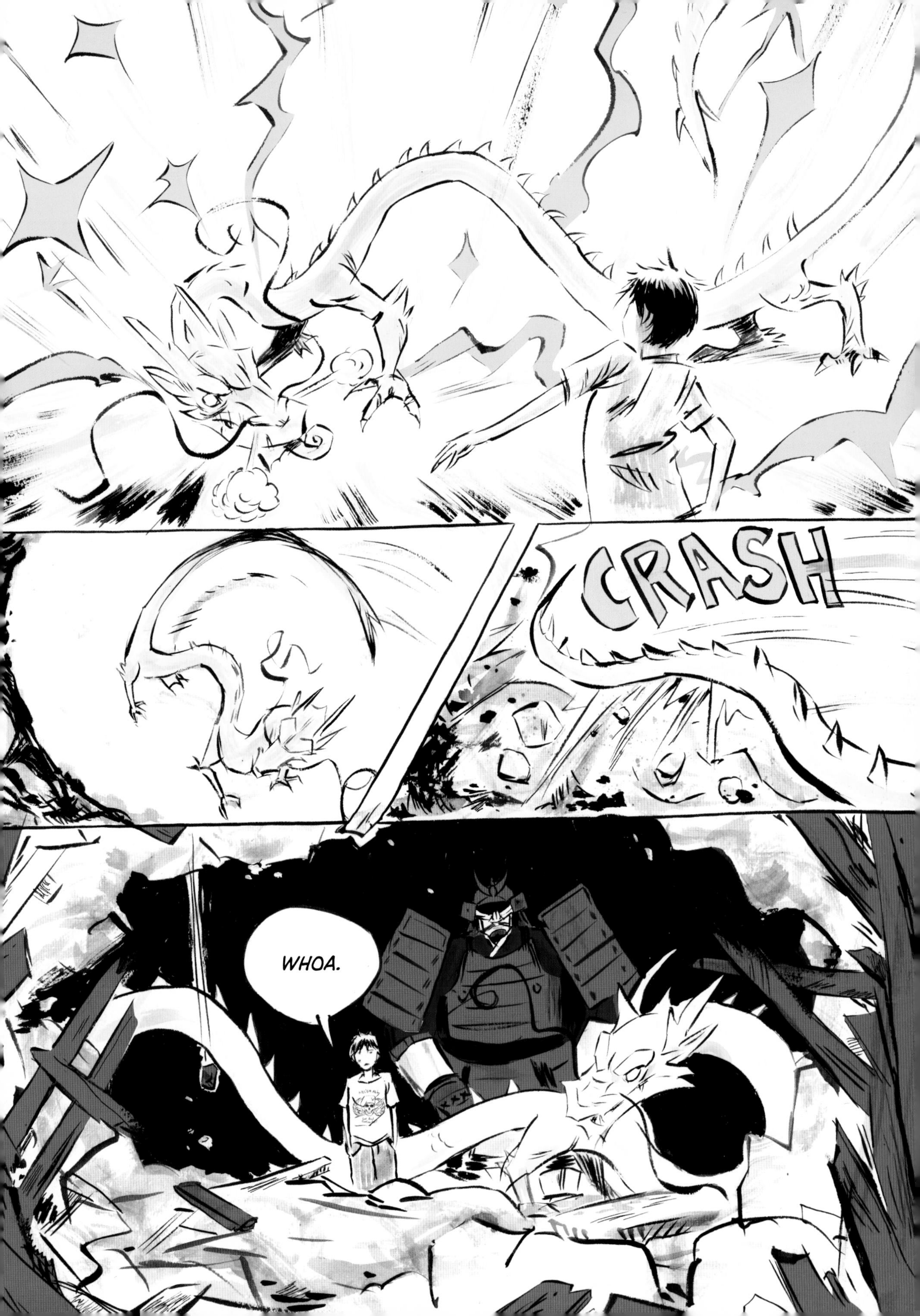
CRASH
WHOA.

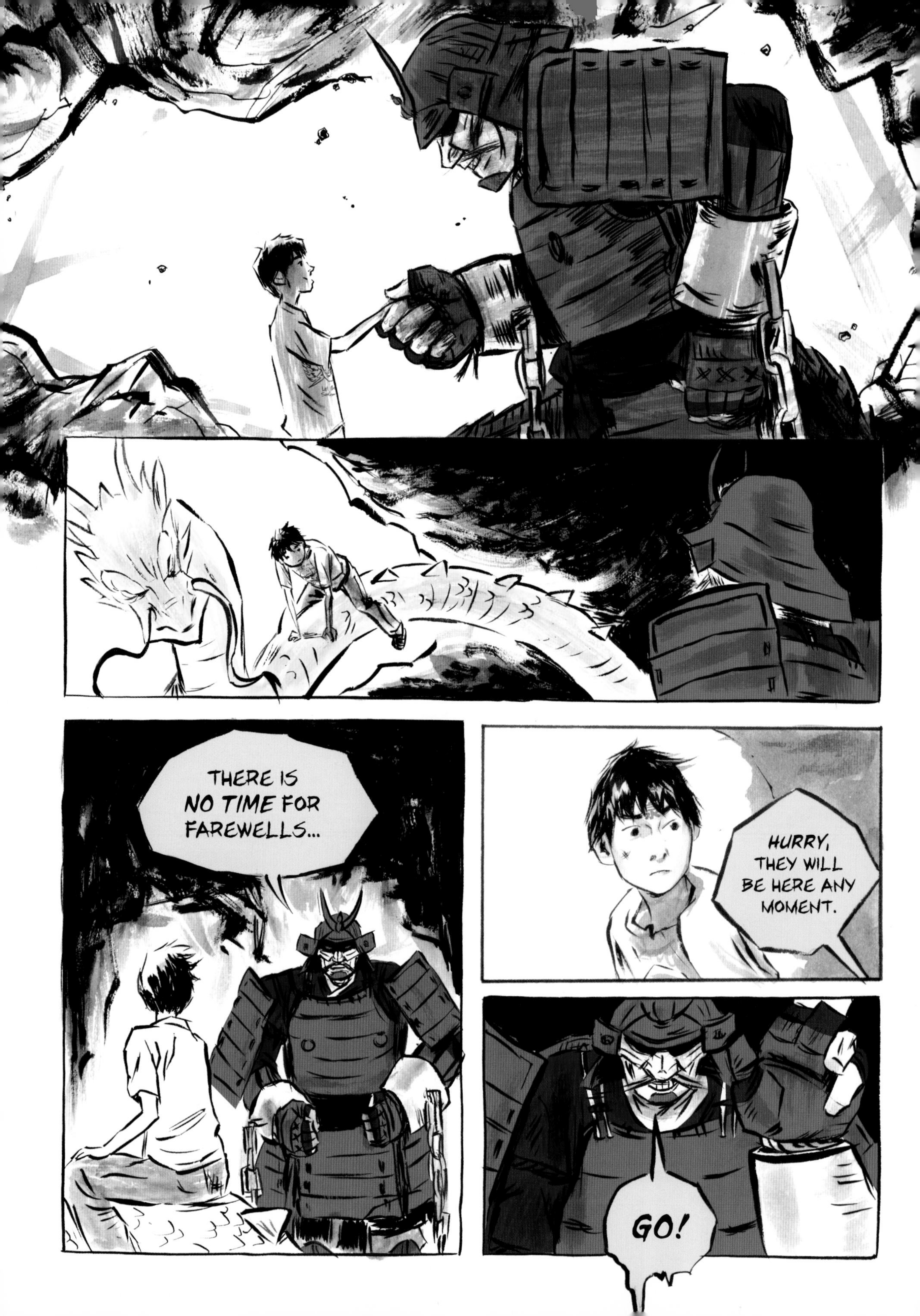
THERE IS NO TIME FOR FAREWELLS...
HURRY, THEY WILL BE HERE ANY MOMENT.
GO!

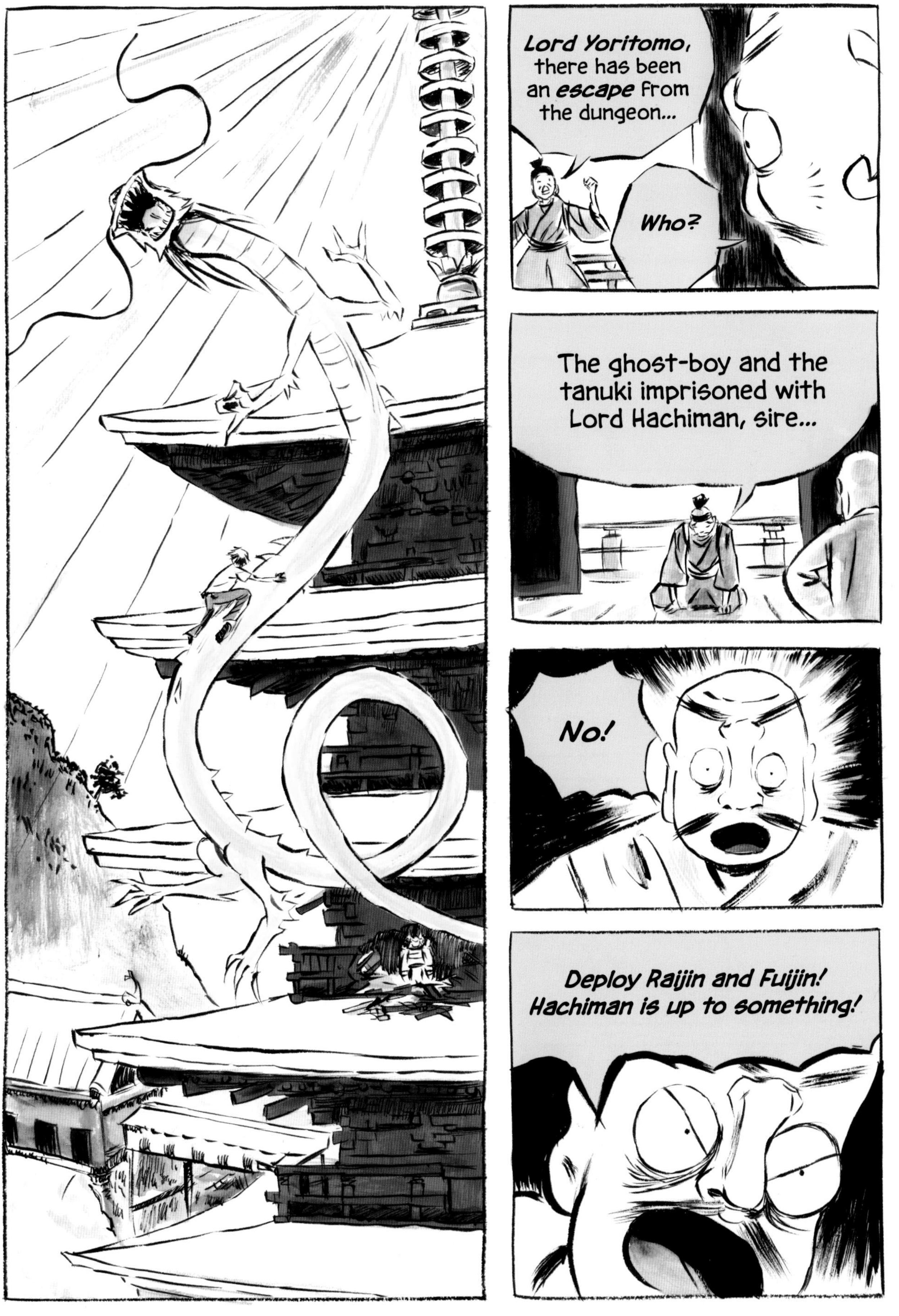
Lord Yoritomo, there has been an *escape* from the dungeon...
Who?
The ghost-boy and the tanuki imprisoned with Lord Hachiman, sire...
No!
Deploy Raijin and Fuijin! Hachiman is up to something!

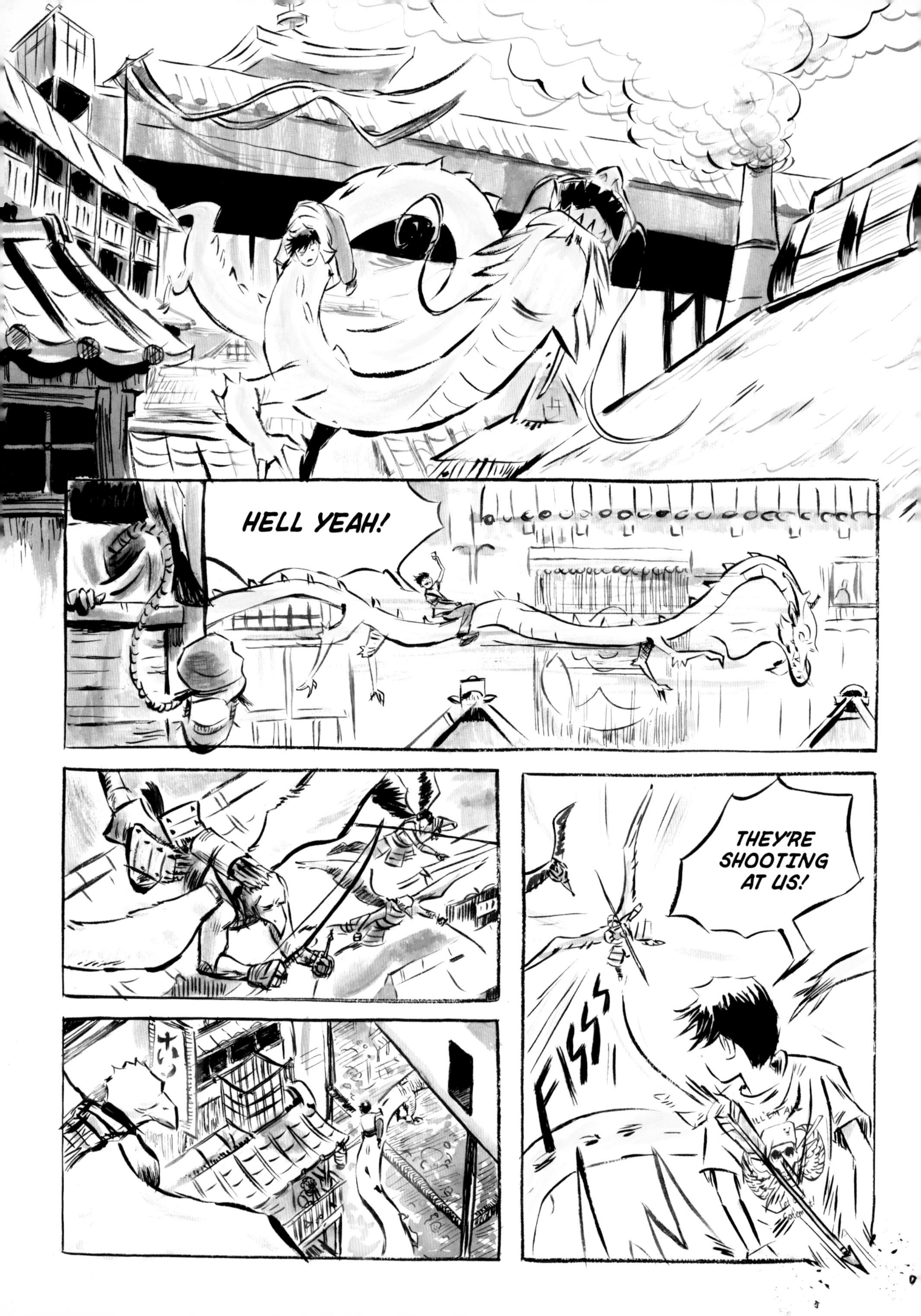
HELL YEAH!
THEY'RE SHOOTING AT US!
FISS

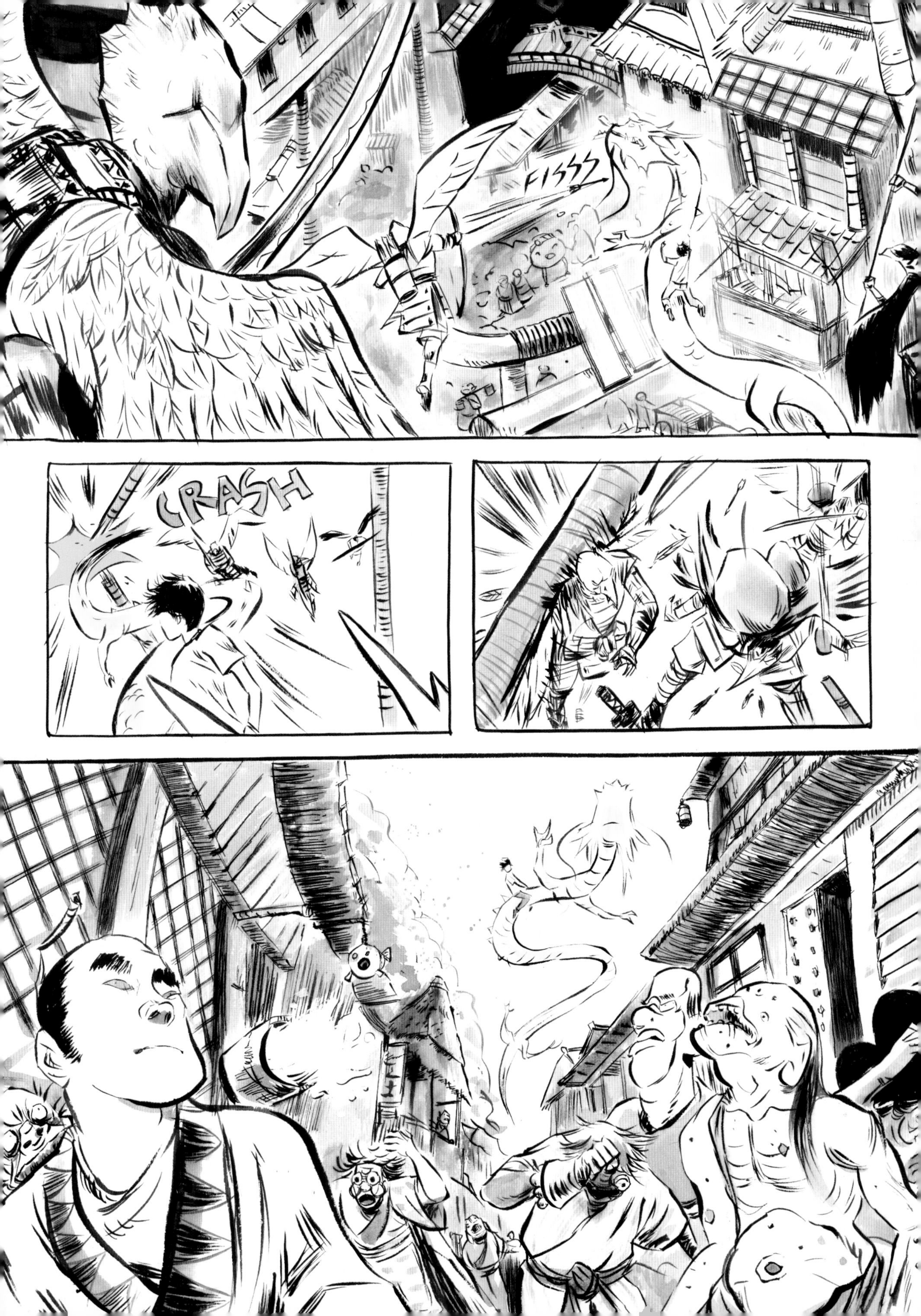
FISSS
CRASH

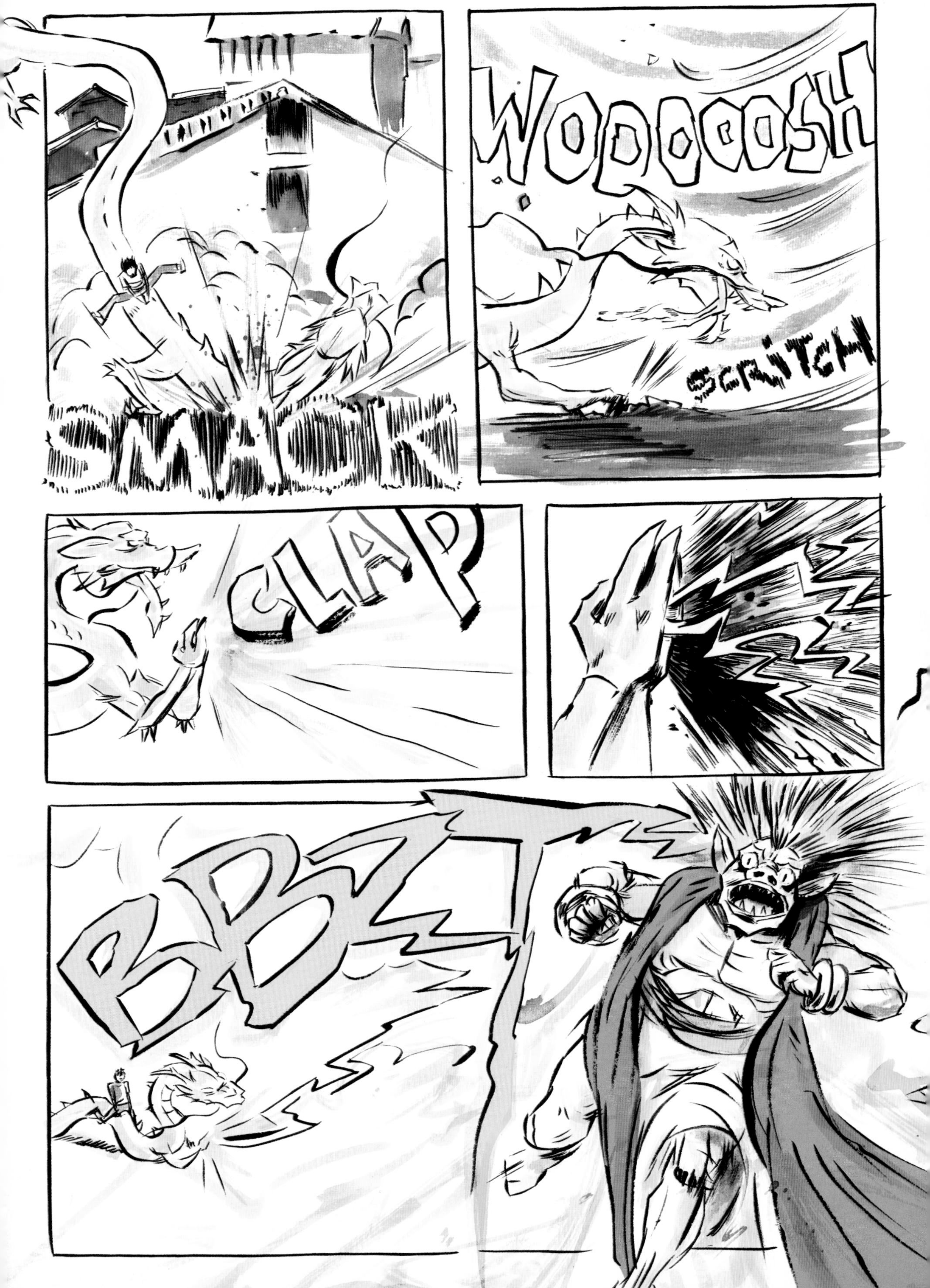
SMACK
WOOOOOSH
SCRITCH
CLAP
BBZT

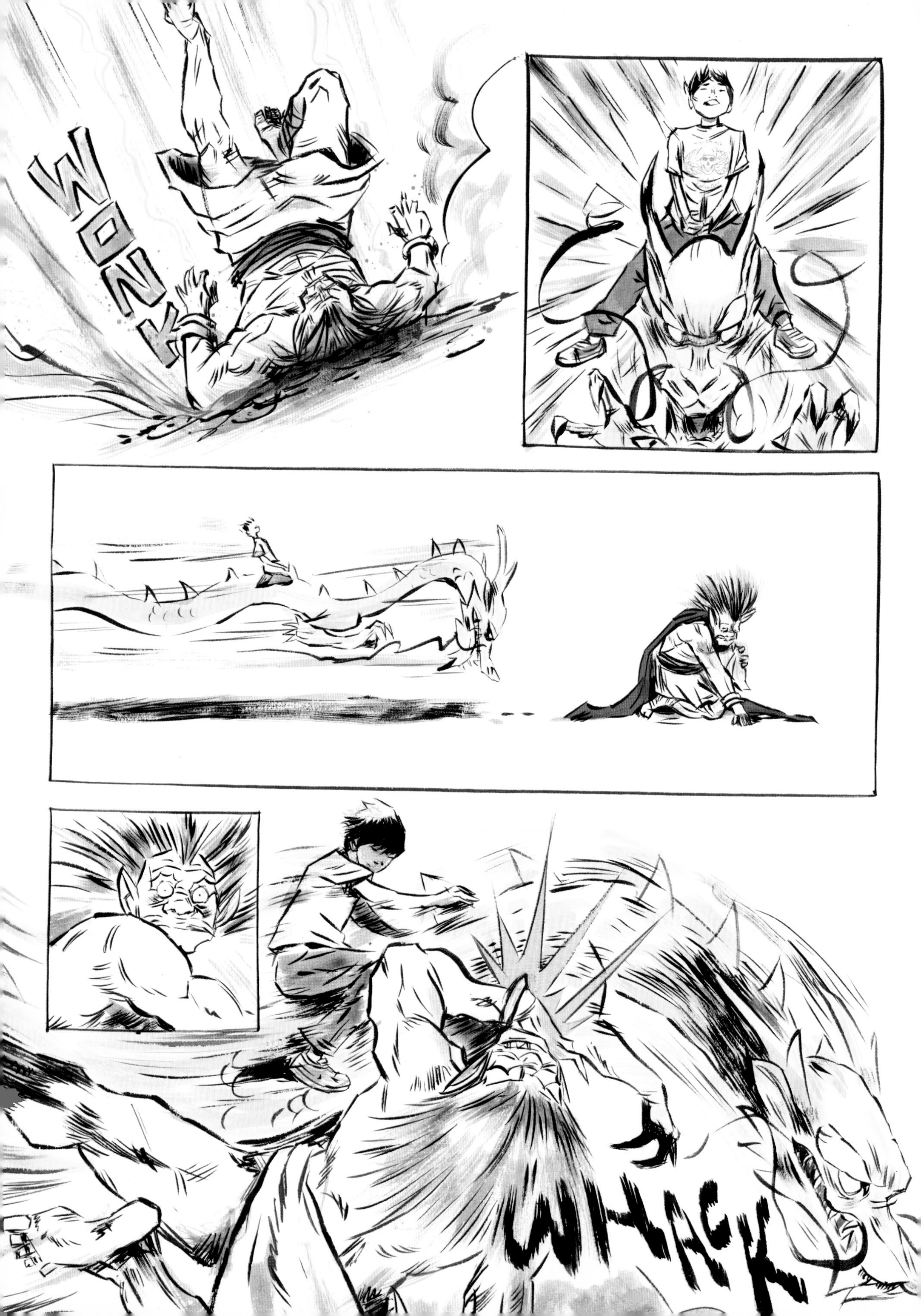
WONK
WHACK

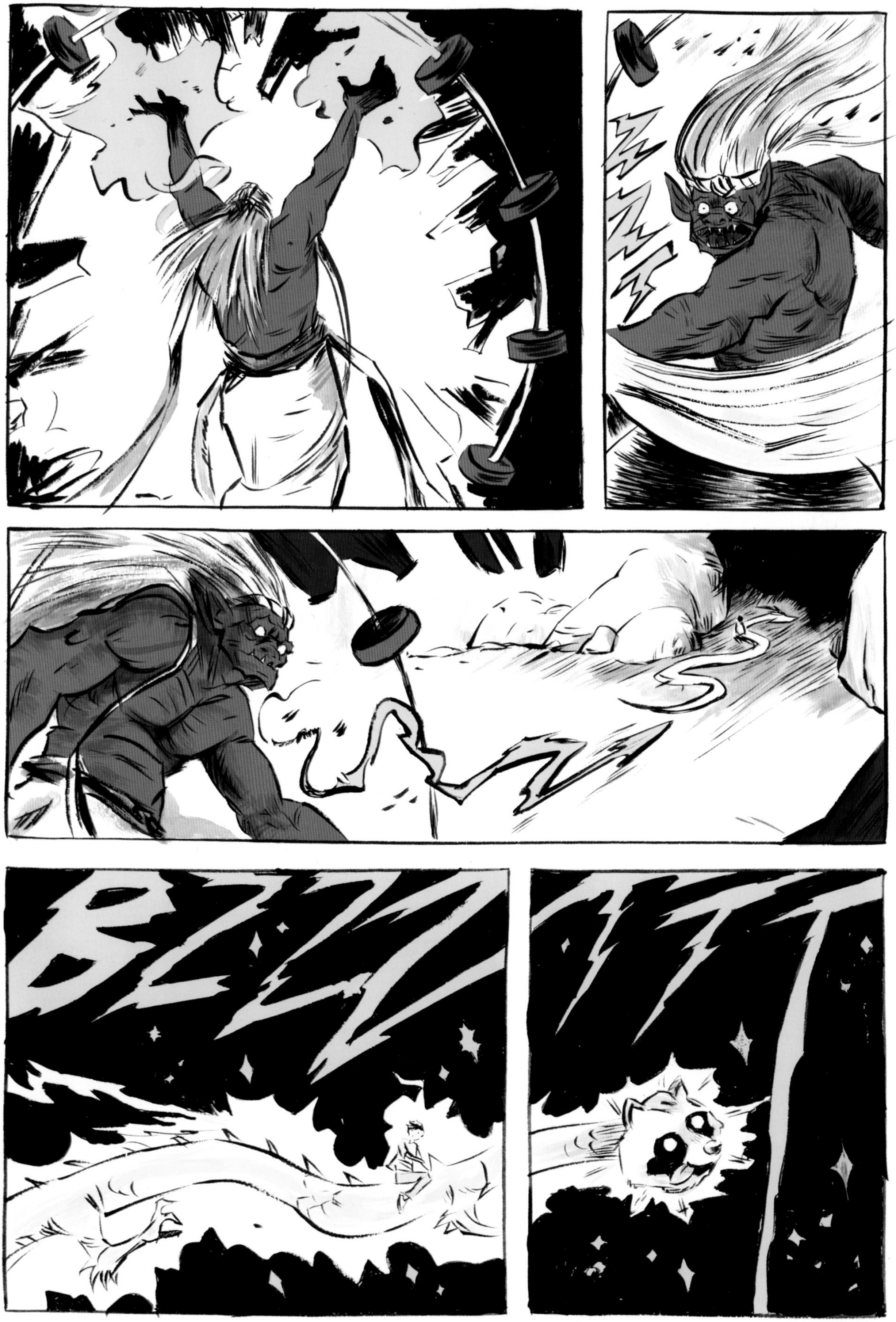
BZZZZZT

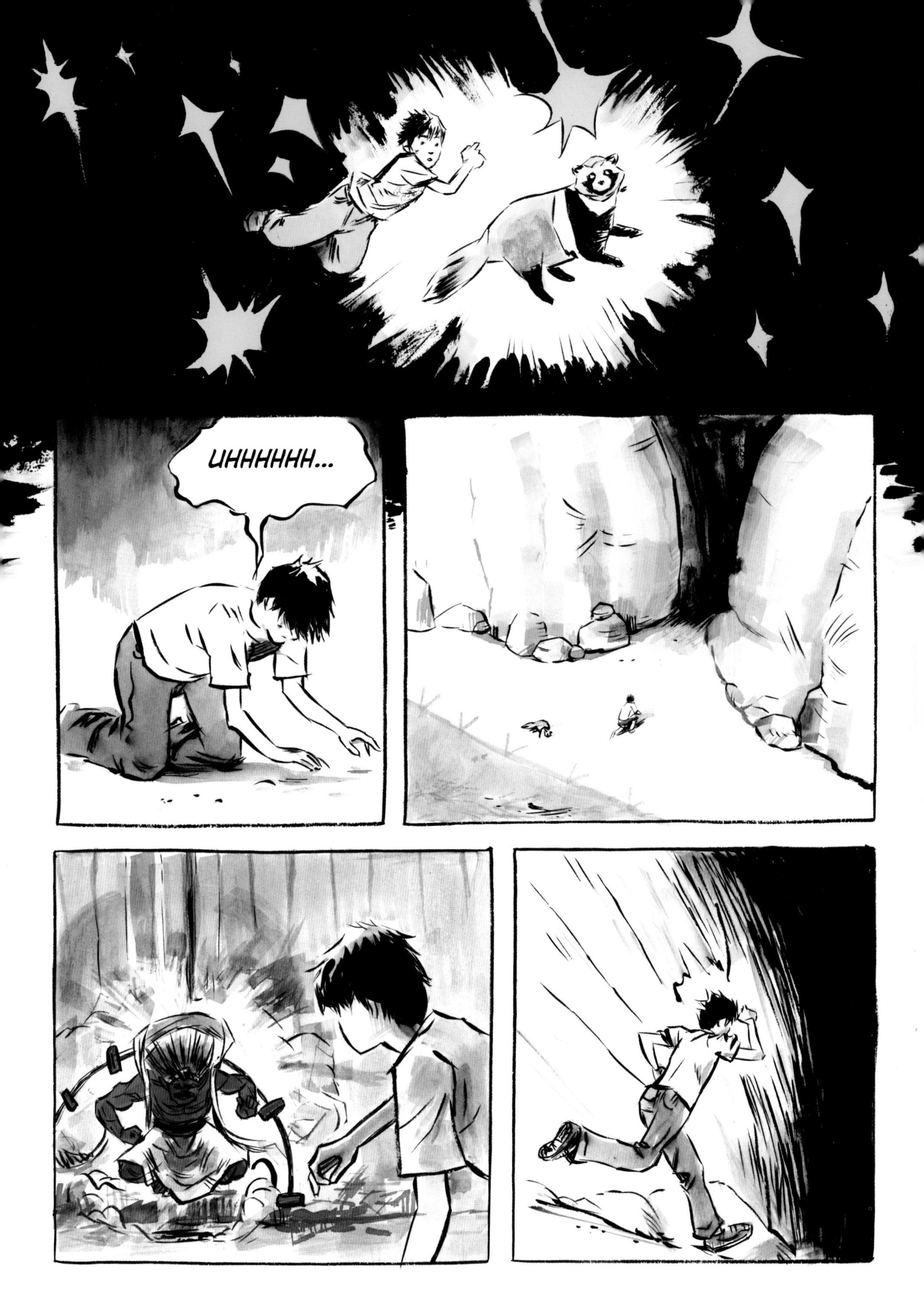
UHHHHHH...

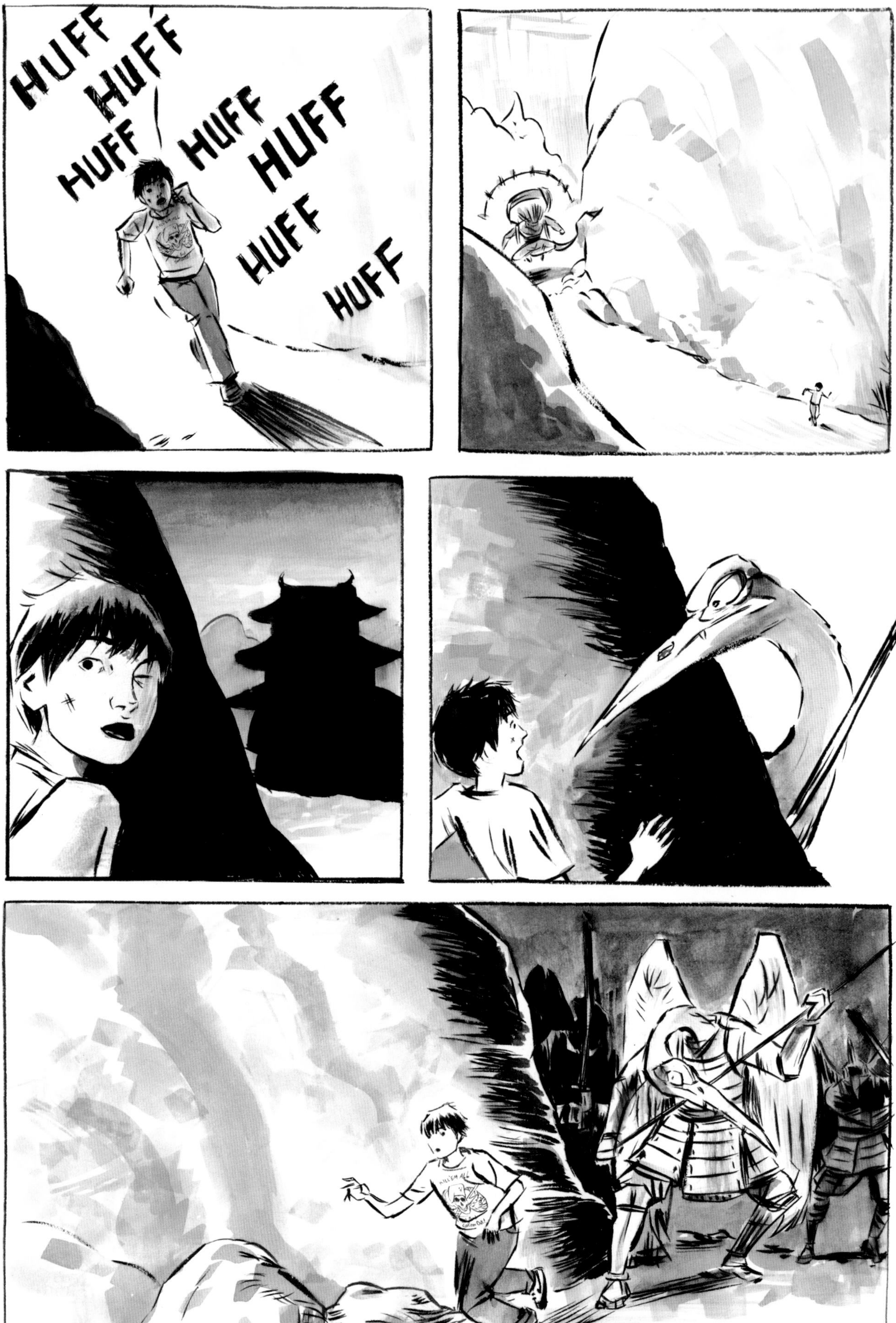
HUFF
HUFF
HUFF
HUFF
HUFF
HUFF
HUFF

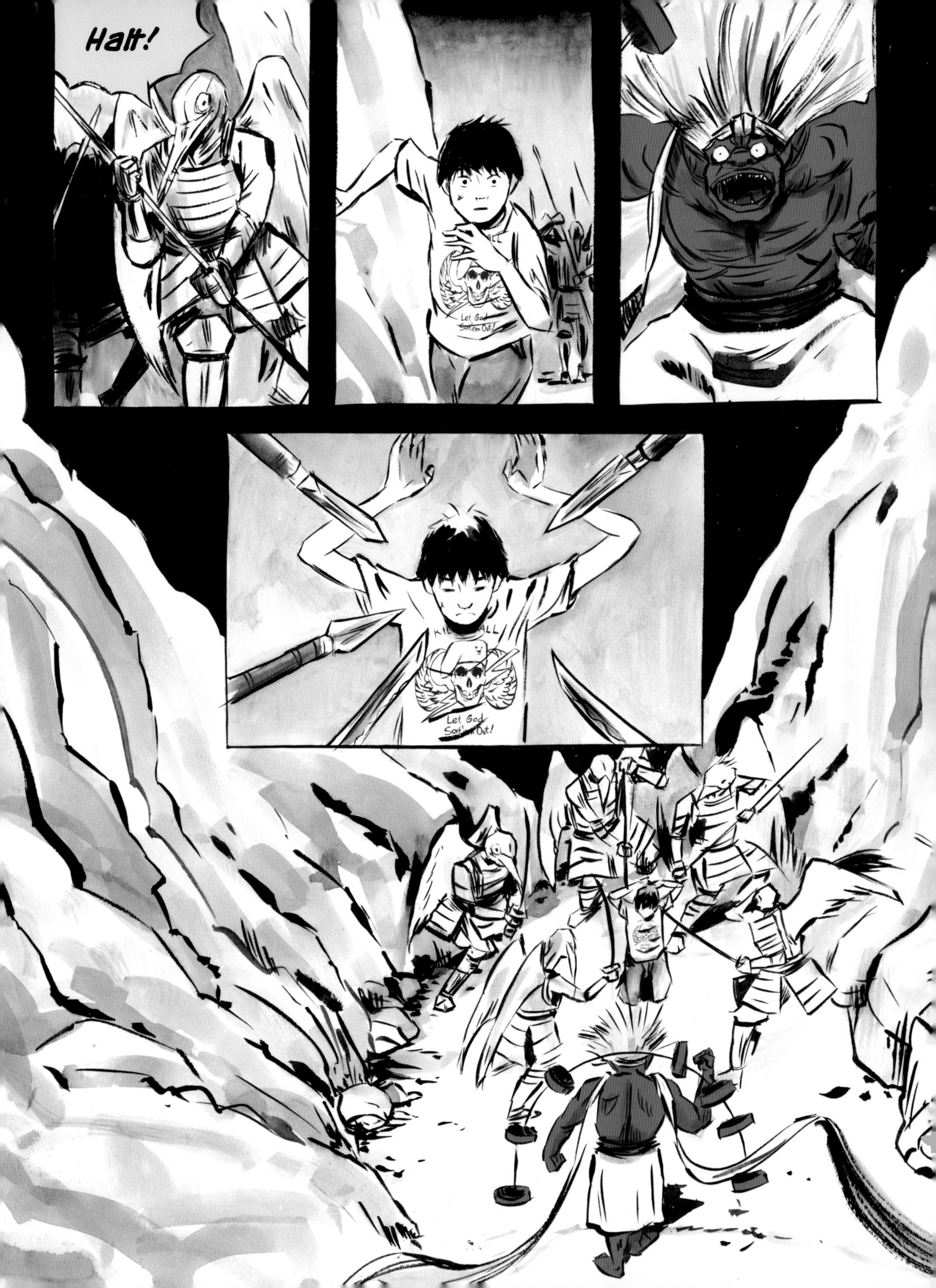
Halt!
Let God Sort'em Out!
KILL 'EM ALL
Let God Sort 'em Out!

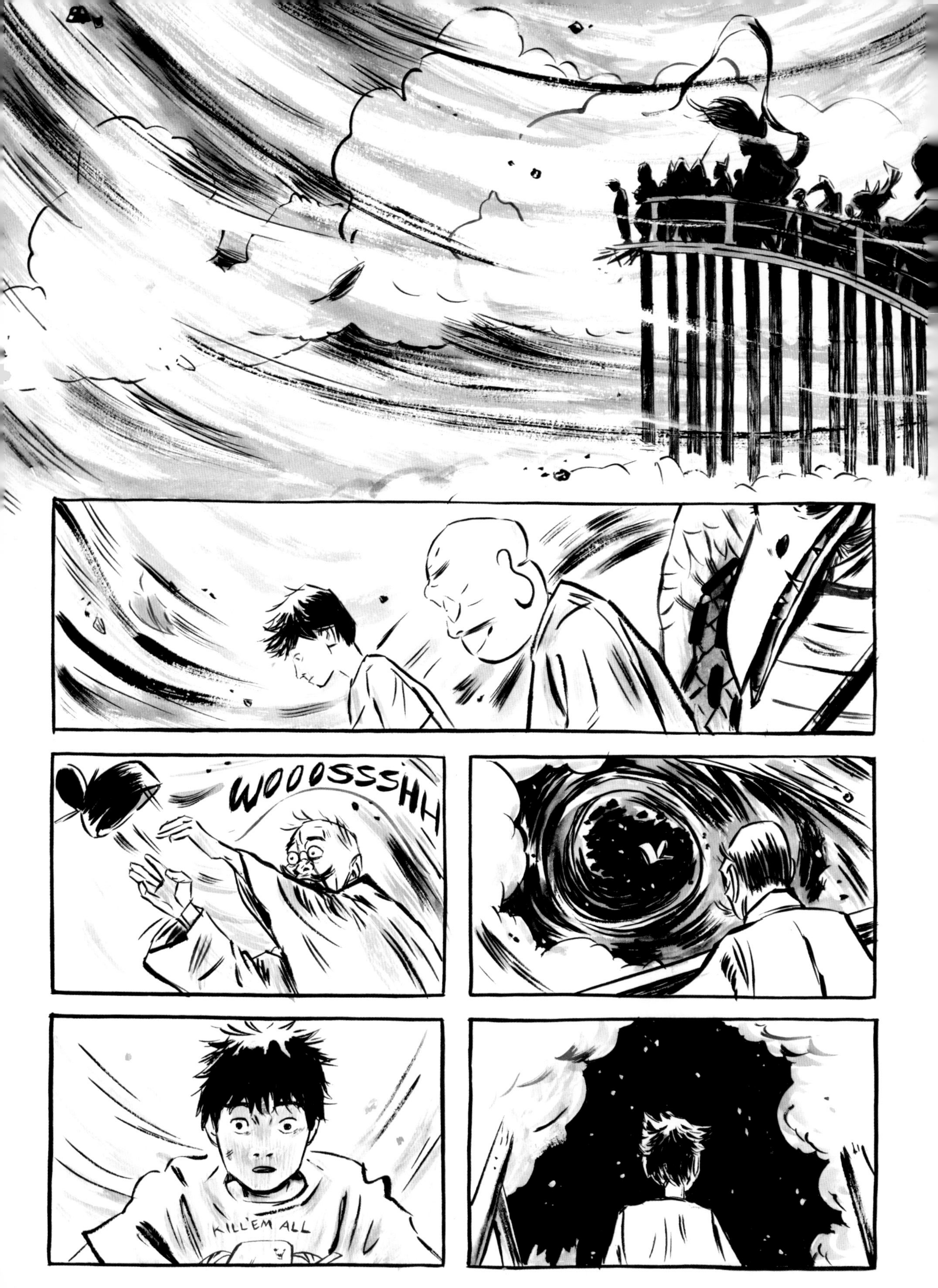
WOOOSSSSHH
KILL'EM ALL

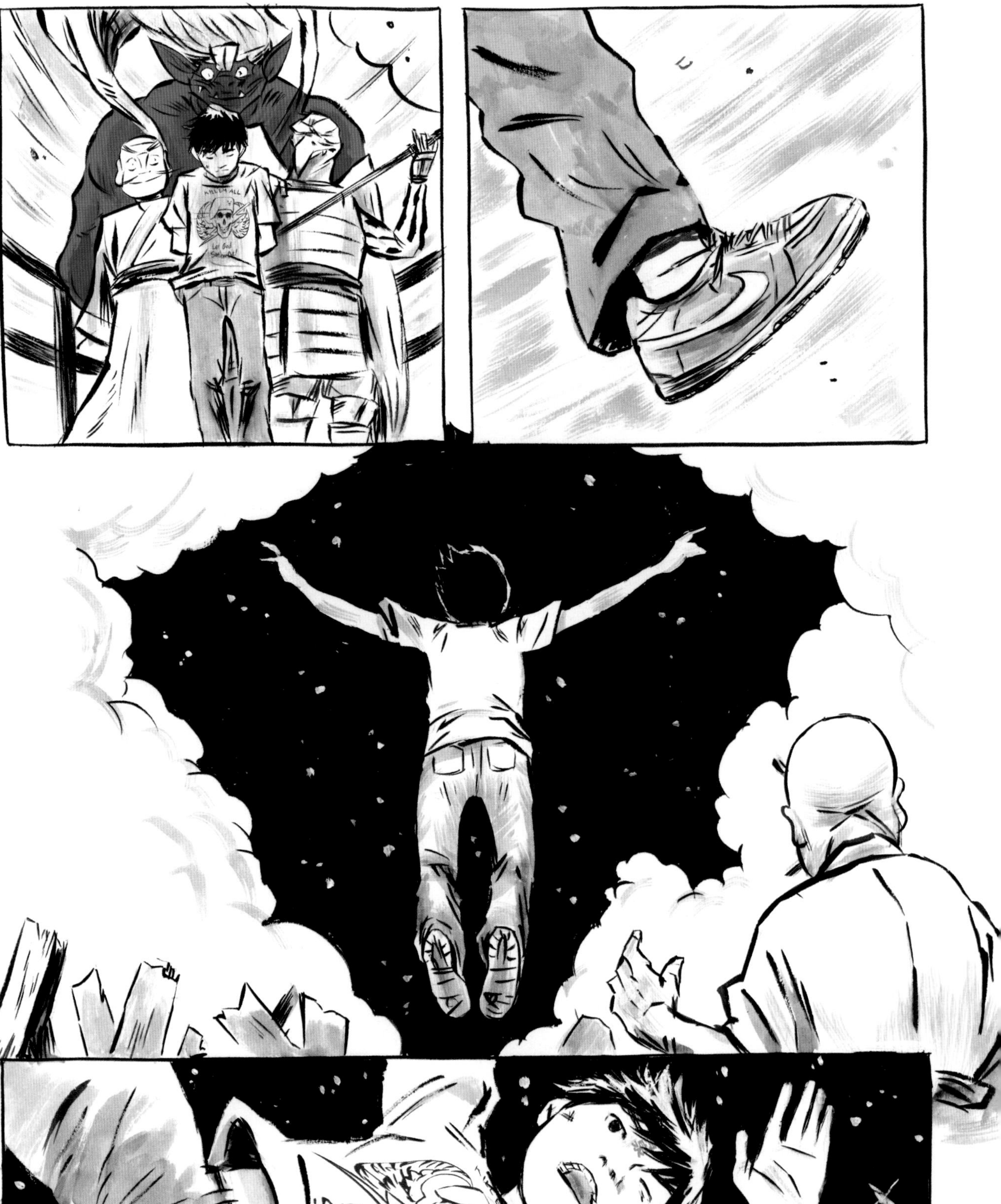
Let God
Sort'em Out!

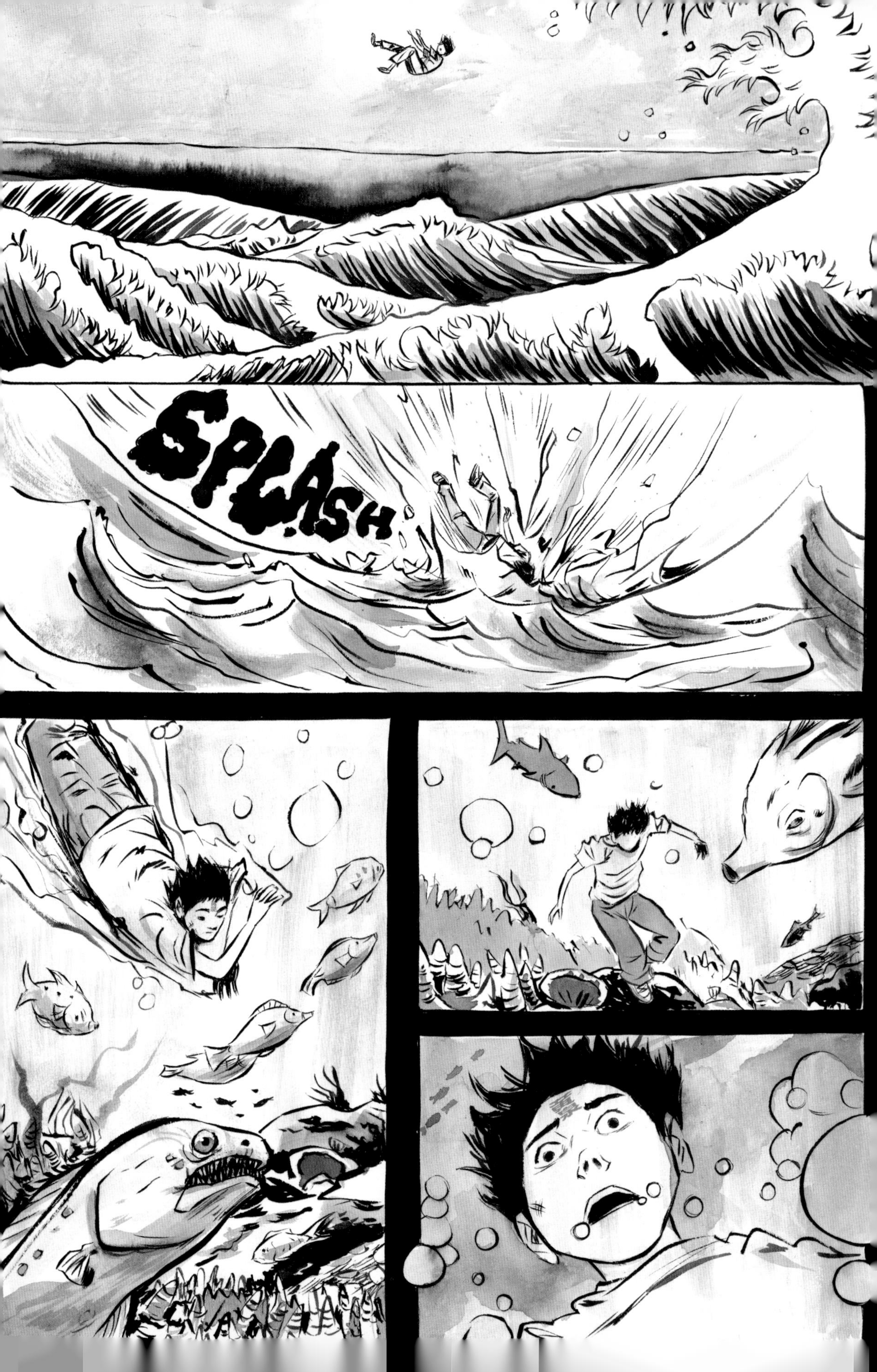
SPLASH

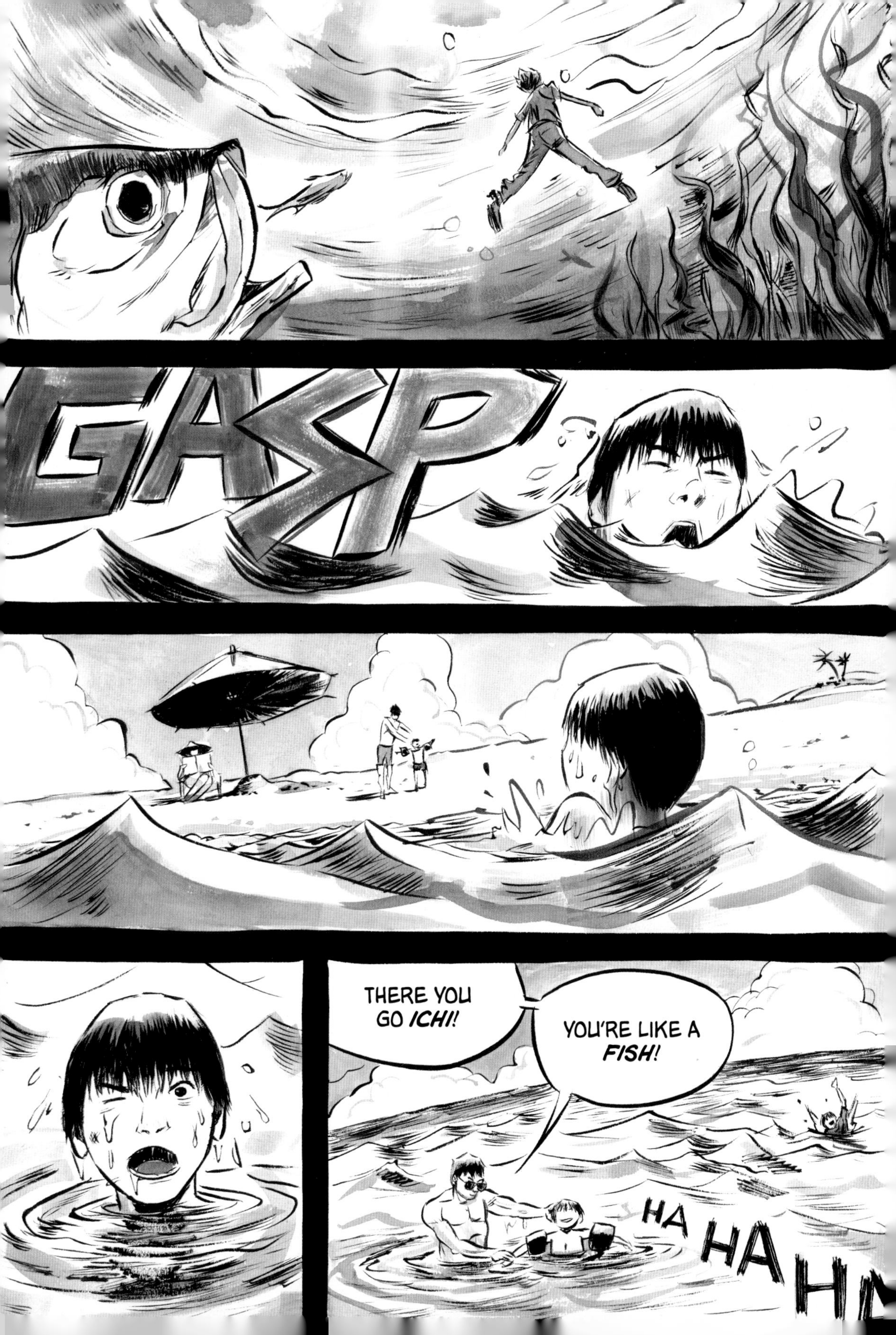
GASP
THERE YOU GO *ICHI*!
YOU'RE LIKE A *FISH*!
HA HA HA

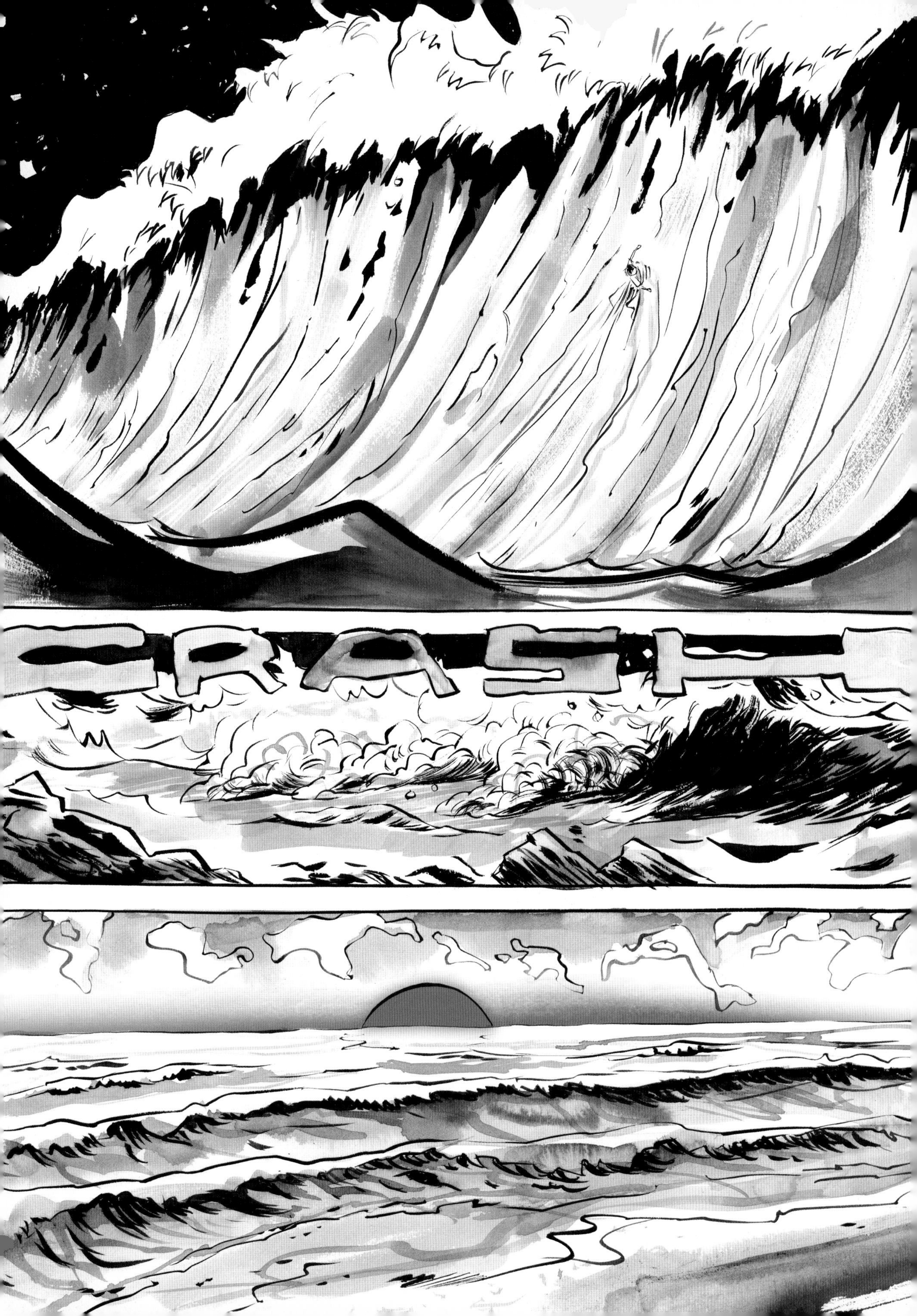
CRASH

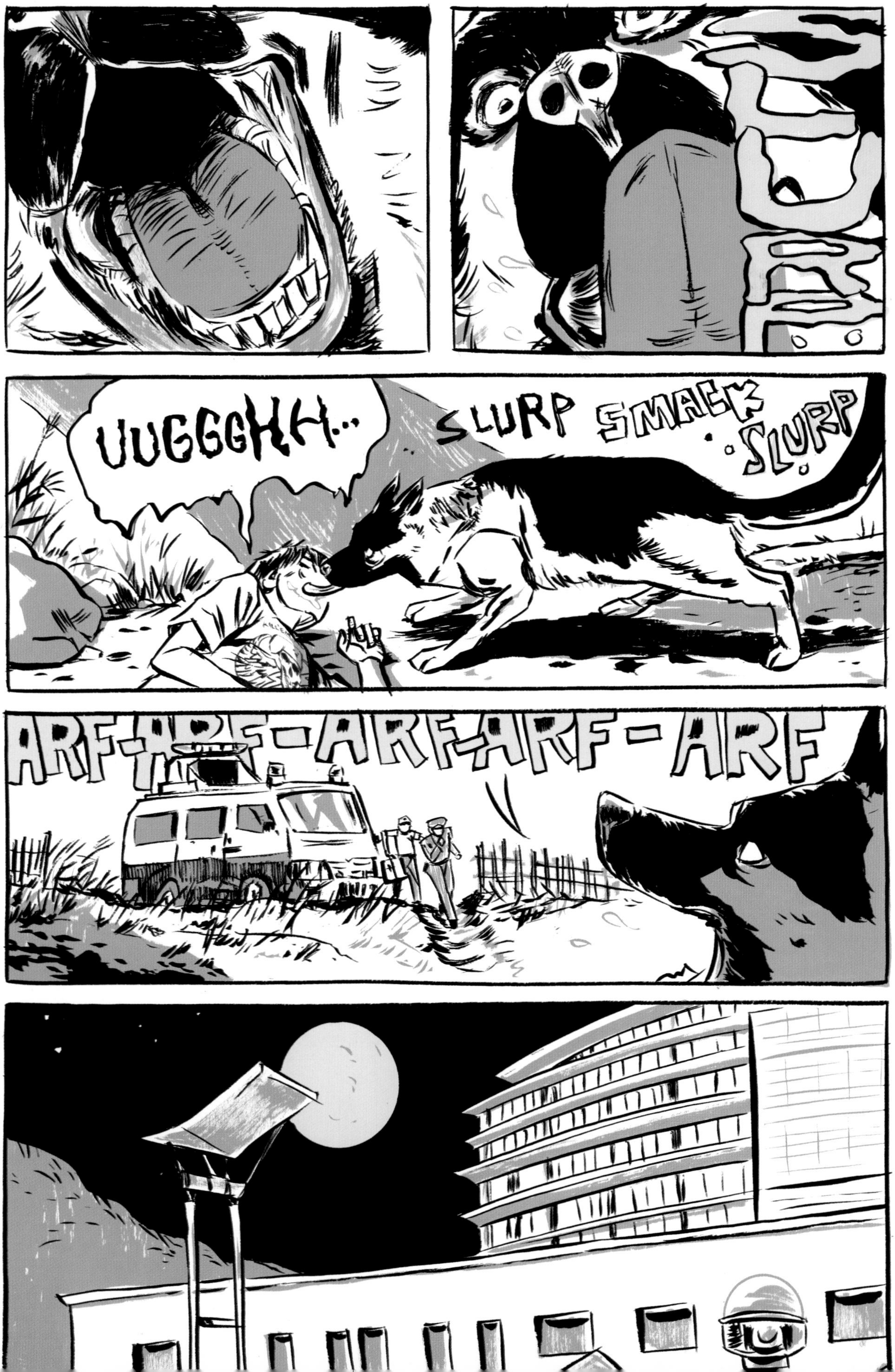
UUGGGHH...
SLURP
SMACK
SLURP
ARF-ARF-ARF-ARF-ARF

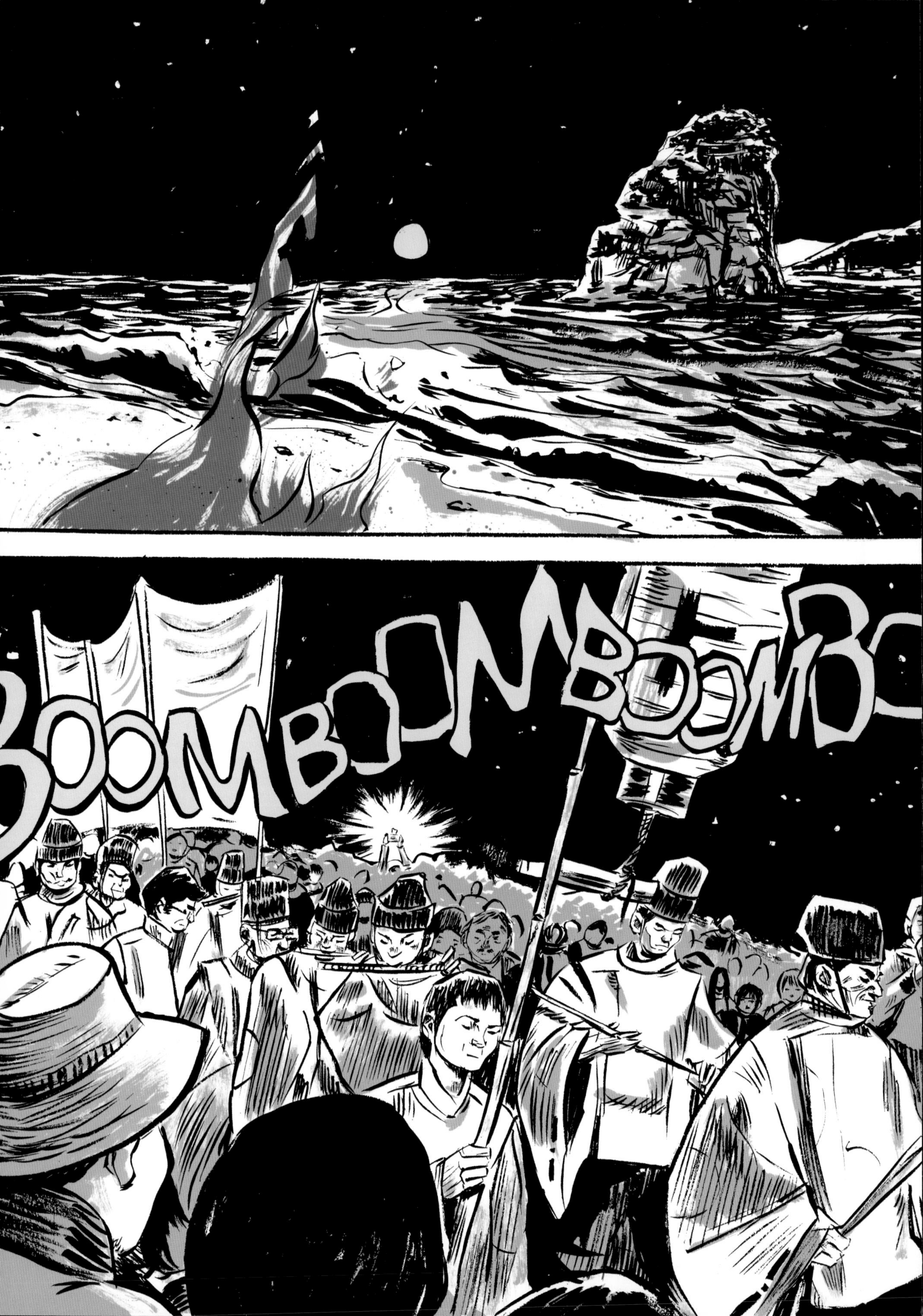
BOOMBOOMBOOMBO

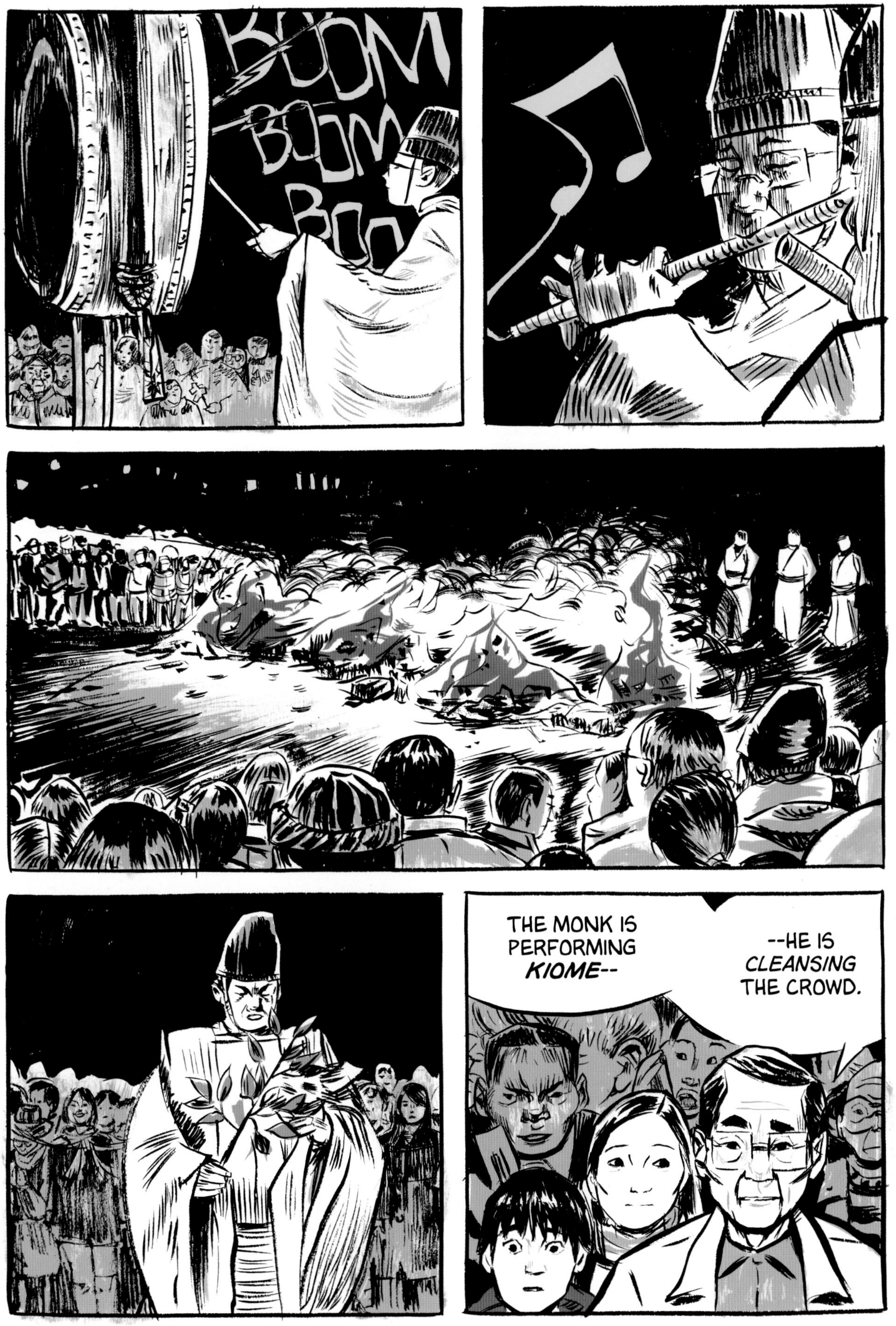
BOOM
BOOM
BOO
THE MONK IS PERFORMING *KIOME*--
--HE IS *CLEANSING* THE CROWD.

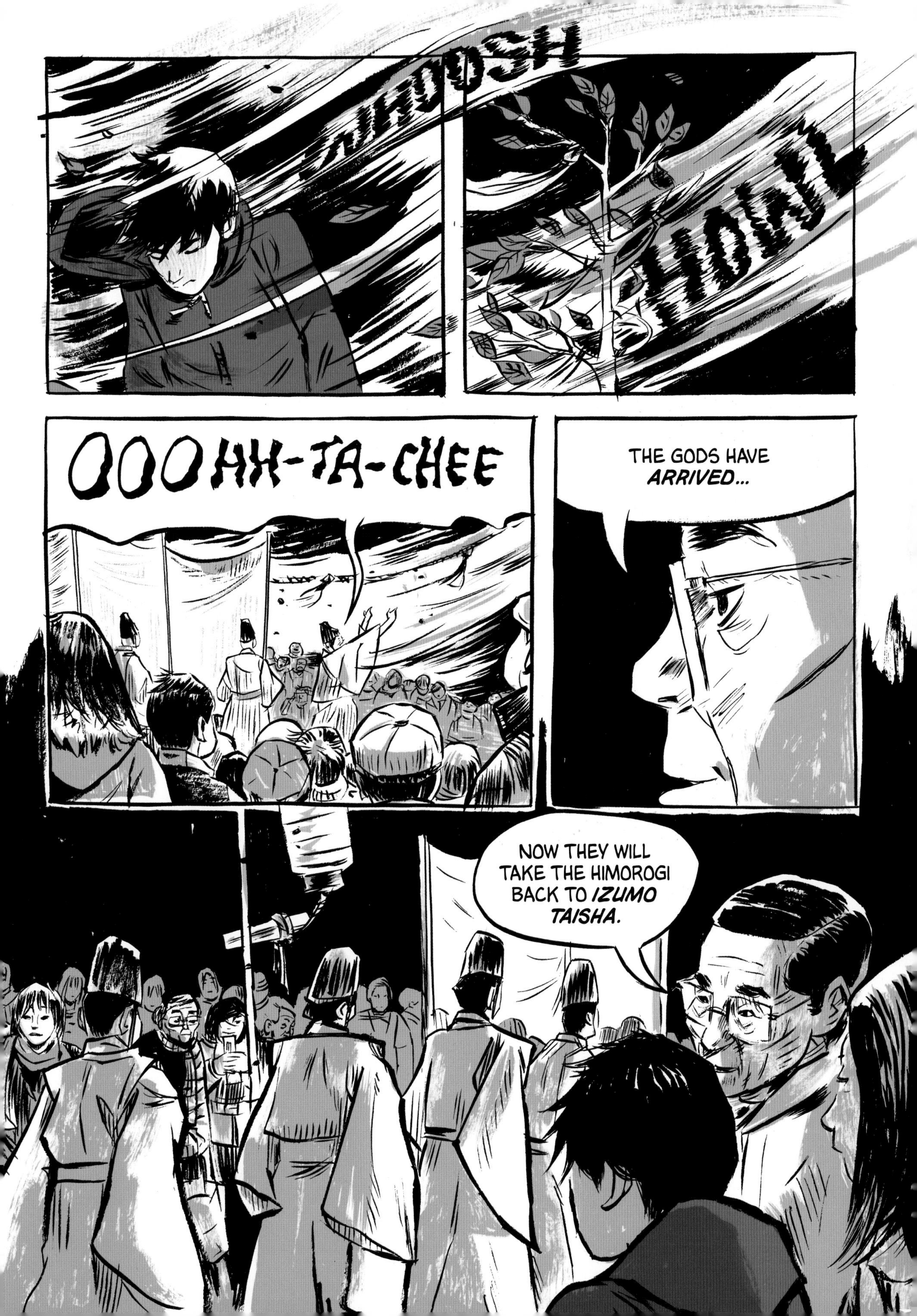
WHOOSH
HOWL
OOOHH-TA-CHEE
THE GODS HAVE ARRIVED...
NOW THEY WILL TAKE THE HIMOROGI BACK TO IZUMO TAISHA.

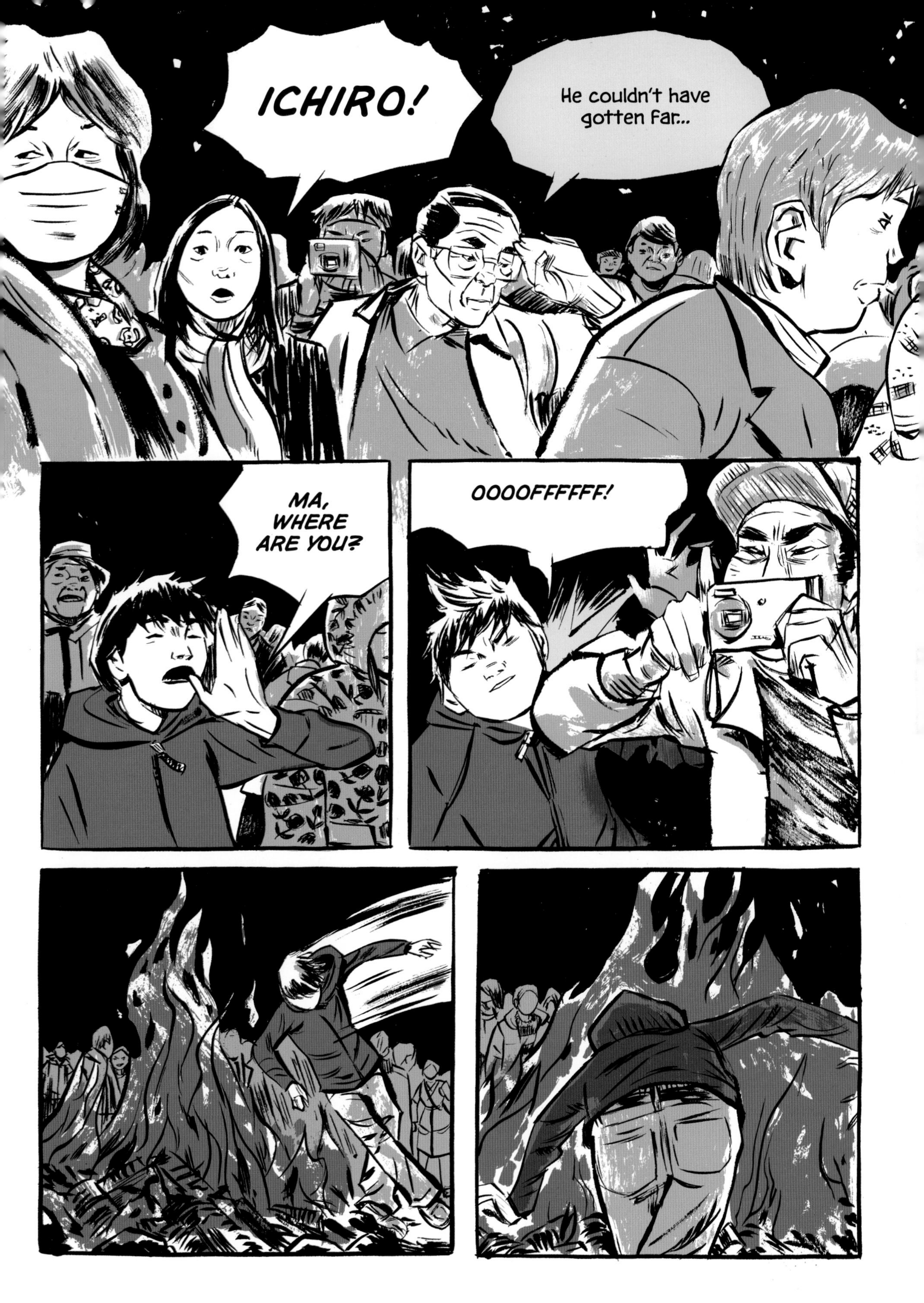
ICHIRO!
He couldn't have gotten far...
MA, WHERE ARE YOU?
OOOOFFFFFF!

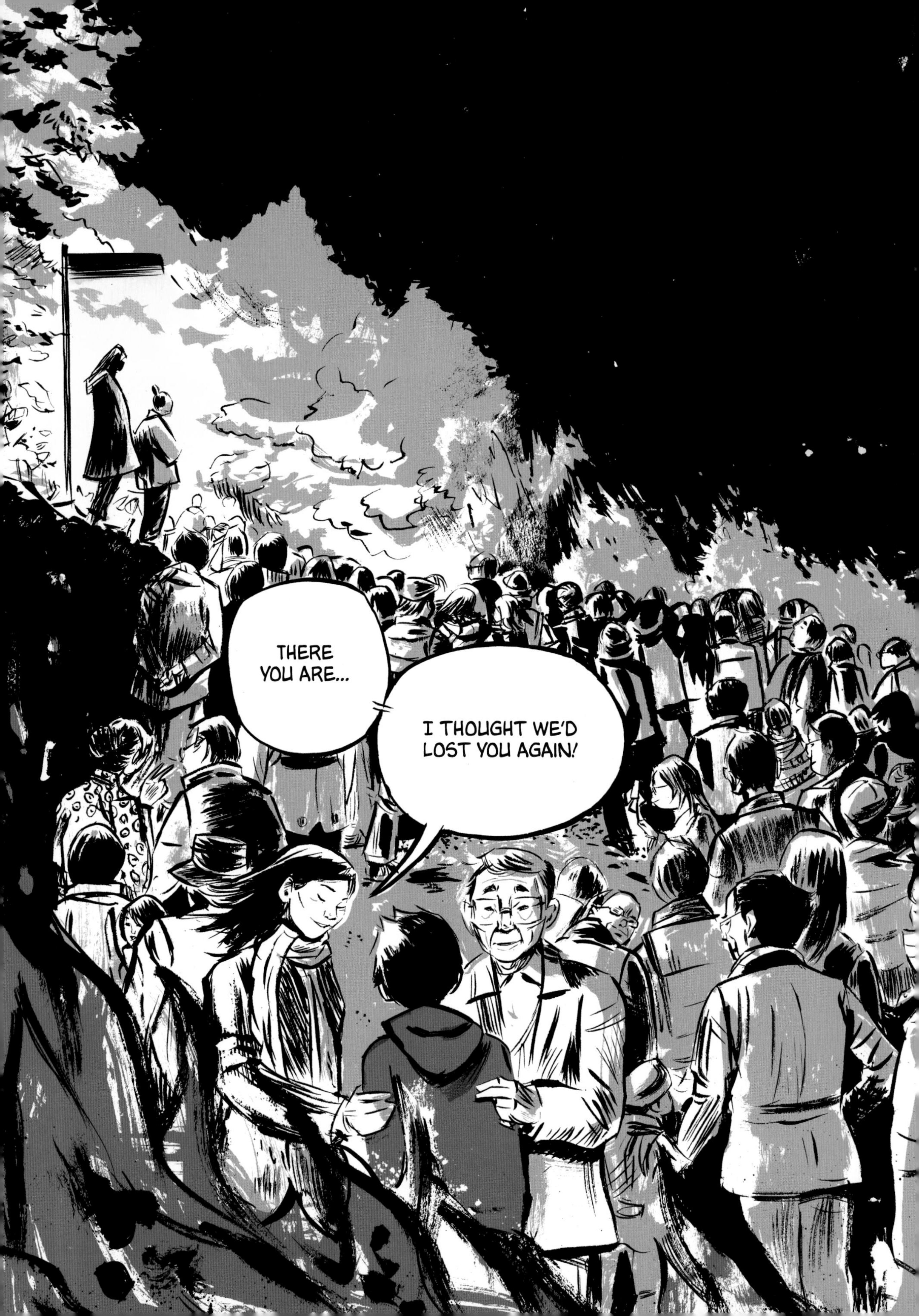
THERE YOU ARE...
I THOUGHT WE'D LOST YOU AGAIN!

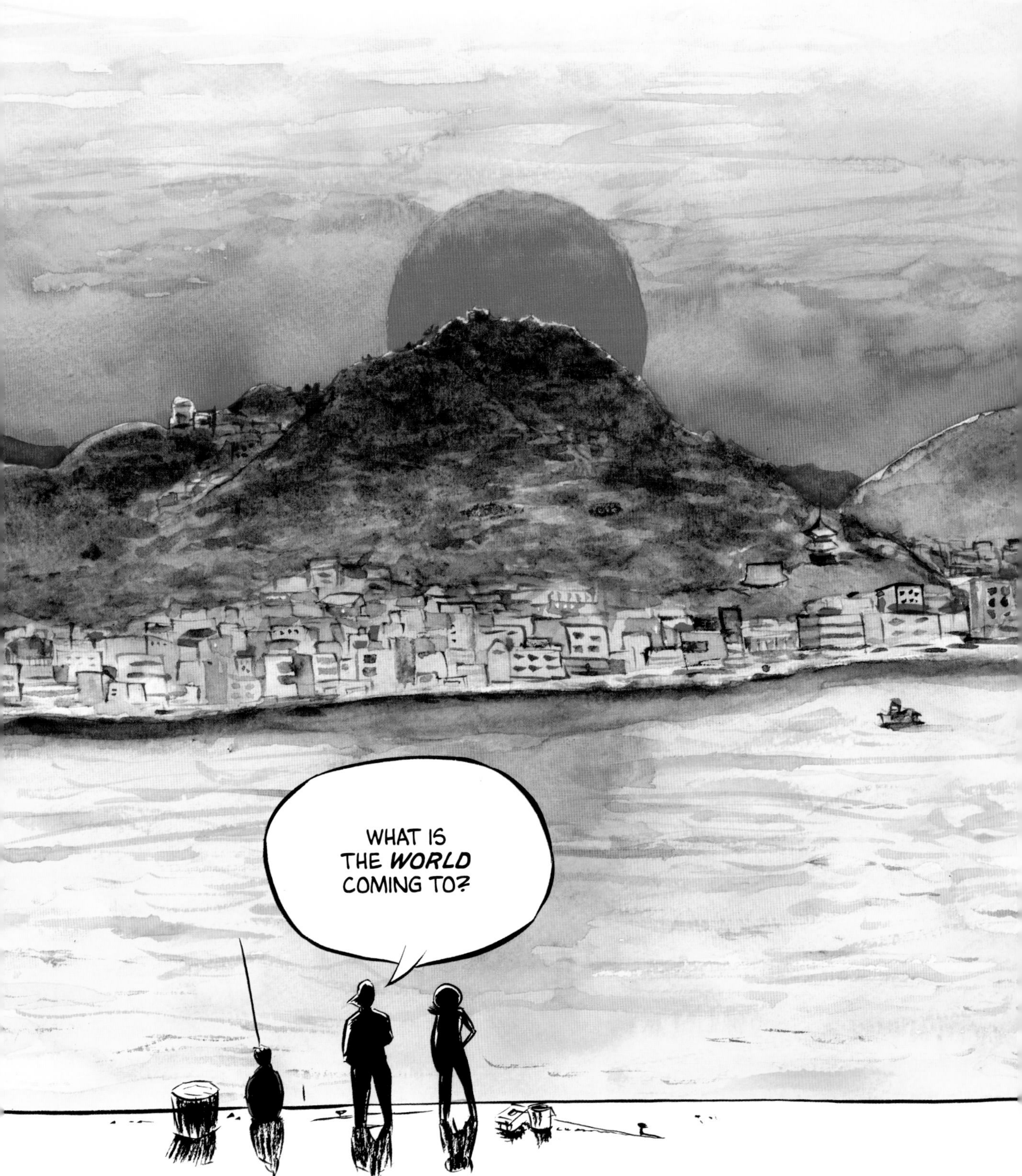
WHAT IS THE WORLD COMING TO?

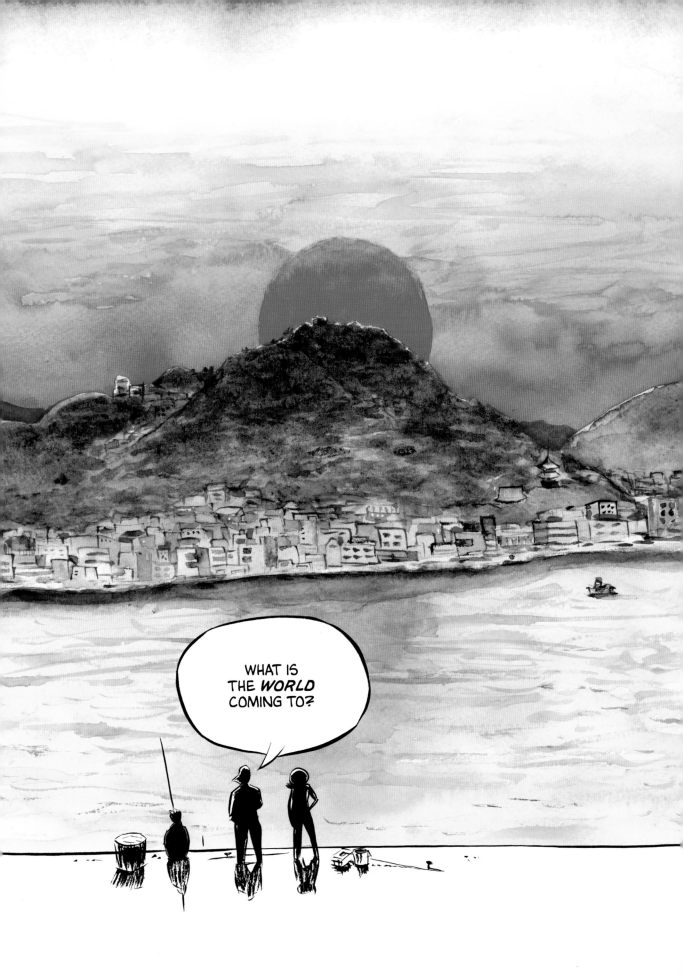

MY DEEPEST GRATITUDE
TO THE EFFORTS OF
CAROL CHU AND JULIA RICHARDSON.
WITHOUT THEM,
THIS BOOK WOULD NOT
BE POSSIBLE.

RYAN INZANA IS A COMIC ARTIST AND ILLUSTRATOR. THIS IS HIS SECOND GRAPHIC NOVEL.

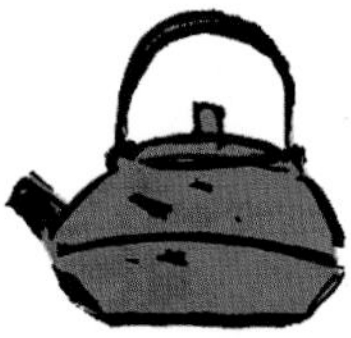